Praise for Julie Leto

"Sexy, quick, and lots of fun."
—Heather Graham, *New York Times*
bestselling author

"Nobody writes a bad girl like Julie Leto!"
—Carly Phillips, *New York Times* bestselling author

"She loves pushing the envelope, and dances on the edge with the sizzle and crackle of lightning."
—The Best Reviews

"Sizzling chemistry and loads of sexual tension make this Leto tale a scorcher."   —*Romantic Times*

"Smart, sophisticated, and sizzling from start to finish."   —Fresh Fiction

"Ms. Leto pulls out all the stops to give readers a double-edged thrill."   —A Romance Review

PHANTOM PLEASURES

JULIE LETO

A SIGNET ECLIPSE BOOK

SIGNET ECLIPSE
Published by New American Library, a division of
Penguin Group (USA) Inc., 375 Hudson Street,
New York, New York 10014, USA
Penguin Group (Canada), 90 Eglinton Avenue East, Suite 700, Toronto,
Ontario M4P 2Y3, Canada (a division of Pearson Penguin Canada Inc.)
Penguin Books Ltd., 80 Strand, London WC2R 0RL, England
Penguin Ireland, 25 St. Stephen's Green, Dublin 2,
Ireland (a division of Penguin Books Ltd.)
Penguin Group (Australia), 250 Camberwell Road, Camberwell, Victoria 3124,
Australia (a division of Pearson Australia Group Pty. Ltd.)
Penguin Books India Pvt. Ltd., 11 Community Centre, Panchsheel Park,
New Delhi - 110 017, India
Penguin Group (NZ), 67 Apollo Drive, Rosedale, North Shore 0632,
New Zealand (a division of Pearson New Zealand Ltd.)
Penguin Books (South Africa) (Pty.) Ltd., 24 Sturdee Avenue,
Rosebank, Johannesburg 2196, South Africa

Penguin Books Ltd., Registered Offices:
80 Strand, London WC2R 0RL, England

First published by Signet Eclipse, an imprint of New American Library,
a division of Penguin Group (USA) Inc.

First Printing, April 2008
10 9 8 7 6 5 4 3 2 1

PUBLISHER'S NOTE
This is a work of fiction. Names, characters, places, and incidents either are
the product of the author's imagination or are used fictitiously, and any resemblance to actual persons, living or dead, business establishments, events, or
locales is entirely coincidental.
    The publisher does not have any control over and does not assume any
responsibility for author or third-party Web sites or their content.

To new beginnings . . .

ACKNOWLEDGMENTS

This book has been a long time coming. I conceived the story line nearly fourteen years ago, if you can believe it, and actually wrote a book with similar characters, setting, and story line, but alas, I was ahead of my time. When I finally had the time and experience to tackle the idea again, I did not do so without help from some very special people. Writing is a solitary business, but not as much as it used to be. And I'm particularly fortunate to have the best people to lean on when I'm in need. I can only hope that I can return the favor a few times over the course of my life.

As always, my love and appreciation go to the Plot-monkeys: Janelle Denison, Leslie Kelly, and Carly Phillips, whose encouragement and plotting expertise helped me take what was a relatively simple story line and turn it into the multilayered novel that is *Phantom Pleasures*. I wouldn't have had the guts to revisit this dream without you. Also, to Helen Breitwieser, my amazing agent, whose unstoppable enthusiasm about my work keeps me going during the roughest times. Of course, to Susan Kearney, who read the original version of this story all those years ago and also encouraged me to bring this concept back into the light. The same goes for my aunt, Rosie Glatkowski, Bobbie Walters, and my sister-in-law, Joy Leto, who read this work in the early stages and never let me forget what they loved about it.

Special acknowledgment goes to award-winning and bestselling author Jo Beverley, who took the time from her own busy writing schedule to help me with the historical aspects of the story. Her knowledge of the Georgian period and all that is England boggles the mind, as does her generosity of time and spirit. Thank you, Jo! Also contributing to my historical knowledge were Mary Jo Putney, Susan Pace, and Virginia Henley. I'm incredibly fortunate to have access to such brilliant women.

I cannot ignore the many "experts" I found on the writer's loop for Novelists, Inc., who have answered my calls for information and resources with complete generosity. One day, I suppose, we might find a topic at the NINC link that no one knows anything about— but I doubt it. Same goes for my friends at the Tampa Area Romance Authors.

And of course, the wonderful team at NAL/Signet Eclipse, especially my editor, Laura Cifelli, who is not only utterly brilliant in story line problem solving, but is also a hell of a lot of fun, too. I'm thrilled to finally work with her. Her assistant, Lindsay Nouis, is also amazing, helpful, and efficient in ways that awe me. Of course, efficiency does that to me.

And if I left anyone out, please know that I will make it up to you in the next book!

Prologue

Austin, Texas
April 2008

His hand shaking, as much from age as from fear, Paschal Rousseau, noted Romani scholar, shut the door to his study and said a silent prayer for more time. He'd once thought he'd had more of that commodity than he could stand, but not any longer. His enemies were closing in on him. Of this, he was sure. He wouldn't go without a fight, of course, but despite his best efforts to remain in good shape, ninety-plus years did take their toll on a man. In the meantime he had to bolster his arsenal with as much information as he could gather in the quickest, if most draining, way he knew.

To that end, he had to act. He had to push through the final barrier of his mind and connect with the past.

Not his past. He knew his own history, his own wild tale, which had led him here to the States to seek the objects he needed to counter the Gypsy curse. No, tonight he had to attempt something more dangerous. He had to seek a path into the distant past—into memories that were not his.

Flicking on the lamp on his desk, he stared at the oil painting he'd propped up on the blotter, knowing it had been the artist's last work. The purplish clouds scuttling across the top of the canvas raged with rain. The whitecaps beneath the listing schooner sparked with anger and turmoil. Paschal had searched for this stormy seascape for years, learning more about the intricacies of art dealing than he'd ever intended. But he'd found the piece, and now it was time to use his so-called gift to take the final step.

He sat. Clutching the curved armrest of his chair with one hand, he reached out with the other and gingerly traced the name of the artist, rendered in bold strokes across the bottom of the canvas. *Damon.* He concentrated on everything he knew about the man, closed his eyes and painted his own picture of the artist in his mind. The only other rendering of the man existed in a place Paschal could no longer reach. Luckily, although he'd lived a somewhat unnaturally long life, his memory remained strong and reliable.

Once he saw Damon's dark hair, steely eyes and rigid jaw in his mind's eye, Paschal spread his fingers and palm over the center of the painting. At first he felt nothing but cool canvas and the stiff texture of dried enamels. But then, slowly, his hand seemed to meld into the painting. His flesh transparent. His mind transported.

The connection made, he pulled his mind's eye out of the schooner in the gyrating ocean and concentrated on the night, more than two hundred and sixty years ago, when the artist and his entire band of brothers disappeared forever.

Valoren
1747

Tonight the war began.

The war? No, the slaughter. And if Damon Forsyth and his brothers didn't reach the town of Umgeben before morning, their cherished sister would die in the impending massacre.

Damon kicked his heels hard into his mount's sweaty flanks, pushing the animal onward despite the blinding rain and rocky landscape. Lightning flashed, briefly illuminating the distant cliffs. They were close to the cursed town. He could feel the vibrations beneath his horse's hooves. The electricity spiking through the sky connected with the magic that pulsed beneath the ground and surged through his soaked clothes.

Valoren, land of the lost, prison to the Gypsies exiled from England by the first King George, was tucked into a mostly uninhabited corner of land between Germany and Bohemia. For nearly thirty years, Damon's father, a British baron, governed the land. But even he had been powerless against the magic—powerless against the enemy who had used sorcery to steal Sarina from her family.

Damon howled a curse and kicked the horse harder. A few lengths behind him, his brothers echoed his battle cry. The chorus of five pulsed with desperation, anger . . . fear. Fear for their sister. Fear for their exiled family. Fear for the very continuation of the Forsyth name.

At the sight of a rider charging toward them from the west, Damon yanked on the reins. He held up his hand, and his brothers stopped alongside, their horses snorting heavily so that their hot breath created a gray mist in the frigid rain. Molded to his horse's back like an extension of its spine, the approaching horseman galloped over the crags and rocks in the road.

Damon immediately recognized his half brother, Rafe, who slid into their circle and tossed back the hood on his cloak. His long, raven black hair merged with the darkness, but his clear blue eyes—so much like Sarina's since they shared the same mother—were bright with fury.

"The mercenary army advances at dawn," he reported.

Damon nodded, though his mind reeled. How had the confrontation escalated so quickly? From his trips to court, he'd known that the second King George often grumbled about reclaiming his land from the wanderers. Over the years, rumors flew that troops comprised of British and German mercenaries were being gathered to cleanse the enclave of the Romani. But Damon had never believed troops would arrive. Or that the offensive would put his family—good British citizens, save his Gypsy stepmother, youngest brother and only sister—in such grave peril.

"Then we have time to find Sarina," Damon declared.

His brother Aiden, next in line to inherit, drew his sword. "Not if Rogan has spirited her away. He's brought this danger on her. On us. He must pay for his betrayal!"

Rogan. Damon's blood froze. He had brought Lord Rogan here to Valoren from London, introduced him to his family—and to his starry-eyed, trusting, barely seventeen-year-old sister—never guessing that the wealthy traveler had designs on taking the Gypsy land for his own. Rogan's machinations had likely stirred the jealous king to action. Damon had unleashed the lion into the coliseum, and now everyone in the Gypsy colony would pay with their lives.

Damon held his hand against Aiden's weapon, which glittered white when another bolt of lightning streaked across the sky. "Remember, we must find Sarina before we kill Rogan. He cannot die until we know where she is."

The brothers said nothing, but their faces darkened, their jaws tightened and their eyes burned with hatred.

"We must ride!" Damon declared.

Once again, their band took off toward the cliffs. Between the rocky jags they narrowed their line, entering through the pass one rider at a time. By the time all six of them emerged in the valley, a cold weight dropped with a thud in Damon's stomach.

The village of Umgeben appeared untouched. Still. Had the Gypsies not received the warning sent a few hours before? Fires flickered in the windows, smoke curled from the hearths of the common houses and music echoed from a faraway *vardo*, an elaborately decorated wagon the Gypsies had been forbidden by English law to move. But John Forsyth, their governor, had rescinded the order hours ago to help the Romani escape the incoming hoard. Why weren't they uprooted? Hitched to mules in advance of the exodus that could possibly spare their lives?

Colin, the third brother, rode up silently, his voice only slightly louder than his usual whisper. "Where is everyone?"

Damon urged his mount through the town's open gates and from his saddle tore open the curtains of the nearest cottage with his blade. He smelled meat stewing on the hearth, yet no one tended the fire. He rode around to the back and saw the animal pens unlocked and empty. He heard his brothers behind him as their horses' hooves sucked in and out of the slick clay, each one riding to nearby houses and announcing the same results.

The Romani had disappeared. The entire population of Umgeben was gone.

"What sort of magic spirits away an entire town?" the elder twin, Logan, shouted to Rafe, who'd dismounted. "They had but an hour's warning. They could not have abandoned their homes without our meeting them on the road."

Rafe, the only brother with Gypsy blood, looked as confused as the others and shook his head wildly. Damon's anger surged. If his youngest brother, so adept at maneuvering through the Gypsy world, was shocked by these events, what chance did they have at saving Sarina?

Aiden raised his sword, pointing east. "Colin, search the chapel in case the citizens have simply taken refuge. Rafe, find the *Chovihano*," he ordered, directing their youngest brother to the Gypsy elder. "See if he's remained, and if so, what he knows. You two," he barked, indicating the twins, Logan and Paxton, "check the storerooms. See if the tinker is about. He alone is allowed to travel from this place. He might have known of this attack long before we heard the news, and warned the others away before our message arrived."

The brothers dispersed, leaving only Damon and Aiden behind. Aiden had just returned home from fighting with the king's army, scarred but alive. Now betrayal hardened his features. Damon reached out and placed a calming hand on his shoulder.

"We shall find her," he said.

"I'll seek out Rogan," Aiden replied.

Damon shook his head. "I brought that viper into our midst. It is my right to slay him. But only after Sarina is back in our care." Damon sat straighter on his mount. He'd allowed his brother to take the reins a moment ago, but now he had to act. He was the eldest. He bore the responsibility of justice.

"Check the armory," he ordered. "See if the Gypsies armed themselves to fight before they left."

Aiden opened his mouth to protest, but then quickly deferred. He sheathed his weapon and rode west.

Alone, Damon cantered through the village, his destination looming just beyond the ramshackle cottages and immobile *vardo*s parked along the main path. Lightning ignited the flecks of glass embedded in the stone of Rogan's castle and shimmered up the tall spires that rose into the sky like snakes about to strike. The large stone structure was intimidating, just as the architect had intended. But Damon wouldn't hesitate to enter. Not when he guessed that this castle would be the most likely place for Rogan to hide Sarina, if they'd stayed behind.

Which Damon suspected they had. He could smell the stench of Rogan's power even through the falling rain. On missions of their own, his brothers would be safe from the battle to come. And when his combat with Rogan ended, they would reunite in victory.

At the entrance to the castle, Damon dismounted, unsheathed his sword and smacked his horse on its rump so it shot into the darkness, out of the storm. Out of danger. He climbed the steps boldly and kicked open the heavy door. Pain shot up his thigh. He cared not. He removed his cloak and balanced his blade in his hands. Rogan would die tonight.

Something crunched beneath Damon's boot as he stepped toward the grand staircase. He bent down and his heart clenched. Sarina's necklace. The chain broken. The charm damaged beyond repair. Who had ripped the ever-present amulet from her throat? Damon's footfalls reverberated on the stone floors until the sound of his steps was muffled by one of the many rich carpets. The only light came from two torches at the top of the stairs.

From there, Rogan smiled down on him.

Damon smirked. Not the man, but the portrait, hung with conceit as the centerpiece of the staircase. The oil on the canvas portrayed the villain with perfect accuracy.

"Rogan!" he shouted.

Damon stomped up the stairs.

"Rogan! Release my sister and face me."

His voice shook the atmosphere, but there was no response.

Only silence. Deadly silence.

The absence of sound was ripe with magic. Damon could taste the metallic flavor on his tongue.

At the portrait, he stopped and stared into the eyes of the traitor, fighting off a chill spiking from the black irises. In the dancing light from the flickering torch flame, Damon spied the makings of a sneer on the man's slim lips, even while he petted the beloved cat curled in his lap. Cursed beast. Black. Long-haired. Amber-eyed. Mean as a devil. The perfect personification of dark and dangerous magic.

Why hadn't Damon seen the evil in his so-called friend before? Damon had once prided himself on his ability to judge people. What kind of charm had Rogan employed to make Damon believe him to be a noble companion? To convince all the Romani exiled to Valoren that Rogan had their best interests at heart?

Pushed by a surge of wind, the manor door behind him banged closed. The torches faltered, then flamed, but in the seconds between light and dark, Damon glimpsed a figure move within the painting.

Not Rogan. In a doorway curved over Rogan's left shoulder.

A woman?

Damon's stomach dropped.

"Sarina?" he whispered.

He stepped closer, sheathed his sword and yanked the heavy portrait off the wall. Startled at the weight of the carved and gilded frame, he took care not to damage the canvas. Even the Gypsy *Chovihano*, the shaman Damon's father had consulted when Rogan's dark intentions had started to manifest, feared that Rogan had mastered the blackest of magical arts. Could the sorcerer have tucked his sister away in a place from which no mortal man could release her— even someplace as inconceivable as inside a painting?

Damon dragged the portrait closer to the torch and stared hard into the shadowy doorway painted in the corner. Again he caught sight of a woman. But her hair wasn't dark like his sister's. This woman's tresses caught and reflected the light from the flames.

In a flash of thought, he remembered his wife back in England. Flame-haired and filled with ice. If he died in the battle with Rogan tonight or with the king's mercenaries at dawn, she'd care not. But his mistress . . . at least she'd weep for his loss, even if only for the absence of his generous purse. For his part, he'd miss her bold lovemaking, her insatiable, curvaceous body and the sound of her pleasured cries bursting in his eardrum. Suddenly he could hear her laughter, raucous and loud, burbling from the painting. His body instantly responded with needs that had no place here, needs that made him forget—momentarily—his missing sister.

He shook his head until his brain cleared.

"Damn you, Rogan!"

Damon lifted his sword high, and then plunged the

blade down into the canvas, precisely at Rogan's black heart. He heard the rip and then pain shot through him. He screamed as a thousand shards of light stripped his body bare to the bone.

And then . . .

Nothing.

1

"What are you doing?"

From behind her, manicured hands coiled around Alexa Chandler's face and pressed gently against her temples. Even without turning around, she knew who'd come up behind her. Catalina Reyes's scent always gave her away. Spicy. Rich. Exotic. Alexa had tried wearing the same fragrance and had come off smelling like the proverbial French whore. On Cat, however, the scent reminded Alexa of pure freedom—of the wild life she could be living if she used her money for evil rather than good.

If simply making more money qualified as "good," of course.

"What do you think I'm doing?" Cat replied.

Alexa sighed. They'd played this game before. "Trying to read my mind."

Cat chuckled softly.

"Only trouble is," Alexa continued, "you don't read minds."

"Says you," Cat countered.

"Oh yeah?" Alexa said, sounding much more confident than her previous experiences with Cat warranted. "What am I thinking?"

Alexa clutched the railing of the hotel suite's balcony tighter and focused on the horizon, on the tiny sliver of land far in the distance, where, with any luck, she'd be exploring sometime in the next few hours.

"You're thinking about how much money you're going to make if that abandoned old castle on that barren little island your father left you is the cash cow in disguise that you think it is," Cat replied.

Alexa turned abruptly, breaking Cat's contact with her skin.

"How'd you know that?"

Cat laughed, the otherworldly tone in her voice completely gone. "Because I've watched you go after properties for six years now. What else would you be thinking?"

Alexa rolled her eyes. "See? Not psychic."

Cat gave her a sly smile. "You're also entertaining some fairly naughty fantasies about finding a mysterious dark knight in that castle and letting him have his way with you."

Alexa's breath caught in her throat. She was fairly sure that she'd never shared that particular fantasy with anyone—not even her favorite drinking buddy. Of course, with all the tequila they'd shared over the years, she supposed she might have gotten a little too tipsy once or twice and spilled her most secret desire to her friend.

As a young girl, castles, headstrong maidens and handsome princes had been her easy, innocent daydream. Her mother had spared no expense in transforming Alexa's bedroom into a perfect princess palace, right down to the step-up four-poster bed with shimmery sheers flowing from the canopy. After her mother had died, Alexa had forbidden anyone, least of all any of her stream of stepmothers, from changing the decor.

In her teen years, the setting had become more private. More sensual. Ripe for a young girl's fantasies. Only she'd never wanted a knight or prince to rescue her. From what? A life of wealth and privilege? No, she'd simply wanted a sweet-voiced young man who could satisfy the torturous, mysterious aches that haunted her in the middle of the night. A man who could steal her away with pleasure and, perhaps, a forever love.

Luckily for her, college had pretty much knocked those delusions right out of her head. Sex, while enjoyable, was no longer a mystifying secret. And as far as Alexa had experienced, men who could weave prince-worthy magic with their bodies were few and far between. No, Alexa had now turned her princess fantasy into something much more practical.

Profit.

"I'm not talking about my sexual fantasies," Alexa said, "until you're ready to spill a few of your own."

"You want the ones I've actually lived out or the ones I'm still working on?" Cat replied quickly, a sculpted eyebrow arched over a sparkling eye.

Alexa steeled herself against a shudder. "Forget I said anything. I don't play games I can't win, and God knows your love life has always been more exciting than mine. Let's talk about something important, like how you'll help me with this project."

Cat stepped back. "God, that hungry look is scary."

Alexa chuckled. "So I've been told."

"You do realize that you already have more money than God, right? I mean, in case you're wondering where your next meal is coming from, I'd say from the nearest five-star restaurant that delivers. Hell, who cares if they deliver? You can buy the place and have the chef come over to make you a peanut butter sandwich. With truffle sauce."

Alexa blanched at the combination of flavors, imaginary or not. "It's not about the money."

Cat laughed out loud. "Come on, Alexa. With you, it's always about the money."

Alexa turned back to the sliver of land on the horizon, shaking her head as she gazed. She couldn't blame Cat for making that assumption. She presented that picture to everyone, even to her best friend. Her father had left her millions—millions he'd made with his own ingenuity and backbreaking determination.

He'd worked his way up from a doorman to become a competitor to the likes of Hyatt, Hilton and Marriott. Crown Chandler hotels exemplified excellent service, meticulous decor and premium prices. Since Richard's death six years before, Alexa had kept the business running with keen precision, as she hadn't been raised to whittle away her legacy without first adding to the pot. She'd worked twenty-four/seven to ensure that everyone from the maintenance man to the top executives knew that Alexa Chandler put the solvency and growth of her business above all else.

When she discovered that in addition to his all-consuming work ethic, her father had also left her this perplexing piece of land off the coast of St. Augustine, Florida, uncharacteristic whimsy had shot through her. What could be more perfect for her than an abandoned island and a castle? Though Richard Chandler had died in the same car accident that had also nearly killed Alexa, no mention of the property had been made in his will, and the deed had only recently been discovered by her stepbrother, who found the paperwork among his mother's belongings—along with a note that had "For Alexa" jotted on the corner. None of his attorneys knew a thing about it, though they'd verified the authenticity of the document and Richard's signature.

The discovery had spawned a series of events that had led her here, to St. Augustine, with her best friend, the occult expert, opening her briefcase in preparation for a meeting Alexa had been anticipating for hours. Initial research revealed that the island—and the castle—were reportedly haunted, which put them right up Cat's alley. A well-known paranormal researcher with a list of degrees as long as her waist-length hair, Cat was the perfect person to delve into the history of the land Alexa had inherited. And if the rumors of ectoplasmic activity were true, Alexa knew she had a real discovery on her hands.

In more ways than one.

"The only reference I could find to Valoren was in

a database run by a Gypsy genealogy site," Cat informed her after placing pointy-cornered glasses on her regal nose.

At the news, a thrill shot into Alexa's veins and she spun, excited and terrified at the same time. The word "Valoren" had been scribbled on the bottom of the deed, with no explanation.

Alexa had tried to research the island—called Isla de Fantasmas by the locals—on her own and had come up with little more than rumors and speculation. She'd learned that the island's reputation as a gathering place for ghosts had been recorded as far back as the Spanish occupation of Florida in the fifteen hundreds. Tales of hostile spirits, coupled with the inhospitable terrain made up mostly of prickly palmettos and thick walls of bamboo, had kept anyone from inhabiting the land. Even sea birds and turtles stayed away. Locals speculated that the tales of spectral activity had been planted by pirates protecting their stronghold, but the tales had remained long after the privateers vanished from the Florida coast.

Then, sixty years ago, according to a local historian, a mysterious speculator had bought an abandoned castle in Germany and began moving it to Florida to rebuild on Isla de Fantasmas.

Piece by piece.

Quietly, almost secretly, the medieval-style stronghold had been rebuilt by a foreign architect and workers housed exclusively on a ship anchored off the island. Armed men in fast boats had kept curious onlookers away. Even the press had been thwarted in their quest to find out more about the project.

And then, in 1950, two years after the work began, the project stopped.

The architect, the workers, the ships, disappeared. The castle remained, but the local fishermen claimed that even if a visitor did find a place to go ashore on the craggy island, the castle was surrounded by a completely impenetrable twenty-foot stone wall. If anyone had made it over the wall, he or she hadn't returned to tell about it. The sheriff had reported that thrill seekers often claimed to have breeched the island's natural defenses, but no one cared enough about an empty scrap of land to provide proof.

Interestingly, the county courthouse contained no record of the land being bought by Alexa's father, though the quitclaim deed had been declared genuine by a local judge. Yet when she'd asked for a guide to take her to her property, the local sailors had scattered faster than a school of grouper startled by a hungry shark.

That's when she'd called Cat.

"So, the rumors . . . are they true?"

Cat shook her head, her ironed-straight hair brushing along her bared shoulders. "That the island is haunted? I'll need to see that for myself," Cat said, her tone, as usual, brimming with skepticism. Though Cat's genetic makeup included a potent mix of New Orleans Creole and Santería-worshipping Caribbean stock, her friend didn't believe in any magic she couldn't prove. So far, Cat had built a reputation for proving more paranormal phenomena than any other researcher in her field—and disproving even more.

"The only other reference I found to Valoren was in a book written twenty years ago by a Gypsy *Chovihano* whose family dated back to the seventeen hundreds," Cat said.

Alexa slid onto the sleek leather couch beside her friend. "And?"

"That book was useless."

"Then why—"

"The writer is dead, the mention to Valoren the equivalent of your father's note on the deed, though it does lead me to believe that Valoren is a place, not a person or a Romani word. The *Chovihano* left no relatives. His publisher was no help. Small press. Out of business. But," she said triumphantly, "in the acknowledgments, the author made reference to an anthropology professor in Texas. A Gypsy expert. I called him."

"And he's heard of Valoren?"

Cat nodded. "And not just an oral history, either. He'd read about the place, though his memory was sketchy. He remembered something about it being a Gypsy enclave. A sort of safe haven."

"I thought Gypsies never stayed in one place."

Cat shrugged. "They don't, ordinarily, which makes the place all the more interesting, doesn't it?"

"Could he remember his source?"

"No, but he seems to think it was a dissertation or an academic paper of some sort. Maybe a diary. Unfortunately, he has hundreds of professional journals and personal memoirs in his private collection and he can't remember which one has the reference."

Alexa cursed. Why she felt so compelled to figure out the answer to this puzzle perplexed her, except . . . she missed her father desperately. This gift seemed so personal, as if he'd searched for a castle for his little princess, remembering how fierce she'd been about her room, about her mother's legacy. And her father had been just the type—loving and whimsical one minute, serious and driven the next—to try to turn her childhood dream into a moneymaking reality. In all practicality, a reputedly haunted, five-star hotel on an exclusive, hard-to-reach island could become the crown jewel for Crown Chandler. If Alexa made this project happen and filled the rooms with celebrities, dignitaries and nouveau riche entrepreneurs who appreciated privacy with their pampering, she might finally be accepted as the shrewd, creative new leader of Crown Chandler Enterprises and not just the spoiled little rich girl who'd inherited her legacy because she'd lived and her father had died.

Or was she simply so hard up for a decent lover that she was pinning all her hopes on some Sleeping Beauty fantasy?

"What's our next step?" Alexa asked, shaking off her apprehension.

"I'm flying to Texas," Cat informed her. "The professor said I could search his collection. I'll check out the island when I get back. That is, if you're still interested in the history of the castle before you move forward with your plans."

"Oh, she's interested."

Alexa sat up straighter, her spine rigid. Ordinarily, she didn't react so icily to her stepbrother walking into a room unannounced. However, she ordinarily didn't allow Jacob anywhere near Cat, either—at least, not since their messy breakup.

"My, my," Jacob said, his nose crinkled as if Catalina's exotic scent offended his delicate sensibility. "Look what the *cat* dragged in."

Cat skewered him with a sharp glare, tore off her glasses and snapped her briefcase closed. "God, Jacob. You're such a drama queen. You could at least make an attempt at being original."

Alexa jumped to her feet. Blood would be drawn if she didn't act quickly. "Okay, now that we've had our warm reunion, can I talk to you, Jacob, in the other room?"

With a sneer, her stepbrother begrudgingly headed toward the suite's bedroom. Just to be on the safe side, Alexa shut the door behind them.

"Why are you still hanging out with that freak?" he asked.

Alexa bit the inside of her mouth. Black pot? Meet kettle.

"Just because the two of you broke up—four years ago, I should remind you—doesn't mean I can't be friends with her."

Clearly, time hadn't lessened the bitterness between her brother and her friend. Catalina had kicked Jacob to the curb once she realized he'd been using her to meet the self-proclaimed witches and vampires who flocked to Catalina unbidden, sometimes because of her research into the occult, most times because of her legacy as the granddaughter of a Santería priest and a voodoo priestess.

From the moment Jacob Sharpe's mother had married into the Chandler family, Alexa had realized that

her new brother had interests that were more than
a little weird. While Alexa herself had always been
interested in ghosts, her reasons leaned toward the
capitalistic and had nothing to do with Cat. Long before Alexa had met her friend, her interests in the
paranormal had always stemmed from how a rumor
of ghostly hauntings in the hotel world nearly always
equaled financial gain. Travelers often paid big money
to have a cold, otherworldly breeze blow across their
cheeks in the dead of night.

Jacob, on the other hand, had proclaimed himself
Wiccan, Goth and anything else that would drive his
parents crazy. After college, he'd stopped trying to
shock everyone. Alexa had figured he'd finally grown
out of his rebellious stage. Cunningly, he'd let the inky
dye fade out of his brown hair, gave up lining his icy
blue eyes with black kohl, and traded his favorite
black duster jacket and Nazi storm trooper boots for
Armani suits and Bruno Magli shoes just long enough
to land himself in her daddy's will. Which was why
she had to deal with him on a regular basis.

"Why are you here?" she asked. "I told you I could
handle this situation on my own."

He had an unnerving habit since the accident of
following her around like a guard dog, despite the fact
that she'd given him an entire division of established,
top-performing hotels to supervise. She'd survived the
car wreck, even if his mother and her father had not.
Therapy for her concussion, punctured lung and broken thighbone had been a bitch, but she'd recovered
with even more strength—and determination—than
she'd had before.

Jacob shrugged in that boyish way that made her
forget he was nearly thirty years old. "Things are running like clockwork as usual. But I'm bored. I need
a challenge."

"You can always look into that ski lodge in Utah."

He scrunched his nose. "Too many Mormons in
Utah."

She blew out a frustrated breath. "Yes, they do tend to gravitate there." And the good Lord knew that Mormons weren't her stepbrother's speed.

"Let me help you here," he said, his tone vaguely whiny. "I am the one who brought you the deed. I didn't have to, you know."

She supposed he didn't. He'd taken his mother's death pretty hard—harder than she'd expected for all the tension that existed between the two of them. Apparently, he'd waited until recently to go through the last of her effects, and Alexa supposed that if he had wanted to be cruel, he could have kept the deed to himself. But while Jacob had nearly always been a pain in her ass, he'd never been underhanded or mean.

"Come on, sis," he pleaded. "I can make myself more useful with your spooky castle than I can approving budgets for bed linens. With your knowledge of hotels and mine of all things mysterious, we can build a property that will make our competitors weep with envy."

Jacob's grin quirked up on the right side of his face and his eyes glittered. They might not have been related by blood, but Alexa couldn't deny that they both suffered from a condition that caused hot flashes at the possibility of growing their portfolios.

"Yes, well, I can't make any decisions until I see the place close-up," Alexa said, wearing her most unengaged expression. She didn't want anyone, even her stepbrother, to know how desperately she wanted this venture to work out. "But since you're here, you can at least come with me. I hate flying."

Alexa's father had taught her everything he knew about hotels in particular, but also about business in general. He'd also insisted that a smart woman adhered to the old adage of keeping her friends close and her enemies closer. She wasn't exactly sure where her stepbrother fell most of the time, but as she was on the brink of a spectacular opportunity, she'd rather not take any chances.

At least not until she arrived on the island.

2

Air rushed into Damon's lungs, nearly choking him. His eyes flew open and he was partially blinded by the sudden light. Had it happened? Had he finally crossed over from the plane of his punishment into hell, where he belonged?

A soft mewling at his ankles convinced him he still was not dead. At least not entirely. And he couldn't suppress a wave of disappointment, an undercurrent against his natural instinct to survive.

He looked down, not surprised to see a long-haired black cat circling his ankles. He kicked out, but the animal merely burst into a cloud of smoke and seconds later reformed into the crafty feline he was.

"Away, beast."

The cat stared at him with amber eyes flecked with gold, eyes that, perhaps, didn't look so evil after all these centuries.

Damon bent down. The cat disappeared. A split second later he felt a warm, furry weight in his arms.

"You enjoy taunting me," Damon said to the cat.

The creature replied by purring and rubbing its flattened face against his arm.

The cat's rumbling vibrations brought Damon a peace he did not deserve. He preferred the state of dormancy he fell into every hundred years or so. Drowsy. Still. Forgetful. Dead, and yet . . . not. A phantom, unable to escape from a prison of his own making.

For long periods of time, he couldn't remember exactly what or who he was, why he was trapped in a world that consisted of little more than a drawing room, a doorway that led to nowhere and a window that looked out on nothing. Somewhere in the far reaches of his mind, he remembered a time when he'd been whole. Virile. Strong. Solid.

And ultimately, cursed.

He remembered a sorcerer. A missing sister. Brothers dispersed into a storm in search of their wayward sibling. A storm. And magic most evil.

But beyond that, his brain felt too taxed to work out the details. How could the particulars matter after all this time?

And yet . . .

What was the smell suddenly invading his nostrils? He breathed in deeply. The cat meowed. Sea salt? He closed his eyes and focused on the sounds teasing the edge of his consciousness. Waves? How could that be? There was no ocean near Valoren. Had he transported back to his beloved England? Or was he somewhere new?

Another sound sent him bolt upright, and after a moment, his surroundings solidified. The brushstrokes faded and his sense of the furnishings in the room sharpened. He could feel the carpet beneath his boots, smell the smoke from the torch in the sconce and the melting wax from the candle above the unlit fireplace. The atmosphere became suddenly dank and cloying, causing his linen stock to chafe against his neck. He reached around and undid the ties, his hand brushing against his long hair, bound with a black strip of leather. Was it his imagination or was he still damp from his ride in the storm?

A loud chopping noise drew his attention away from the state of his body and clothes. Despite the cat purring in his arms, Damon stalked to the window. He tore aside the heavy drapery, shocked that the view outside was no longer blank canvas. Below, angry waves crashed against a shore of sharp boulders at the

base of the castle. Blue skies, devoid of clouds,
gleamed all around him. And then swooping in from
above him, something hovered in the sky. The sun
glanced off the monstrosity, forcing Damon to look
away. The cat scrambled out of his arms, arching and
hissing, its claws sharp through his sleeves.

Damon froze, enthralled. The metallic bird turned,
and through what looked like glass, he saw a woman
trapped inside the belly of the beast. He reached out
to brace himself on the window, but his hand slipped
straight through.

Yet no glass shattered.

Damon jerked away from the window, his breath
sapped and his eyes clearly deceiving him.

"Where am I?"

He shouted his question, but just like every other
demand he'd made since his entrapment, this one
went unanswered.

"Did you see that?" Alexa said, her heart clenched in
her chest. She almost couldn't breathe, but she wasn't
sure if her reaction was from the dizzying, bumpy
movement of the helicopter or the flash of a face she'd
seen in the window of the supposedly abandoned
castle—followed by a solid hand materializing, briefly,
on the outside of the window and then disappearing
from sight.

"See what?" Jacob replied.

Alexa removed her headset, adjusted her sunglasses
and looked again. The noise of the helicopter was
deafening, but she ignored the pulse against her ear-
drums. The curtain inside the window had fluttered
shut. The glass was old but surprisingly clean of grit
and grime—and unbroken.

Her skin crawled with memories. Having Jacob as
her stepbrother and Cat as her best friend ensured
that Alexa had seen all manner of odd things in her
lifetime. Some easily explainable. Others not so much.

And this time, she'd seen a man.

Hadn't she?

She replaced her headphones. "Can you bring us any closer?"

The pilot responded quickly. "Negative. The wind is picking up. Ms. Chandler, we need to go back."

"Not yet."

"Alexa, I'd prefer not to die out here. You've seen the castle. The structure looks sound. Let's go back," Jacob insisted.

His face had turned a pasty white. And she was the one who hated flying?

"Circle the island one more time," she ordered the pilot. "There has to be a place to land."

The pilot complied, just as she knew he would, thanks to the more than generous incentive she'd offered him after takeoff to land safely and allow her to explore the island. Every nerve ending in her body flared and quivered. Imagined man in the window or not, Alexa planned to survey the inside of her castle. Today.

She grabbed the seat as the pilot swerved into a turn. Once more, he remained high above the trees, brush and bushes that filled the area between the reputed stone wall and the house. In many places, they couldn't see any hint that the wall still existed. For all she knew, the salt air had broken down the stones until nothing existed to keep her out of the castle—if only they could find a place to land.

Jacob scooted away from her, flipped aside the microphone hanging near his lips and muttered, his mouth against the glass. She rolled her eyes. Let him pout.

Since she'd ordered the pilot to search for a place to land, circumnavigating the island took a little over five minutes. The pilot's voice crackled over the headset when a strong wind slammed the helicopter. They dropped ten feet. Alexa screamed. Jacob seemed frozen in his spot until the pilot regained control and lifted the helicopter back to its original altitude.

"Sorry, folks. Man, that gust came out of nowhere. Ms. Chandler, I'd love that bonus, but it isn't going to

be worth much if the chopper goes down permanently.
Maybe we can come out earlier tomorrow, get a better look. . . ."

Despite the direct input into her ears, the pilot's
words faded as Alexa stared out the window. A cluster
of tall palms bent backward in acquiescence to the
blustery air. In the cleared space, she saw something
that everyone had told her didn't exist.

A lagoon.

"Jacob!"

She grabbed his sleeve. He slid over to her side of
the seat. She pointed. His eyes widened.

"You're right, Captain," Alexa said, nearly unable
to contain the bubbles of excitement popping inside
her. "Let's head back to the airport. I think this challenge is best attacked by sea."

The minute Alexa stepped onto the tarmac, she cursed
herself for sending Catalina to Texas in pursuit of the
documentation on Valoren. If her friend had been in
the chopper, she could have verified what Alexa had
thought she'd seen. Or, perhaps, what she actually *had*
seen, but was having trouble wrapping her mind
around.

A man. A flash of a man.

A man whose hand had solidified on the other side
of an unbroken window, and then, just as shockingly, disappeared.

A man . . . or a ghost?

She swallowed hard. She'd wanted a haunted castle,
hadn't she? She had no business getting all freaked
out and scared now.

Behind her, Jacob was in deep conversation with
the pilot. She scurried through the executive airport
and into the waiting limousine. Using her satellite
phone, she dialed her private plane and was immediately patched in to Cat.

"We haven't landed in Texas yet," Catalina announced, sounding amused by Alexa's eagerness.

"Not why I'm calling," Alexa replied, fully aware

she was about to knock the humor out of Cat's attitude. "We made it close enough to the castle to see into a window. And I think"—she took a deep breath—"I saw someone."

"Someone?"

"A man."

"Inside?" Cat asked.

He'd worn white. The image suddenly flashed in her mind. A white shirt. Long sleeves. "The place is supposed to be deserted. I only caught a glimpse, but I swear, there was a man inside my castle. And his hand . . ."

She recounted what she'd seen. The thrill tripping through Alexa's bloodstream caused her to shiver deliciously. Driven by excitement, curiosity and fear, her emotions skimmed just beneath the surface of her skin. Her body zipped with an electric current she didn't think she'd ever felt before.

The connection crackled. "No one pays much attention to that island," Cat reasoned. "You could just have a squatter."

"And the hand?"

"The sun is bright. It could have been an optical illusion or your overactive imagination."

Alexa smirked. "Or a ghost."

Realizing she wasn't entirely alone in the car with the driver at his post in the front seat, Alexa raised the glass partition.

"That's your first guess?" Cat asked. "You're starting to sound like your brother, always jumping to the occult to explain a simple anomaly."

Alexa whistled out a breath. She couldn't argue. Cat was right. "Explain the disembodied hand."

Cat remained silent.

Alexa cleared her throat. "I know I sound crazy, but I've had the oddest feelings about this place since Jacob brought me the deed. And what with all the legends and rumors . . . maybe I'm caught up in the hype, but could you imagine? A real ghost?"

Cat still didn't respond, and Alexa realized she'd

probably scared her best friend half to death. Cat had seen many people slip over the sharp edge that separated reality from fantasy. She wouldn't be entirely surprised if Cat ordered Alexa's pilot to turn the plane around immediately so she could return to Florida and slap some sense into her.

"Yeah, I can more than imagine," Cat said. "However, I can't help but kick around a few more earthly scenarios that include a serial killer hiding out in your castle, not some soul who hasn't crossed over."

"Well, I'll find out soon enough."

"I thought the island was inaccessible," Cat reminded her.

"During our flyover, we found a small lagoon. All I need is a boat, and I'm on my way."

"Take someone with you," Cat warned.

Alexa glanced out the car window and spotted Jacob moving toward the limo. "Jacob's with me."

"Take someone else."

Alexa rolled her eyes. Four years and these two still couldn't shut off the antagonism. "Right now, he's all I've got. Besides, I can take care of myself. And oddly enough, I'm not afraid."

"That's what scares me most, *mija*. That's what scares me most."

Cat disconnected the call, sat back in the plush seat of Alexa's corporate jet and considered canceling her research trip to Texas. But by the time she landed in Florida again, Alexa would have already stormed willingly into a potentially dangerous situation. Though Cat didn't trust Jacob as far as she could throw him, she had to admit that to date, he'd been very protective of his stepsister, as if his narcissistic brain somehow registered that Alexa was the only family he had left.

And Alexa wasn't exaggerating when she said she could take care of herself. Cat had sparred with her enough times at the *dojang* to know her friend could fight. Maybe not with a crazed serial killer, but Cat had learned long ago that despite her intrinsic abilities to catch visions of the future, she couldn't alter the destiny of her friends, her family.

Or, most especially, herself.

Once fate cast its lot, nothing and no one could change the outcome, even when the outcome meant tragedy.

3

"There's no one here, ma'am."

Alexa glanced over her shoulder, her lips pursed and her jaw tight, as the Coast Guard seaman shifted from one foot to the other, clearly uncomfortable with breaking the news. The discovery wasn't unexpected. The minute she'd squeezed through a crack in the wall, broken through the sixty-year-old padlock on the front door and witnessed six decades' worth of dust and sand on the cracked stone floors of the castle, Alexa had known no one had been inside.

No one corporeal, at least.

At Jacob's insistence, she'd allowed the crew of the closest Coast Guard UTB to escort the boat they'd chartered to the island and search for possible tres-passers. Now that they'd completed their mission, she wanted them gone. She had exploring of her own to do, starting with the lone furnishing—a painting hang-ing alone on the landing above the grand staircase.

A painting that had captured her interest as if the man in the portrait had reached out from the canvas and was even now curling his fingers in a silent, rhyth-mic beckoning.

She gave the seaman a curt nod and returned her gaze to the portrait. Despite the dust and the cobwebs, the man in the oil on canvas was nothing short of magnificent. Piercing eyes the color of a storm-tossed ocean—a swirling mix of green and gray—stared straight into her. His hair, long, deep chocolate brown, seemed to have caught an unexplainable wind in a drawing room decorated with candle and torchlight. As if wet, his stark white shirt and scarlet waistcoat molded to his skin. A single droplet of water slid down his square jaw, threatening to splash down at any moment.

The artist's realism stunned her. The plush face of the cat on his lap. The velvety folds of the cloak tossed carelessly across the back of an ornate chair. Even the fired tips of the candles in the sconces blurred as if photographed rather than painted. The fact that the portrait was the only furnishing in the castle further piqued her interest. Had the mysterious builder in the forties reconstructed the abandoned German castle simply to house a single piece of artwork that no one would see?

"Time to go, Alexa," Jacob announced after the rest of the Coast Guard contingent had congregated in the foyer.

"No," she said.

"What?"

He marched up the stairs. She could hear his loafers crackling across the layer of sand encrusted on the floor.

"I'm not leaving," she said. "Not just yet."

"The place is deserted, Alexa. And thanks to our seafaring friends, we know the structure is relatively sound. Let's get back to the mainland, call in our structural engineers and our designers and—"

She turned and faced her stepbrother squarely. "I said no, Jacob. I want some time to look around. I . . ."

She faltered. She *what*? Wanted to know if the figure of the man she'd seen in the window had been a figment of her imagination or, as she suspected, a ghost? Could he be the man portrayed in the painting?

Despite the sudden difficulty she had moving her legs, she took a few steps away from the canvas. "I want to get a feel for the place."

With perfect timing, Jacob's cell phone trilled

loudly, the noise jarring. There was nothing to soften the sound. No carpets. No furniture. No draperies. Even the room upstairs where she'd been so sure she'd seen a man yank a curtain closed just after she spotted him from the helicopter had ended up having an entirely bare window.

While Jacob was distracted with the call, she thanked the Coast Guard seamen for their time. After assuring them that she and her brother would return to the mainland on their chartered boat and would exercise the utmost caution while on the island, they left.

"Finally," she said.

"Yes, she's here with me," Jacob replied to the caller. He moved to hand the phone to her, but she waved him away, her gaze captured again by the portrait. His nose was as interesting as the rest of him, the nostrils flared ever so slightly and his lips, she noticed, were curved almost imperceptibly upward. As if he was on the verge of a sneer.

"I'll make sure Alexa is accurately informed," Jacob insisted, his volume increasing.

She stepped farther away from Jacob and closer to the painting. She had no interest in the obvious crisis at the office. The urge to get rid of Jacob, too, and experience the castle while alone overwhelmed her. She raised her hand and realized her fingers were shaking.

Touch him.

Touch me.

"She's asked me to handle it," Jacob said.

He laid his hand on her shoulder. Alexa nearly jumped out of her skin.

She caught her breath and acknowledged his assumption with a quick wave.

Jacob walked down the stairs and toward the main entrance, but Alexa's heartbeat didn't slow. She removed the backpack she'd filled prior to leaving the marina and double-checked her stash. Bottled water. Energy bars. Dried fruit and nuts. A very large knife.

Two emergency flares and a flare gun. A portable GPS and her satellite phone.

Enough to keep her safe and sound for a few hours, right?

She glanced up at the painting. Had that tiny sneer eased into a smile?

Below, Jacob's voice grew increasingly perturbed. She was the CEO of Chandler Enterprises, not an operations manager like him. If she didn't have the quality staff to handle a problem without her intervention for a few hours, then how could the company remain successful?

She'd just zipped up her backpack when Jacob returned the phone to his waist and marched back up the stairs.

"I lost the signal, but I got an earful. There's a storm blowing through Boston," he explained.

"And I control the weather, how?" she asked.

Jacob frowned. "We're hosting that big convention this weekend."

She took a few steps closer to the painting. Away from Jacob. Away from the Crown Chandler crisis. Away from her everyday life. Just for a moment. Just for one, brief moment.

"And?" she asked reluctantly. The sooner the situation was explained, the sooner she could order Jacob to handle the solution.

"The hotel lost power."

"That happens in storms," she pointed out, even as a dip in the pit of her stomach warned her there was more to the story.

"The hotel is booked to capacity and there isn't even enough light to run the bar."

She took a deep breath, and then exhaled slowly, tempted to find a stone pillar to hide behind. "What does the city say?"

"They can't send out crews until the storm passes, and this apparent pseudo hurricane isn't showing any meteorological signs of moving one inch. We need to send in buses and move the guests to other properties in the area or we need to get the generators up and running."

"Why aren't they?"

"It's bad, Alexa." Jacob said, his mouth drawn in a tight line. "Looks like sabotage."

Her chest tightened. "Sabotage?"

Jacob leaned in close, his voice hushed as if they were in the office with a half dozen prying ears rather than in an abandoned castle with only a haunting portrait to intrude on their privacy. "The generators have sustained severe damage. The police have been notified. They don't want maintenance to touch anything because they'll be destroying evidence and—"

"Stop!"

This couldn't be happening.

Not again.

He arched a brow.

"Go back to the mainland," she ordered. "Organize a conference call with all the managers of our properties in the area. We can't bus the guests anywhere until the storm dies down, but we need transportation in place. At the hotel, move the guests to the grand ballroom, where there aren't any windows or exterior doors. Have the kitchen break out all the ice cream and desserts we'll lose anyway and serve it gratis, as well as all the booze they can pour. And then . . ." Her mind swam. God, didn't she pay her staff huge salaries to handle this type of crisis?

But sabotage? Again?

She leaned back against the wall, the portrait's frame skimming her shoulder. "Jacob, you know what to do as well as I do. Handle this, okay?"

She closed her eyes. The stone against her back, so cold only moments before, suddenly warmed. The heat eased through the thin layer of her clothes and ignited her skin. She could feel the gray eyes of the man in the portrait staring down at her. Into her.

Jacob stepped nearer, his gaze darting with annoyance to the portrait as if the man were intruding on their conversation. "Are you crazy? You want me to leave you here alone?"

Fingers of warmth curled around her shoulders. Alexa allowed her head to drop forward, and the sensations smoothed over her neck, then eased down her spine. Yes, she wanted to stay. Yes, she wanted to be here alone.

"Alexa?"

Jacob grabbed her arm and tugged her away from the wall.

"What's wrong with you?"

Alexa shook her head. Wrong? Nothing was wrong. Was it? She was simply tired. Overwhelmed by her experience earlier in the helicopter and now in the castle.

"Look, you'll only be gone for a few hours, right? The Coast Guard knows I'm here and I have the portable GPS. I can activate the distress signal if I need to and our friends will come running, I'm sure. And I have my phone."

"I just lost the signal on mine," he said, his expression incredulous.

Guard dog.

"A cell, not satellite. And you had the phone working long enough to hear the complicated and business-threatening tales of woe from Boston. If I call you and all you hear is 'help,' get here quick, okay? I've got water and supplies. Just come get me before dark."

His eyebrows slanted together at a hard angle. "I can't just leave you here."

"Why not?" The farther she walked onto the landing, the more the warmth seeped out of her, the clearer her mind focused on the possibilities of the castle as a Crown Chandler resort property. The stairs would be polished, the cracks repaired. Lush tapestries would keep out the drafts and keep in the cool air that seemed trapped in the stone walls. She'd insist on electric or gas-powered torches to provide ambience and just enough light to keep the shadows sufficiently spooky.

This could work.

She just needed time alone to concentrate. To allow the ideas to flow uninterrupted.

She spun and lifted her chin. "Just take care of business on the mainland and let me do my stuff here."

Jacob made no move to leave.

She stared at him intently.

He groaned. "There's no arguing with you when your chin tilts up that way."

She smiled. He was right.

"I'll be back in two hours or less," he promised. He jogged down a few steps, then returned, removing a necklace from around his neck. "Wait. Wear this."

Alexa eyed the offering warily. She wasn't sure she'd seen Jacob wear this particular trinket before—a gold triangle with a jagged corner, as if it were ripped off a larger design.

"What's this?"

"A talisman," he answered.

She crossed her arms.

He rolled his eyes. "Take the damned thing, Alexa. It's for luck. I'm betting this charm kept us from falling out of the sky today on that helicopter."

She shook her head. "I don't need a good-luck charm."

He thrust the necklace at her. "Take it or I'm not leaving."

Alexa knew how to assess an opponent. From across a boardroom table or on the landing of an ancient castle staircase, she could estimate with amazing accuracy when her adversaries would back down and when they would not. Jacob had correctly assessed her stubbornness a moment before. Now he was the one who wasn't budging. Which meant the crisis at Crown Chandler would only snowball. Sunlight would slip away. Her chance to roam the castle halls would be lost.

She yanked the necklace out of his hand and, while he watched, twisted the chain around her neck.

"There," she said. "Satisfied?"

After a quick kiss on her cheek, Jacob told her to be careful and left.

Instantly, Alexa turned to the painting. Fingering the triangle now dangling from her neck, she approached the portrait with soft, measured steps. The closer she got, the more intensely her body reacted. Her chest tightened. Sweat curled along the back of her neck. Her breathing shortened. His eyes seemed to rake over her. She jolted when her nipples hardened in response.

Whoa.

She stopped. "Just who are you?" she asked the painting.

Touch me and find out.

She staggered backward, then spun around. The door at the bottom of the stairs remained firmly closed. The voice had been a whisper in her ear, a hot breath along the nape of her neck . . . and yet, she was alone.

Alexa swallowed hard and turned sharply. She hadn't come this far to be afraid. She marched to the canvas and balanced her fists on her hips.

"Say again?"

She waited.

Nothing.

"Just when things were getting interesting, you turn shy?" she quipped.

His expression remained stoic, unchanged, but his eyes brimmed with wild fury like thunderclouds rolling over white-capped waves. Even through the layers of grime coating the canvas, masking what she anticipated was a rich depth of color, he intrigued her at the same time that he unnerved her.

She shrugged out of the silk shirt she'd worn over a lacy chemise and approached the canvas.

Hung high, the painting remained mostly out of reach. She stretched on her tiptoes and flicked the shirt at the corners, removing most of the powdery dirt and spiderwebs that had accumulated on the surface and in the corners of the once-gilded frame. With a shiver, she tossed the ruined material to the floor, but admired her handiwork nonetheless.

He was gorgeous. The fire of male strength and power had been captured in his eyes, in the set of his shoulders, in the broad width of his chest. The fabric and detail in the cut of his clothes reflected money. Perhaps influence. The time period eluded her, but she'd have experts tackle that question. She was more concerned with who he was—and if he was the man she'd seen in the window. Was he the type of man who would defy time, space and, perhaps, death?

She closed her eyes and concentrated.

Who are you?

She ran her fingers over the frame. Once again, she felt a surge of warmth. Funny. Ghosts were supposed to announce their presence with cold, weren't they? Clearly, this was no ordinary spirit.

Or she was taking this fantasy thing way too seriously.

She nearly pulled her hand away when she heard the whispered baritone once again.

Touch me.

She kept her hand steady. "I don't go around touching strangers," she countered.

The air around her swirled with heat.

I'm not a stranger. We've met before. In a dream. In your fantasy. Touch me and see.

Alexa couldn't resist. She slid her hand off the frame, then up the portrayal of his waist. She stretched as high as she could on the balls of her feet and reached until her palm settled on the spot where his heart would beat.

Did beat.

Strong.

Hot.

Heat seared her hand, and yet she couldn't pull away.

The temperature rose. Her skin seemed to melt into the canvas.

She opened her mouth to scream, but darkness dropped over her and pulled her into a vortex. She scratched out, stretched and twisted, fighting to keep from falling . . . but lost.

4

This time the awakening came slowly.

No rush of air.

No blinding light.

Just the gradual saturation of life into his body, the gentle peeling of his skin away from the moist oil and canvas that had held him captive for what he guessed must have been centuries. The moment his boot hit stone, his vision cleared. The redheaded woman was sprawled on the ground at his feet.

He hoped she wasn't dead. Pity if such an enchanting female perished only to set him free.

On bended knee, he reached to touch her, but stopped before his fingers made contact with her alabaster cheek. Her hair, pulled back tightly from her face, gave him pause. How many centuries had elapsed since the Gypsy woman had warned him that a woman with flames in her hair would be the instrument of his destiny? Her predictions had thus far proved ominous. He'd married his wife, Anne, partially because of her station and dowry, and partially because her burnished tresses garnered renown among the whole of King George's court. He'd been so curious to see if the Gypsy's prediction would prove true, he'd sacrificed his bachelorhood.

Yet despite the fire in her hair, Anne had proved as cold as the Thames in winter. He'd then found himself with Renata, his mistress, drawn by her passionate mien and crimson curls. Too late he'd learned she'd used henna the first night they'd met and changed her hair color on a whim. Sweet natured and warm, Renata had been a welcome distraction during his sojourns to London, but she had not affected his destiny in any way.

Except on the night of his imprisonment, when he'd thought—for a brief, insane instant—that Rogan had trapped her in a painting.

He glanced from the woman on the floor to the portrait on the wall, now devoid of subject. On the night of his sister's disappearance, there had been a redhead in the portrait. In a corner shadow. In a doorway that did not exist. She'd lured him in and yanked him out of his time and into this new world where machines flew in the sky and women, like the one now crumpled on the floor, ordered men in uniform about as if she were queen.

At that thought, he touched her. A lock of hair had escaped the severe queue she'd tied at the nape of her shapely neck, so he merely brushed the hair aside. She moved, made a sound quite like a cat's mewling.

He looked up.

No, it was only Rogan's cursed cat.

Golden eyes ablaze, the flat-faced feline leaped out of the portrait, landing on its paws with a skilled bounce. The infernal animal stared at him accusingly, as if to suggest that Damon had once again developed a soft spot for a woman with red hair.

Despite the animal's uncanny presence, Damon dismissed its omniscient look. He cared nothing for this woman except that she had somehow freed him.

She was, admittedly, beautiful. And before the force of the magic had knocked her unconscious, responsive. He hadn't missed how her nipples had hardened beneath her blouse or how her breathing had changed when he'd entered her mind with his sensual suggestions. She might have made a worthy conquest, if not for the fact that he had only one thing on his mind at this moment—escape.

"What do you think, beast?" He scowled at the

animal, still unsure after all these years if the animal was friend or foe. "Is she the one who shall be the instrument of my destiny?"

The cat replied by licking its paw.

With a frown, Damon stood and assessed his surroundings, his eyes drawn instantly to the door across the great hall.

"Or perhaps she already is."

He strode down the stairs, invigorated by the stretch of his muscles, the power in his thighs and shoulders. He breathed in deeply and the smells of the sea were unmistakable. With a backward glance, he noted that the woman who had freed him remained on the floor. A pang of something he assumed was guilt nearly caused him to pause, but he managed to push the intrusive emotion aside and concentrate on his goal.

Freedom.

Nothing would delay him.

Nothing and no one.

Not even the beautiful flame-haired woman who'd freed him from his prison.

At the top of the stairs, the cat howled.

Damon continued to the door.

He grasped the latch but didn't yet pull. What manner of insanity existed outside these castle walls? He touched his waist. His sword was long gone. Machines that flew might be just one insignificant hint of how the world had changed. Damon was an educated man, a resourceful man. But even he understood that a man out of time would be vulnerable in ways he might not adequately anticipate.

Still, he couldn't remain here any longer. Rogan's castle brimmed with dark, evil magic. Questions ranging from the deep and philosophical to the shallow and mundane coursed through his mind. Were his brothers still alive as was he? Had they found his sister? Vanquished Rogan? There was no ocean near Valoren, so he knew the castle no longer existed there. How did one move a castle? And was he now in England? He'd heard the strangers speak as they milled beneath his portrait prison. They did not sound like any of his countrymen, but they spoke the mother tongue. At least, a bastardization of the language. Had his country changed so much over the years?

He pressed down on the latch.

Nothing happened.

He tugged and pulled, bracing his arm on the door-jamb to create leverage. He buoyed all his strength against the lock, straining until sweat broke out on his brow.

From across the hall, the cat hissed.

With a curse, Damon stopped. Apparently, the witch on the landing had released him only so far. What magic did she brew that kept him entrapped?

He crossed the hall in seconds, then took the stairs three at a time, catching her as she raised herself on her arms and groaned.

A sensual sound, even when laced with pain.

"Move slowly, my dear," he said. "You've suffered a great shock."

She defied him instantly, spinning to face him with a decided bounce on her backside.

A rather lovely backside, truth be told.

"Who are you?" She winced as she smoothed her hand over the back of her head. "Or should I ask, *what* are you?"

She slid her palm over her forehead, squinting beneath her fingers despite the dim light on the landing. Damon glanced at the torches, unlit for all these centuries. He wondered if there was a way to light them when, suddenly, they flamed to life.

Interesting.

"I could ask you the same question," he said, extending his hand to her.

She looked at him defiantly, her expression crisp with suspicion.

"I mean you no harm," he emphasized.

"Then explain the knot on the back of my head."

"A consequence of the dark magic imbued in these castle walls, I suspect."

"Your magic?" she asked.

He sniffed derisively. "Hardly. I wouldn't have trapped myself here, would I?"

Though her wary expression did not falter, she accepted his help in standing. Her hand was small in his, but her intrepid comportment compensated for her lack of size. The minute she regained her balance, she yanked her hand from his and stepped back to establish distance.

"I apologize, my lady. As for what I am, I cannot yet say. As to who, I am Damon Forsyth."

She popped the tie holding her hair in place, releasing the red strands in thick, shiny waves. She sighed. Apparently loosening her hair alleviated some of the pain in her head. Her jaw relaxed, but only slightly.

"So, Damon Forsyth, are you dead?"

Damon glanced down at his body, examining the coarse texture of his breeches and the slick leather of his boots. "I do not believe so, madam. Quite frankly, I've not felt this alive for centuries."

"Then what are you?"

"I'm quite certain I do not yet know. Previously, I was the son of John Forsyth, a British baron and governor of a Gypsy colony in a land called—"

"Valoren?"

Damon gaped. "You know this place?"

She shook her head. "No, I don't know it at all. Just the name. And you're not in Kansas anymore, Sir Damon. Then again, neither am I."

Wavering on her feet, she reached out to find her balance. Luckily, Damon was the nearest solid object. Her hand gripped his powerfully, and for a split second he imagined those same fingers seizing his naked shoulders or raking across his back.

He cleared his throat and shook the bawdy image from his mind. "What is this . . . 'can sis'?"

She snickered. "It's Kansas. *Wizard of*—oh, never mind. Okay. You're not dead. And unlike when I saw you in the window earlier, you are now solid. Which means?"

Damon took a second before he realized he was supposed to provide the missing information to her supposition. "I know not, my lady. My last memory includes a powerful anger toward a dark sorcerer. I must suppose that this anger led me here."

She blew out a breath and managed to stand solidly on her own. "So, you pissed off some magician who locked you in the painting?"

Damon winced. Such language from a woman of breeding was wholly unexpected, but nonetheless intriguing. "What makes you think *I* angered *him*?"

She broadened her stance in a pose that looked vaguely defensive. "He wouldn't have trapped his best friend in here all this time, would he?"

Damon thought of the cat. "I would not be so sure." Eyeing her skeptically, he wondered at the breadth of their conversation. For a woman who'd just confronted someone whose presence could not be explained scientifically, she appeared mostly unruffled. Did such occurrences happen daily in her century?

"You have no trouble accepting that I am a man out of time?" he asked.

She laughed. Not a tinkling, genteel giggle, but an out-and-out guffaw. "I have a lot of trouble, believe me. But I can't ignore what is right in front of me."

Nor could he. She was hauntingly lovely, with eyes the color of leaves in spring and skin that, despite a natural pale hue, glowed with life. But mostly, she possessed a fire he'd never witnessed in a woman so young, so lonely. She'd reacted to him too easily to be a woman who warmed herself regularly in any man's bed.

"Perhaps I am not real at all," he offered, wanting to verify his suspicions, "but a figment of your powerful fantasy?"

Her shock, followed by a quick flash of anger, told Damon more than she intended, he was sure. That she *was* lonely. That she was in need of a lover. And that she wasn't happy about it. Not, at least, when someone else voiced her innermost desires.

She pinched him on the arm. Instinctively, he stepped back and voiced his displeasure with a random curse.

Her chuckle infuriated him, but he had to admit, she possessed a wealth of courage. She'd turned the tables, saucy wench.

"You're as real as the knot on my head," she insisted. "At least, for my purposes. Question is, *why* are you here?"

Damon took a deep breath, invigorated again by the rush of air into his lungs. This, coupled with his attraction to this beautiful, headstrong woman, was a sensation he never wanted to forget. "I have no idea, my lady, but I do intend to find out."

Her hand shot out and grabbed his wrist before he could react. He squelched his instinct to twist out of her grip, startled by the heat of her flesh. She turned his hand and pressed her fingers tightly on his palm. Satisfied by what she felt there, she quickly scratched her nails across his skin.

He winced. "Is this a new form of greeting?"

She pulled his hand closer and watched as nail marks swelled.

"You feel pain; you have a heartbeat and blood flow," she assessed.

Damon attempted to gently remove his hand from her grip, but she held tight. With no need to demonstrate his power at the moment, he simply arched a brow.

She released him but showed no repentance for her audacious behavior.

"You have not yet reciprocated," he reminded her.

"Excuse me?"

Absently, he rubbed the spot where she'd marred his flesh. "Your name?"

"Oh." She thrust her hand at him. "Alexa Chandler, president and CEO of Crown Chandler Enterprises."

He glanced skeptically at her hand. He gave her a sweeping bow, then stepped aside.

She pulled her hand back. "You weren't solid before," she said.

"I daresay you know nothing of who I was before, Miss Chandler. Or is it Lady Chandler?"

She snorted. "I take it you're from England originally."

"We are not in Britain now?"

"You're in the United States."

He searched his brain but found nothing. "Where?"

"Sorry. The colonies. Only we're our own country now. You are now in the United States of America. But," she said, her eyes narrowed as she dismissed the information she offered as insignificant, "when your hand went through the window upstairs, you were not solid. Now you are. Care to explain?"

Damon pursed his lips. This woman was incredibly observant and wholly single-minded, and didn't exhibit the least indication of fear in the face of the unknown or supernatural. Either the world had changed completely from when he last lived free, or else she was a remarkable woman of courage. From the painting, he'd watched her command the crew of sailors that had searched the castle for signs of his existence. He'd heard her negotiate and issue orders to the young man who'd shown concern over her safety, which she'd promptly dismissed. Clearly, this Alexa Chandler was a woman of importance and power.

Just the sort of woman who might be able to set him completely free.

"Yes, 'twas I in the window, but no, I was not solid then as I am now."

"What changed?"

"You. You unlocked my soul from the portrait."

"Your soul? You said you weren't a ghost."

"I do not believe I ever died."

"How can you be sure?"

He took a deep breath. "How can a ghost, whose body has perished, take solid form?"

She nodded, chewing on her bottom lip charmingly while she pondered the situation. A thinker, this one.

Practical and logical. He wasn't sure he knew many women of her ilk in his day. Clearly, he was frequenting the company of the wrong women.

"Okay, I'll give you that one. Ghosts are not, to my limited knowledge, ever solid. Then what are you?" Her luminous eyes fixed on him, even as her voice pitched with desperation to understand. "Some sort of lunatic?"

He smirked, though he supposed the possibility existed. The whole of the situation teetered on the absurd, but he knew enough about Rogan's black magic to accept that this situation did not exist within a damaged mind. "I cannot say, but since you are presently the only person who can see or hear me, the onus of sanity would be on you, would it not?"

She nodded. "Right. Can't argue there. However you became trapped in the painting, you certainly aren't stuck there any longer."

His gaze darted toward the door. The reins had loosened, but he was still trapped by Rogan's curse.

He'd emerged in a different era, but he doubted that outcome had been part of Rogan's grand design. More than likely, the sorcerer had laid magical traps in his castle to stop anyone from interfering with his and Sarina's escape. Rogan had known about the coming horde, just as he'd known Sarina's brothers would come for her. The trap may not have been meant for Damon specifically, but it had been sprung nonetheless.

"There's so much I don't understand," she admitted.

"I'm sure I'd be additionally fearful for your sanity, my lady, if you did comprehend my situation fully."

She snorted, but he found the sound quite charming.

"Because of the Gypsy curse, I have stepped out of my time and into yours. When I was entrapped in the painting, the year was 1747, a year after the defeat of the Great Pretender at Culloden."

Her eyes widened.

"What year is this?" he asked.

She bit her bottom lip, drawing instant attention to the fullness of her mouth. "Oh, only 2008. I think I need to sit down."

Even as she made the confession, he saw no weakness in her. Her skin had bloomed with color. If she swooned now, he'd have to suspect her action was a weak attempt at gaining his sympathy.

Yet why would she need to play such games? As far as he knew, she could leave the castle anytime, the same way she entered—unencumbered and free to move about at will. But if she left, how would he escape? He needed her. She'd already helped him breech one barrier. Chances were, she could help him progress further once he determined the means she'd used to get him this far.

Unless, of course, her touching the painting had trapped her as well.

"I'm sorry," he said, gesturing to the empty landing, "there is no furni—"

A chaise appeared a few feet behind them.

She spun around.

"Where did that come from?"

He arched a brow. "I'm not entirely sure," he replied, glancing at the flames flickering in the sconces.

Rogan had built this castle. On more than one visit, Damon had suspected that a common magic allowed the sorcerer to keep the place running with only a small number of servants. Perhaps the magic still existed, now at his beck and call.

What did that mean about Rogan?

What did it mean to the curse?

Anger and confusion surged through him, but Damon held his emotions in check. First, he had to ensure that Alexa Chandler didn't leave until he was able to follow.

"The chaise looks comfortable enough," he assured her. "Why not have the seat you so desire."

He allowed his voice to deepen at the word desire, and he could tell from the indignant flick of her eyes that she felt the effects of his suggestive tone.

Sharp, this one. And sensitive to sensual hints. She'd prove either woefully easy to seduce or ridiculously resistant. Either way, he didn't doubt his ultimate victory. He was, after all, the Forsyth heir. Challenges fed the men in his family with as much nourishment as meat and wine.

At the thought, a table appeared beside the chaise, laden with steaming brisket, a pewter decanter and two matching goblets.

"Stop that," she ordered, spinning on him with fire in her decadent green eyes.

He crossed his arms tightly over his chest. "I'm afraid that is easier said than done."

She matched his stance, tilting her chin in a valiant attempt to mask her lack of height. "Why?"

"Because, my dear lady, I have no idea what, exactly, I am doing."

Alexa Chandler narrowed her gaze, assessing him with cunning worthy of a man, but incredibly alluring when coming from a woman. "I find that incredibly hard to believe."

His gaze locked with hers in a battle Damon knew could have serious repercussions.

For both of them.

"Then I'll just have to convince you."

5

"Clearly, you're a man who likes a challenge," she assessed. "Should make life in this little dreamworld of yours very interesting."

His chuckle echoed off the bare stone all around them, then injected directly under her skin. The sound skirted the edge between sinister and genuine mirth. Perhaps she should have heeded both Cat's and Jacob's warnings for caution. Maybe—just maybe—for the first time in her life, she was in over her head.

"I assure you, Miss Chandler—"

"Alexa," she corrected, ignoring the sudden acceleration of her heartbeat.

"Yes, of course. Alexa."

He exploited every vowel, his accent emphasizing the keen feminine sound of her name even as he stepped an inch or so closer. Her instincts battled between running like hell and leaning in those last few inches, to see if his skin was indeed as warm and his muscles as hard as she imagined.

"I assure you that this dreamworld, as you call it, can be very real if you so wish."

She locked her feet in place, determined to remain unaffected by his proximity. And yet, anticipation thrilled through her, electrifying the space between them with a raw, natural magic that she understood very, very well—even if she hadn't experienced it firsthand for a long time.

To cover her attraction, she eyed him with as much

skepticism as she could muster. "A moment ago you told me you didn't know how the magic worked here."

" 'Tis true," he said, "but I did not say I would not attempt to manipulate the magic to my advantage."

His curve of a grin emphasized the sharp angles in his cheekbones and square jaw. His snug breeches, loose-fitted sleeves gathered at the wrist and finely embroidered waistcoat conjured images in her mind of Jason Isaacs in *The Patriot*—or better yet, from the richness and quality of his garments, of Richard Chamberlain in *The Slipper and the Rose*. She remembered swooning over that particular video during her incredibly romantic and tragically lonesome youth.

Well, she wasn't a starry-eyed Cinderella wannabe anymore. This castle belonged to her. And she wasn't going to let some superhandsome ghost or whatever he was trick her into believing this situation was anything less than real and, therefore, primed for her control. She was here. He was here. And he was not from this time.

Not. From. This. Time.

The realization struck her hard and she dropped onto the chaise, her brain spinning. With a tilt of his head and a practiced gesture with his hand, he asked permission to sit beside her—which she granted after scooting over to provide a safe distance.

"You have no reason to mistrust me, Miss Chandler."

"Please, call me Alexa. I like to be on a first-name basis with all the . . . phantoms I free from cursed paintings."

He chuckled again, the sound no less effective the second time around. "You have a sharp tongue."

"You have no idea," she quipped. "Look, I'm not afraid to admit that I'm feeling a little bit foggy. Maybe we need to take a deep breath and back up and try and figure this all out."

He leaned across her to the table and retrieved the goblet and decanter. His linen sleeve brushed against her skin, injecting the air with a tantalizing scent that was decidedly male and inherently intoxicating. Before she could stop herself, she'd inhaled deeply.

He smelled exactly as she'd expect of a man of his time and station. Like leather and spices and pure maleness. No designer fragrances or masking colognes. Once he took a draft of the wine, his kiss would return the full-bodied flavor of the vintage, with nothing minty or artificial to impair the taste.

"Perhaps this will help," he said, pouring the scarlet liquid into the goblet.

She eyed him skeptically. "I don't think drinking magic wine is the answer to my problem. Water will suffice."

He took a long sip from the pewter cup himself, humming with pleasure. Her mouth watered, then, with a swallow, quickly dried.

"You'll not trust any water I conjure, true?"

"I have some in my bag. Just there."

After a pause, he moved to retrieve her backpack. Clearly, this wasn't a man accustomed to fetching items for anyone, much less a stranger. He placed the pack at her feet, and while he sipped his wine, she fished the bottle out and unscrewed the plastic cap.

The crisp flavor of the water refreshed her, but the continued cloudiness in her mind made her wonder if maybe she was trapped in some sort of dream. Certainly that would make playing along with him easier. She was used to seductive dreams, wasn't she? She'd had little else in her love life lately. Of course, she couldn't deny he was solid, at least in her imagination. She'd felt his pulse and the heat of his skin all at the same time—and muscles like his didn't fill out pants the way his did unless there was something rock hard underneath.

But the bump on the back of her head was the size of a Ping-Pong ball. She knew as well as anyone that head trauma could cause all manner of problems.

Including powerful hallucinations.

"Tell me why you're here," she said.

"My best guess?" he asked casually, as if sitting on

a chaise lounge with a woman from his future and sipping wine was something he did on a daily basis. "I was trapped by a sorcerer's curse, and somehow you freed me. What do you know about this castle?"

"That I own it," she replied.

His eyes widened. "Truthfully?"

"I never lie about real estate."

He sat forward, clearly intrigued. "Do you know its history?"

While toying with the cap on her bottled water, she decided there was no harm in telling him the truth. Whether he was a figment of her imagination or a real manifestation of a man who'd been trapped by a curse, the facts were the facts. "About sixty years ago, a mysterious and as yet unnamed entrepreneur bought the castle in Europe and had it moved, piece by piece, to this island off the Florida coast."

"Florida? Isn't Florida controlled by the Spanish?"

Luckily, researching the castle's origins had allowed her to brush up on her history. "Not for about one hundred and fifty years, give or take."

He swirled the wine in the goblet, then took a hearty swig. "This world is very different."

"That's an understatement" she said, taking a long drink of water. "According to my sources, this man rebuilt this castle in as much secrecy as he could manage, hung your portrait and, apparently, disappeared. I don't suppose he showed up in the painting with you?"

"I would have noticed," he said ruefully. "I have a vague memory of a journey. Of darkness. Of being enclosed. But nothing I can hold on to."

She frowned. When Jacob had first brought her the deed, she'd never envisioned that the land would bring with it such a perplexing puzzle. And in this case, she wasn't even sure which pieces—if any—were entirely real.

"At some point," she continued, "this man transferred the ownership of the island to my father, and I inherited the land and everything on it from him.

Property I intend to use as soon as I can make it habitable."

Damon looked scandalized, and Alexa couldn't help grinning. She supposed if he really was from the seventeen hundreds, he wasn't accustomed to dealing with a woman like her—one who owned property as opposed to one who *was* property. Well, he'd have to catch up to the twenty-first century sometime or another.

"So, do you want to be my resident ghost?"

It was so easy to fall back on her original plan, no matter how distant the scheme seemed now. But she couldn't allow herself to fully accept that Damon Forsyth was now a real force in her life, or at least her castle. That would change everything. *He* would change everything.

"I told you previously, madam," he said with a haughty sniff, "I am not a ghost."

"Phantom, then," she decided, with equal snobbery. "Here, but not here. Can you make yourself transparent?"

Alexa really should be careful what she wished for. In a split second, Damon disappeared. She dropped her water and threw herself off the chaise lounge, scooting away from where he'd vanished even as her lungs struggled for breath.

Slowly, like a ray of sunshine gleaming through a window, he rematerialized. He was staring at his hands, as if he were as surprised as she was.

Once he was completely solid again, he crossed his arms on his chest. "The answer to your question, my dear lady, is yes."

Alexa squeezed her eyes shut, then opened them again, all pretense gone. Damon still stood above her, his expression handsomely smug.

"Maybe this is a dream," she muttered.

"Perhaps. There is also the distinct possibility that instead of you freeing me from the portrait, I sucked you in with me."

"You're just trying to scare me."

His brow furrowed as he considered the possibility. "Frightening women for sport is not the measure of a true man."

"What is?" she asked, annoyed at the unwelcome fear coursing through her.

His smile was pure sin.

She scowled to mask the sudden flare in her blood. "I can't be in the portrait. Can I?"

"Can't say for certain. I appear to be free of the portrait," he said, nodding toward the painting of the room that no longer had a sexy, sardonic man in the center, "yet I cannot leave this castle."

"How do you know?"

"While you were unconscious, I attempted an escape. I was not successful."

"Can I leave?"

"I've no idea," he admitted, then leveled his ocean gray stare at her. "Why don't you try?"

A sudden wave of dizziness struck her. She braced her hands on either side of her, willing the sensation away. She'd experienced enough vertigo for a lifetime after the wreck. She didn't need a reminder of the pain and discomfort now.

She was healthy. She was strong. She was a survivor. She repeated the mantra silently in her head until the wooziness subsided. After blinking away the last of the fog, she shot a glance down the stairs and to the door, then back at Damon.

His hopeful expression vanished nearly as quickly as he had.

But not quickly enough.

"No," she said.

"No?"

She arched a brow. "Not used to being contradicted?"

His glower was powerful. "Of course not, but I assumed you'd want to ensure that freedom was still yours to take."

She smiled. "You let me worry about my freedom. You'll soon discover that I'm very good at taking care of myself and getting precisely what I want, when I want it."

He wanted her to try the door. Desperately. He was clever and commanding, this man, and he wasn't as adept at hiding his emotions as she was at reading them. For all she knew, the wave of vertigo she'd just experienced was from him trying to exert his will on her with the same magic he'd used to disappear and to conjure the chaise lounge and the wine. But she'd fought him successfully. If she played her cards right, the game could be hers.

Bottom line, she wanted this man.

To be her personal phantom. This idea, so entrenched in her psyche for oh so long, blossomed into something tangible for the first time in her life. She'd turned quite a few of her more pragmatic fantasies into reality using her wealth and influence, but she'd never brought a fantasy to life with just her touch.

"What could possibly be more pressing than finding out if you are free of this curse or trapped by it?" he asked, incredulous.

"Finding out more about you."

The atmosphere shifted. The power play ended and the blaze in his eyes kindled from a spark of frustration to a slow, steady sexual heat. He reseated himself on the chaise and held out his hand to her.

"You say that with seduction in your voice, my lady."

She accepted his hand. This time, when he drew her onto the chaise, he allowed no space between them. His thigh crushed against hers, igniting a wildfire of sensation through her.

She traced an invisible crazy eight on his knee. Crazy, as in completely insane, touching a man who, by all tenets of reason and logic, couldn't possibly be real. "Wishful thinking, perhaps?"

He smiled with hooded eyes. "Simple observation. There's no shame if you want me. In the most classical sense."

She licked her lips, unwilling to deny his assertion. She did want him. She had wanted him—or, at least, a man like him—for all of her life. Gallant, powerful, intense. A master of magic.

And best of all, he wasn't entirely real. By his description, he could not follow her out of this castle or disrupt the ordered life she'd built for herself on the mainland. He was a fantasy. A diversion. A sexy, sensual secret she'd discovered and, perhaps, only she could keep.

"I won't deny that I find you incredibly attractive," she responded.

"How can you? Even now, your body tightens for me."

She swallowed a gasp. Even in her century, such talk pushed limits. And yet, as his gaze brushed over her breasts, her nipples responded instantly. Her thigh muscles clenched with anticipation.

Maybe he was simply like her. Honest. Insightful. Observant.

Hot for magical sex.

"Is this magic?"

He leaned closer so that his breath, wine scented just as she'd imagined, teased her cheek. "The most elemental magic of all."

She tilted her chin to match his sensual stare. "You were a playboy in your former life, then?"

He ran his tongue over his lips, drawing her attention to the fullness of his mouth. "Circumstances of my youth dictated that my boyhood was rather brief and did not include much time for play," he informed her, his words crisp and factual while his tone lazed with sensuality. "My pursuits of pleasure began when I was very much a man."

"And you've been a man a very long time," she said, her voice breathy with possibilities.

Their lips were mere centimeters apart.

"I've been a man trapped without a woman even longer," he warned.

Their noses brushed. "Should I be afraid?"

"If you have to ask," he said, sweeping the edge of his lips over hers, "the answer is decidedly no."

Alexa couldn't remember the last time she'd kissed a man, but the moment her mouth clashed with Damon's, all thoughts of former lovers or the lack thereof flew out of her head. As she'd anticipated, he tasted of a fine claret—and so much more. Tobacco. Time. Experience. His tongue smoothed against hers with coaxing skill, but she didn't need to be cajoled. She speared her hands into his hair, freeing the dark strands from the leather tie, and climbed onto her knees so she had to tilt his chin toward her to fully devour him.

He grabbed her by the shoulders and pulled her away. His eyes narrowed in suspicion.

"What manner of witch are you?"

She supposed she should be insulted, but instead she laughed. "Don't try to convince me that all the women in your day were prim and proper maidens with no passion. I know things about history and I won't believe you."

He scowled slightly. "I would not attempt to perpetrate such a lie. Yet only moments ago, you doubted my good character."

She balanced her hands on his shoulders, massaging the thick muscles with greedy hands, waylaying her need to rip the soft linen of his shirt away from his skin. "I still doubt your good character. All the better for what I want from you."

He quirked a grin. "You're sure you're not royalty?"

She laughed. "Depends on who you ask."

"I prefer to keep our interactions private."

"Good," she said, leaning forward and teasing his lips with hers once again. "I was thinking the very same thing."

6

Alexa hardly knew what had come over her.

Okay, that was a bald-faced lie. Lust had come over her. Years and years of fantasizing about a mysterious, ghostly stranger fading into her room late at night and introducing her to decadent pleasures of the flesh. Hot dreams. Wet dreams. Dreams that had haunted her with particular vigor since her monthlong stay in the hospital, when she'd had little to do but sleep and surrender to the medications coursing through her body.

But now she was healthy. She could have exactly what she wanted with a lover who wasn't completely real—if only she took the leap.

The room darkened around her. She leaned away from Damon and watched candles and torches in iron sconces and elaborate candelabras materialize all around them. Silk draperies and tapestries unfurled from the stones on the wall. In seconds, the landing was transformed into a sensual hideaway, with the cushioned chaise as the centerpiece.

"You're getting the hang of using the magic," she whispered, awed by the finery glowing around her.

"Wondrous what a man can do when properly motivated," he replied.

Alexa sank to her knees, knowing she'd lost her mind in pursuing this mysterious phantom—and not really caring. "Maybe the magic is what is making me so hot for you."

He quirked a half grin. "Do you truly believe that?"

Leaning back fully against the chaise, Damon locked his hands behind his head and stared at her with those stormy eyes that sucked her in like a watery vortex. She didn't know what to think—until she realized that was her problem.

Alexa didn't want to think anymore. Day after day, hour after hour, minute after minute, Alexa Chandler was expected to use all of her brainpower to ensure that her father's legacy didn't falter. One hundred and thirty-five luxury hotel properties in eight countries fell under her responsibility, along with thousands of investors and employees. Not to mention hundreds of thousands of premium guests.

Even at home, someone always needed her. Jacob. The staff. Various and sundry members of her extended family who had no use for Alexa until they needed a suite for a good friend for their wedding, an advance on their dividends from the company or even her opinion on their latest vacation destination—which was only a roundabout way of bucking for a free room. Even the men she'd dated came up short in fulfilling her most basic desires. Or else she'd been too afraid to accept what they had to offer, so she'd found lame excuses to send them away.

The only peace she ever found had been alone in her bedroom, in the hour between when she slipped into bed and finally fell asleep, fantasizing like a schoolgirl about a mysterious man who would slip uninvited into her room and ask her for nothing while he gave her everything she ever wanted.

Girlish, yes.

But damn it, Alexa grasped escapism when it came, which wasn't often. How could she now deny what she so desperately wanted? Her entire body thrummed with the gravity of her need. In every other aspect of her life, she'd always taken what she wanted without looking back. Why not here? Why not now?

"Make love to me, Damon," she said.

He sat bolt upright, touched his fingers to the straps

of her blouse and, in a blink, the material disappeared, leaving only her bra to cover her breasts. And under his heated gaze, even that seemed too much.

"I will make love to you, Alexa, but not because you order me to. As a man, looking at you, feeling you against me . . . I have no other choice."

The soulful longing in his voice sparked a flame inside her that raged the minute he grabbed her by the waist and pulled her down atop him. Whether their clothes disappeared completely via magic or through the insistent ripping away of fabric, Alexa wasn't sure. In a haze of heat, she knew only that her skin had ignited where every nerve ending in her thighs, stomach, breasts and arms moved against his. Instantly, the fire melted her insides until liquid warmth seeped from between her pulsing labia. She stretched her body completely over his; his sex jutted against her, hard and ready.

She couldn't wait. What if she awoke before she'd had her fill? What if someone roused her prior to the fantasy playing out? She'd been there before. The frustration had been maddening. No, she wouldn't wait. Not a minute. Not a second. Instead, she pulled her knees beneath her, took his cock boldly in her hands and guided him inside her.

An explosion of sensation rocked her. She cried out from the blast of ecstasy, burying her fingers in his chest hair, holding on for dear life as her body rode the wave until it crested, then fell. She was nearly unaware of his presence until he spoke.

"Why the rush, my lady?"

He curled his hands over hers and softly loosened her grip. Panting, she opened her eyes and saw a smile twinkling in his eyes. She'd used him for instant gratification.

Embarrassingly instant gratification.

Wonderful instant gratification.

"I didn't want you to disappear," she admitted, breathless.

He shifted so that the thickness between her legs

jolted her with another wave of pleasure. "I'm certain I have no better place to be than here."

He felt so real. So solid. Unlike the lovers from her dreams, whose very insubstantiality had haunted her. Climaxes while in the throes of sleep left her wanting more. Like just now. Her body, so starved for satisfaction, had taken the least he had to offer.

And from the look in his eye, he clearly wanted to give her so much more.

She smiled shyly, keenly aware of how their bodies were still merged and how she'd reacted like she'd never had sex before in her entire life. "I suppose I jumped the gun."

He clucked his tongue. "Clearly, you jumped something."

Surprisingly, his chuckle didn't send her running.

"Some*one*, you mean."

He arched a brow. "Not that I mind, but such haste defies logic. Had you waited, I could have done this."

Lifting her hands to his lips, he kissed her fingers one by one, then lolled his tongue along the inside of her palm, flicking down her wrist to stir her pulse points. He then guided her hands to her breasts and smeared the moisture over her nipples until the tight pucker of arousal no longer ached, but instead pearled with needy vibrations she knew only he could alleviate.

"Your breasts are perfectly lovely. So sensitive. May I?"

His polite request left her stunned, but she dropped her hands to her sides and managed a nod, her eyelids drifting closed as he applied his singular touch. He smoothed his roughened fingertips over her, weighing the fullness of her flesh in his palms, using his thumbs to draw tiny circles around her areolae, then flicking the tips of her nipples with his thumbnails until she cooed from the sensations.

She found herself running her hands over his stomach, reveling in the resistance of his abs and in the soft pelt of hair arrowing down his chest. In a dizzy swirl of sensation, he pressed his hands against her shoulders, pulled her close, then flipped her beneath him.

"Ah," he said, his grin wide, "that's more like it."

She blinked rapidly. "Women on top threaten you?"

His chuckle spawned another wave of sensations within her, each more delicious than the one before. "Threaten? You have an odd view of men, my lady."

"You haven't lived my life."

"No, but I have lived mine. Trust me when I tell you that nothing you do, nothing you say, will threaten me in any way."

She grinned and laced her hands behind his neck. "You said yourself that I'm a powerful woman."

"Yes, and this intrigues me. Challenges me. If the men in your life have run from you because of your strength, you are simply pursuing the wrong men."

She cradled her cheek against the pillow as she laughed. "You've said a mouthful," she agreed.

He eyed her breasts hungrily. "Ah, but a proper mouthful has nothing to do with words."

Damon proved his point by scooping his arm beneath her back, arching her body so he could wrap his lips around her erect nipples. Instantly she reacted, boldly scrambling her fingers into his hair and tugging him closer. Had he not been certain of her station in life, he might have thought her a courtesan, at the very least—or more likely a queen. From the moment she captured his cock, shoved it within her moist folds and milked instant pleasure from him, she'd snared him. Now it was his turn to enslave her. Only through their mutual delight would he find his way to freedom.

He flicked his tongue across the tight tip of her breast. She writhed beneath him, impatient. Needful. His tentative control slipped from his grasp. He needed to orchestrate this seduction to his advantage, but more than that, he needed to feel her, taste her, lose himself inside her until the wasted years refilled with new, glorious memories.

He'd been alone too long. Longer than his entrapment. Longer still than his married life, mistress or no. He dropped lower and bathed Alexa's naked belly in hot kisses. She spread her legs so that her feet dropped over the sides of the chaise. Her need crystal clear, he thought he'd lose his mind.

And he did. In the taste of her. In the feel of her. The heat of her desire and the fire of his own tossed all thoughts of freedom and captivity, magic and evil, from his brain. He wanted nothing more than to learn her, brand her, make her his in ways neither of them would ever forget.

She was panting hard when he finally looked up from between her thighs. She grabbed him by the cheeks and pulled him close.

"I can't wait anymore. You're driving me mad."

He kissed her hard, loving how her flavors mixed and mingled with his. The tightness of wanting her made his whole groin ache, particularly when she clasped his buttocks with both her hands and drove her fingernails into his flesh, urging him inside her once again. He saw no reason to prolong the agony and immediately complied, though he did not impale her swiftly as she expected. Instead, he pressed the head of his sex into her just an inch, waited for her to gasp in pleasure, then withdrew.

"What?"

He drove into her a little deeper, relishing the sensation of her hot, moist skin against his hardened flesh and the way her breath caught in her throat when he teased.

"You are too hot," he chastised.

Her eyes widened. "I'm too—?"

He eased back, leaving the top of his penis nestled in her tight opening, but denying her—and him—the full sensation they both so desperately sought. "Slow and steady wins the race," he claimed.

She grabbed his buttocks and pulled him hard inside her.

"Not in my century," she claimed.

His laugh soon turned to unbidden groans as need overtook him and he could think of nothing else but pumping them both to climax. She wrapped her legs around his waist, and the tilt of her womb nearly drove both of them mad. In a haze of pleasure, Damon felt centuries of control slip out of his grasp. Around him, candles blinked in and out of existence. The tapestries and silk sheaths rustled from an unseen wind and the music of her gratified bliss rang in his ears.

The moment of climax came hard, and Damon's entire body tensed, then released. He crumbled atop her, sated and stretched to his limit. The gentle way she curled her fingers in the long strands of his hair nearly lulled him to sleep.

"I can't believe this is real," she said on a stilted breath.

He pulled up onto his elbow and watched how the reflection of the flames from the sconces flickered in her emerald eyes. Her beauty truly was unsurpassed. Her intense passion enhanced her attractiveness to the point where it almost pained him to look at her. Against the pillow, her burnished hair taunted him, reminded him of the Gypsy's promise. He could only wonder how deep Alexa Chandler's influence would remain over his destiny. She'd already released him, albeit partially, from Rogan's cursed painting. Now she'd brought him intense pleasure in an act so simple and basic, with any other woman, the physical actions might as well have been by rote. Yet with Alexa, Damon felt renewed. Invigorated.

Alive.

Completely. Not a shadow of a man, but solid to the core.

"This is amazingly real. A few hours ago, I was trapped in a single room, staring out at nothingness for centuries on end, too exhausted by monotony and emptiness to dream about either my future or my past."

She released the lock of her legs around his waist,

but he remained inside her. Now lax, a single movement enough to separate them, he remained perfectly still.

"And now?"

He brushed a lock of her hair from her dark eyelashes. "The present has grasped my attention in a most amazing way."

As their bodies readjusted to normalcy, Damon shifted beside Alexa, and after untangling legs and arms and slick skin, they spooned. He placed his hand protectively on her belly, splaying his fingers to possess the maximum amount of skin. He concentrated, and seconds later, a silk coverlet draped over them, chasing away the chill. Surprisingly, he felt the muscles in his shoulders and arms go completely lax. His legs barely seemed to exist. The only part of his anatomy having trouble embracing this laziness was his cock, and with her buttocks snuggled so tightly against him, he could hardly blame his intimate anatomy for attempting to regain its strength.

He leaned in and, burying his face in her tousled hair, took a deep breath. When he pulled back, he felt a scrape across the bridge of his nose. Brushing aside her burnished locks, he found that a gold chain twisted the tight strands at the nape of her neck.

"What's this?" he asked, tugging on the necklace.

She attempted to turn toward him as he worked to untangle the chain. "Oh, it's a good-luck charm."

He chuckled, thinking the talisman had clearly done a brilliant job for both of them.

Working as nimbly as he could, he eased the hair from the chain, twisting and tugging until the charm came free. Only once the torn triangle fell across his fingertips did he realize what Alexa wore.

Sarina's necklace.

The one given to her by their father.

The one she'd lost on the night of her disappearance.

7

The chain snapped, abrading the skin on the back of Alexa's neck. Her hand flew to press against the pain, and when she removed her fingers, a light streak of blood slashed across her skin.

"What the hell do you think you're doing?" she demanded.

"Where did you get this?"

Damon's naked body gleamed with sweat even as he stood in an attack position. Legs balanced, knees slightly bent, arms at the ready, one hand clutching the delicate charm Jacob had given her as if his decision to murder her or not depended entirely on her reply.

She pressed her lips tightly together and reminded herself to breathe. She wasn't going to let some ghost on the edge of insanity intimidate her, no matter what they'd just done or how delicious the experience had been.

"You need to calm down," she insisted.

He lunged forward, and with a squeal, Alexa tumbled off the chaise and remained out of his reach. Damon was easily twice her size and clearly in a rage. She couldn't protect herself from a prone position. If he caught her, she wouldn't stand a chance, martial arts training or not.

His chest heaved with barely checked emotion, only the chaise between them—a strip of furniture he could make disappear just as easily as he'd conjured it.

"Tell me how you came to possess this charm, witch!"

Infuriated, she slammed to her feet. "You'd better watch your tone, mister. I took you out of that painting. I'm nearly positive I can find a way to put you back in."

Damon leaped over the chaise, his hand reaching toward her. She effectively deflected his first move but wasn't quick enough for the second. His hand tangled tightly in her hair, and if she moved, she knew it would hurt.

"Let go of me."

"Tell me how you possess my sister's necklace," he demanded through clenched teeth.

"What? You're insane!"

"That remains to be seen, but I know this charm. Sarina was wearing it the night she ran away, but I found this very broken piece only moments before Rogan's curse locked me in the portrait."

"That's impossible," she explained, her heart pounding. "Jacob gave me the necklace just this afternoon. He told me it would protect me."

His eyes blazing, Damon moved his face closer to hers. "He lied."

With a shove, he released her. Alexa's knees hit the cold stone with a jolt, but she swallowed a painful gasp and instead concentrated on reaching her backpack. Inside, she had a gun. A flare gun, but a weapon nonetheless. She wasn't sure the exploding cartridge could do any damage to a cursed phantom, even one with corporeal form, but she'd be damned if she didn't try.

Damon clutched the necklace as he stalked around the landing like a caged predator. One by one, the accoutrements he'd added to the room faded out of sight. First the plush tapestries and velvet screens, then the table and wine, and finally, the chaise. Still naked and struggling with a shame she refused to feel, Alexa was completely exposed to his cruel gaze. Luckily, he no longer seemed interested in looking at her at all. His eyes remained locked on the charm in his palm.

The sconces and candles faded last, dousing them in shadows that deepened and darkened as the sky outside the far windows swirled with grays and blacks. An ominous rumbling rolled across the ocean, announcing the coming storm. Alexa took advantage of the darkness and dashed to her backpack, fished out the gun and turned to point the wide orange barrel at Damon.

But he was gone.

Down the stairs.

"This is the key," he said triumphantly, mindless of his nudity and looking every inch as strong and powerful as he charged down the stairs as he had when robed in his Georgian-era clothes.

Alexa kicked into her trousers, sans undergarments, and punched into her blouse, fastening only one button before she flung her backpack over her shoulder and headed toward the stairs. A storm was coming, but she preferred to stare down Mother Nature in all her ugly glory rather than stay with a madman in the castle—her castle, she thought with a quiet growl— one minute longer. Staying close to the railing, she went down the stairs barefoot, grateful for the silence.

"This is where the magic originated," he bellowed, spinning and stopping her dead when his ocean-storm eyes burrowed into hers as lightning flashed around them. "Instrument of my destiny?" he shouted. "Not today. Not ever again."

Alexa's legs shook, but she continued downward, the gun clutched tightly in her hand, her eyes darting alternately between Damon and the door. She'd never get past him. Not unless she fired. And she couldn't justify shooting an unarmed man unless he lunged at her again. She'd have to find another way.

Lightning strobed, the bolts so intense, they brightened the inside of the castle so that the stones practically glowed with electricity, sparking off the tiny flakes of glass embedded in the walls. Thunder blasted immediately after, shaking Alexa straight through to her bones.

With his left hand clutched around the necklace, Damon grabbed the door handle with his right. With a mighty curse that rivaled the sounds of the squall outside, he pulled hard. The door flew open. Raising his fists triumphantly, he moved to step outside, free to unleash his bitter rage into Alexa's very real and vulnerable world.

A second later, blue light crackled against the blackness outside. The castle shook from the boom that instantly followed. Instinctively, Alexa looked away, her eyes tightly shut, but the howl of pain that accompanied the thunder forced her to look. Damon flew across the slick floor, landing hard against the stone.

Rain shot into the grand hall like a million needle-tipped arrows, but Damon didn't seem to care. He crawled on his knees until he was standing again, but before he got within even ten feet of the door, another burst of blue light invaded the hall, striking him directly.

Alexa screamed, but his agony made her reaction sound like a whimper. Electric fire burned into him. His body nearly floated upward as the strike continued, longer and longer than any ordinary force of nature. The whites of his eyes and his teeth glowed with cobalt fire.

She reacted on instinct, bolting down the remaining stairs. Sliding behind the massive door, she pushed with all her might. The heavy wood panel resisted for only a second, then flew into place, cutting off the searing pain that had flung Damon's body backward until he slid across the wet stone and slammed into the bottom stairs.

Any mortal man would have been knocked out cold. Hell, any mortal man would be dead. But, apparently, neither the force of a hurricane nor the blackest magic could kill a phantom. But it caused him pain. Blinding, excruciating pain, judging by how he writhed on the floor.

Outside, the storm continued to rage. The mournful wind and the slam of tree limbs against the windows grew in volume until the cacophony nearly had Alexa running for cover. Instead, she reached for the door but didn't touch the handle. What if she was struck, too? She might have cheated death once in the car accident, but chances were she couldn't pull off such a miraculous escape from the Grim Reaper a second time. Instead, she headed toward the nearest window to the right of the hall.

Unfortunately, the grimy stained glass wouldn't open. She swung at it with her backpack, but the window repelled her strike, even with the water bottles and portable GPS tucked inside. From the hallway, she could hear Damon groaning. She didn't care. She had to get out.

Reaching inside her pack, she retrieved the slicker she'd tucked inside and wrapped her fist, even while clutching the gun. With a shout that mixed determination, anticipated pain and fear, she punched at the glass. The pane held. Pain shot up her arm like hot fire, throbbing even as she staggered back.

She unwrapped her hand, stepped back a few feet from the window and fired. The cartridge hit the window with shattering force and exploded in a burst of red fire, but once the smoke cleared, she saw that the window remained intact.

Shaking, she reloaded. Aimed. But she had only one flare left. Did she really want to waste it on a window that would not break?

Instead, she bolted across the hall in search of another exit. She tried not to look at Damon, crumpled and naked at the bottom of the stairs, his arm tilted at an odd and painful angle. But the minute her mind registered his injury, she stopped.

Glancing back at the door, she approached Damon cautiously, the gun aimed at his chest.

"Why is this happening?"

He struggled to pull in a satisfactory breath. "I . . . don't . . ."

He didn't know. Big surprise. For an all-powerful phantom who could conjure an orgasm with a single stroke, he certainly wasn't much help against the big, black magic encasing this castle. This island. Her island, damn it. She wanted it back. Now.

"Give me Sarina's necklace," she demanded.

His narrowed gaze burned with unchained resentment. "Never."

She aimed the gun at his stomach.

"Give it to me or I'll blow a hole in you that will last for eternity. Obviously, you can feel pain. I'm betting a flare gun exploding in your gut might be considerably worse than a lightning strike. You really want to try and heal from both? I won't hurt the damned necklace. I don't know anything about it except what my brother told me. I want out. I want to get the hell away from you."

His breath ragged, Damon threw the charm and chain. It slid across the floor at her bare feet. Careful to keep her aim steady, she retrieved the charm.

"The magic. Will. Kill. You."

"I don't believe you," she spat. "The castle doesn't want me. It wants you. This necklace protected me before, allowed me entrance. Now it'll let me out."

"You don't know. You don't know for sure."

Alexa straightened to her full height. "I'll take my chances."

She darted toward the door again, her insides roiling with uncertainties she'd never show him. Not in a million years. All evidence pointed toward the charm providing her with the protection Jacob had promised. Her world hadn't turned from fairy tale to nightmare until Damon had ripped the chain from her skin.

Tossing her backpack to the ground, Alexa pressed the charm against her chest and reached for the door. Though lightning and thunder continued their raucous dance outside in the darkness, none came shooting toward the castle. She clutched the latch and tugged hard.

Nothing happened.

She dropped the gun and tried again.

The latch was frozen in place.

She turned toward Damon, fury and fear fighting for dominance.

"Let me out!" she screamed.

But no one listened. No one but the phantom lying at the bottom of the stairs, filling the castle with his cruel laughter.

8

Damon knew he shouldn't laugh at her, but to survive the excruciating agony of having his shoulder dislodged, he'd take what jollies he could. A thousand colors swirled in his eyes, each more sickeningly bright than the last. His skin burned. The act of breathing scorched the inside of his lungs.

Unfortunately, laughter hurt nearly as much as being thrown fifty feet by a wild bolt of lightning. He remained conscious by focusing on how Alexa had been so sure of herself, issuing threats as if her paper deed to this castle somehow gave her true ownership. She would learn. The rights and title to this structure belonged only to Lord Rogan and his evil magic.

He'd learned that the hard way himself, hadn't he?

"Shut up," Alexa ordered, the strange, wide-barreled gun aimed accurately at his midsection.

Perhaps she should shoot him. Maybe with a gaping hole in his belly, he could forget about the torturous separation of his shoulder from its socket.

"You're trapped," he coughed out. "This magic won't release you. Not until it is ready."

"When will that be?"

He shook his head, trying to remain conscious even as his vision blurred and his instinct for breathing faltered under the increased pain of his inhalations.

"Your shoulder is dislocated."

He managed a nod. Damned horse-riding accident. Since being thrown by a skittish mare at age thirteen, he'd suffered this residual condition more than once. His brother Aiden had become incredibly adept at popping the joint back into place. But what could a wisp of a woman like Alexa do except shoot him and put him out of his misery?

She tossed her pack to the ground and threw the gun atop it. "Let me take your hand."

"What?"

She held out both of her hands to him, palms up. "Let me take your hand. Trust me. I know what I'm doing."

"A moment ago, you threatened murder," he reminded her, trying to squelch the agony in his voice. What he wouldn't do right now for a shot of brandy. Hell, a whole bottle.

A flagon appeared beside him, and he wasted no time using his good hand and teeth to tear off the cork and imbibe a fortifying swig. The fire of the alcohol barely registered after the pain of the blue flame.

Her scowl faltered, revealing a flash of a grin. "I reserve the right to shoot you later if you piss me off again. Now, let me take your hand."

With no other immediate options at his disposal, Damon complied. Perhaps he had acted too hastily in accusing her of somehow procuring Sarina's necklace through evil means. He had been the last person to possess the chain and charm. While he was certain the jewelry had not come into Alexa's ownership coincidentally, he'd had no real cause to accuse her of witchcraft. Not when he was the one who controlled the magic.

"Wait," he said, just as she was lifting her foot against his chest to use as leverage in what he anticipated to be a horribly painful way of restoring his shoulder.

She nearly stumbled. "I said you can trust me."

He nodded. "I know. I just . . . want to try. Shoulder, heal."

Since she hadn't released his hand, he could feel the tension in her touch. And the warmth. How could he have tossed her aside so callously? He truly was a cad of the first order.

But before he could offer recompense for his callous behavior, he had to be able to think straight. Channeling all of his concentration, he called to Rogan's magic again.

"Anything?" she asked.

Pain still throbbed through his arm, accompanied by a growing numbness that would only lead to a deeper pain. "No. Apparently, I cannot use the magic to heal myself."

"That's what you get for yanking that chain off my neck and calling me a witch."

"A justified consequence," he admitted.

"Paybacks are hell. Now, brace yourself. This isn't going to tickle."

With her foot pressed against his chest, she used the counterbalance of her body weight to pull his shoulder fully forward. Surprisingly, the pain did not increase, though nausea flooded his insides and turned his stomach into a roiling mess. Little by little, she rotated his arm, pushing gently until the ball of the joint slipped back into the socket. The pain spiked, then subsided to a dull ache.

"Better?" she asked.

He managed a nod. He really was a complete idiot. "You didn't have to help me," he added.

"No kidding. You certainly didn't deserve it."

He watched her gingerly touch her hand to the back of her neck and then glance at the broken chain in her hand.

"Did I hurt you?" he asked.

"Yes." Her eyes bored into his with venom, then quickly softened. "But it could have been worse. Are you truly certain this necklace belonged to your sister?"

She handed him back the gold chain and triangle charm and he stared at them cupped in his palm. Knowing that moving his injured arm immediately after repair wasn't wise, he shifted the jewelry in his hand until it dangled from his fingers.

"Yes, I'm certain," he assured her. "My father gave Sarina this necklace on her twelfth birthday. The triangle is but a corner of a handmade star wrought by a Gypsy artisan of some repute. She wore the star daily and I found the chain, broken, and the torn charm, near this very step on the night I became trapped by Rogan's dark magic."

Centuries couldn't fill the well of loss that widened every time he thought of Sarina and his failure to rescue her from a man he'd once considered a friend. Damon swallowed thickly, knowing now was neither the time nor the place to indulge regrets and sorrow. He had to reassess his situation. Proceed with more caution. His rage had nearly destroyed him—and his tentative bond with Alexa, his only link to the outside world.

Though he couldn't seem to lock back into his cold feelings toward her. Making love to her had affected him, and not only because he'd been without a woman's touch for so long. Alexa presented a rare combination of woman—one with wealth and breeding, and yet fearless in both her passion and her self-defense. He'd never met anyone like her, and, use her though he must, he had no desire to hurt her intentionally.

He handed the necklace back to her, and after a second's hesitation, she slipped it into the pocket of her slacks.

"I can't imagine it is coincidental that you've come into ownership of the charm, Alexa," he said, forcing his gaze away from where she'd placed the jewelry, thinking, but not saying, that the hiding place she'd chosen seemed hardly fitting for something of such value. "Tell me more about this brother of yours."

In a move that seemed more instinctive than deliberate, Alexa placed a protective hand over her pocket. "Why?"

"So I can decide whether or not to kill him."

* * *

Alexa stared at Damon, wondering how she could have made love to a man she most definitely did not know. From any other guy, she might have dismissed his comment as an idle threat. But this guy? He was serious. She only hoped the protective properties of his sister's busted chain and charm didn't fail her now.

"How long has it been since your sister went missing?" she asked. "Two hundred and fifty years? I hate to be the one to break it to you, but it's time to get over it."

"At times, it seems like yesterday." Damon glanced down at his lap, which completely reminded her that he was naked. Not that she could really forget. While his skin remained on the pale side, he was otherwise formed in the image of a Roman god. Explosive temper or not, he knew how to use that body.

Man, did he ever.

"That may be," she said, glancing anywhere but at him, "but that doesn't give you the right to threaten me or my brother just because we somehow ended up with a necklace that belonged to your sister three centuries after she lost it."

Leaning forward, Damon captured her gaze, a smile teasing the corners of his lips. "My nudity unnerves you?"

Alexa squeezed her fists tighter, then slowly relaxed them. She had this very bad habit of denying her weaknesses, even when they were painfully obvious.

"Yes," she replied.

"My nudity did not disconcert you when we were making love."

She turned and eyed him boldly. "That was before you assaulted me, called me a witch and threatened to kill my brother."

He nodded. "I allowed my emotions to best me, and for that, I apologize." Damon closed his eyes and, seconds later, his loose-sleeved shirt, snug breeches and glossed boots were back on his body. " 'Tis a failing of mine three centuries have not cured."

Alexa rubbed the back of her neck. The cut still smarted, but she'd certainly lived through worse. "Apology accepted. I suppose my brother having your sister's necklace is peculiar, but then, my brother is one of the most peculiar people I know."

"Is that said lovingly?"

Alexa shrugged. She wasn't entirely sure. She certainly cared about Jacob and didn't want him murdered by a vengeful phantom, but they'd lived at odds so long, and old habits died hard.

"I see the magic works again?"

Damon chuckled at her topic switch but left the matter alone. "Apparently, conjuring clothing and furniture and food are still within the realm of my power."

He tried to lift his arm, and the exertion caused a pained grunt.

"But you clearly can't heal yourself. You're going to need to rest your shoulder for a while," Alexa instructed. "Maybe conjure up some ice?"

From the perplexed look on his face, she knew she'd confused him, but he did as she asked. After several tries through which he conjured everything from a large block of ice to a bucket of snow, she finally explained the concept well enough for him to produce enough crushed ice to wrap in cloth. She fished a couple of ibuprofen out of her bag and convinced him to swallow them. He winced at the cold ice and nearly choked on the pills, but after a few minutes of allowing the compress to numb the soreness and the drugs to work their magic, he sighed and relaxed.

"You know, my brother is into all sorts of occult stuff," she explained, adjusting the ice against his joint. "It really doesn't surprise me that he got his hands on something so precious, something he clearly thought offered me some sort of protection. He's not perfect by any means, but he's never been anything but loyal to me. Particularly since I nearly died."

Damon's gaze prickled her skin, so she scooted a few inches away.

"Nearly died?" he asked. "How?"

Alexa instantly regretted her remark. She hated talking about the accident. She'd come to terms with the pain she'd suffered, but not the loss. Her father. Her stepmother. The last vestiges of her childhood. She'd been an adult when the truck had smashed into their limousine, but while her father lived, she still had someone to rely on, advise her. Be proud of her.

"An accident in a car. My injuries were extensive, but I survived. My father and Jacob's mother did not. That event bonded Jacob and me in ways you can't imagine. I won't let you hurt him."

Damon did not reply, but from the shadows in his eyes, she knew her point was made.

Outside, the storm still raged, but the crash of the thunder had softened with increasing distance. Within a few hours, the deluge would pass. She wasn't sure if the tempest had been just an example of Florida's often violent weather or a manifestation of the castle's dark magic objecting to Damon's attempted escape. Either way, she was stuck here for the night with a centuries-old phantom who'd made wild, passionate love to her one minute and then threatened to kill her brother the next.

Now he'd gone back to showing concern. Riding such an emotional roller coaster with a stranger who wasn't even supposed to exist sent her mind reeling.

"Stop staring at me," she said.

"You're beautiful."

"Don't," she said, shaking her head. "You can't threaten to kill my brother one minute and then compliment me the next."

He shifted and she readjusted the compress, squeezing the water from the melted ice onto the floor.

"I apologized for my hasty words," he reminded her. "But know this. If your brother is uninvolved with Lord Rogan, I will have no reason to kill him."

Gooseflesh prickled her skin. He might have meant the words to be reassuring, yet they were anything but.

"Rogan is long dead," she argued.

"Many likely believed me long dead as well, Alexa. I cannot make such assumptions."

"Even about your sister?"

"Especially not about her. Her necklace still exists, after all this time, and falls nearly immediately into my hands. This castle has been rebuilt with every last stone in the exact place it was on that fateful night. Rogan's magic pulses through here and allows me to do this," he said, once again divesting himself of his clothes. "And this."

Seconds later, she was naked as well.

She cursed. With a devilish smile, he clothed them both again and she had to call on all her self-control not to slap him hard.

"Don't—"

"How can I assume the past has not affected the present deeply?" he went on, ignoring her protest. "For all I know, it was Rogan's magic that brought you here to free me, to renew our battle until one of us finally wins."

The keen resolve in his voice chilled her, but she shook off the cold and pressed the ice pack tighter against his skin. She'd heard determination like his before—out of her own mouth. Why should his attitude frighten her when she so often sounded just as single-minded and resolute?

"This is going to be a long night," she said. "Maybe we should go somewhere more comfortable."

She moved to stand and suddenly found herself floating in a vortex of color and light. Before she had a chance to cry out in surprise, her feet steadied on a plush carpet in a warm room that smelled of ocean, books and charred wood.

Damon was sitting on a hand-tooled leather chair, one knee curved over the arm, looking rakish and dangerous and as sexy as hell.

He'd just magically moved them into another room.

"Can you warn me before you do that?" she asked.

"If you wish," he replied.

"I do."

She nearly jumped out of her skin when something furry brushed against her leg. She looked down and saw nothing, then spun in her search for the animal or large, hairy insect that had caused the sensation.

"What was that?"

Damon laughed heartily. Clearly, he was feeling better.

"Show yourself, beast."

In a puff of black smoke, a cat as diaphanous as the fog appeared.

"Is this yours?" she asked.

Damon sneered. "I abhor the creature, but he has been my only companion all these centuries. He belonged to Rogan."

Alexa knelt down and attempted to assess the cat on an equal level. She hadn't owned a cat since she was in college, but liked the animals nonetheless— even scary ghost cats with long black hair and ominous yellow eyes.

"What's its name?"

"Dante," he replied.

"Like the guy who descended into hell?"

"The beast lived with Rogan," he answered. "The name is highly appropriate."

From experience, Alexa knew not to reach for the cat if she wanted its attention. Cats liked best the people who worshipped them least. Which is why she wasn't surprised when the feline disappeared and then reappeared in Damon's lap.

"He likes you," she said, amused by Damon's put-out expression. Still, he gave the cat a scratch behind the ears.

"He is only used to me, as I am to him."

"Is he dead?"

Damon shrugged. "I cannot be sure about the cat any more than I am about myself."

He shifted in his seat, but the cat did not scamper off or, more likely in its case, burst into a puff of smoke. Odd how she was becoming accustomed to the wild world she'd discovered inside these castle walls.

As time passed, she was feeling more and more like Alice after she'd fallen down the rabbit hole. Alexa walked the perimeter of the room, noting the fine furnishings, such as handblown glass and fascinating statues molded in striking bronze and untarnished silver. Where silk didn't festoon the walls, bold tapestries did, providing a richness of color and texture that nearly stole her breath. Even the cloak draped across the back of Damon's chair flowed with rich opulence.

Ideas took form in a swirl. How she'd decorate the presidential suite. What flowers she wanted in the lobby. How she'd present even the smallest guest room with the finest touches of history and wealth.

"You bear no scars," he said, his voice intimate.

She looked up, surprised. For an instant, she'd forgotten she wasn't alone.

"Excuse me?"

"You spoke of an accident. In a . . . car? You bear no scars."

She scoffed. "You weren't looking in the right places."

"I looked everywhere," he insisted, his voice dipping into naughty territory.

She took a deep breath. She couldn't go there with him again. She'd had her fantasy and it had been amazing. But she was too confused and conflicted to surrender to such intimacy again. She was stuck here for the night, at the very least. She had to make conversation, but making love was out of the question.

"I had excellent plastic surgeons," she replied.

His brow furrowed. "Surgeons, I understand. But what is plastic?"

She had to think. How could she explain something that was so elemental to her, yet so foreign to him? "A synthetic material. Man-made. Like rubber," she offered, guessing that the natural material was available to some degree during his time period, "but harder."

"They attached this to you to cover scars?"

She laughed, shaking her head as she joined him

near the chair, then reached to give the cat, who'd curled up comfortably in his lap, a gentle stroke. She didn't really understand the instant rapport she shared with this mysterious man from the past, but she was too tired and emotionally spent to fight her instincts. In the morning, she'd likely wake up and discover the whole interaction was nothing more than a dream. Or a very stupid mistake. For tonight, she had to wing it.

"No," she said. "Plastic surgeons specialize in removing outward signs—scars and such—after major injuries. And they do the occasional boob job."

He arched a brow. "Do I want to know what that is?"

She swallowed a snort. "If you stick around in this century, you'll find out soon enough."

"My plans do not include returning to my own time," he said, and after looking around, he added, "Or to my banishment in this infernal room."

"I think the room is rich and warm."

"Try remaining here for nearly three centuries."

"I get your point."

With a push, he moved the cat off his lap. It hit the ground on all four paws, then poofed into nothingness.

"That's very unnerving," she said.

"Everything about the animal is. Rogan loved the beast, so I advise you not to trust it."

"Can you trust a cat? I mean, like, ever?"

He chuckled, stood and offered her the chair.

She was tempted. Her shoulders ached. Her legs throbbed. She glanced at her watch and discovered that her nine-thousand-dollar Franck Muller had stopped working. She had no idea how long she'd been here, trapped in the castle or perhaps even in this dream, but the experience had drained the last of her energy. She dropped to the ground, and sitting, as her nanny used to say, "crisscross, applesauce," she stared up at Damon, who looked entirely shocked by her collapse.

"Please, my lady," he said, extending his hand.

"Sit down," she said, crossing her arms.

"I will not allow you to sit on the floor."

"See, that's the best part of the twenty-first century. You don't get to *allow* me to do anything. I make my own choices. And I'm tired. And right this second, I'm comfortable, so I'm not moving." He scowled, so she added, "But I thank you for your concern over my comfort. Sometimes, it just feels right to sit on the floor."

After a moment of deep consideration, Damon plopped down beside her and, after examining her position, twisted his limbs until he was sitting in the same fashion. "I do believe I was much younger the last time I attempted this."

Alexa tried not to laugh. "I'll see to it that my next Crown Chandler property offers daily yoga. You'll enjoy it."

He shook his head. "There are so many words you speak that I do not understand. Plastic. Yoga. Car. That's how you knew how to heal my shoulder. The accident in the . . . car?"

Alexa yawned. "It's a mode of transportation. A horseless carriage."

Damon's brow arched. "This I'd like to see."

She shook her head. "Not on this island. We'll probably use golf carts."

His face reflected his additional questions, but he remained silent.

Alexa grinned and patted him on the knee. "Okay, Damon Forsyth, I get the hint. You've got a lot of history to catch up on. Got anything better to do tonight?"

His grin bordered on sinful as his eyes darkened sensually. "That is entirely up to you, my lady."

She slapped his knee again, this time harder and with obvious denial.

"Then why don't you magic us up some coffee. It's time for a history lesson, and two hundred and sixty years' worth will clearly take us the rest of the night."

9

"This ruler of yours, also George, you're sure he's not the king?"

Alexa instantly burst into laughter, leaving Damon to wonder what he'd said that was so amusing. He was merely making an assessment based on the facts she'd provided. Over the course of the night, he'd done precisely as she'd asked, conjuring a collection of cushions on the floor for them to lie upon while they imbibed pot after pot of brewed coffee, a drink he'd learned to appreciate during his travels to Italy. As they drank, he listened while she ran down the basics of technological and political advancement over the past three centuries. Her knowledge of the British, outside their failed battle to squelch the revolution of the colonists, was less than comprehensive, and yet *she* was laughing at *him*? He failed to see the reason for her amusement.

She noticed his displeasure and quickly rebounded. "I'm sorry, Damon. Honestly, you're not the first person to ask that question and you likely won't be the last. But unlike in a monarchy, we have—"

"Elections. Yes, I understand your two-party system and the basics of a representative democracy. Thank you. Perhaps we should take a break from any further explanation of politics," he said, sliding his empty china cup away from where he'd reclined on the carpet surrounded by thick, tasseled pillows. The setting he'd conjured using Rogan's magic was much more conducive to seduction than instruction, but so far, none of his attempts to sway Alexa to forget her history lesson in lieu of more pleasurable pursuits had worked. He was either losing his touch, or exhaustion and the medication she kept forcing him to swallow at the slightest twinge of pain was playing on his skills.

"Shall we go over the principles of capitalism again?" she asked, earnest.

It was his turn to laugh. "I was hoping for some relaxation, but now I'm leaning toward rest. Once I was freed from the portrait, I did not ever think I'd want to sleep again." He yawned noisily. "I was wrong."

"Am I that boring?" she asked, unsuccessfully attempting to cover her own exhaustion.

"Boring?" he asked, surprised. For a woman who claimed to be nothing more than a hotelier, she'd done a fine job explaining what might have taken him weeks to learn on his own. And she was much more delightful to look at and listen to than any of the scholars he'd studied with in his youth. "Not likely, my lady. But I must say that for all the learned tutors my father employed over the course of my boyhood, none tried to cram my brain with so much information in such a short time."

She curled a pillow underneath her breasts, forcing Damon to look away or risk molesting her despite her protestations. Two buttons kept her blouse from breaking open. Two measly buttons.

Before, he'd found her merely beautiful and alluring and powerful. Now that he'd discovered how her intelligence not only matched, but surpassed her beauty, he couldn't imagine resisting her, no matter the cost.

"Are you still afraid to sleep?" she ventured.

Damon frowned, but noted silently she might not be too far from the mark. "I cannot deny the emotion has niggled at me, particularly when there's a chance I might not wake again for another century or two. Of course, you might be experiencing the same reluctance. If you sleep, you may discover that once you wake, our meeting has been nothing more than a dream."

Alexa pressed her lips tightly together, lips that were now pale. They'd been rouged darkly when he'd first seen her from the other side of the painting. All of the color she'd applied to her face to enhance her large green eyes and striking cheekbones had faded, and her hair, still brilliantly red of course, was now a tangled mess.

And yet, he still found her undeniably desirable. Educated beyond most men of his station, Damon had met many knowledgeable women in his time, yet none took their educational prowess lightly. Women in his age who'd been lucky enough to know things beyond husbandry and housekeeping either flaunted their superior intellects or hid them furiously. Alexa did neither. She simply enjoyed the things she knew and joked about the things she didn't.

And underneath the fair skin, rumpled appearance and sharp mind resided a woman of unparalleled passion. Perhaps this was his ultimate punishment— meeting a woman he could have only until he was free. Because once he could leave this castle, he would spend the rest of his days avenging Rogan's evil.

As she rolled over, her hair fanned across the pillows and caught the dying light of the fire's embers. "I'd likely be better off if this were all a dream."

"Why?" he asked, scooting nearer. Unable to help himself, he wished for the torches and candles to dim, and instantly, they complied.

She stretched, raising her arms over her head and arching her back so that her breasts curved against her barely buttoned blouse. The outline of her dark nipples caused his mouth to water. What he wouldn't give for another taste of her heavenly flesh.

"A lot of people rely on me," she answered. "They need me to think clearly and logically all the time. Indulging in an affair with a man who might not be real? Doesn't exactly qualify as clear or logical."

"You cannot be beholden to others all of your life."

Mindlessly, she toyed with the cuff of his shirt, her fingers grazing over the inside of his wrist. If she knew how the tiny action was driving him insane, would she stop? Could she?

"You were the eldest son," she pointed out. "Are you trying to say you didn't put your family obligations above your own needs most of the time?"

Damon glanced aside. "I upheld my responsibilities, yes. But that's not to say I didn't indulge my own needs. On a regular basis, I might add."

He was tempted to tell her of his mistress, but thought better of it. He'd gathered from her earlier diatribe on marriage in the twenty-first century that the taking of a lover while legally wed to another was no longer universally acceptable, though the practice still existed. What a strange world she lived in. She had no trouble sleeping with a man without benefit of marriage, but breaking marriage vows was unacceptable. He wondered if he'd ever grow accustomed to the new morality—or if he'd even get the chance.

Suddenly noticing how she was touching him, she yanked her hand away and tucked it beneath her head. "What about the night you went after Rogan? Was that for you or for your sister?"

Damon had avoided admitting too much about the situation that had led him to his entrapment, but her question struck him deeply. He supposed he'd never questioned his motivation for seeking out Rogan that night because his sister's kidnapping and the oncoming mercenary horde had taken precedence above all else. "A bit of both, I suppose. Lord Rogan had been introduced to me at White's by a mutual friend a year before I brought him to Valoren. The man was utterly fascinating, I must admit. Nobility from some far-off land, knowledgeable in all manner of science and literature and politics. Handsome. Wealthy. Engaging, I dare say."

"Charming?" she asked.

Damon frowned. To women, yes. Undeniably, to many men as well. In Valoren, company rarely changed.

Damon had relished the time he'd spent in London tending to his family's interests and, when not paying attention to familiar concerns, seeking out new and interesting entertainments. From their first encounter, Rogan had brought an exotic excitement into Damon's often tedious life. First, he'd been fascinated. Shortly thereafter, disgusted.

"Most who met Rogan fell immediately under his spell. I had no idea at the time that his magic was beyond this world."

"You had no idea he was a sorcerer?" Alexa yawned again; this time she managed to curl her fist in front of her mouth before she rolled onto her side and watched him intently, despite her heavy-lidded eyes.

"One hardly believes such things, does one? The magic I'd witnessed in my childhood had been of Romani origin—healing and such. Hardly more than an intense knowledge of herbal remedies, good luck and superstition, or so I believed," he said, adjusting a few pillows to accommodate the stiffness growing in his shoulder. "But when Rogan heard that my father was the governor over the only recognized colony of Gypsies in Europe, he was the fascinated one. He entreated me to invite him on my next journey. I had no idea that he would not only set up housekeeping within the Gypsy enclave and attempt to usurp my father's authority with the king, but also entice my sister to run off with him on the eve of what would have been a very bloody attack."

Damon filled in the rest of the story, marveling at how his anger still seemed so fresh.

"Rogan must have been very charismatic," she concluded at the end of his tale.

The dreamy sound in Alexa's voice raised the hairs on the back of his neck. "He was evil personified. Romanticize any other portion of my life, my lady, but not him. Never him."

Alexa's eyes widened at the intensity of his speech,

but her shock surrendered to yet another yawn, and slowly, her lids began to drift closed.

"I doubt I'll ever have to deal with your Lord Rogan, Damon. Neither will you. Yes, you survived all these centuries because of magic, but what are the chances this Rogan did as well? And if he did, wouldn't he be here, in his own castle, seeking to regain the magic you now command?"

Alexa curled into a ball and closed her eyes. Apparently, Damon thought too long before he replied, because just as he opened his mouth to present a theory on Rogan's whereabouts, he heard the sweet purr of her sleeping. Indulgently, he brushed aside the hair that had fallen across her cheek and wondered at the soft sensation of his skin against hers.

His skin. His touch. His blood, bone and muscle. He was alive again, Rogan be damned. And if he survived all these centuries on account of his nemesis's dark magic, chances remained that Rogan had somehow cheated death as well—no matter how unlikely Alexa thought such survival could be. Rogan had been an extraordinary man and an even more clever sorcerer. Damon had underestimated him once. He would not do so again.

And then there was Sarina. His heart ached, knowing that the protective talisman she'd once worn had been torn away on that fateful night. Did she escape with Rogan? Had another of their brothers found her? Or had the mercenaries destroyed her with the coming dawn?

Damon surrendered to the softness of the pillows all around him. Sleep teased the edge of his consciousness, and he didn't have any further energy to fight. If sleep meant the end of this folly, he'd at least have the memories of making love with Alexa to last him for the next few centuries. If he awoke with the dawn, however, he'd have to push those memories aside. For as much as he relished the idea of seducing her again, he had to keep his emotions in check. He enjoyed her.

And he'd use her. Just as he'd used his mistresses before her. Because only with her help could he answer the questions burning through him—and only by betraying her would he finally find retribution.

Farrow Pryce tapped his fingers along the windowsill, the rhythmic drumming marking his impatience. Yet again, for the good of the cause, he'd operated with maximum stealth, never moving in for the kill, no matter how many opportunities he'd watched come and go. He waited until he could utilize the old man to ultimate effectiveness. And according to the spies he'd placed in the Crown Chandler organization, the time was now.

After a barely audible knock, the door behind him opened with a soft whoosh.

Farrow didn't bother to turn around. "Is our guest tucked in for the evening?"

"He thinks so, yes," was the reply, the male voice tremulous, a contrast to the man's large size. He could break Farrow in two with his bare hands, and yet he followed his every order to the letter. Farrow's jaw twitched into a smile. Power really was delicious.

"Good," he replied. "Wait until the drugs have him nearly asleep, then wake him. Ice water ought to do the trick."

With the appropriate affirmative response, his minion shot out of the room. Funny how none of the men he'd brought into his service ever dawdled. Farrow never blatantly asked for quick service and immediate obedience, but somehow they all knew his expectations. Subtlety could be a powerful motivator, when skillfully applied. But not for his guest. With Paschal Rousseau, he was done playing games.

"Rousseau is old," Gemma said, her sultry tone creeping out from where she lounged on the leather chair behind his desk. She was, as always, the lone voice of constant contradiction.

"Why do you care?" he asked.

"Care? Hardly. But torturing him with traditional

methods could result in his death. And then where will you be? He's gone to a great deal of trouble to hide the diary. He's not going to give it up just because you put bamboo shoots under his fingernails. At his age, he's likely made peace with dying, don't you think?"

Cold, hard and sapphire blue, Gemma's eyes taunted him, challenged him. Though he supposed lesser men would find her endless opposition threatening, Farrow instead entertained a surging rush of lust. Loyal to the last, Gemma provided keen insight and clever council to his cause. Not to mention what her bloodline added to his bid to rule the followers of the sorcerer Lord Rogan. With a direct descendent of their master at his side, Farrow would rule the K'vr like none other before him. And under his leadership, the truest power—imaginable only to the followers of the great magician—would be his for the taking.

He reached out with both hands, curling her outstretched fingers in his. "What do you suggest, love? As you said, Rousseau is over ninety years old. I doubt he'd fall prey to your particular brand of persuasion."

With sleek elegance, she slid off the chair and coiled into his arms, her breath teasing along the edge of his collar. Her short, cropped hair, highlighted in colors that ranged from white blond to inky black, hugged her sleek cheekbones and emphasized the luminous blue of her irises. "You think age makes a man immune to a woman's charms?"

Farrow laughed, wondering how Gemma's brother would react to witnessing this scene. Keith Von Roan fancied himself the true heir to the K'vr—which wasn't exactly untrue. But what he possessed in bloodline, he lacked in vision. Over the centuries, many a coup had taken away the leadership from Rogan's direct descendents, though they remained influential. So with Keith's sibling at his side, Farrow would take the title of leader. Once he had Rogan's magic in his possession.

He swiped his lips across Gemma's, reveling in the feel of her sleek red mouth against his. "Is charm what they're calling your talents these days?"

Her grin reflected her iniquitous sensuality. "No, but it's what they called it in Rousseau's day. I know all about a man like him. The chivalry. The denied passions. Allow me to work my magic on him and I'll get you what you want. Perhaps more. And he'll be in a condition to use him later on, if necessary, which he won't be in if you keep turning him over to those goons of yours. If I fail, you can try your preferred approach with nothing but a few more days lost."

She pressed her taut breasts fully against him and he enjoyed the thick feel of her feminine flesh, the hard tips of her nipples swiping across the silk of his shirt. He couldn't resist leaning into her hair and inhaling the lingering scent of her bath. Her tongue grazed over his chin, igniting a simmering need for her that never truly abated—and, unfortunately, was never fully satisfied. And now that he was on the brink of taking over the leadership position he'd sought for more than a decade, his best interests were served by keeping her on his side.

"Do what you must," he instructed.

With a felinelike growl, she tugged free of him and proceeded to the door.

"Try not to give him a heart attack," he reminded her.

She glanced over her shoulder, her eyes glittering with lusty expectation. "I'll see what I can do, but I'm an awful lot of woman for just one old man."

"You're an awful lot of woman for any man."

Even after she swung out of the room, Farrow could hear her laughter echoing down the long hallway.

10

Cat peered around the darkened corner inside the university's humanities building and involuntarily drew her hand to her nose. It wasn't that she didn't appreciate the smell of old books every once in a while, but in the last twenty-four hours she'd achieved maximum overload. For the entire afternoon and evening yesterday, she'd pawed through the extensive collection of professional journals and diaries owned by Professor Morton Gilmore. Her hands still needed a few more coats of moisturizer to counteract the dryness caused by constant contact with old paper and fading ink. To top off the experience, she'd come up entirely empty in her search for the dissertation or memoir that supposedly contained the reference to Valoren. After a hot shower in her hotel room, she'd finally cleared the scent of old books out of her nostrils. But now she was about to charge headfirst into another professor's dusty office in search of documentation she wasn't entirely sure existed—and if it did, might not help her on her quest.

Ordinarily, she wasn't this wimpy. Dealing with musty scents was chicken feed compared to the things she'd done to hunt down evidence in her search to either prove or disprove paranormal phenomena. She'd rappelled into the hidden chambers built beneath ancient adobe structures in the Southwest during a heat wave. She'd slept alone, tucked in a three-foot-by-three-foot closet, in an abandoned New Orleans plantation house for seven nights straight in search of an elusive ghost. She'd even armed herself with a self-whittled wooden stake and several atomizers' worth of holy water to confront a coven of self-proclaimed vampires in a back alley in urban Detroit.

She didn't scare easily.

And yet, yesterday, she'd been overwhelmed by such a powerful feeling of dread, she'd nearly flown back in the middle of the night to Florida to check on Alexa and break the news that her expedition had, so far, been a bust.

Shortly before she'd zipped up her suitcase, however, Professor Gilmore had called her hotel, finally remembering that the diary he'd read with the reference to Valoren had never been in his possession after all. He'd read it while conferring with a colleague at a nearby university. A colleague named Paschal Rousseau, who'd written the academic paper about Valoren years before. The same Paschal Rousseau who apparently didn't rate high on his university's relevance list since his office had been tucked in the farthest, darkest corner of the school's humanities building with little to no ventilation. And while Cat was no expert in Romani academia, she'd never heard of the guy. His name had not come up in any of her research. No articles like the one Gilmore claimed to have seen. No dissertations. Only one listing as a secondary resource that might have been regarding the paper he'd supposedly written, but which no longer existed. She had found a Ben Rousseau listed as a fellow of the same university, but not a word about Paschal.

Still, he'd been important enough for a tenured expert in Romani culture like Morton Gilmore to confer with. And if the mysterious professor had the diary that explained the significance of Valoren to Alexa's castle, Cat had to push her antsiness about Alexa out of her mind for a few hours more.

Alexa.

The dreadful feeling overwhelmed her again, pressing in on her like a vise, weighting her shoulders, chest and stomach. Shrugging her briefcase to the floor, she yanked her cell phone out of her pocket and tried calling Alexa again.

"I'm sorry, but the subscriber you are calling is unavailable at this time. Please call again or press the star key to leave a message."

Damn.

Cat disconnected. She'd already filled Alexa's mailbox with multiple messages both last night and again after receiving Gilmore's lead. She'd contacted Alexa's hotel manager and was told that Ms. Chandler had not returned to her suite for the night, but that her brother had. Frustrated, Cat decided she had to break down and call Jacob. Much as her fingers ached with each punch of his cell phone number, she had to make sure her friend was safe.

"If you're calling to tempt me back into your bed, you're wasting your time," Jacob said by way of greeting.

Cat blanched. God, she hated caller ID.

"In your dreams, Goth boy. Where's Alexa?"

"Would you like to know the content of my dreams, Catalina? You might be very interested to find out exactly how you play a role nowadays."

"I'm not interested in any of your sick fantasies, Jacob. Remember? That's why I dumped your freak ass. Now, tell me where your sister is."

"Or what?"

"Or I'll clue your beloved sister in on the real reasons I sent you packing. Do you think she'd still be so keen to let you run even that tiny, insignificant division if she knew what a wannabe you were?"

Silence ensued, tension crackling over their connection like electrical interference. For the millionth time, Cat wondered why she hadn't already confessed to her best friend all she knew about Jacob and his tastes for the macabre, and again remembered her reasoning. Jacob dabbled in the black arts, true, but he had no true power. He couldn't hurt anyone. At least, as far as she knew, he hadn't hurt anyone who hadn't been anxious to enjoy the experience. And since he was Alexa's last remaining family member, Cat had decided it was in Alexa's best interests for Cat to keep her mouth shut regarding Jacob's sadomasochistic tendencies. As an orphan raised by a grandmother who had never valued her progeny above her religion and a grandfather who saw Cat simply as an extension of himself, she knew that family wasn't something to be thrown away simply because they didn't measure up to classical standards. Not when you had no one else.

"Alexa isn't here," Jacob finally answered. "She's on that new island of hers."

"Again? What's so interesting that she had to go back?"

"She never left the first time."

Despite the dank, uncirculated air of the hallway, Cat shivered. "What are you talking about? You left her there all night long?"

"She insisted," he replied, his voice brimming with boredom. "We had a crisis at our Boston property and she ordered me back to the mainland to handle the mess. I did, but when I was ready to go back and retrieve her, a storm popped up out of nowhere."

"How convenient," Cat said, doubtful.

"Check the local news, Catalina. It was freakish. Just your speed, actually. No captain in his right mind would have taken a boat out in that weather, but I'm on my way to fetch her now. She had supplies and a sound roof over her head. Stop worrying."

"Maybe you should start worrying," Cat snapped back. She knew that if the castle had survived hurricanes over the last sixty years, one weird storm wasn't going to knock it down now. And yet, she couldn't shake the feeling that Alexa was in trouble. Problem was, Cat didn't know if the danger came from the island or from someone closer to home. "By the way, who gets the Chandler billions if Alexa meets with some freak accident?"

She knew the answer. The hotels would go to the shareholders and the fortune to a charitable foundation. Jacob's take was minuscule in comparison. He was richer with Alexa alive than dead—one of the few facts that kept Cat off his case.

"Only you would think something so disgusting," Jacob replied, sounding genuinely insulted.

Good. Catalina didn't much care about Jacob's feelings as long as he remained loyal to his sister.

"Even if you reveal my proclivities to Alexa," he said with an audible sneer, "she'll forgive me for indulging in less-than-traditional extracurricular activities. Will she forgive you for trying to drive a wedge between her and the last blood tie she has?"

"You're not tied by blood," Cat pointed out.

"I'd like to get you tied up one time," Jacob said, his leer palpable in his voice.

"You're a pig."

"And you are entirely too loud!"

That voice didn't come from the phone, but from a tall, lean, rather snotty gentleman glaring at her from the doorway to Paschal Rousseau's office.

Cat pressed the phone to her chest to respond until she felt the vibration of Jacob's voice on her skin. Creeped out, she disconnected the call.

"Excuse me?" she asked.

"Please take your lovers' quarrel to the other end of the hall," the man said, his tone dripping with disdain. "Some people have work to do."

With a self-satisfied smirk, he slammed the door shut.

Cat gaped. If this guy was Paschal Rousseau, her quest to find the diary with a minimum of fuss just went down the drain. If he wasn't Paschal Rousseau, then he was about to learn a very hard lesson about pissing her off.

Cat shoved her cell phone back into her pocket, grabbed her briefcase, stalked down the hall and banged on the professor's office door, hoping Mr.

Tight Ass who'd just had the nerve to complain about her volume jumped in surprise and banged his head on a low shelf.

She heard a crash and a curse.

She knocked again. Harder.

When he swung the door open this time, he was pressing his palm tightly to the top of his head.

"Office hours aren't until Monday," he ground out through clenched teeth.

"I'm not a student," she said evenly. "I'm here to see Paschal Rousseau. Dr. Morton Gilmore sent me."

Tight Ass eyed her from head to toe, but his assessment, oddly enough, was purely academic. His eyes reflected no hint of male-to-female interest—which meant he either was gay or possessed inordinate amounts of self-control. Cat didn't flaunt her body, but reactions to her curves remained constant all the same. Although, clearly, her pink wraparound blouse and loose-fitting, cuffed gray slacks didn't do it for him. With a sniff that suggested she reeked more than his ancient books, he met her gaze boldly. "Morton Gilmore, you say? What are you, his new research assistant?"

She squared her shoulders. "I'm a colleague."

"In what? His cooking class?"

Cat realized she was standing straighter than normal, so she shifted her weight to her right hip and huffed audibly. "I'm not some lowly coed, asshole, so your attempts to intimidate me with your superior attitude are a waste of your time and mine. I need to speak with Dr. Rousseau, so could you please tell him I'm here?"

"He's not."

"He's not what?"

"Here," he replied, a smile teasing his lips.

Either he enjoyed pissing her off or bantering with her gave him some sort of thrill. Must be lonely in the dungeon.

"He's unavailable," he explained further. "You'll need to make an appointment."

He flipped a business card from his pocket and thrust it toward her. She didn't accept it.

His mouth tightened into a thin line. "Do you want an appointment or not?"

"Not," she said. "I want to see him. I need to return to Florida immediately, but first I need to discuss a paper and a diary with Professor Rousseau. Both, according to Dr. Gilmore, reference a Gypsy safe haven called Valoren."

Had she been a less observant person, she might have missed the flash of emotion behind his eyes— eyes a slate gray that he kept hidden behind glasses she now suspected were only for show. Right down to the tweed jacket with the leather patches on the elbows, his look screamed academic, but in that brief spark of surprise, she caught sight of something more—something interesting. Mysterious, in a "he's hiding something" sort of way. Glancing down, she noticed a rip across the thigh of his jeans, which he wore loose in the front and slightly snug around the hips. And instead of tasseled loafers or the dime-store sneakers favored by grad students, he wore boots. Scuffed boots. Dusty boots. Boots that had seen action.

"You must have the wrong professor," he replied.

He stepped back into the office, his hand tight on the edge of the door. He was going to slam her out again. Cat jammed her heavy briefcase into the opening.

"Is there another professor at this university who is a Romani expert? Because I'm thinking most institutions don't need more than one."

The man's scowl might have been intimidating to someone else. Luckily for Cat, she'd been around the block enough to know when a guy was more bark than bite.

Though, so far as bites went, this guy had potential. Once he lost the jacket. Mussed up his hair a bit. Tore off the glasses à la Clark Kent. Or he could keep the gold wire rims. They were sort of sexy, now that she saw them up close and personal. Her mind drifted to images of Harrison Ford as Indiana Jones. When he was in the classroom at the start of the first film. Before he donned the fedora. Before he grabbed his whip.

To his credit, Rousseau's assistant didn't back away when Cat pressed closer. The aroma of old books clung to him like musk, but didn't smell quite so musty when mingled with his woodsy cologne.

"Paschal Rousseau is a leading expert in all things related to Romani culture," he informed her, "primarily in the British Islands during the eighteenth century."

"Eighteenth?" she asked. "Well, that narrows down my search."

"What exactly are you looking for?"

She'd piqued his interest. Leaning saucily against the doorjamb, she licked her generous lips and shrugged prettily, cast her eyes downward, then glanced up from beneath her lashes. "Information, that's all."

"And I'll bet you're willing to do just about anything to get it, aren't you?"

"Depends," she replied, deciding to play the innuendo in his voice to her advantage. "What are you suggesting?"

Unexpectedly, he encircled her arm with his hand. An instantaneous spark crackled through her body. He had rough hands and a strong grip. Evidently, this man did more in his daily routine than turn pages and type on a keyboard.

When he kicked her briefcase out of the office, she yelped. He tightened his grip, then practically dragged her out into the hall. "I suggest a ten-minute head start before I call security and accuse you of stalking."

"Stalking? For one visit? Sensitive much?"

"You don't know what you're dealing with," he warned. "Go back to Florida. Don't contact us again."

The power in his grasp belied his reaction to her presence. He had no reason to fear her—so she had to assume he feared what she sought.

The diary?

Valoren?

With a determined yank, she tore her arm from his hold. "Fine. I get the message."

"Make sure that you do." His eyes, while gray, contained a strong hint of blue that turned icier and icier the longer he stared at her. "Someday, you'll thank me."

With a curt nod, he shut the door. Seconds later, Cat heard the sounds of classical music. Loud classical music. Straight down to the screaming violins, crashing cymbals and pounding bass drums. If she knocked again, he wouldn't hear her. Or, at least, he'd pretend not to.

As if Mozart was enough to ward her away.

With a snort, she rubbed the spot where he'd grabbed her, somewhat surprised by the electric thrum on her skin. In those boots and ripped jeans was a man who didn't scare easily. So why had he reacted so strongly?

"Someday, very soon," she said to the door, picking up her briefcase and heading back toward the commons, "you'll learn not to manhandle me. And, that I don't give up quite so easily."

11

Ben waited a full twenty minutes before he turned down the head-splitting classical racket his father loved so dearly and checked the hallway. Except for a few coeds chatting with a professor near the front exit, the building was deserted.

She'd left.

With a satisfied nod, he returned to the office. But over the course of the rest of the day, his gaze had returned to the door. Easily, this woman had been the most fascinating distraction he'd had in days. Straight dark hair. Flashing obsidian eyes. A body that tortured his inadvertently celibate self even though she was covered in fabric from neck to toe. Curves like hers were impossible to hide completely. She reminded him of Jennifer Lopez but with half the ass and twice the attitude.

Although . . . she had given up without much fight, which raised the hackles on his neck. Though he'd tangled with her for only a few minutes, she'd struck him as a woman who didn't surrender. Her business in Florida must have been important. Still, she could come back. And if information on Valoren was what she sought—she'd return eventually. No one else possessed the secrets she sought.

Not even him.

He'd never anticipated that anyone outside the small circle of Romani academics would come to the university to ask his father about the mythical Gypsy sanctuary. Once was odd enough. But twice?

The topic had been verboten between father and son. Paschal had presented one paper on Valoren early in his career as an academic—and it had nearly destroyed his chances of tenure at any institution with a serious reputation. Ben had questioned his father about why he'd go out on a limb with such a crazy tale, but the older man had reacted to his questions with uncharacteristic anger, and then hadn't spoken to him for a week.

Clandestinely, Ben had learned that only a select few of Paschal's colleagues in the study of Romani history, lore and sociology had ever heard of the place, and nearly all had gotten their information, scant as it was, from Paschal himself.

According to legend, Valoren was a Gypsy safe haven tucked into some forgotten region between Germany and Bohemia in the mid–seventeen hundreds. Nothing remained of the place except a few whispered stories about a powerful, deadly curse.

Ben shut off his laptop and tucked it into its case, wondering why Morton Gilmore had chosen to help the woman who'd barged into the office when he knew how protective his father was about this particular topic. Not content to let the mystery lie, he made a phone call.

"Son, are you going to tell me you could resist those eyes?" Gilmore said after the initial pleasantries. "I'd have ducked into another room and forged a diary outlining the details of this Valoren nonsense myself if I'd thought she'd fall for it. Smart cookie, this Catalina Reyes. Don't underestimate her resolve."

Great. The last thing he needed was some sexy woman on a mission. Been there, done that. Had the scars to prove it. Inside and out.

"I couldn't help her if I wanted to," Ben admitted. He'd done an independent study under Gilmore during his undergraduate years and respected the man immensely. Because Gilmore was an old friend of his father's, he didn't mind admitting the truth. "I've never seen this diary. And I never read the paper father wrote all those years ago. Can't even find a copy anymore. You know Paschal has never told me much about this Valoren myth."

"Your father claims the myth is real," Gilmore insisted. "I'm quite certain he has more proof than he's ever shared with either of us. You can thank a couple of bottles of Crown Royal for the fact that I saw the diary for myself. Took a hell of a time to bring the memory out of this old brain of mine, but Ms. Reyes's persistence was compelling. Her perfume helped, too. You did notice the exotic, spiced scent, I gather?"

Old coot. With apologies for his haste, Ben ended the call. He preferred not to think about the soft, tangerine scent still lingering on his hand from where he'd touched her, a fragrance potently mixed with exotic spices that lured him, for just a moment, to forget the vow he'd made to his dying mother to protect his father and his work above all else—even his own personal interests.

He checked his watch. Paschal was likely out gardening, but he called the house anyway. As expected, there was no answer. Still, it couldn't be a coincidence that Catalina Reyes had come looking for the Valoren diary so soon after one of Paschal's seemingly disinterested undergraduate students had come sniffing around for the same information. Packing up as quickly as possible, he locked the office and headed to his car.

With few evening classes on a Friday, Ben's car sat in the lot nearly alone. He tossed his bag on the passenger seat, then bent in to turn on the air conditioner and roll down the windows before subjecting his body to the solar temperatures inside the El Camino. Waiting for the car to cool, he glanced around. Other than a few students waiting for a bus inside a covered booth on the corner, no one was around.

So why did he feel like he was being watched?

Casually, Ben strolled to the passenger side of the car and, using the key, unlocked the reinforced glove compartment where he kept his gun, a souvenir from his old life. Before his mother died. Before she made him promise to give up his explorations and return to the university as Paschal's assistant and, frankly, keeper. Turning his back so no one could see what he was doing, he checked the safety and ammo, then shoved the weapon into his waistband and untucked his shirt to cover the fact that he was armed. He was probably overreacting, but after the scene he'd witnessed between his father and one of his undergraduate students, who was accompanied by a mysterious stranger, just a few days ago, he preferred to err on the side of caution.

The minute the temperature in the car dropped below eighty, Ben roared out of the parking lot. He glanced several times into the rearview mirror but saw no one follow. Once he was embroiled in busy, Friday afternoon traffic, he couldn't be so confident. Something was up. Something weird.

He pulled his cell phone out of his bag and punched the speed-dial number to his father's house again. Old man wouldn't carry a cell, though Ben supposed he couldn't blame the guy. Paschal Rousseau might be in prime physical condition, but he was more than ninety years old. His technical know-how was limited to tools that helped him with his research.

The phone rang several times, with no answer. The voice mail took over, and this time, Ben punched in the codes to retrieve the messages. Nothing new. He accessed the saved messages and nearly wrecked his car.

"Professor Rousseau, this is Amber Stranton. I'm really sorry about that scene the other day on the quad. I know that my cousin is creepy, but he wouldn't hurt a fly. I wish you'd reconsider looking over the items he told you about. I really think they could help you with your research on Valoren."

Ben had witnessed the scene the girl referred to—

cheerleader-sweet Amber leading his father to a man in a dark overcoat entirely too stifling for Texas weather. From a window in the faculty lounge, he'd watched Paschal exchange a few words with the couple, and then, after looking at some item handed to him by the man, he'd grown agitated. Angry. The skin on his face had reddened as if sunburned and his arms flew as he shouted and stormed away.

Amber had looked terrified during the whole exchange, yet by the time Paschal had returned to his office, he'd calmed down to his usual jaunty self and refused to discuss the matter with his son.

So what was new?

Ben had made it his business to track down Amber Stranton and question her about the situation. She'd been tight-lipped, mentioning only that her cousin had been interested in some Gypsy hideaway his father had been researching. Without mentioning Valoren by name, Amber had invoked a sore topic between Paschal and Ben. He'd warned her off broaching the topic again with Paschal, and yet, she'd called his private, unlisted home number. This couldn't be good.

His father, despite all signs to the contrary, was not going to live forever—especially not with added stress. Ben turned left onto a side street and tapped on the accelerator until the car reached a fast but manageable speed. In less than five minutes, he found himself in front of Paschal's house. Seconds later, the hairs on the back of his neck prickled. The security pad at the end of the driveway, which, once coded, would allow him past the iron gates, had been smashed to bits.

Grabbing his phone, Ben dialed the security company. After supplying the correct passwords, Ben listened as the service rep rattled off details about receiving a signal the night before indicating a problem at the address, but a call to Paschal had stopped any further investigation.

"How do you know it was really him?" Ben asked, his heart shoving its way up his esophagus even as it attempted to pound out of his chest through his ribs.

"He gave us the correct codes, sir. Should I alert the police?"

"Yes," Ben replied, his stomach as hard as stone.

He should have checked on his father earlier. Friday was the old man's day off, and since he was a notorious night owl, he preferred to sleep in. Ben normally didn't stop by to check on him until late afternoon, a practice waylaid by one Catalina Reyes.

And anyone who made note of Paschal's routine would know that, wouldn't they?

Was she connected?

"Are you inside the residence?" the rep asked.

"Not yet," he answered.

"Please stay outside until the authorities arrive. We don't want any con—"

Ben disconnected the call, switched the phone from ringer to vibrate and shoved it in his pocket. Retrieving the gun, he approached the gates behind the cover of his car and, using his key, gained access to the property.

Everything looked relatively normal, though the setting sun cast elongated shadows across the carefully tended lawn and gardens. His father didn't have much time for a life outside of his research and travels, but he insisted on keeping a neat yard—a holdover from Ben's mother, who never started a morning at their chateau in France without puttering in her flower beds before breakfast.

After creeping up the wraparound porch, he found the front door not only unlocked, but open a few inches. Again, the security alarm had been disengaged. No lights—green, red or otherwise—blinked on the control panel. Ben pushed the door completely open and called out his father's name.

His voice echoed across the entryway. Leading with his gun, Ben moved into the house as stealthily as possible. While ornate and usually well kept, the house had been turned upside down. Cushions and books vied with carpets for spots on the floor. Statues were overturned and swept aside. Luckily, his father's place wasn't overly large. In two minutes, Ben knew the bottom floor was deserted, with no sign of his father anywhere. And if his instincts proved correct, nothing was missing.

"Do you know how to use that thing?"

Instantly, he spun toward the voice, then pulled up on the gun, aiming the barrel toward the ceiling. He wasn't entirely surprised to see Ms. Reyes standing in the doorway, her arms folded beneath her ample breasts.

"Do you have a death wish?" he asked.

"You don't seem the type to shoot first and ask questions later."

"You've known me for, what, five minutes? I could be a serial killer."

"Not with that dimple," she replied.

Instinctively, Ben touched the indentation on his chin. He hated that dimple.

"I believe Ted Bundy had dimples," he snapped.

She slipped into the house and boldly swiped a finger over the depression on his jawline. "Trust me, I've met a few serial killers. You, sir, are no serial killer. But I am wondering why a pedantic graduate student is packing a .357 magnum with his pocket protectors."

Graduate student? He had his PhD. Two of them, actually.

"Who are you?" he asked.

She set her briefcase down beside the door and extended her hand forcefully, ignoring both his weapon and the upturned state of the house. Ben glanced up the stairs, uncertain what he'd find there, though he was nearly sure the house was deserted. Either that, or his father was . . .

"Catalina Reyes. I'm a paranormal investigator."

Absently, Ben gave her a nod, unwilling to part with his weapon simply to exchange pleasantries.

"Ben Rousseau. *Dr.* Ben Rousseau," he said unabashedly. "Paschal is my father. Perhaps you should wait outside until I'm sure it's safe here. Obviously, someone came in uninvited."

"And left in a hurry. There are ruts in the driveway. Looks like they were put there by a rather heavy vehicle, too."

Ben kept his eyes on the staircase, hoping for a sign of life. "What are you, CSI?"

"No, but in my line of work, it pays to be observant. And I'm totally addicted to cop shows on television. Speaking of cops, shouldn't you call them instead of running around like David Caruso?"

"The security company has alerted the authorities, but I need to see if my father is safe. He was supposed to be home, catching up on reading. Relaxing. There's no sign of him. Stay here."

Catalina surprised him by closing her eyes for five long seconds. When she opened them, a relative calmness darkened her eyes from dark chocolate to complete and utter blackness. "He's not here."

"And you know that, how?"

"Just call it instinct."

"I'd rather rely on proof, thanks."

Upstairs, he discovered she'd been right. His father's bedroom, while completely ransacked, contained no sign of the man. Neither did his bathroom, the guest room, the guest bath or the upstairs study. All were torn apart from top to bottom, but did not contain a single sign of Paschal Rousseau's presence.

"Damn it, Dad," Ben muttered, "what have you gotten yourself into this time?"

12

Alexa wasn't sure what woke her first—the cold stone beneath her cheek or the sound of someone calling her name. Groggy and stiff, she forced herself into a sitting position and tried to open her eyes. Her left-over mascara had fused her lashes, so she rubbed until tears flushed her vision clear.

Great. Just great. She'd gone to sleep without washing her face. She was going to have one hell of a blemish in a day or two. And her teeth. Ugh. Her tongue, pasted inside her mouth, tasted horrible. She reached around for a bottle of water and found nothing.

As in absolutely nothing. The furnishings, at first a reflection of the portrait hanging in the hall and then brimming with pillows and cushions, had completely disappeared. Nothing remained. No chair. No fireplace. No cat.

No Damon.

"Alexa!"

The voice, not Damon's, came from downstairs. She attempted to stand, but the aches in her body nearly left her paralyzed. She'd recovered from her car accident, but her body would always bear the scars, even if no one could see them.

Reaching behind her neck, however, she winced when her fingers touched her skin. The flesh, swollen and sensitive from the ripped necklace, still stung.

The pain contradicted the barrenness all around her. Had last night been a dream?

"Alexa!"

"Jacob?"

Her throat parched, her voice barely carried. She stumbled across the cold stone, her muscles throbbing first in the usual places, and then in spots where a flash of pain wasn't quite so bad. At the mere thought of the bliss Damon had given her, an instantaneous, pleasurable tremor rippled between her legs and across her breasts. As if he still stood beside her, she heard his voice cataloging the decadent things he intended to do to her the next time they were alone. A warmth not unlike body heat chased the stone-cold chill away.

Her muscles relaxed. Her aches subsided. Every nerve ending in her body shifted its focus until nothing but anticipation ruled her brain. She closed her eyes. Her nipples, bare beneath her blouse, pricked against the fabric. When the rich scent of leather and man sneaked into her nostrils, she had to squeeze her legs tightly together to offset the sweet, raw response.

Her eyes flashed open and she spun, expecting Damon.

The room remained bleakly empty.

She blew out a frustrated breath. Damn. She'd experienced a few intense wet dreams in her lifetime, but never anything like this—especially not while awake. Still, despite the lack of evidence, she had to believe that what had happened last night—hell, what had happened a moment ago—had been incredibly real.

"Alexa!"

With a reluctant groan, she picked up her backpack and headed into the second-floor hall. Her feet scraped against the cold stone, but after a few steps, she found her stride. Now, if she just had a latte with an extra shot of espresso, she'd be able to survive the sunlight streaming in through the highest windows.

The minute she touched the top step that led down to the landing of the main staircase, the smell of freshly brewed coffee caught her nose. Either Damon's magic was still working or her brother had come bearing Starbucks.

When she looked up, Jacob stood in front of her, staring at the painting where Damon used to be, a green-and-white-logo cup in his hand.

How was she going to explain the sudden disappearance of the portrait's subject?

Or would she have to?

Jacob immediately dashed toward her, took her by the hand and, once she reached the landing, enfolded her in a typically stiff hug. "I'm so sorry, sis. I couldn't believe the storm. I couldn't—"

She placed a soft palm over his mouth. He was rambling, and she had no patience for chatter before she'd been bolstered by a jolt or twelve of caffeine.

"It's okay. I was prepared. I knew you'd come as soon as you could."

Arm still wrapped around her protectively, Jacob led her across the landing.

"Your satellite phone didn't work?"

Alexa frowned. Hell, she hadn't even checked.

"I guess not. Did you try to call?"

"A dozen times. I would have called the Coast Guard, but we'd—"

"No, I'm glad you didn't." If he only knew how glad. "I don't want the local authorities pegging us as a nuisance. I had everything I needed to make it through the night. I've never camped before, but despite the lack of twelve-hundred-thread-count sheets and a proper mattress, I survived."

He rubbed her shoulder, and while the sensation was relaxing, she silently wished for Damon's hands instead. "Did you sleep at all?"

She pressed her lips together to hide a sexually satisfied smile. "Not much."

"Can't blame you," Jacob said, his voice a wry mixture of sympathy and repulsion. He stopped in the middle of the landing, right under the cursed painting. "Staring up at this man all night? It's enough to give you nightmares."

Alexa's breath caught tight in her throat. Damon was back in his prison, dead center, as handsome and intimidating as ever. Maybe even a bit more so.

Had it all been a dream?

As she stared into his eyes, intense and stormy gray, her chest ached. If last night had been just a sexual fantasy, she could make the memories last a lifetime. But damn it, he'd told her about his sister. About his quest to exact retribution on the sorcerer who'd cursed him inside the canvas and oil. She couldn't have dreamed all of it. Could she?

Even as a phantom, Damon Forsyth possessed more life than most men she knew. The magic containing him had to be incredibly powerful. And dangerous. Too dangerous for her to go forward with her plans?

Jacob nudged the coffee cup into her hand. She inhaled the bitter aroma through the tiny spiral of steam that escaped through the top.

"Two sugars and cream," Jacob said with a wink. "Just the way you like it."

Half the time, Jacob could be a real pain in the ass. The rest of the time, he was a certifiable prince. She often didn't know what to make of him, but for today, she could certainly drink his coffee and be thankful for his company. "Doctors said I should stick to soy," she reminded him before taking a sip of the perfectly delicious, ultracreamy brew. Leave it to Jacob to know just when she needed a decadent indulgence.

She glanced up at Damon.

Relatively speaking.

"The doctors didn't stay all night in a dark and dank castle on a godforsaken island in the middle of a freakish storm," Jacob added. "You can run off the calories in the hotel health club later."

"No health club for me. We have a meeting to plan. I want a team of contractors here by two o'clock."

"Here? Or the hotel?"

Glancing at the painting, Alexa forced herself to think beyond the swirl of conflicting emotions coursing through her. No matter what had transpired between her and Damon the night before, her goals hadn't changed. The castle would become her premiere property. Whether or not the hotel had a resident ghost, she supposed, was up to Damon.

If he was real.

If, she supposed, she could find a way to free him again.

Closing her eyes, she tried to listen, in case Damon spoke to her again from within the painting. Unfortunately, the castle seemed colder and emptier than it had yesterday during the Coast Guard's search, and the portrait lacked that spark of fire that had ensnared her attention shortly before she'd touched the canvas. Damon had still been trapped in the painting then, but he'd somehow reached out to her. She'd heard him. Felt his presence. Now?

Nothing.

She chased off a chill with another sip of coffee.

"You've got to be as stiff as a board," Jacob said, his lip curled up to his nose. Alexa covered a snicker.

"Wondering how I could possibly have stayed overnight in a stone prison without the creature comforts?"

"Plush velvets, rich tapestries and a warm body beside you in bed are always a nice touch," he lamented.

She covered a chuckle with another sip of coffee. "I'll remember the part about warm bodies when we open the hotel."

"You're not thinking of giving a new definition to room service, are you?" he asked wickedly.

Not for all the guests, no, but the owner's suite might be a different story. "Ask me after I've had a shower and brushed my teeth. As for last night, the bottom line is, I survived."

"Yes," he said, his eyes glittering, "you have a nasty habit of doing that. Did the talisman help?"

His eyes darted to her neck, and instantly, Jacob's

face fell. Instinctively, Alexa reached for the charm, but thanks to the broken chain, she could no longer wear the trinket. She smoothed her hand down her slacks, relieved to feel the triangle tucked within.

"It must have fallen off," she said, not wanting to return the charm to Jacob when she knew how important it was to Damon. And to her. She might not be able to reenter the castle without its magical properties. "I'm sure it's around here somewhere."

Alexa grabbed Jacob's arm. She could feel him shaking beneath his tailored shirt. Did he have any idea of the value of the necklace, magically speaking? Or was he simply being his dramatic self?

"Jacob, seriously," she reassured him. "I wouldn't lose something you gave me. I'll find it. I promise."

After a moment, he shook the worry off his face and forced a smile. "You didn't leave the castle, right?"

She hadn't had the choice. "Not even for a second. And clearly, no one else has been here. I, um, camped out in a room upstairs."

Jacob raised an eyebrow.

"One selling point of this new property is that the stone seems to generate a nice chill against the Florida heat, but in the storm, it got a little icy. I ventured upstairs where I found a room that seemed warmer than the rest. I'm betting the necklace is up there somewhere. Stay here. I'll go—"

"No," Jacob said firmly, glancing once at the castle's keeper in the painting. "I'll go. Which room?"

Oh, this was ridiculous. Still, she couldn't bear to return the necklace to Jacob. Not yet. Not without Damon's . . . what? Approval? The charm did, more than likely, belong to his sister, and the protective properties Jacob had believed in had been quite real, judging by the fact that she'd survived the night. No, she couldn't give the jewelry back. Not until she knew more.

While she hesitated, Jacob took a step toward the second level of stairs, but his foot missed and he tumbled onto his knees. He yelped when his shin scraped over the hard stone.

"Jacob!"

He turned on her in a flash, his eyes watering and his lip curled into a snarl. "Why did you push me?"

"What?"

"Alexa, I know I should have tried harder last night to get to you, but—"

"I didn't push you, you moron. You lost your footing."

He stared at her, his eyes wild with accusations he trapped behind clenched lips. Without a word, he headed upstairs once again, making it all the way to the top before he tripped over nothing and once again went flying.

Alexa spun around, spilling her coffee. Suddenly, she sensed a third presence. A larger-than-life presence. An "I cheated death and I don't trust anyone" presence.

"Damon?"

Jacob groaned.

She put down the cardboard cup and charged up after her brother. "Stop it," she commanded through tight teeth.

Jacob had twisted onto his ass, his gaze trained on the spot where he'd tripped—a spot with nothing but the slick, stone floor.

"Stop what? Falling down? I'd like to obey, Alexa, but—"

"No, not you."

"Then who?"

"Never mind," she snapped. She had to get Jacob out of here. Perhaps Damon's entrapment in the painting wasn't as absolute this time, and perhaps despite his promises the night before, he intended to seek retribution against the man who had somehow come to possess his sister's necklace. She certainly wasn't going to lend a hand in the phantom's quest for revenge. Not toward Jacob, at least.

"Jacob, I'm tired and hungry. I want to go back to the hotel. Now."

"But the talisman?" Jacob asked, his voice shaky.

He could be such a twit sometimes. "We'll find it later. This island has been uninhabited for sixty years. I doubt we'll suddenly have a rush of interlopers in one afternoon."

Jacob's hesitation sparked a chill that ran along the edge of her skin. Why was he so attached to the necklace? Sure, he'd thought the charm would protect her, but his stricken look spoke of something deeper. Did he know the powerful magic that made the charm so valuable? How could he?

Either way, she had to get him out of here before Damon threw him down the stairs. She grabbed Jacob's elbows and helped him stand. He hesitated, but then finally submitted to her tugging and followed her down.

As she reached the grand front door, blue, electric images from the night before flashed in her brain. She held her breath and reached for the latch, hoping the door would open.

It did, but not before a whisper blew across her ear. *You'll be back.*

Not a question. Not a request. Just a simple statement of fact.

"I own this place," she whispered. "Of course I'll be back."

Jacob eyed her suspiciously, looking around to see whom she was talking to. "Alexa, are you all right?"

She glanced up at the landing. The distance between the door and the painting was substantial, yet though she couldn't see the sneer of a smile on Damon's face, she could feel it.

She could feel him.

A brush of her sleeve. A breath across her neck. A flick of a fingertip over her nipple and her body's traitorous response.

"I'm fine," she insisted to her brother. "Just lead the way out of here."

She stepped out of the way and Jacob strode through the door unhampered. Alexa couldn't resist peering at the seemingly clear blue sky before she attempted to put one foot over the threshold. When no angry storm brewed out of nowhere with winds that would knock her on her ass and slam the door closed, she smiled and strode into the warm Florida sunshine.

Then she realized she'd forgotten her backpack.

Jacob was halfway through the thick palmetto bushes that led to the stone wall surrounding the castle when she called out for him to stop.

"I forgot my pack."

Jacob rolled his eyes indulgently as he returned to her side. "I'll get it."

She grabbed his arm. "No. I mean, you're not my servant, Jacob. I can get it myself. Wait here."

Since she hadn't yet shut the door behind her, she slipped back into the castle and made certain to leave her exit unblocked. Jacob stood in the doorway peering after her, which inspired her to hurry across the entrance hall and up the stairs to where she'd dropped her pack underneath the portrait.

She grabbed the canvas bag by the strap and, as she spun to exit, spied Damon's intense eyes staring down at her. Eyes that looked glossier than before.

She moved in closer. The whole of Damon's body seemed glossier, as if the oils . . .

She reached up and swiped at his breeches, not at all surprised to find dark paint smeared on her fingertip.

"You're quite the trickster," she said softly.

"Only when I need to be," Damon replied.

She looked around, but he was nowhere to be seen. Not, at least, until she peered into a shadowed corner just a few feet away. There she saw the outline of a man. A large man, leaning against the cold stone with a cocky assurance that belied his transparent form, barely visible in the shadows.

After a quick wave to Jacob, she moved toward the corner, which was outside of her brother's sight.

"Alexa?" Jacob called from downstairs.

"He watches me like a hawk," Alexa explained to the shadow.

Damon chuckled, and the sound simmered through her body like warmed wine. "I can't blame him."

"Give me a second," she shouted over her shoulder. She heard Jacob grumble in response.

"So you are still free?" she asked.

"I am free from the painting."

"But not from the castle?"

The sense of his pushing through the space around her spawned a sensation not unlike a chill, but decidedly warmer. He moved into the light, and no trace of him remained except his scent and the remnants of his body heat. She remained facing the wall even though she guessed he was now standing directly behind her.

"I cannot leave the castle without your help," he said, his voice skimming down her neck on a ghostly breath.

A wisp of a touch reached beneath her blouse and glided over her skin.

She swallowed deeply. "What makes you think I'll help you after you tripped my brother?"

Pressure built between her legs, not from within, but from without. "Because I'll return the favor a hundred times over. Remember? I told you this morning. In the room. You didn't realize then that I was there, did you?"

"Telling me all the sexual things you want to do to me?"

"Oh, yes. I want, Alexa. And I will. Every single delicious sensation will be yours if you help me."

She started when a jolt of stiffness crashed against her buttocks, as if he was pressing his sex right into the crease, snuggling his thickened cock against her. He might as well have magicked away her clothing, the sensation was so strong. In her mind, he'd stripped her bare. The buttons remaining on her blouse popped open, the fingers that manipulated the fasteners unseen. She looked down and watched her breasts undulate as he attended them with invisible hands.

The sensations were decadent and delicious and too tempting to ignore. She closed her eyes and cooed, even as a teardrop of need moistened her sex and blood rushed to the places he touched—and the places she wanted him to touch. For more of this, she'd do whatever he wanted.

The thought burst into her mind like fireworks, and she instantly spun around and stepped back, breaking the contact between her body and his intangible form. She grabbed her blouse and punched the buttons into place.

"You can't seduce me into doing your bidding," she insisted.

She gasped when a whoosh of warm air pushed her fully against the wall. Ensconced in the dark corner, she could see his outline again, right down to his fathomless eyes, now swirling with gray mist like angry storm clouds.

"Every woman can be seduced," he claimed, his lips mere inches from hers.

"Not me," she claimed. "Not if you're going to be crass about it."

He chuckled and backed away, blowing like a puff of smoke out of her path. "Then I'll simply have to exercise more finesse."

Alexa pushed off the wall and, with a swing of her backpack, marched to the staircase, excited and unnerved at the same time. "You do that."

Before her foot touched the bottom step, she jolted as the sensation of an intimate kiss burst between her legs, right down to the tongue slipping inside and sucking her clit in one explosive pull. She nearly tripped, but instead fell backward into Damon's invisible but waiting arms. He guided her to the floor, and by the time Jacob arrived, the hot surge of pleasure had subsided and Damon was gone.

"Are you all right? What happened?" Jacob asked.

Alexa shook her head. "Dizzy spell."

"This place isn't right, Alexa. Maybe you should forget about this for a while. Find a property that is more . . . hospitable."

With a narrowed gaze, Alexa stood, dusted her pants and handed her backpack to her brother. "No way. Nothing's changed, you hear that?" She spoke to Damon but knew her brother needed to register the message as well. "I know what I want. I'm willing to do whatever it takes to get it. Makes two of us, right?"

Jacob's smile was uncertain, but Alexa didn't say another word. The message wasn't for him anyway. It was for the phantom who'd become her lover and who'd just issued her a challenge she'd be a fool to ignore.

13

Gruff voices below, accompanied by the crack and whistle of police radios, forced Ben to tuck the gun into a drawer in the guest room and head downstairs. He had a license to carry, but he'd rather not deal with questions. Once in the foyer, he found Catalina chatting with the cops.

"Ms. Reyes here says this is your father's house?" asked a female cop with a ponytail.

Ben nodded. "There's no sign of him upstairs. I hadn't heard from him since yesterday, so I came to check on him. The security alarm by the driveway was destroyed."

As the other officer went upstairs to verify his father's absence, Ben repeated his conversation with the security company. After answering a few more questions, he found himself shuttled outside onto the porch with Catalina while the police called for backup and began an investigation. Evidence at the scene pointed toward only one possibility—kidnapping.

"He's all right," Catalina said, her voice gently melodic.

"You know that the same way you knew he wasn't at home?"

With a shy smile, she nodded. "Yeah. Great parlor trick to have in the repertoire. Makes you very popular at parties."

Despite her jokes, he knew she wasn't kidding around.

"How long have you been psychic?"

She eyed him skeptically. "You seem awful quick to jump to that conclusion."

Ben jammed his fingers through his hair. "I've been around the block. Seen things." Weird shit, too. Shit most people blew off as hallucination.

"I could be a scam artist," she warned.

"You could. But with Paschal gone, you'll never get the one thing you claim to really want—the diary. So for now, I'm willing to take my chances. Seriously, what can you feel about my father?"

She shook her head sadly. "Not much. Especially not out here. Can you get me something of his? Something he cherishes?"

Ben leaned into the doorway and, without entering the house, saw a hand-carved flute lying among the debris near the door. A flash of a memory assailed him. He'd been four. Maybe five. He'd been treasure hunting, complete with pirate kerchief and cardboard cutlass. He'd followed the scribbled map he'd drawn himself to the trunk tucked into his father's closet. Inside, he'd discovered the ancient musical instrument. Fine booty indeed. Of course, he'd no clue how old the flute was or how fragile. He'd only known it made funny noises when he blew into it, making his triumphant find all the more exciting.

His father had probably taken the stairs three at a time when he'd heard the trills and tweets coming from his room. But he hadn't yelled or screamed. He'd taken the instrument away gently, explained how fragile it was—how special.

How Ben was never to touch the things his father kept hidden.

He snatched the flute from the floor and shoved it into Catalina's hands. "Best I can do on short notice."

As if naturally sensing the flute's age and delicacy, she handled it gingerly. "This is very old. Older than your father could be. Much older."

"He told me he found it in an antique shop in Dresden sometime after he married my mother. Claimed the style called to him, like something from his youth. Only, he doesn't ever talk about his childhood. I believe the flute is . . ."

"Romani, yes. Distinctive vibrations come off objects made by people who believe in magic."

"Do you believe in magic?"

Doubt lilted his voice, but Catalina smiled, though whatever emotion hid behind the soft curve of her lips didn't reach her eyes. Her gaze darkened with an innate sadness—one he'd seen in his father's gaze more times than he could count.

"Isn't that a song?" she teased.

"Not from my era. Or yours."

"Still," she said, humming as she walked the length of the porch, the flute cradled in her hands.

Ben tried to ignore that he knew nothing about this woman except that she'd charmed Morton Gilmore, a known rapscallion, but otherwise brilliant man.

"He's worried," she said finally.

"Worried? Not afraid?"

She shook her head. "No, not afraid." Looking up from the flute, she grinned. "Your father isn't an easy man to intimidate."

Ben stood up straighter. Man, she got that right. He supposed a man couldn't reach the ripe old age of ninety-five without possessing a great deal of grit, which his father had in spades. He'd run with the French Resistance during the war. He'd traveled off the beaten path all over Europe. He'd moved his entire life, from France to Texas, and took up a whole new career when most men were wasting away in nursing homes. He could live through this.

Shutting his eyes, Ben willed away the wave of emotion threatening to break him down. He was made of the same tough stuff as Paschal. And his mother hadn't exactly been a hothouse flower, either. Damn if he was going to lose it now.

"Can you find him?" he asked.

Catalina shot over to a bench, sat down and

clutched the flute tightly. After a long, tense minute, she looked up and handed him the instrument.

"Not from this. I'm sorry. I have a natural ability, but I don't practice much. If my grandfather were here, he'd likely be able to conjure a street address, but I'm not nearly as talented."

"Can you call your grandfather?"

"Yes," she answered ruefully, "but since he's been dead ten years, I don't think he'd be much help."

Ben looked at her oddly, and the tiny smile on her lips revealed nothing about her level of seriousness. He couldn't question her further, though, since the detectives had arrived. Their interrogation was much more thorough and took nearly half an hour. Ben answered their questions with as much honesty as he thought prudent. He told them about the phone message from Amber Stranton and the meeting on the quad. He provided the most accurate description he could of Amber's mysterious cousin. With his laptop, he found Amber's phone number on the class rolls. She was, right now, their only lead.

Or was she?

Catalina sat, quietly clutching the flute, the entire time.

Just as the detective was closing up his notebook, one of the beat cops poked his head out the door.

"Detective, you need to see this."

Ben stood, but Catalina caught him by the arm and kept him in place. After an interminable absence, the cop finally returned.

"Mr. Rousseau, we need for you to come with us downtown."

"What?" he asked, enraged. The accusatory sound in the guy's voice was unmistakable.

"Calm down," the detective instructed. "We just found some evidence that requires further investigation."

Ben's insides clenched. "What kind of evidence?"

The detective frowned and gestured toward the steps. "We can discuss the details downtown."

The distinct scent of accusation hung heavy in the air. Cat sent him a fortifying smile and stepped forward. She wanted him to go. And she was going with him.

Ben pressed his lips tightly together, well aware that his actions were being scrutinized. He nodded to the detective and followed him to his squad car, Catalina touching him lightly on his arm the entire way. He pushed all supposition out of his brain and concentrated on one goal—satisfying the police so he could get back to the task of finding his father.

Blood. Four drops on the back porch near the driveway, fresh enough to have come from a wound on his father. Luckily, between Cat vouching for Ben's whereabouts at the college campus (admitting that she'd secretly watched his car all day and then followed him home) and a neighbor reportedly seeing Paschal in his garden that morning, Ben was cleared of suspicion and immediately released. He and Cat didn't arrive back at Paschal's house until the next morning, but by then, the police had released the crime scene and they were free to venture inside.

Ben slid the remains of his father's knickknacks and collectibles out of their way as they walked. The house echoed with emptiness. Paschal was gone, and it was up to Ben to get him back.

"Want me to help you clean up?" she offered.

"You don't have to stay."

"Actually, I think I do. I'm a firm believer that life isn't random. I think I'm supposed to help you."

"Perhaps you're the reason my father was taken."

"Excuse me?"

He'd offended her, but he didn't care. He was angry, scared and tired. So far, Catalina had been indispensable, but he had to know now if he could trust her completely—and this was the only way.

"My father lived a perfectly anonymous life until people came around asking about Valoren. You're one of those people."

She removed a collection of boxes from a velvet chair, then collapsed into it. "You're right."

"And maybe you know that he hasn't been hurt not because of some psychic ability, but because you're in on the whole thing."

She nodded. "Makes sense."

"So you don't deny it?"

"Of course I deny it! You can check me out, Ben. You'll find that the woman I'm working for is above legitimate and beyond reproach."

"Who is she?"

"Alexa Chandler."

Ben had to think. He'd heard the name before but wasn't sure where.

"Of the Crown Chandler hotels?" she prodded.

"You work for an heiress?"

Cat rolled her eyes. "Alexa isn't just an heiress. She's more Ivanka Trump than Paris Hilton, I assure you. She's also my best friend. Trust me, her interest in Valoren is completely legitimate, and while she's widely known as a shark in the boardroom, she'd never resort to kidnapping an elderly man to get the information she needs."

Before he'd become his father's assistant, holed up in a tiny office poring over undergraduate research papers and flipping through maps and course material, Ben had lived an entirely different life. He'd learned then to rely on his instincts—and his instincts told him Catalina Reyes was telling the truth.

He stepped over the remnants of a collection of vases and sat in front of her on an ottoman. "You heard what I told the police. It can't be an accident that some stranger in a trenchcoat came looking for my father to ask about Valoren, and then he's kidnapped."

Cat smirked. "I'm no longer a suspect?"

He cleared his throat, wondering if he was making a huge mistake. "For the time being, no, you're no longer a suspect."

"And you think Amber's so-called cousin took your father?"

"Seems like the most likely lead. My father doesn't run with a dangerous crowd."

"But you told the police your father was quite wealthy. Wouldn't that make him an ideal target for all sorts of criminals?"

"His wealth is hardly common knowledge. Nearly all his money is in foreign banks. To the world, he's an eccentric college professor who teaches a few classes a week in topics most students wouldn't be interested in, except he's known as an easy A."

"Easy A? Why is that?"

Ben agreed with Morton Gilmore's assessment that Catalina Reyes was a smart woman. Most professors at the university would hate the designation, while his father enjoyed his popularity.

"He's not interested in teaching, really. He likes talking and the kids like listening. He's actually quite a good storyteller. But he works with the college because his association with the university allows him access to sources he needs in his mission."

"Mission?"

Ben paused. Since his mother's death, Ben had discussed his father's true calling in life with no one, just as Paschal had barely discussed the matter with his own son. But it didn't take a genius to figure out what his father meant to do with all his collecting and research and trips around Europe, mostly in Germany and England. His father was trying to prove Valoren once existed—and the quest compelled him to the point of near obsession. Now his interests might have cost him his freedom. And if Ben didn't act soon, perhaps his life.

"Why are you looking for information about Valoren?" he asked.

"Alexa inherited an island called Isla de Fantasmas, complete with a Gothic castle, from her father."

"Isla de Fantasmas? That's Spanish."

"The island is off the coast of St. Augustine."

"And how is this related to Valoren?"

"That's what I'm trying to find out. The place name was written on the letter bequeathing the property to Alexa. The castle was reportedly moved to the island sixty years ago, possibly from Valoren."

Ben's chest tightened. Sixty years ago? His mind flashed to the paperwork he'd found among his mother's things shortly after her death. Bills of lading. Customs forms. Deeds and documents from the state of Florida. At the time, his parents had still been living in France and he'd assumed the documents had simply been a part of his father's research. All the names and most of the contents of the cargo had been blacked out.

"What can you tell me about this castle?" he asked.

"Not much. I haven't seen it myself. One roadblock to the development of the island is that it is hard to get to. However, Alexa was able to reach the island yesterday by both helicopter and boat."

"And she wants to develop the castle as a hotel?"

"That's her plan. The castle is large enough for an exclusive, privacy-oriented resort, but she'll need her big investors and stockholders on board for such an expenditure, so she needs more information. What she knows now is scant, at best, but since there are reportedly ghosts involved, she asked me to investigate."

"Ghosts?" he asked skeptically. He'd seen odd things back in his adventurous days, but not much pointing to the existence of spirits of the dead.

"Alexa thinks so, but I have my doubts."

"Well, ghosts didn't kidnap my father and leave drops of his blood on the driveway. Tell me precisely what you know about Valoren."

"Only that it is a legendary gypsy safe haven. There seems to be no definitive documentation, either modern or historical, that proves the place ever existed. According to my research, if Valoren was real, there is nothing left, artifact-wise, to give us any information."

Ben shook his head, glancing at the detritus surrounding them. His father had gotten himself into a serious mess by keeping his knowledge and research about Valoren a secret. The time to bring things out into the open was now. He could send her away and get down to the real business of breaking his father's code of silence. Or he could join forces with the determined and knowledgeable—not to mention psychic— Ms. Reyes and perhaps find his father before the old man met his maker at the hands of obvious thugs.

"Well, that part certainly isn't true," he said.

"What part?"

"That nothing is left. Look around you, Ms. Reyes. I suspect that everything you see here is connected to Valoren in some way."

"Why?"

"My father's entire life has been one long obsession with the place, though he worked hard to keep it all a secret from me for reasons I can't begin to explain. He admitted, to others, that the so-called Gypsy safe haven was cursed. From what I gathered from his colleagues, sometime in the eighteenth century, the entire community vanished, along with everyone who lived there. All that was left were knickknacks and furnishings he found in private collections, secondhand shops and antiques stores all over Europe. Men of my father's ilk aren't the types to believe in curses and magic, but Paschal has always spoken with utter certainty that black magic exists. Yet despite his dire warnings of danger, he's persisted in his quest to locate as many items associated with Valoren as he can. That's why he's never allowed me on his junkets. Why he never wants me to stay in his house with him or linger too long over his personal possessions. And judging from what's happened today, I'd say his luck at remaining free of the Valoren curse finally ran out."

14

Catalina waited, silent, marveling at what Ben had admitted so far. "Guarded" didn't begin to describe the man's aura, and yet she felt certain he'd told her everything he knew—or close to it. He didn't trust easily. Wise man. But he trusted her. Also wise.

"Do you think the police will find your father?"

"I have no idea, but look around. The people who took my father want something, something I don't think they found. I don't know how much time my father has if he doesn't give them what they want."

"It could just be a robbery. For money. Maybe someone followed him home from the grocery store and wanted bank codes or some such."

Ben shook his head. "The police found Paschal's checkbook upstairs. My father doesn't keep financial information for his accounts in Europe here in the house. It's at the university office. And the police already contacted security at our building on campus. Nothing was disturbed after I left."

"Maybe it's a disgruntled student," she hypothesized.

Impatience flared in his eyes, but Ben managed to keep his tone even.

"Students with As aren't disgruntled. The only disgruntled student he's had has been the one whose cousin wanted information about Valoren."

"You don't know that for sure."

"I'm his assistant. Students talk to me before they

talk to him. And the only clue we have is the phone call from Amber. In a situation like this, it's best to have a working hypothesis. And so far, Valoren is the best we have."

Exhaling loudly, Ben turned toward Cat, his knees knocking against hers. The contact jolted her, but she fought not to react, not to slide away. The atmosphere in the room instantly changed, just like the emotion in his eyes. Where moments ago his gray eyes reflected guarded trust, now the curtains fell.

"It's time to look for his secret room, and you're going to help me."

"What?"

Ben hopped over the mangled artifacts and locked the front door. Extending his hand, he invited Cat to join him, which she did, slipping her fingers into his grasp even though she certainly could have maneuvered through the mess without his assistance. The vibrations of Ben's skin on hers provided ample reward. For a split second, she forgot why she was here.

"Since he moved to Texas, I've believed my father has a secret room somewhere in the house. Maybe the clues we need to find him are there," he said, guiding her toward the stairs.

"Why would you think your father would go to such an extreme?"

"We had several hidden rooms in the chateau in France where I grew up, places even my mother wasn't allowed to go. I wasn't even supposed to know about them, but I was an only child and keenly observant, though ridiculously discreet. I grew up shuttled between New York and France. In Manhattan, we had a brownstone with at least one secret room, and my father was very particular when he shopped for real estate here in Austin. He wanted the oldest house possible. I always suspected there was something about this place he was hiding."

"Just because he appreciates lasting workmanship doesn't mean he has a secret room."

"No," he agreed, stopping as they reached the

second-floor landing, "but look around. The layout of the house is strange, isn't it? And there have been times when I couldn't find my father anywhere, but then he'd suddenly show up. He's a wily old guy, but even I don't believe he has the power to disappear and reappear at will."

"You've never looked for the room?"

Ben frowned wryly. "Of course I looked. But not with much enthusiasm. Mild curiosity isn't a good enough reason to break trust with a parent. But now? Now we need to tear this place apart."

Since Ben reported that he'd most often found his father in the small upstairs study after his unexplained disappearances, they started their search there. Following the dictates of every spooky movie they'd ever seen, they began by pulling back the tops of the spines of the hardcover books lining the shelves in the cramped thirty-square-foot space. Nothing happened. They worked the wall sconces next, then tilted paintings and fiddled with the hardware inside the fireplace. Ben's frown deepened from annoyance to chagrin. He stood in the middle of the room with his hands on his hips, emphasizing the slimness of his waist, hinting at a swagger she'd bet her shrunken head collection would taunt her mercilessly as long as they remained in the same room, pursuing the same goal.

"Any ideas?"

Cat concentrated, trying to locate a vibration within the room that would point them in the right direction. If Paschal Rousseau had been in his secret room, hiding, she might have been able to locate the entrance. Her talents leaned more toward sensing people and their thoughts than finding objects or locations, and even then, her skills were rusty. Concentrating on debunking or proving other people's paranormal powers had forced the development of her own powers to the backseat.

Hell, more like to the trunk.

"Sorry," she said. "I've got nothing. Maybe we should start looking in another part of the house."

Ben whipped off his glasses, nearly causing Catalina to dissolve into a puddle of utterly charmed female right there. Luckily for her, she had excellent control over her body. Or at least, she had until she'd met Ben Rousseau.

"No, it's here. I've always known it's here, but respecting my father's privacy is something I've been taught since birth."

"Is your father secretive?"

Ben snorted. "He invented the concept. My mother never questioned him, never challenged him, so I never did either. Now my politeness could cost him in ways I don't want to think about."

Standing stationary in the middle of the room, Catalina looked around one more time, clearing her mind of her emotions and concentrating only on what she saw with her eyes—a skill she'd perfected in her job. Grabbing Ben's hand, she guided him to the doorway, so they could see the whole room unimpeded.

The chandelier caught her eye immediately. Wrought from cast iron, the light fixture resembled twisted tree branches. Crystals cut like raindrops dangled just underneath each pointed lightbulb. Turning her head to the side, she noticed that while most of the crystals sparkled, one did not. One was muted.

With fingerprints.

"There!" she said.

She pointed to her discovery, and Ben's eyes widened in instant recognition. He strode forward and, after a fortifying glance toward her, tugged on the crystal.

The panel in the wall beside them slid open silently. Barely a whoosh rent the air.

"You've got good instincts," she complimented.

"On par with your eyes?"

"Sometimes you just need an objective observer and a new perspective."

"Right now, what we need is a flashlight."

Which they found just a foot from the panel, sitting

on a nearby shelf. The gleam from the light was slightly dim. "Needs new batteries," Ben commented.

Cat arched a brow. "Afraid of the dark?"

With a glare, he squeezed into the dark corridor, undoubtedly built for one person. The thought of climbing in after him shot a thrill through Cat that wasn't exactly unwelcome. On the surface, Ben Rousseau was so not her type. Slightly nerdy. Superior attitude. Driven by a blind devotion to a father who was, at the very least, secretive and, more than likely, emotionally cut off from his child. But he was incredibly good-looking, and his hidden adventurous streak appealed to her on a very deep, very personal level—a level that usually, if not always, led her into trouble.

She stepped into the darkness, feeling around with her hands while her eyes adjusted to the lack of light. "Not a cobweb in sight," she whispered. "Your father must be very meticulous."

"He has his moments," Ben said, his voice deep and surprisingly sensual when echoing off the thick wood panels that lined the passageway. In the enclosed space, Ben's scent, rich with the aroma of freshly tanned leather and sandalwood, assailed Cat mercilessly, especially when paired with the warmth of his hand curled around hers as he guided her in the relative darkness. Fortunately, the secret hallway wasn't long, and in seconds, Ben opened a door that led into a surprisingly well-lit room, only slightly smaller than the den they'd just left.

And similarly decorated. Books lined the shelves, though these were decidedly older, or at least in less pristine shape than the ones displayed in his study. Tapestries covered every wall, two and three deep. Portraits and paintings, mostly done in oil on canvas, and likely by the same artist, leaned against every available surface. The only clear space was on a small desk lit by a colorful Tiffany lamp.

"He's been here recently," Cat commented, running her hand over the surface of the desk. In temperature, the polished teak was cool, but in psychic vibrations, the wood simmered with a familiar warmth, similar— if not identical—to the tremors she'd felt when she'd held the flute.

"How recently?" Ben asked.

Cat slapped a thin layer of dust off her hands. "I'm not sure. It's so strange to be with someone who believes in my powers, maybe even a little more than I do."

"Like I said," he replied, "I've been around the block. Before I started holing up in my father's office as his glorified gopher, anyway."

Regret laced his tone, piquing Cat's interest. Crossing her arms over her chest, she watched him as he stalked around the room, assessing carefully, not touching anything until he had the lay of the land. He had the instincts of a cop. His hands hovered at his sides, as if he itched to disturb the crime scene but had the self-control to resist.

"What did you used to do?" she asked.

Ben turned his face into the shadows. "Let's just say that I took my father's interest in antiquities in a slightly different direction than academia."

The wry lilt in his voice, not to mention his elusiveness, turned her suppositions down a dark path. Not a cop. A criminal.

"You were a smuggler?" One swipe with a feather would have knocked Cat right off her feet.

When he faced her again, his gray eyes reflected a dash of unexpected charm. " 'Smuggler' is an ugly word. Let's just say I was in the import-export business."

"With an emphasis on export," she quipped.

He didn't deny it, but he did have the grace to change the subject.

"You said you were a paranormal researcher. I suppose you must be more used to dealing with skeptics when it comes to your psychic ability."

Cat poked into the drawers of the desk, all of which were unlocked except for one. "Actually, no. Usually,

I'm the skeptic. Very few of the people who put themselves 'out there' as mediums actually have any talent that isn't explainable by heightened intuition. For all I know, that's where my talents lie. I don't use them enough to know for sure."

Ben lifted one of the tapestries and extracted file folders that had been stacked on a chair behind the fabric. "Really? Why not?"

"A psychic who relies too much on her gift can become a slave to it. I've seen it happen."

Cat waited for Ben to press further, but luckily he seemed caught up in the files and lost interest in her personal admission. Since the people she dealt with daily either didn't know about her talent or, like Alexa, preferred not to believe in it completely, this wasn't a discussion she'd had many times before. Mostly, extolling the evils of ignoring her powers was a lecture she endured from her grandparents. At least, until Grandpère died and Yela, her grandmother, succumbed to the ravages of Alzheimer's.

In the largest drawer at the bottom of the desk, she found a thick bound manuscript. Flipping through, she discovered a collection of hand-drawn calendars dating back to the seventeen hundreds. Most pages were blank, except for a few penciled-in notations along the lines of "painting, *Schooner at Dawn*, Damon, Versailles at Antronique's," most written after 1946. A quick flip through the paintings stacked near the door revealed a rendition of a two-masted ship with three billowing sails, each reflecting the oranges and pinks of the sunrise. Paschal Rousseau must have found the painting in Versailles at a shop named Antronique's in April of 1947, according to his notations. She paged through and found references to hundreds of items. Crockery. Books. Children's toys. Interestingly, nearly all the paintings were attributed to an artist named Damon, whose work she found compelling, bold and unapologetic.

She replaced the calendars. Then, tucked into a cubby, she found another book. A catalog. Hundreds of photographs of swords, with information jotted on the back. The location of origin. The type of metal. The current collector and asking price.

"Was your father into swords?" she asked.

Ben shrugged. "No more than anything else. Why?"

"Not sure yet," she replied, replacing the book and wondering about the locked drawer. She checked the most obvious places for a key, then turned to the less obvious. Under the chair or taped to the bottom of another drawer. Inside a vase. Maybe mixed in with the paperclips?

Nothing.

"What did you find?" she asked, noticing he was still wrapped up with the files.

"Maps."

"Of?"

"Looks like Germany."

"You were born in Europe, right?"

Ben shook his head. "Actually, no. I was born here in the States when my mother and father were visiting old friends from the Resistance."

"The French Resistance?"

"None other. My mother's delivery was difficult, so my father bought an apartment in Manhattan and we lived there until I was nearly a year old. Then we returned to Paris. We lived between the two places for most of my childhood."

"And Germany?"

Ben's face skewed with deep thought. "I've been, but not with my father, though he traveled there quite a bit. He never took us with him, and after my mother died, he never went back."

"How long ago was that?"

Cat tried not to notice how Ben pursed his lips when concentrating. His fascinating mouth drew her attention more than warranted, and she couldn't help suspecting that Alexa's romantic notions about her mysterious ghost had rubbed off on her. But Ben's eyes—reflecting both a wild curiosity and a tempered worry—snared her as effectively as a metal noose. "Ben?"

He answered without meeting her eyes. "Too long ago. What's the deal with that drawer?"

He tossed the files back onto the chair, flipped the tapestry down and joined her at the desk. Bending on one knee, he examined the drawer carefully, running his fingers over the lock and around the handle before giving it a firm tug. When it remained closed, he pulled harder, but the compartment wouldn't yield.

"How are you at picking locks?" he asked.

"Rusty," she replied. "You?"

"About the same. Is there a letter opener or a paper clip on the desk?"

Cat found both, and he worked the tools with precision. She continued to look for a key. Scanning the shelves, she found a title that seemed more worn along the top of the spine than the others, as if it had been handled often. With a tug, she released the book and inside found a cutout in the pages that contained a small gold key.

"I found—"

With a grunt, Ben yanked open the drawer. The letter opener flew into the air. The force of the lock's release sent him tumbling backward. Cat winced and tried not to laugh.

"Tell me that's not the key," he said dryly, climbing to his feet as he swiped at his backside.

She dangled the tiny treasure from the satin ribbon tied to the end.

"Great," he said. "We're going to have to synchronize our efforts more effectively next time."

Cat pressed her lips together and fought down her laughter. God, he was cute. Nerdy, inventive, stubborn, snobby. A collection of qualities that didn't ordinarily combine into a desirable mix for her, but Ben Rousseau was certainly doing a number on her libido.

She put the key, no longer needed, back in its hiding place. "After our first meeting earlier, I'm surprised you want me around at all."

Ben's expression grew utterly serious. His eyes darkened so that the silver rings of his irises contrasted sharply against the intense blackness of his pupils. "I didn't want you around," he admitted. "At first, just because you were loud and disturbing my work. But once you mentioned Valoren, I knew I had to get rid of you."

Her breath caught. All hints of wry humor vanished. He was dead serious.

"Even now?"

He grabbed her by the arms, and the tension in his fingertips fried her nerve endings. His fear for her safety was a palpable, living thing. Powerful. Fierce.

Fear for his father.

Fear for her.

Without letting her go, he glanced at the drawer, now half open. Whatever lay inside was wrapped in bright red tissue paper. Like a gift—a gift that could change them both forever.

"Especially now," he concluded.

"Why? Because of what might be in that drawer?"

"Yes. I don't want to be responsible for putting you in danger, too."

"No one is responsible for me but me."

His fingers clutched her tighter. "Maybe that was true before, but trust me, it isn't anymore."

15

"Do you think there's something wrong with us?" Alexa asked Jacob, who'd been poring over the rudimentary blueprints and sketches of her castle with surprising concentration for the past twenty minutes.

Alexa, on the other hand, had decided that after four hours of intense meetings—which had been preceded by a surprisingly Damon-free four-hour visit to the island with a crack team of contractors and architects—she preferred to nurse a vodka gimlet rather than look at lines and angles until her eyes blurred. The booze, unfortunately, triggered her reliving all the weirdness that had happened over the past two days. Hell, the past thirty years.

Jacob didn't look up.

"Jacob?" she asked again.

"What? I'm sorry. Did you say something?"

Alexa grabbed the plans and slid them onto the floor, out of Jacob's reach.

"I asked if you think there's anything wrong with us."

"Us? What do you mean? Are you having second thoughts about this property?"

Shockingly, he sounded disappointed. She'd had the distinct impression that Jacob had been less than enthusiastic about this venture until today. There was something invigorating about standing in the middle of a hollow castle and watching with awe as her experts assessed and brainstormed life into her dream project.

She had been so caught up, she'd nearly forgotten about Damon and his plight, as well as what they'd done in the dead of the stormy night on the landing where she'd stood for most of the afternoon.

Nearly, but not quite.

"This isn't about the property," she admitted.

Jacob arched his eyebrow.

Alexa sighed. "For five minutes, can we not talk or think about business?"

Jacob slid into a chair and reached for the gimlet he'd left untouched for the last hour. "Fine with me. You're the workaholic, not me."

"Yeah, I know," she acknowledged. "I guess being abandoned on that island made me think a bit about my personal life. Or lack thereof. And yours, too. I mean, we're two wealthy, attractive, interesting adults. Why aren't we attached?"

"To each other?" His other eyebrow had now beat the first in curving ability.

She chuckled at the absurdity. "No, thank you. We may not be related by blood, but you're still my brother whether you like it or not."

He took a dainty sip. "I plead the fifth."

"Smart strategy. Look, be serious, Jacob. Why aren't you married?"

He made a face as if the vodka in his drink had suddenly gone rancid. "I'm not the marrying type. Lord, Alexa. What's gotten into you? And since when have you been interested in my personal life?"

Especially since his breakup with Cat, the topic of who Jacob slept with and why had become completely off-limits. And she couldn't really remember Jacob showing any interest whatsoever in the men she brought home, so long as they were independently wealthy and weren't wooing her into bed as a means to access her bank accounts. But without Cat here or even reachable by phone to kick around her problems with, who else did she have? At least she knew Jacob cared about what happened to her. Everyone else in

her life pretty much looked at her as the signature on
their paycheck and nothing more.

"Who do you discuss your personal life with?"
she asked.

"No one. I'm a guy. We prefer action over discussion."

She nodded. This much was true, judging by Damon's delicious actions the night before.

"Shouldn't you be talking about this crap with that
weirdo ex of mine? As much as I think the woman is
entirely a fraud, you seem to like her well enough."

"She got your number rather quickly."

He sneered. "All the more reason for me to de-
spise her."

"And the feeling is mutual on her part, so at least
you have one nonfamilial relationship in your life that
is an emotional match."

"Bully for me." This time, Jacob's sip wasn't dainty
at all. In a thick swallow, he downed the rest of the
vodka and lime concoction and reached for the pitcher
room service had delivered an hour ago, along with
the crudités they hadn't touched.

"I'm serious," Alexa insisted.

"I get that," he said, popping a grape tomato into
his mouth and chewing. "I also get that since Madam
Morose is not available to you, you're installing me
as your personal Dr. Phil. I should point out here that
with your bank account, if you called the real deal,
he'd fly here in a heartbeat."

She stuck out her tongue. She didn't need a therapist. Yet. She needed a friend. "I just wonder why
neither one of us has made a personal attachment with
a member of the opposite sex. I mean, our parents
loved each other enough to die together."

Jacob froze, then after a long minute, reached
across and patted the top of her hand. "That wasn't
your fault, Alexa. If this is survivor's guilt talking
again, I think you need to call someone with more
expertise than mine to work it out."

She shook her head, though the tightening in her chest belied her denial. But she'd had enough therapy—both mental and physical—to last a lifetime. She'd grown beyond blaming herself for the fact that she'd lived when they'd died. Accidents happened. But the event that should have made her embrace life more fully had instead made her cautious. Except in business. With her father gone, her ambition to not only prove herself but protect the legacy left to her had consumed her.

To the point where she'd ignored every other aspect of her life.

Everything except her fantasies.

"I'm fine," she assured Jacob when it looked like he was reaching for his cell phone, undoubtedly to give her long-abandoned therapist a call. Or maybe Dr. Phil.

"You sure?"

With a nod, she poured more gimlet for herself and decided that her attempt to draw her stepbrother into an intimate conversation had been a fool's errand. Jacob's loyalty to her was something she could pretty much count on, but he did have his limits. And since Cat was still entirely out of touch, she had only one other person she could talk to.

The one person who had caused all this angst in the first place. She should have known that going directly to the source would be her best strategy.

"I think I'm going to get some sleep," she said.

Jacob nodded, finished his drink, then stood. "Good idea. I'll call the pilot and make arrangements for us to return to Chicago first thing in the morning."

Twisting and turning the crystal glass in her hands, Alexa found herself fascinated by the prismed light reflecting onto the polished table. It was like magic, wasn't it? Magic that fascinated her. Called to her. Unlike the call of returning to her hometown. She loved Chicago, but other than a great big mansion she rarely used and a business that leeched every ounce of her soul out of her, what did she have to go home to?

Clearly, nothing as exciting as what she'd get if she stayed.

"You can go back," she replied, straightening in her chair as determination coursed through her, replacing the void left by questions and uncertainties and regrets. "I'm talking to the board tomorrow morning via conference call, but I'm sure they're going to embrace this project once they hear from the architectural and marketing teams. Once that approval goes through, the contractors will need at least a week to assemble the first team of workers for the castle while the architects finalize the plans and the designers start descending on the place needing direction. I'm not dallying with this. Once the word gets out in the press about this new hotel, the buzz will be huge. We need to be ready to go. I'm going to stay behind and supervise the renovation myself."

Jacob eyed her suspiciously. "Don't you have some lackey that can handle the mundane details until the real work begins? That assistant of yours, perhaps?"

Alexa stared boldly at her brother. "Of course I do."

"And what about the crisis in Boston? The police are fairly sure the damage to the generators was sabotage. This is the second incident that we know of. If someone is out to get us—"

"You can handle it," she interrupted. "You came here seeking something interesting to do, didn't you? And you've handled the Boston situation so far. I don't see any reason why you can't continue."

Jacob scowled. "So you can stay here and supervise construction workers? I know you think you're hard up for male companionship—"

Alexa cut him off. "This project is important to me. The land is mine. Personally. A gift from my father. I'll have the hotel manager arrange for office space here first thing in the morning. You can either stay and help, or go back home and take on all that responsibility you've been bucking for all these years. Either way, I'm running this show from here."

Jacob waved his hand at her, as if he'd heard her unbreakable determination before—which he had—and it bored him. "Whatever. You're impossible to deal with when you have dollar signs in your eyes. I'll see you in the morning."

Jacob ambled out of the room without another word, which struck Alexa as somewhat odd. Jacob usually wanted to be in the thick of things, just off center of the main action of running the corporation so he could constantly remind people, even if only visually, that he was the heir apparent to the fortune she managed. She wondered briefly how her father had truly felt about that, even if his estate attorney and all documentation proved that Richard Chandler wanted Alexa to teach her stepbrother the ropes. Richard and Jacob had never gotten along, but Richard had loved Jacob's mother with a passion Alexa had resented as a daughter, but admired as a woman.

She supposed she should outgrow such romantic notions someday, but after last night, Alexa didn't think she'd be forgetting her fairy-tale fancies anytime soon. No, the only way she was going to move beyond her fascination with Damon and the pleasures he promised was to confront her fantasy directly.

He knew the minute she'd entered the castle. The cold chill that had clung to his skin since nightfall evaporated in a wave of warmth, followed by a vibration that shook the air around him and halted the magic he'd been wielding. Dante, the cat, had taken up residence atop a large armoire and now screeched loudly.

"Hush, beast," he ordered, waving his hand. He'd discovered this afternoon that adding the physical gesture accelerated the magic. As if blown by a concentrated wind, the cat disappeared in a puff of smoke.

From below, Alexa called his name. Even from that distance he could hear the longing in her voice. The need. The fear. He supposed he couldn't alleviate her suspicions and anxiety. He had no reassurances to offer her. Though not a man considered ruthless during his lifetime, his imprisoned state required him to adopt a new morality. He would employ whatever means necessary to escape the castle. He had to find out if any clue remained that would lead him to his family, even if they'd all since died.

Not knowing would be more torturous than his imprisonment, of that he was certain.

Her voice echoed against the stone as she climbed the stairs. "I'm here," he called, knowing she'd follow the sound.

A few moments later, she leaned in from the hall, her hands clutching the thick oak door of the room he'd chosen for his first exploration.

He turned, smiled and, with a flourish, showed her what he'd accomplished with only a few hours of work.

Her eyes widened to bright green discs.

"Wow," she said.

"Is this expression positive?"

"Positively amazing." She entered the room cautiously, stopping to admire the silk dressing gown curved across the foot of the well-appointed bed he'd conjured only an hour ago. "What is this? A re-creation of your bedroom?"

Damon frowned. He had little memory of his own master suite. And of which house? The town home in London? The estate in Cumberland? Or perhaps the home of his boyhood in Valoren, the land of the exiled, the only true home he'd ever known.

"No, a re-creation of Rogan's. I mean to uncover the mystery of my release. And if I know Rogan, which I did, quite well, he would have kept his secrets close to him. In this castle, if not in this very room."

Alexa crouched and ran her fingers over the plush pile of the handwoven rug, dropping the bag she carried on the floor near the bed. Rising, she followed the thick lines of the teak bedposts and then palmed the velvet coverlet and satin pillows. Rogan had enjoyed the trappings of luxurious living, as Damon had once. Odd how such details meant little to him any longer, except when Alexa was near. Without uttering a word, she demanded the finest of everything. She might be a common businesswoman in her century, but in his, she'd be a queen.

"This is amazing," she said, her voice breathy. "How did you remember all the details of Rogan's private quarters? I can't imagine you spent a great deal of time here," she ventured, her voice dipping into suggestive territory that spawned an immediate growl of annoyance.

"I admit I saw the room once or twice. Rogan could be a notorious slugabed when the mood suited him, so he often took visitors in his dressing gown."

"Still," she said, cupping a pewter goblet she'd removed from the bedside table, "the detail is glorious."

Damon nodded with satisfaction. "I could not remember every element of the decor, but the magic could."

"The magic?"

"The place is rife with it, as you discovered last night. The more I open my mind to the possibilities, the more the magic serves me."

She stepped toward him, her hand outstretched. "But it's black magic, isn't it? Can't it harm you?"

Damon took her hand and pulled her close. He'd considered her expressed fear carefully before determining his course of action. While he had no ambition to follow his former friend down an evil path, he had no choice but use the resources at his disposal to achieve his goal.

"I know not," he admitted, "but if I find the answers I seek, the danger is negligible."

Unable to be in her presence for more than a few minutes without tasting her, Damon lowered his head and covered her mouth with his. The scent of her perfume intoxicated him—a clean scent that conjured images of fresh citrus and ocean breezes. Her skin, so warm and soft, yielded to his touch. When she cooed, he knew she'd come to him for the most basic reason.

She wanted him.

And yet, she pulled away.

"We need to slow down," she insisted, pushing him aside.

He arched a brow. He never could resist a woman of contradictions.

"Did you not come here tonight to make love with me?" he asked.

She planted her fists on her hips indignantly. "What happened to your finesse?"

"I see no reason to pretend with you, Alexa."

She narrowed her gaze. "Don't you?"

"That I want you is no secret. That I want *something* from you is no secret, either. I want my freedom. And I want you to help me gain it."

"I don't know how to do that," she said.

"Not yet, perhaps," he insisted. "But you freed me from the painting. I know the magic exists somewhere within these walls that will ensure my release entirely."

"What if your release means your death?"

Surprisingly, he heard regret in her voice. "Everyone must die. I only wish to do so after I've found my family. And to do this, I must explore every nook and cranny of Rogan's magical realm. This castle has always been the source of his power. The minute he declared the structure complete all those hundreds of years ago, his abilities grew exponentially. The key is here. I know it within my soul."

"Then you plan to rebuild every room?"

" 'Tis the only way."

"That's going to be interesting for my workers," she commented.

Damon had considered this point. All afternoon, he'd watched the parade of builders and architects examining the castle. He'd listened intently, learning much not only about modern construction, but also of the modern world. He'd learned the true scope of Alexa's wealth and power and ambition. The men under her command respected her family name but had doubts regarding her ability to live up to her father's high standards for success.

What firstborn son of a nobleman wouldn't have felt instantly connected with her on that point alone? But Damon had had the luxury of a humble father, one who took his banishment to a Gypsy enclave not as the punishment of a foreign king, but as a grand adventure. He chuckled, remembering how his father's humor had matched his wealth and how his optimism had turned what might have been a shameful assignment from the king into a triumph.

Even the first King George had been pleased. The Gypsies had left London without bloodshed, and the sale of their wares around Europe through intermediaries brought in a tidy sum to the Crown. Abandoned land he'd inherited in his native Germany now produced an income. But then the monarch had died and his ambitious son had sought to reclaim his lands by sending in the ruthless horde to murder the Romani Damon's father had sought to save.

A dark thought crossed his mind. If the horde had descended on Valoren and found it deserted, had they ridden out to his father's estate on the other side of the mountain and massacred his family instead? Only his father, his stepmother and a collection of servants had remained behind, hidden in a cellar with provisions to last them a week. Had they survived?

"Damon?"

He blinked, then glanced down at her as she eyed him with bold curiosity.

"I apologize," he said with a short bow. "The atmosphere draws me deeply into the past."

He cleared his throat. A past he needed to unravel, and to do so, he had to master the magic, as well as ensure Alexa's loyalty so he'd have access to her vast resources. Now, who was the mercenary?

"Reminds me of dreams I had," she said wistfully. "Not so long ago."

A wicked flash of green lit her eyes.

Instantly, his body reacted, tight and hard. He'd satiated his long-ignored desires with her last night, yet he wanted her again with renewed vigor. In more ways than he could name. "What kind of dreams?"

Her eyes darkened and her mouth curved downward in a serious frown. "You're a man straight out of my fantasies, Damon Forsyth."

"Does that not please you?"

"Last night, it did. You did."

"Thank you."

"But it makes me wonder."

"About?"

"Why you're here. If you're here, really. Can't you simply be a figment of my imagination?" Her voice softened with a dreamy quality he couldn't recall hearing in her tone before. "You're what I want most from a man. You have character. Power. You come in the night and pleasure me, but you disappear by morning and don't interfere with my everyday, crazy life."

Taken aback, Damon stopped to think. "Do you mean to suggest that your fantasies drew you to me?"

She shook her head. "No, I'm suggesting my fantasies created you."

He clutched her arms. "I assure you, Alexa, that in the night, I am very real and very solid."

"But you're still the perfect man. And until I prove otherwise, I won't be able to walk away from you."

"Why should you wish to walk away? For the time being, I'm trapped in a property you own. I shall be at your beck and call."

"I can't have a man in my life."

Damon took a step back. That was a phrase he'd never heard from a woman before. "Why on earth not?"

She squared her shoulders. "I have a lot of responsibilities. Several billion to be exact."

"You have chosen money over your personal happiness?"

She shrugged. "Sort of chose me. But it's not the money entirely. It's the Chandler name. It's the hundreds of investors and thousands of employees and guests and extended family and—"

Damon cut her off with a kiss. The sound of a sensual, beautiful woman eschewing a fulfilled life so she could meet the expectations of society cracked his soul. Is this what the future held for him? A reversal of roles that would tear at his core?

When breathing became necessary, she pulled away. "My father wanted to give me the world," she explained.

"And he gave you this castle, with me inside."

"He didn't know that," she argued.

"Maybe he did; maybe he did not. But for the time being, I am here. Perhaps fate drew us together. Perhaps—"

Her eyes drifted downward as she extracted his sister's necklace from her pocket and dangled it in front of him.

"Something more powerful than even destiny?"

Her eyes reflected the same surprise he felt. His hands itched to take the charm back, in case the residual magic would somehow help him in his quest to break free of the castle's hold. But if the charm was meant for protection, Alexa needed it more than he.

"I can't keep this," she said.

He twined his fingers with hers, the charm dangling between them. "The value of the piece is inconsequential."

"That's not why I can't keep it," she said. "When I'm here with you, I don't need protection. And if it did belong to your sister, then you should have it."

If only she were safe. If only he knew without question that Rogan's black magic wasn't seeping into his soul. "I want you to wear it."

Confusion turned her china-doll face into a mask of indecision. "I'm not afraid."

He buried a chuckle deep within his chest, allowing his passion to override his misgivings about the magic. He had to do what he must, and if the necklace provided her with a counteragent against the evil, so be it. He could manage with his own store of charms, couldn't he?

"You should be," he warned. "You deny your passions on the odd risk that you might have to challenge your vision for your future, when my existence has already changed your destiny. Take a lesson from me, Alexa. What we work toward our entire lives may come to nothing with one tear of a sword."

Her gaze locked with his. Her irises darted from side to side as she searched, in vain, for words to counter his logic. She took a deep breath, pocketed the charm and exhaled. The moment the tension in her shoulders released, he knew he had her.

16

Damon surveyed his handiwork in Rogan's room and decided he could not risk jeopardizing all he'd accomplished. He grabbed Alexa by the arms, stood flush against her and warned, "Let us not make love in a den of evil," then magically whisked her to a room he'd discovered at the top of the west tower.

When they materialized, she wavered and inhaled quickly, her eyes still shut tight.

"We are here, my lady," he informed her. He'd been materializing and dematerializing in different parts of the castle all afternoon. He'd become accustomed to the sensation.

She, on the other hand, clutched his arms tightly and her eyes remained closed. "Where?"

"Open your eyes. No, wait."

Damon extracted one arm from her grip and after concentrating on the atmosphere he wanted to create, waved his hand. More than one hundred candles appeared in the tight, circular room, each atop a standing sconce or tall candelabra of varying heights and clusters. The heat around them flared instantly and Alexa gasped, though her eyes remained closed.

"What did you do?" she asked.

"Open your eyes, my lady."

She shook her head. "I'm dizzy."

"And I'm about to make you dizzier."

The flames flickered from the breeze sneaking in from outside. Through the loopholes, the night sky twinkled with a thousand stars. The scent of the ocean curled into the tower, and for a moment, Damon imagined the freedom of riding along the shoreline and making love to Alexa on the sand.

Not tonight, though. Perhaps not ever. But for now, he would indulge her fantasies—and his—until he knew she'd help him, no matter the personal cost.

He manipulated the magic until they were naked to the wind, but even as her eyes flashed open, he took her in his arms and kissed her. Seducing her came at the price of his sanity. In seconds, he was hard with need. His cock jutted against her belly and his knees wavered when she took his sex in her hands and stroked.

"No," he gasped, but she didn't listen. She continued to pull hard on his flesh, up and down, cupping his balls even as his mouth ravished hers. He could feel his seed building inside him, and when she dropped to her knees and took him in her mouth, he lost all ability to think. He felt the candles flame hot and high, singeing his shoulders as he reached down and speared his hands into her hair.

Every sensation rocked him. The pressure of her mouth over his sex, of her tongue across his flesh, brought him to the brink of climax. He pulled her off, nearly coming when he spied the sinful, triumphant look in her eyes.

"That was for what you did to me on the staircase," she said, licking her lips lovingly.

Panting, he managed, "You mean this?"

She cried out when the sensation of a tongue licked between her legs. Though he hadn't bent down, her flavor unfurled in his mouth, and he couldn't help but hum in appreciation. Oh, yes, this magic was pure wickedness.

"What?" she asked, her tone breathless. "How?"

He smoothed his hands over her body, buoying her buttocks in his hands and lifting her high against him.

"I'm entertaining the most delicious thoughts about how to please you."

Her eyelashes fluttered even as he could feel the tip of her clitoris against the tip of his tongue.

"Not . . . fair," she breathed.

He chuckled. "No, not at all."

Bracing his hands against her backside, he pulled her up high, engulfing her breasts with his mouth. She wrapped her legs tightly around him, unintelligible words spilling from her lips as he pleasured her with his hands, his mouth and the magic. When his balance started to waver, he knocked through the candles and leaned her flush against the cold stone wall.

If she minded the biting roughness against her flesh, she did not complain. Instead, she moved so that he had nowhere to thrust but upward, inside her, deeply. The head of his cock crashed within her, and she accepted the impact with moans of satisfaction. She urged him to strike harder, faster, with hot words and blissful groans, until both of them were spent and a quarter of the candles had toppled to the floor.

After regaining his senses, he pulled her away from the wall, spun until his back bit against the stone and slid them both to the ground. She curled in his arms, her breathing raspy and unsteady until the remnants of wild climax subsided and she found words to speak.

"It's a wonder we didn't burn this place down," she commented.

Damon chuckled. "The night is still young."

Cat pulled away from Ben, her skin on fire with a rush of emotions all related to Ben's fear for her life. Well, she didn't need to feel his fear. She had plenty enough on her own. But not fear for her safety. Cat had become incredibly adept at taking care of herself in the face of physical danger. It was the emotional entanglements that terrified her, especially with a man she hardly knew.

"You need my help," she reminded him.

"My father has been kidnapped and probably injured, his house ransacked. You can see what his interest in that cursed place has caused."

"Perhaps it has, or perhaps it hasn't. But if the curse or Valoren is to blame for your father's disappearance, then that's all the more reason for me to help. Curses and black magic are right up my alley."

He crossed his arms tightly over his chest. "Is the diary so valuable that you're willing to risk your life for a stranger?"

Impulsively, she grabbed his hand. His fear subsided, replaced instead with a sense of utter surprise. And something more. Something tightly contained and controlled.

Something like excitement, perhaps?

"I've risked my life for strangers many times. Paranormal researchers often find themselves in dicey situations. You have to think on your feet. Be creative. Yes, I want the diary. I've made no secret of that. But I want to help you find your father, too. Not just because it's the right thing to do, but because I need to know what he knows. If my friend's castle is tied to Valoren, it may well be cursed, too. I need to know how to protect her. We both have a better shot at succeeding if we work together."

Ben gave a curt nod, then twisted around her and dug in to the drawer he'd worked so hard to unlock. His snort alerted her and she leaned around to see what had caused his sardonic reaction.

Out of the tissue paper lining the drawer, he withdrew a leather-bound book, complete with a flap where a keyhole used to be. The pages, edged in gold, had long since faded, but the purpose for the book was clear.

"Looks like you've found what you're looking for, at least," he said, handing the journal to her.

Cat accepted the book gingerly. A wash of guilt ran over her, but she'd meant what she said. No matter what information the diary contained, she would help Ben find Paschal.

"May I?" she asked.

"Please do. If my father went to all this trouble to hide this book, the contents must be important."

Cat settled into Paschal's chair and flipped open the diary. The ink was faded but still readable. The date on the top of the first page seemed to read "1746," but she couldn't be sure about the language within. A few words were familiar, clearly English, but notwithstanding the flourishing handwriting, the combination of letters didn't always form words. At least, not words in any language she recognized.

"Is this Romani?" she asked.

Ben leaned over her shoulder. "Yes. Looks like a dialect favored by Gypsies who lived in Britain." He flipped the page. "See here. This is actually broken between English and the Gypsy's native tongue."

"Like Spanglish," she quipped.

He grinned. "Same concept, yes."

"Is that a usual way for a Gypsy to write?"

Ben arched a brow. "Most Gypsies wouldn't keep a diary at all. Their tradition is oral."

"It's written by a woman," Cat said, turning a few more pages and scanning the words for phrases she recognized.

"How can you tell? The fancy quality of the handwriting is typical of this period for all genders, and most women, I'd guess, especially those of Gypsy origins, wouldn't have been taught to write."

She pointed to a few words on the page. "Here, she's complaining about having to wear a corset."

"Men wore corsets."

"And wigs?"

"In the eighteenth century, absolutely. Think George Washington."

She kept reading, finally stumbling on a passage that was unmistakeably female. "I can't see George Washington worrying if he'd ever find a husband."

Ben took the diary from her and wandered away while he read. With a keen knowledge of Romani, she guessed he could traverse the minefield of Georgian English, as well as Romani, with more skill than she.

With each minute that passed, he flipped the pages

more quickly. At about the halfway point, his eyes narrowed and his brow knitted with worry.

"This is it," he said.

Cat stood. "What?"

"The diary that mentions Valoren." He turned the page. "She hates living here. She wants to go to London, like her brothers. She wants to see the world outside of the Gypsy safe haven. Meet fascinating people. Eat exotic foods. She feels guilty about leaving her people, but only half of her is Gypsy. Her hunger to learn about her English half makes her want to defy her father and run away to London on her own."

"The desire to wander isn't unusual for a Gypsy, is it?"

"No, but the British and the Gypsies rarely, if ever, mixed. If this woman was half Gypsy and knew how to write English, chances are her father was British."

"And that's unusual?"

"She's educated, so she's probably wealthy. In that regard, yes, it's very unusual."

Cat blew out a breath. She'd always wondered how she would have survived in another time period, living under rules and expectations that dictated a woman's status and whether or not she received any sort of useful education. A half-breed with Gypsy blood would probably have been crucified in London, a city renowned in all centuries for adhering to strict codes that decided who was valuable and who was worthless based on birth, rank and wealth. Did this girl have any idea how she would have been scorned in the city she dreamt of so romantically?

With yet another reason to be thankful for being born in the twentieth century, Cat changed places with Ben, reading over his shoulder as he flipped through the diary, the dates spanning over a year.

"What else does it say about Valoren?"

Ben paged through, his head shaking from side to side the more he read. "Her oldest brother travels back and forth between Valoren and London. He must be of the peerage, though I'm not exactly an expert in these matters."

"A half Gypsy serving in the House of Lords?" she asked, surprised.

He looked at her oddly.

"I read romance novels, okay? And not just the juicy parts."

"Though I don't suppose you skip them."

"Would you?"

Ben chuckled and continued scanning the pages. "He must be a half brother, though she doesn't seem to make any distinction. His name is Damon."

"Like the artist?" Cat asked, pulling out the painting of the schooner.

Ben gave an affirmative hum, then returned to the book. "She might be adopted or a ward raised with the family," he went on. "She's wildly jealous of his ability to go where he wants whenever he wants to," he said, humor lilting his voice. "She must be nearly eighteen because she laments never going to balls and meeting men."

Cat couldn't help but smile. She'd been dating since she was around thirteen. There were some advantages to being raised by grandparents who had more pressing interests than supervising the daughter of their own wayward child.

"If only she knew how much trouble men were, she wouldn't be so anxious to leave her nanny behind," Cat commented.

"That's stopped you?"

She slapped him on the shoulder, and after an exaggerated "ow," he returned to his reading.

"Wait," he said.

Cat bent closer. The little room behind the wall had adequate ventilation . . . for one person. The two of them together, coupled with the lights, increased the temperature from comfortable to . . . uncomfortable. Perspiration glistened along the back of Ben's neck, intensifying the scent of his cologne.

"Here. She's talking about a stranger coming to town with her brother, one who wants to make Valoren his home. He's . . . Rogan. Incredibly handsome, I take it. She spends several pages here just on his eyes alone."

"Rogan," Cat repeated. "Damon. It's not much. Are there last names?"

The sound of crackling pages added to the tense atmosphere. The diary contained the deep, dark secrets of a swooning young girl whose biggest complaint in life was that she'd never had a date. How could the contents possibly be dangerous or even valuable? Why the secrecy? Why the locked drawer?

"No last name," Ben informed her, "but she refers to him as Lord Rogan here."

"Think he's British, too?"

Ben shrugged. "We could find out more if we had *her* name."

"Check the inside cover," Cat suggested.

Ben went back to the beginning of the diary. A label identifying the antique-book shop in Dresden where the journal had been sold hid nearly the entire inside cover. Ben reached into the desk and found a razor-tipped knife. He poked at the edges of the label, prying away the paper centimeters at a time.

"Do you still think this book is why your father was kidnapped?"

As he worked on the label, Ben snared his bottom lip in his teeth. For a split second, Cat imagined snagging his lips with *her* teeth. Never one to apologize for her sexual nature, Cat rolled her eyes at her reaction nonetheless. Ben wasn't giving off a single signal to indicate he entertained any interest in her. At least, not beyond the help she offered in finding his father. And she made it a rule never to pursue a man who wasn't pursuing her twice as vigorously.

So why was the room getting so damned hot?

"I can't see how this diary contains any valuable information," Ben groused. "It's the ramblings of a silly child."

"She's not so silly," Cat defended. "She's a product of her time and circumstances."

Ben acknowledged her comment with a jaded snicker. "I still can't see where she'd have any information that anyone would need."

"Maybe she cursed the place. She certainly hated living there. But we won't know for sure until you read the entire diary."

"No, I suppose not."

Luckily, the label had been applied many years before, so once Ben loosened the toughest streaks of glue, the identifier peeled off with ease. Beneath, the inscription remained intact, though the words beneath the adhesive were faded and somewhat illegible.

"The diary was given to her by her father. 'My daughter,' " Ben quoted, his voice stilted as he stumbled over the writing. " 'For here you shall write your secret dreams. Fondly, Father.' "

"But what's her name?" Cat asked impatiently. "Or the pop's name. I'm not picky."

Ben grunted and pushed away from the desk. Cat took over, carefully turning pages and scanning for anything recognizable. Ben had been right—the diary was mostly the ramblings of a sweet young woman who dreamed of exploration and discovery, but who had little opportunity to reach out of her life experience. Except in books. Again and again, she wrote about her privileged life, contradicting her Gypsy bloodlines. Finally, about three-quarters of the way through the journal, Cat found a series of drawings. Sketches, really, of a grand estate.

Or more like . . . a castle?

Cat gasped.

"What?" Ben asked, returning to her side instantly.

Cat hadn't yet seen the castle Alexa had inherited, so she could only speculate that the places were the same. How many castles would one Gypsy safe haven have?

But more important than the architecture was the name at the bottom of the sketch.

"Sarina," Cat said, tapping her finger just above the artist's signature. "Sarina Forsyth. Now we have a place to start."

"You mean *you* have a place to start," Ben said. "That name will help you in researching the origins of the castle your friend inherited, but it won't help me find my father."

"You don't know that," Cat insisted.

Ben pressed his lips together, his pewter eyes assessing and intense.

"No, I suppose I don't. But we won't find my father if we stay holed up in here."

Cat closed the diary. "Let's check in with the police. They've had time to interview Amber Stranton and identify the blood on the driveway and any fingerprints by now. Then we'll know what we should do next."

Ben gestured toward the diary, which she held clutched to her chest, his disappointment at their discovery unhidden. "Shouldn't you call the heiress and give her the name in the diary, maybe fax her the drawing of the castle, see if it's the same place?"

Cat grinned guiltily, her thoughts running in the same direction. She would contact Alexa, of course. Alexa was, after all, the reason she had come to Texas in the first place. The reason she'd met Ben. But now the stakes were higher. Paschal Rousseau was in serious danger. The professor had unwittingly provided the diary, but more than that, he'd provided the impetus for her to use her psychic gift for something more than entertaining her friends.

Her progress had been small, but the thrill surging through her couldn't be ignored. Of course, she couldn't discount that the feeling was simply caused by Ben alone.

"Alexa can wait a few hours, but I have a strong feeling your father can't."

17

With her eyes firmly closed and her brain existing on some plane between consciousness and deep sleep, Alexa decided that being roused by a lusty man beat alarm clocks any day of the week. Damon's wispy kisses along her exposed belly were warm and insistent . . . and just a little ticklish. When his chin lowered, his hands pulling aside the sheet to the bed he'd conjured so he could apply his wicked tongue even lower, she nearly jolted off the mattress.

"Hey," she said, though her protests were half-hearted at best.

He looked up at her expectantly, without the least repentance in his stormy gray eyes.

"You require too much sleep," he complained.

She yanked the sheet back into place and with her foot on his shoulder, kicked him away.

"You don't require enough."

With a chuckle, Damon rolled aside. The bed was plush and round and filled the entire tower space. He'd left a few candelabras against the wall, but most of the candles had burned out. With satin sheets and velvet coverlets, the space brimmed with decadent luxury. After all these years sleeping alone, Alexa didn't think she'd like sharing a mattress with a man. Clearly, she simply hadn't found the right man.

"Were you so insatiable when you were alive or is it a symptom of your phantom state?" she asked.

"Life is too precious to fritter away to sleep," he

replied. "Or at least, life *was* too precious. I'd like to think it will be again, once I am free."

A note of longing, perhaps even regret, tinged his voice. Instantly, Alexa wanted to roll over to him, wrap her arms around his chiseled chest and offer some sort of comfort. But the truth of the matter was, he could be dead. He didn't remember dying, but he did remember pain. And his unfinished business regarding his sister's disappearance could be the ultimate factor in his entrapment in this world. The solid form he took each night thanks to Rogan's dark magic might be temporary—or at the very least, limited. If he could never leave this castle and never have corporeal form during daylight hours, what kind of life was he reduced to?

Alexa stretched her hand to him and gave him what she hoped was a fortifying squeeze on his arm. "Trust me, you're living life quite well, at least from this side of the bed."

"I'll take your compliment, my lady, but I'll need more than sexual prowess to release myself from this prison."

Alexa curled back beneath the covers. "So far as prisons go, this one isn't so bad."

" 'Tis true," he agreed. "But the ocean below calls to me. I'd give my finest sword to feel the sunlight on my face."

The tense, emotional moment shifted to surprise when Alexa's satellite phone buzzed from inside her bag. Damon eyed the pack suspiciously.

"Can you hand me that?"

He grabbed the bag, but rather than giving it to her, he eyed it as if it were a hissing snake. "What is that noise?"

"My phone."

"Your what?"

She leaned forward and grabbed the bag herself, afraid she'd miss the call. Only three people knew her satellite number—her assistant, who'd been instructed not to contact her unless one of the hotels was burning down; Jacob, who slept like a rock and would have no reason to contact her before dawn; and Cat.

"Alexa Chandler," she said.

"Where the hell have you been?"

Cat. Alexa's heart slammed against her chest and she pulled the sheets high on her neck. Shit. Cat was going to kill her. Believing in ghosts was one thing. Sleeping with one?

"I'm at the castle," she said. It wasn't a lie. It wasn't the whole truth, but hey, she was doing the best she could.

"In the middle of the night?"

Alexa gazed appreciatively at Damon, who'd suddenly discovered something fascinating about her painted toes. "I decided to stay over."

"With no electricity, no running water and no feather mattress?"

"I'm not that spoiled."

"Yes, you are."

"Well, I'm making do. How are you? I tried calling you earlier and your cell phone was off. Did you find the diary?"

"I found more than that."

As Cat started to talk, Alexa drew the covers closer around her, trying to ignore the delicious massage Damon had begun on her feet. Her mind drifted to the question of how a man of Damon's station learned such delicious ministrations when Cat informed her that the man who owned the diary, Paschal Rousseau, had been kidnapped.

Involuntarily, she yanked her foot away from Damon. He grumbled loudly.

"Who's there with you?" Cat asked.

"No one," she said quickly. "Have you called the police?"

"Yes, but Ben, his son, is afraid the kidnapping is related to Valoren and the curse."

"Curse?" she repeated.

Damon looked up, but Alexa glanced aside. One conversation at a time.

"Do you want me to call in my private detectives? I have several good ones."

Cat whispered to someone with her, clearly Ben Rousseau, the missing professor's son. "Not just yet. He's trying to protect his father's privacy."

"He should be thinking only about protecting his father," Alexa sniped.

"The police aren't going to take their search seriously if we start spouting off about magic and curses," Cat argued.

"Good point," Alexa concurred.

"I'm glad you agree. Look, I know you wanted information quickly about your castle and you're probably still curious about that supposed ghost you saw—"

Alexa nearly interrupted but decided against it. Now wasn't the time to tell her that not only had she found the ghost, but she'd made love with him.

Several times.

"—but I want to stay with Ben and try and help him."

"Of course," Alexa said quickly.

"Which means I won't be able to help you," Cat clarified. "I did find the diary, and as soon as I get back to the hotel, I'll have your manager scan it and forward the pages to you immediately, but I want to keep the journal with us. Just in case."

Despite the warmth in the room, Alexa felt a chill creep along her skin like a swarm of icy centipedes. She wanted the diary. She wanted definitive proof that what Damon had told her so far was true, but she had to defer to the more pressing situation—Paschal Rousseau's kidnapping. "Just make sure the file is sent encrypted. The business services manager at the Austin property is a longtime employee. Very knowledgeable. He'll know what to do. But do you have any idea why this journal warrants attention from anyone other than us?"

"I wish we did," Cat lamented. "Ben says his father rarely talked about the existence of Valoren to anyone but a few close colleagues. But the young woman who wrote the diary had a hell of a lot to say. Mostly day-to-day stuff—complaints about her overbearing father and brothers, wondering if her mother understands her. Fantasies about going to London and exploring the world. It's mostly a young girl's dreams and ambitions, truth be told, but there's a drawing I'm betting is of your castle. I haven't had time to read much more."

By now, Damon was starting to pay closer attention to the phone call. His eyes had grown darker and stormier and he'd removed himself from the bed and dressed with a thought. He was pacing near the spiral staircase, and his heavy steps echoed on the stone floor.

Sarina's necklace, which she'd tied to her wrist at Damon's insistence, warmed against her skin, drawing her attention to the dangling gold charm. Her mind raced and she wondered if the talisman was responding to increased danger or to the phone conversation.

"What do you know about this young woman?"

"Not much," Cat replied. "She was born in Valoren and her mother is Romani, her father British. She has six—"

"Brothers?"

"How did you know?"

Alexa swallowed deeply. "What's her name?"

"Sarina. Sarina Forsyth."

Damon stopped pacing when she repeated the name out loud. He faced her squarely, and for an instant she suspected he had the ability to look straight into her soul.

"You're sure?" she asked Cat.

"Yes, it's right here in black and, well, seriously yellowed white. Sarina Forsyth. Is that name significant?"

Alexa met Damon's gaze, and in an instant, he seemed to know that she'd made a connection to his past.

"More significant than you can imagine. Remember that ghost I told you about?"

Damon's eyes widened. Alexa hadn't had the opportunity to tell Damon about Cat and her extensive knowledge of the paranormal, but she'd remedy that situation soon enough.

"Yes," Cat said, but she drew out the affirmation on a long, suspicious breath.

"Well, he's real. And his name is Damon Forsyth. Sarina was his sister. Forget the scan and fax, Cat. I need the diary here. First thing tomorrow."

Damon had to bite his tongue and lock his knees in place to keep from tearing over to the bed at the mention of his sister. He clenched his fists when Alexa spoke his name into the device she called a phone and nearly burst when she admitted to the person she spoke with that he was a ghost. He managed, albeit with great difficulty, to remain still even when the conversation turned into an intense argument.

When a numbness developed in his hands, Damon turned away and examined his fingers more closely. The sensation, not unlike the electric current that ran through him whenever he used Rogan's magic, tingled in his joints and fingers. In addition to making love to Alexa all night long, he'd employed more of the magic than ever before. He couldn't help but wonder about the aftereffects.

A loud beep from the perplexing instrument Alexa spoke into drew his attention. She'd tossed the phone on the bed and now raked her hands through her mussed hair. When she looked up at him, her eyes reflected dire circumstances.

"She won't bring the diary."

His chest tightened. "I heard you order her."

"Unfortunately, Cat isn't one of my employees," she explained with a sigh. "She's a friend. A good friend who is doing me a favor. But the good news is she found your sister's diary. That's a huge step forward. She will send a copy, though. That's something."

Pressure built behind his eyes, and only squinting alleviated the strain.

"Are you all right?" she asked.

He squeezed his eyes tightly shut. "I suppose I need more sleep than I wish to think," he offered, though the explanation seemed hollow. Something was happening. Something that had nothing to do with the coming dawn, but was related to the magic nonetheless. He could feel the currents surging through him, even though he'd done nothing to call the magic into his body.

"Where did she find the diary?" he asked, hoping to deflect his attention from the tiny pinpricks of power poking through his skin.

"With a Romani expert named Paschal Rousseau. He had the book very well hidden, which suggests it's much more important than just a young girl's personal thoughts."

"Sarina fancied herself in love with Rogan, and he worked quite diligently to gain her trust. He may have told her things . . ."

A dizziness swept through his body. Damon clutched the wall to keep from toppling onto the bed.

Alexa crawled across the bed and placed her hand gently on his arm.

A rush of warmth swirled beneath her touch, then slowly eased through his veins, dispelling the magical sensations so that suddenly he felt normal again.

For a phantom. He glanced out the slim window and spied a glow across the horizon.

"Are you sure you're all right?" she asked.

He took a deep breath, then patted her hand. "I think breakfast is in order. Tell me more about this man . . . Paschal?"

"Rousseau. He was kidnapped yesterday and his house ransacked. He did, however, own several of your paintings. Were you an artist?"

Damon shook his head. "A hobby. I cannot believe any of my works still exist. And why would anyone track them down?"

She shrugged. "No idea. Clearly, his interest in your family runs deep. Cat said something about a curse?"

"The few Londoners who knew of Valoren thought

it cursed. I sidestepped many such rumors when I returned to court, but I never saw evidence of any dark magic until Rogan settled there. I suppose the disappearance of the Gypsies and the mystery of what became of me and my brothers might have set tongues wagging. I was not there to know."

"Well, that's the scoop now. Apparently, Paschal didn't speak openly about Valoren, even though he researched the place quite thoroughly. But since your sister's journal was hidden so well, Cat suspects the diary is at the heart of Paschal's kidnapping. She wants to keep it but will get us copies of the pages as soon as possible."

Damon's mind swirled. He remembered Sarina sitting in a corner of the family drawing room, her fingers stained from the quill she used to scribble in the leather-bound journal their father had given her. She'd guarded the tome with her life, and while Damon had never had the least interest in the journal of a wide-eyed child, Sarina's full-blood brother, Rafe, had made it his mission in life to not only find her hiding place, but expose all the secrets Sarina poured onto the pages. As far as Damon knew, Rafe had never accomplished his goal. Had he found Sarina's diary, Damon had no doubt their youngest brother would have been dead, or at the very least, maimed.

Sarina might have been impressionable, romantic and naive in the way only a girl raised in a household of men could be, but she had a formidable streak, thanks in great part to her dominant Gypsy blood. Like her mother, Alyse—Damon's father's second wife—Sarina understood well the power of the feminine. She'd never been afraid to use that strength when the situation warranted—even against her own family when planning her escape. He could only hope her wiliness had ultimately saved her from Rogan and his black magic, even if she died. He preferred to hope her soul had moved on, free of evil, rather than imagine her trapped, like him, in a web of vile sorcery.

Alexa toyed with the necklace she'd bound by the

broken chain to her wrist and Damon experienced a second surge of warmth at the sight of her cradling the gold close to her pulse point.

"So," he said, sitting on the bed beside her. He heard her stomach rumble and knew he should conjure food, but the residual effects of the magic and the odd way the vibrations had clung to his insides made him reluctant to act again so soon. Perhaps in a few minutes. After he'd had a moment to clear his mind. "Tell me more about this Paschal Rousseau."

Alexa released a breath he hadn't been aware she was holding. Had she expected his temper to flare as it had the day before or even, though she hadn't been aware, a few moments ago? He couldn't understand his extreme behavior. He'd always been intense and passionate, but he'd never been one to lose control.

"He's a Romani expert," she explained. "A professor at a university in Texas. It's a state. Remember, we talked about states?"

He waved his hand, unwilling to broach the topic of politics yet again. Right now, he only wanted to know about the diary.

"Well, he's the one who knew about Valoren, and he owned your sister's diary and your paintings." A shy smile curved her well-kissed lips. "I didn't know you were a painter. Is that how you put your image back onto the canvas?"

Damon felt an itch in his hand again, this time in the center of his palm. He rubbed the skin over the sheet, but the sensation didn't subside. A ringing began in his ears, and no manner of shaking would free him from the sound.

"Yes," he answered, then stood in the tight space between the wall and the circular bed. More than anything, he wanted to wisk the mattress out of his way. But the magic—he couldn't risk it. He needed the power to rebuild the rooms within the castle and find the secrets he sought. He needed to be free. Free of this castle. Free of his imprisonment. Free of his anger and hatred toward Rogan, who had effectively destroyed his life.

Outside, the sun's glow turned the edge of the sky deep plum with streaks of lavender and pink. Perhaps this was what he was feeling? The dawn erasing his corporeal form from sight?

Alexa stretched to take his hand, but he moved out of her reach. Instinctively. Without knowing why.

"You need to go," he ordered. "Come back when you have the diary."

She sat up straighter. "I think you forget whose castle this is, sir," she said teasingly. "I can come and go as I please. And besides," she announced with a playful bounce on the mattress, "I'll have a houseful of workers here in a few hours. When I make up my mind about something, I don't mess around. I'm going to have this castle opened as a hotel within a year if it kills me."

Damon couldn't contain the seething anger that shot through him like a bolt of fire. In a flash, the bed disappeared and Alexa dropped to the floor in a naked heap.

"Hey!"

He stepped back, but reached out to her with his hand. Not surprisingly, she didn't take it, but stood on her own accord.

"What was that about?"

A bright streak of pink glowed across the horizon outside. He'd used too much magic the night before. He needed rest. His daylight transparency could be the symptom of rejuvenation. Perhaps he *was* dead. Perhaps he was the one who was dreaming, not Alexa. Perhaps his punishment in the castle was not that he could not go free, but that he could not be the man he'd been in his previous life—honorable, resourceful and, above all else, kind.

Though he anticipated a shock of pain, he used the magic to return Alexa's clothes. But he didn't feel weaker. He felt stronger. And that frightened him to his core.

"You must go," he ordered again. "And no one else can enter here until I am free."

She threw up her hands. "That's impossible! There's too much planning to do. The measurements the architects took yesterday were just preliminary. The foundation needs to be tested, the walls explored and mapped so we can install plumbing and electricity. The roof needs a good once-over. The renovation needs to start as soon as possible, so I need my experts—"

Fury flooded through him. His freedom was vastly more important than some silly hotel. "I forbid it!"

Her eyes widened to bright green circles of outrage. "You what? Someone is forgetting what century this is again and whose name is on the deed to this castle."

He stepped forward until he was mere inches from her. His hands tingled again and his arms felt as if someone had poured lead into his veins. "I've forgotten nothing. Be forewarned, my lady," he said evenly, "if one of your workers sets foot inside this castle, they'll have me to deal with. What I did to your brother on the stairs was child's play. Cross me and you'll suffer much, much worse."

The sun broke the horizon and Damon saw his body fading under the light. Never in his life had he been so relieved to simply disappear.

18

For a man of advanced age, Paschal Rousseau wasn't entirely unappealing. In fact, unless Gemma's eyes were deceiving her, there was no way in hell this man was over ninety years old. Seventy was pushing it. Even unconscious, his face possessed a wealth of fascinating planes and angles. His hair might have been shock white and his skin shaped by deep furrows and lines, but an inherent strength radiated off his sleeping form. Maybe Farrow's thugs had shanghaied the wrong guy?

Gemma eased to the side of the bed and more closely examined Paschal's profile, defined by a strong, square chin and a perfect nose she was certain had never been broken or even bruised. The hollows around his eyes were deep and she wondered about the color of the irises beneath his thin lids. She drew a finger along his temple, marveling at the thickness of his hair. Would Farrow age so well? Would she still be acting as his handmaiden in their so-called golden years?

Hell, if her plan progressed as she hoped, she wouldn't be his handmaiden by the end of the week.

Farrow Pryce thought her an insatiable hanger-on. The fool would soon learn that the Von Roan bloodline was more powerful than any man's sexual appeal. And Paschal Rousseau was the key to her success.

Gently, she laid her hand on Rousseau's shoulder. He didn't move. She plied her fingertips over the surprisingly sinewy muscles of his arm and glanced furtively around the room. As she suspected, a surveillance camera was embedded in a vase on the top shelf. Farrow was quick and wily, she'd give him that. They'd procured this hideaway less than a day before they'd grabbed Paschal Rousseau and spirited him outside Austin to this Hill Country fortress, to the previous home of a Texas oil baron with dicey Venezuelan ties. If Farrow wasn't always so paranoid, she might have thought him exceedingly clever.

"Monsieur Rousseau?"

She gave him a little shake. He didn't move. Bending down, she timed his breathing. Slow was an understatement. Fools. The man had been unconscious since yesterday. Farrow's followers had likely given their captive a larger dose of the sedative than necessary. Just her luck if the man died before she had what she wanted. To secure her place as the leader of the K'vr, she needed not the diary that Farrow initially wanted, but the Queen's Charm—Rousseau's most prized Romani find.

She leaned close to his ear. Her voice was barely a whisper. "If you are playing dead, *monsieur*, please continue for a few minutes longer."

As she turned to watch the steady rise and fall of his chest, his breath fluttered the hairs along the nape of her neck. Well, well, well. Paschal Rousseau was alive. And she'd keep him that way . . . if he cooperated.

She wandered around the room with seemingly aimless purpose, as if waiting for Rousseau to wake. Designed in a southwestern style, colorful curtains fluttered through the open window, the breeze hampered only by the iron bars on the other side. Tiny collections of hand-painted pottery and a shelf full of skillfully woven baskets provided the sparse decoration. From what she knew of Paschal Rousseau, the decor would not please him. He preferred to surround himself with items purchased, pilfered and pawned from across the greater European continent.

In a panel beside the door, she found the intercom system access. With a twist of two knobs, she connected to the stereo she'd left on downstairs and turned the volume up high. Rousseau stirred. Not only would the music drown out any listening devices; it would help her wake Rousseau out of his drug-induced sleep.

With a groan, he moved again. She wasted no time, swinging a leg over his midsection on the bed and buoying herself just above him. Leaning forward, she braced her hands on either side of his head and pressed her lips hard against his mouth.

She expected him to wake with a start. To bolt against the restraints Farrow's men had banded around his wrists and secured to the bed. To, at the very least, protest against his capture or shout in shock.

She didn't expect him to kiss her back.

And with such an expert tongue.

With a start, she flew backward.

Eyes still closed, the wrinkled rake had the nerve to grin like a schoolboy.

"You're awake?"

He peeked one eye open. "I may be old enough to be your grandfather, but I'm not dead. Drugs or not, no man can sleep soundly when a woman mounts him so boldly."

Her wits recaptured, Gemma leaned forward again, hoping that all Farrow saw in his monitor was the actions of a woman hell-bent on seduction. In truth, she had so much more in mind.

"I simply know what I want when I see it," she explained.

"And you expect me to believe you want a man who will have been alive for an entire century in just a few years?"

So he was still claiming to be in his nineties. She had swampland in Florida she'd sell him if that were true. "Everything still works, doesn't it? It's common knowledge that a man can perform until the day he dies."

He snickered. "Or he can die trying."

"Is that how you envision your final hours?"

With a flick of her gaze, she noted that he was tugging at the wrist restraints. Not hard enough to be a waste of energy; just enough to test the strength.

"You aren't going anywhere, Monsieur Rousseau. Not without my help."

His eyes, which she noticed were a clear, silvery gray, narrowed. "And why would you help me?"

"You fascinate me."

"My dear, you do not know me. The moment you figure me out, which won't take long, you'll toss me aside for someone more interesting. And decidedly younger."

He'd just described the pattern of her dating habits since age fourteen. Smart man, this one.

"You've lived a long life," she countered. "I'm drawn to you in ways I can't explain. Perhaps we met in a previous incarnation."

"I have no reason to believe in reincarnation," he scoffed.

She shifted her weight, pleased by the thick hardening of his sex beneath her. If all men were in Rousseau's shape, Viagra's makers would go out of business. "And yet, you believe in Gypsy magic, don't you?"

"I'm a renowned Gypsy researcher. I'd hardly be worth my salt if I didn't acknowledge the existence of supernatural phenomena attributed to the Romani. Their knowledge of herbs, roots as well as—"

"Spare me the lecture, Professor." She speared her red-tipped fingernail against the hollow beneath his Adam's apple, then drew her touch downward, across his chest. "I'm not interested in the magic that can be traced to a strong knowledge of natural remedies or the power of suggestion that fueled many a Gypsy curse. I'm talking about the real thing."

The clock by the bedside alerted her to the duration of her stay. Farrow wouldn't expect her to close the deal quickly, but he was not a patient man. Sooner or later, Paschal's son would realize his father was missing. That could only mean trouble.

Farrow had indulged her so far, but she had one, maybe two more encounters with Rousseau before Farrow expected her to produce the information he so desperately wanted. His men had searched Rousseau's house from top to bottom and had not found the diary or the necklace. If Rousseau had the golden talisman and the journal—and all of their intelligence told them that he had been the last one to possess both—he'd hidden the objects very well.

"How can magic be real? It defies the laws of nature," he argued, though she suspected he was faking the sincerity in his voice—blatantly faking, which in her mind, was the equivalent of a taunt.

Wily didn't begin to describe this man. Her respect for him elevated a notch.

She pressed her sex against his crotch. "This defies the laws of nature, too, but you don't see me denying what's happening. In fact," she said, grinding mercilessly against him, "I'm rather enjoying the fact that you want me."

"Don't flatter yourself," he said, his voice dripping with dangerous intensity that belied both his advanced age and his prone position on the bed. His eyes, pale and silvery, flashed with contempt. "Purely biological functions don't reflect any power you have over me."

"I have the power to decide whether you live or die," she told him, then swung off the bed and headed toward the door. When she turned, he was yanking against his restraints, clearly infuriated.

Good. She exited without another word. Maybe if he was frightened enough, desperate enough, he'd cooperate. Because only through a double-cross with Paschal Rousseau at her side and the Queen's Charm in her custody would Gemma take her rightful position in the K'vr—the organization that had bound her family for centuries with promises of ultimate power.

Too bad the empty promises had lost their luster for her when her gender had cost her direct ascension to the leadership. Now she'd have to take the power that was rightfully hers—and Paschal Rousseau would either help . . . or die.

His choice.

"Look, I told the police everything I know. I have a date. So, if you'll, like, leave?"

Cat and Ben exchanged doubtful glances. Finding Amber Stranton had been easy enough, but clearly, getting the coed to talk was something else altogether. Under other circumstances, Ben might have tried turning on the whole professorish-charm thing, but the strategy was useless with Cat around. She likely had no idea how intimidating other women found her. Even now, Amber couldn't tear her eyes off the dark-haired, dark-eyed beauty. Cat made Catherine Zeta-Jones look ordinary in comparison. So much like Mariah.

Funny how he'd managed not to think about his ex in more than a year, but the minute Cat stormed into his life, he'd been fighting memories of her all day.

They were nothing alike, really. Where Mariah was slim but devious, Cat was curvy and sly. Mariah preferred jumping out of airplanes, surfing onto fortified island hideouts and dodging hit men hired by foreign governments. Cat . . . well, he didn't know what Cat liked. Besides keeping her nose in his business. Which, to be completely honest, he didn't really mind.

Right now, however, her presence was a detriment to their mutual goal. They needed Amber to tell them more than she'd told the police about her cousin—which hadn't been much. Under Cat's scrutiny, Amber looked ready to crawl under a rock.

He stepped back, formulating a different tactic when Catalina's entire demeanor shifted. She changed from a ballbuster to a sympathetic ear in the span of six seconds.

She snagged her bottom lip in her teeth and eyed Amber from head to toe. When she spoke, she softened her voice and laced her words with genuine concern.

"You're not going to wear that on your date, are you?"

Amber glanced down at her cropped T-shirt and skintight jeans that flared at the calf. "Yeah. With these killer sandals I found at the flea market, but are totally awesome Choo knockoffs." When her enthusiasm failed to infect Cat, it died a quick death. "Why? What's wrong with what I'm wearing?"

She spun halfway around, trying to catch a glimpse of her backside, and then checked her front to see if something private was hanging out. Neither was the case. To Ben, she looked sort of cute, in the way coeds did. She wasn't his type, but then he hadn't had twenty-year-old preferences for a long time.

"Well, nothing's *wrong* with it," Cat said assuredly, sugared sweetness dripping off her words. "I think you'd look great in a potato sack with a drawstring. But, I don't know. This is . . ." She waved her hand around Amber's body and then pressed her lips together tightly, as if trying to contain some salacious bit of fashion information. Amber stepped toward her and nearly grabbed her hand.

"This is what? Too slutty? Too casual? I thought about wearing this killer skirt I got from my ex-roommate, but it's kind of dressy and I don't want to scare him away."

Cat took Amber's outstretched hand and invited herself inside. "Well, where are you going? That's always the first question."

Amber exhaled noisily. Ben could practically hear the vibrations of her nervousness. "Movie. Dinner. Club afterward. The usual."

Cat crinkled her nose and suddenly looked ten years younger. She was a chameleon who could think on her feet. And more than that, she was trouble with a capital *T*.

"Is this your first date?" Cat guessed, leading

Amber into the living room. She sat on the couch and her new best friend instantly followed.

"Third," Amber replied, her voice tremulous.

Ben stepped inside and shut the door behind him.

Cat clucked her tongue. "Then this definitely is *way* too casual. I mean, third date," her voice dropped, and in an instant, images of hot, sweaty sex popped into Ben's mind . . . hot, sweaty sex that had nothing to do with Amber and her unnamed third date.

"My roommate's gone," Amber said, suddenly panicked as she popped off the futon. "I have a couple of things. Do you mind?"

Cat's grin oozed with graciousness. "I'd love to help out."

Without a backward glance, Amber disappeared into her bedroom, shutting the door firmly behind her.

"How did you do that?" Ben asked, looking around the previously forbidden domain. For a young woman barely out of her teens, Amber was ridiculously neat. "Or perhaps I should ask, *why* did you do that?"

She rolled her eyes. "You want her to kick us out again?"

"No, but maybe this is a waste of time," Ben supposed. He found Amber's cell phone on the table near the tiny kitchen. He pressed two buttons and was scrolling through her address book. "I don't want to sit here playing *What Not to Wear* when I could be out finding my father."

Cat's gasp scared the shit out of him. He slammed the cell phone on the table and expected to see Amber staring agog at him, caught in the act.

Instead, Cat arched her carefully sculpted eyebrows. "*You* watch *What Not to Wear*?"

Ben growled and retrieved the phone, causing Cat to laugh as if she'd just been told a hilarious joke. He gave up on the address book—too many names—and switched to incoming calls. Taking a notebook from his pocket, he jotted down the names and numbers of the dozen or so people who'd called Amber in the last twenty-four hours.

"Keep your khakis on, Professor." Cat joined his cursory search, checking out the innards of Amber's tiny backpack purse. "Our little fashion diva knows something. She has to. We'll chitchat about clothes and men for a few minutes and she'll be eating out of my hand. Just sit back and watch how it's done."

Cat didn't disappoint him. Amber had the good manners to announce her oncoming fashion exhibition, so Ben and Cat both had time to stop snooping and take their seats for the runway show. Cat immediately went to work critiquing and offering suggestions that led them to Amber's closet while Ben explored the kitchen and her laptop. Half an hour later, Cat had Amber looking older, more sophisticated and decidedly more desirable to a guy of any age, and when they walked the coed to her car, not only did they have the name and phone number of the so-called cousin who'd confronted Paschal on the quad, but they also had the name and addresses of the bar she'd met him at—information she had not shared with the police.

"Don't tell T that I ratted him out, okay?" Amber begged as she popped her lime green PT Cruiser into gear. "I needed the money, okay?"

"So you took money from a stranger and passed him off as your cousin to set my father up?" Ben asked. Now that he had the information he needed, he saw no reason to be polite. Cat, however, stomped on his foot to get him to shut up.

"What?" he asked. "She did set Paschal up."

"I didn't!" Amber insisted. "Topher convinced me that he was a Gypsy himself. That he was working on some sort of family tree and needed Professor Rousseau's help, but he wouldn't take his calls. He thought if one of his students introduced him, he'd have an in. That's all I knew. He said he had information about this Valoren place that the professor would want. Then, after the professor turned him down, Topher got all weird. Really, really angry. I wouldn't have helped him at all if I'd known what a prick he was."

Cat leaned forward and patted Amber's arm through the open car window. "Dr. Rousseau will be fine. You did the right thing by telling us the whole truth."

Ben turned away, unable to watch as Amber peeled out of the lot without a care in the world beyond what kind of martini to order at dinner and if her shoes matched her purse. She'd led a man she'd now admitted was dangerous straight to his father, and he was supposed to care if she and her third date had a good time?

In silence, they headed back to his car. Ben opened the door for Cat. She slid by him with only centimeters to spare, and the attendant thrill of her clothes brushing against his removed a layer of anger from his body. Without Cat, he never would have finessed the information. She'd worked Amber with a cool style that had his blood simmering. Before she got in, he grabbed her by the shoulders and kissed her.

After a long, luxurious, luscious moment, she pressed a hand to his chest and pushed him back, but only a few inches.

"You don't give a girl much warning, do you?" Her words came out in a breathless rush.

In her eyes, Ben witnessed a mixture of surprise, shock and, perhaps, pleasure? Well, damn. Of course she'd found the kiss pleasurable. Wasn't like he was new to the art form.

When the corner of her mouth quirked up into a saucy grin, however, his mind flashed with images of Mariah. So cocky. So self-assured. So impossible to deal with.

"Maybe if I thought before I acted, I wouldn't make such boneheaded mistakes," he said.

"Kissing me was a mistake?"

"Without a doubt," he muttered, gesturing her inside the car so he could slam the door on his foolish moment of weakness.

However, after he'd slid into the driver's seat, she wasted no time reintroducing the topic. "In my experience, it's the things we *think* we know that usually get us into the most trouble."

He snorted. "You think you know more about trouble than I do?"

"There's a very good chance," she replied.

Though he opened his mouth to speak, he thought better of engaging in this conversation and opted for silence instead. Catalina Reyes clearly knew a great deal about a lot of things, but when it came to trouble, anyone with the last name Rousseau had the market cornered.

"So, now we know that Amber's fake cousin is a drifter named Topher Pyle who can't afford a decent pair of shoes, according to her, but he can spare two hundred dollars to pay a college sophomore to introduce him to her professor," Cat recapped.

"What we don't know is why some low-life is interested in my father."

"Or Valoren. Maybe this Pyle guy really is Gypsy."

"Or maybe he's just lying through his teeth."

"For a place that's supposed to be so secret, an awful lot of people know about it," Cat commented.

"Too many fucking people," Ben muttered, tamping down his anger at Paschal. Maybe if his father had told him a thing or two about the place, Ben wouldn't be operating so blindly. Maybe if he knew . . . something . . . he'd be closer to finding his father before he died.

"Well," she said softly, "at least the information isn't readily available."

"If Topher Pyle really had information about Valoren, my father would have helped him in exchange for it. I think that's a lie. That punk must be working for someone—someone who knows about Valoren and believes in it as much as my father. Question is, who?"

Cat pulled her cell phone out of her purse. "Shouldn't be too hard to figure out who."

"You don't think so?"

After pressing a speed-dial button, she gave him a

jaunty wink. "You're in luck, Ben. You want your father back and so does my friend. My *rich* friend. Whether its ransom or payoffs, we'll get Paschal back. You just have to trust me."

"I have so far," he griped.

"Have you?" she shot back.

"Isn't that obvious?"

"Well," she replied, settling into the seat as if they were going on a long, leisurely drive rather than on a hunt for the man who might have taken his father, "it was to me. I was just wondering about you."

Ben didn't reply. Anything he might add or deny would only bury him deeper in a personal maelstrom he'd rather not confront. Because the truth was, he did trust her.

And the only thing trusting a beautiful woman had ever gotten him was hot sex—nearly always followed by a brush with death. With a resigned shake of his head, he realized he was probably—and hopefully— heading for both with Cat.

19

"Hold my calls."

Jacob barked the order over his shoulder, knowing his assistant would comply whether or not he made eye contact. He tossed his briefcase by the door, removed his jacket and stalked around the office, his skin on fire. No, not his skin. His brain. He glanced at his watch. He had five minutes. Five fucking minutes. What was he going to do?

Five minutes ended up a generous estimation. Five seconds later, an alarm sounded from his computer. Incoming message. He didn't move. Narrowing his gaze, he tried to see if his monitor revealed the source of the alert, but the twirling crown that comprised the Crown Chandler logo continued to spin against the dark screen. E-mail? Interdepartmental instant message? Or what he'd been dreading—a highly encrypted message from the kid who held his future in his hands.

He checked his watch again. He'd said noon, right? Noon?

The console beeped again, and this time, the automated voice on his computer announced the source: Incoming conference call notification.

Reluctantly, Jacob moved toward his desk. He reached for his mouse, hesitating before the vibration of his touch activated the machine. What was he going to say?

The third beep jolted him to action. He straightened his tie, then boldly pressed on the mouse.

Keith Von Roan's face filled the entire screen. Round, light eyes with girlish lashes. Smooth forehead and cheeks, but acne pocked the skin along his jawline. A strip of fuzz over his top lip was mistakenly considered a moustache. His lips moved, but no sound came out. Jacob scrambled to adjust the volume.

". . . flight didn't suck?"

Jacob slid into his chair. Keith was only nineteen. A kid. So why was Jacob sweating bullets underneath his starched cotton collar? Try as he might, he couldn't muster the superior attitude he'd perfected with everyone else. Keith knew too much. And soon, Keith would have more clout and cash than even Alexa. Jacob wasn't a fool. Guys like him stayed on top by hitching their future to the star that would rise the highest—not to the one who would burn out from messing with shit she didn't understand.

And if all progressed as planned, Keith Von Roan would soon be at a zenith.

"Flight was great," Jacob responded. "No turbulence, great mimosa." He prayed the words came out with his practiced lackadaisical air rather than reflecting his heightened nerves. "What more can a man ask for?"

Keith nodded absently, his eyes downcast as he typed away on his keyboard and fiddled with his mouse. Probably playing another round of World of Warcraft. "I don't know," the kid mused, his hands still flying. "I'd rather have limitless power before concentrated orange juice and cheap champagne."

Jacob rolled his eyes. Clearly, the kid had a lot to learn about living large.

Keith looked up, and instantly Jacob popped his expression back into enthusiastic agreement. "Of course."

"So, are we any closer?"

We? Some *we*. Jacob was doing all the work. Jacob was putting his fortune on the line so the kid could take over as leader of the K'vr. The death of the previous Grand Apprentice had split the group into two factions—one led by Keith, catering to those who believed in blood succession, and the other headed by Farrow Pryce, whose money and power lured an equal number of followers. Jacob, who had plenty of money and power on his own thanks to the Chandler legacy, had chosen to ally himself with Keith. Though Farrow had more experience, Keith had the bloodlines. And if Jacob had learned one thing after his mother had married into the Chandler family, it was that blood counted above all else.

Jacob pretended that someone had come to the door of his office. The gesture bought him a few moments to think. How much did he want to tell his eventual lord and master? For the longest time, Jacob's loyalty to the K'vr had been his sole focus. The group had formed centuries ago, solely for the purpose of obtaining the supernatural power once wielded by Lord Rogan, a European nobleman who'd discovered an ancient source of magic in his vast and varied travels, though the power had ultimately destroyed him.

But until now, the K'vr had never been so close to obtaining their goal. And before yesterday, Jacob had also never been manhandled by a ghost. He'd known at that moment that he'd found what hundreds of followers before him had failed to discover. The magic he'd once thought only a pipe dream now loomed larger than he'd ever imagined. And he was at the forefront of the search. Because of *his* cunning. Because of *his* sacrifices. Not due to some pimply kid who'd had the luck to be born to the right father.

"I believe we've made great progress," Jacob replied.

Keith's bushy eyebrows rose high over those feminine eyes. "Can you verify that the castle still possesses the magic bequeathed to me by my uncle?"

More like great-uncle, nine times over. Lord Rogan had lived in the eighteenth century, his tale chronicled by his younger brother, a minor landowner, who'd used his brother's reputation as a formidable sorcerer to keep his tenants and serfs in line. Even after Lord Rogan's mysterious disappearance after he'd traveled from London to a Gypsy enclave tucked into a corner of what was now Germany, Lukyan Roganov continued to spin tales of his brother's magical prowess. Possessing a few tricks of his own, he'd rallied a collection of followers, who had, through the centuries, become known as the K'vr. The group's goal from the very beginning had been to retrieve the reported source of Rogan's great power. Trouble was, none of them knew what the source was.

But the discovery of Rogan's castle, reported to have been built by the sorcerer shortly before his disappearance, had become their strongest clue.

Yet even the nineteen-year-old heir to the Roganov legacy knew not to get his hopes up. The key to Rogan's magic was, to the K'vr, as equal in legend, lore and legacy as the Holy Grail to Christians—and just as elusive. Even though Jacob had been initiated into the group only five years before, his extensive knowledge of the occult had helped push him to the forefront of the search. And with the Chandler family's resources behind him, he'd found more than any other devotee before him.

"I cannot verify that the source exists there, but I highly suspect it does. I actually entered the hallowed halls myself yesterday."

At this, Keith stopped typing. "The necklace worked?"

Now the teen was paying attention. The K'vr had long known the location of Rogan's fortress when it was still in Germany, but had been unable to gain entrance to the structure, or so the legend told. Doors wouldn't unlock. Windows would not break. Stone remained impervious to even the most destructive explosives. Then, more than fifty years ago, a man with a well-armed contingent of masons and bricklayers had somehow torn the castle apart and spirited it away. Though loyal and devoted, the K'vr lacked the money to pursue them. Only recently had they discovered where the castle had gone.

"Yes," Jacob replied. "My stepsister stayed the night there, and I suspect she might not have left if the spirit hadn't attacked me."

"Rogan?"

Keith's jaw slackened at the overwhelming possibility. The way the wraith had knocked Jacob on his ass, he wouldn't have been surprised if the notoriously vindictive sorcerer had returned. But he expected if the K'vr's patron had manifested himself, Jacob wouldn't have simply been knocked down a few stairs. He'd be dead.

"I don't know. But Alexa does, I'm almost sure. But of course, she won't say a word to me."

Keith's lip curled into a snarl. "Sisters suck."

Jacob understood the kid's vitriol. Keith's older sister, Gemma, pissed off that the leadership passed her by simply because she was a woman, had defected to Farrow's side. But as much as Alexa cramped his style and lorded her superior position within the company over him, she'd never betrayed him or left him out in the cold. Not the way he'd betrayed her.

"Without Alexa, we wouldn't have come this far," Jacob pointed out.

"She's in the way."

"She might yet prove useful. I think she's in contact with the spirit there. I think it listens to her."

Keith's eyes narrowed threateningly. "I hate how she has the deed. The castle should be mine."

"It will be," Jacob reassured him. "You can't tip your hand to Alexa or to Pryce too soon. You know he's watching every move you make. By allowing my sister to act as our unwitting emissary to Rogan's castle, we've bought more time. With *her* money."

Keith frowned over Jacob's argument. Jacob glanced at his door. The milky glass panels on either side would reveal anyone listening from the other side. He could see the outline of his assistant at her desk, chatting on the phone as she moved file folders and consulted her computer.

"Time will run out soon if you don't get back to

Florida. Why are you back in Chicago, anyway?" Keith asked.

"I can't raise my sister's suspicions or she'll toss me off the project altogether. There are a few matters I have to take care of here."

Keith's grin bordered on creepy. "You mean the sabotage in Boston?"

Jacob's throat constricted. He had to cough to clear a passage for air. "That was you?"

His laugh was almost childish. Almost.

"When you told me your sister had found a way to land on that haunted island after so many others had tried and failed, I figured it was time we took her out of the mix. A quick check of the Weather Channel and I chose my target. You're not the only K'vr follower in the Chandler organization, buddy. Using your sister's resources to finance our project was brilliant, but I've taken out some insurance that she won't get in our way. Once we have the source of the magic, we'll be unstoppable."

With as much casual ease as he could fake, Jacob sat back against the cold leather of his chair. "I don't want my sister hurt," he said.

All the warmth and guilelessness in Keith's eyes disappeared, replaced with something hard and cold and ugly. "You can't back out now. You tried once to have your sister killed. Now you'll get what you want."

The slice through his heart stabbed Jacob to his chair. He fought to keep his expression blank. He could feel his nostrils flaring as Keith threw his darkest shame back in his face. Of course, this is why the teen would make the perfect leader for the K'vr. He showed no mercy.

Jacob swallowed thickly. "You know I won't get the company if Alexa dies."

"No, but her will stipulates you receive the bulk of her personal assets."

"Not everything," he grumbled, remembering how

much Alexa had designated to go to Cat, the rehabilitation center she'd used after her accident and the staff at their home in Chicago. More than anyone in their right mind would leave to servants, honestly.

"But you'll be set for a huge chunk of change. And once we have the source of Rogan's magic, we'll have everything we've ever needed. Now," Keith snapped, the greedy sound popping out of his voice, "tell me about the castle. What did you find inside? Did you take pictures? I want pictures."

Fed by eagerness, Keith moved even closer to his webcam so that Jacob could practically see the whitehead on top of the blemish beneath his nose.

"The designers took a boatload. I'll forward them as soon as the file is sent to me, but otherwise, the place is barren. Nothing but an old painting on the landing."

"A painting? Of Rogan?"

"No, I don't think so. This man's eyes are pale. A follower maybe?"

Keith's tapping on the keyboard renewed. The kid had lost interest again. Jacob kept his expression steady.

If Keith had gone so far as to place spies within the Chandler organization, the kid likely had more up his sleeve than Jacob had ever imagined.

Maybe Farrow Pryce was not the only cunning one.

"We could ask Rousseau to identify the painting," Jacob suggested.

Keith frowned. "He's useless."

"He's the only expert we know of—"

"He's missing."

"Missing? Did you?"

A whirling sound from the other side of the connection indicated that perhaps his computer game wasn't progressing as planned. "Nah. He's been more useful to us at the university. Led us to the charm, didn't he?"

"Not on purpose," Jacob reminded him.

Keith waved his hand dismissively. "Whatever. But there's only one person who'd want to make sure he didn't lead us to anything else."

"Pryce," Jacob said with a sneer.

The kid nodded, but boredom glazed his eyes. "Yeah. And if Farrow has the old man, he likely won't be alive for long. Farrow's ruthless, you know."

He said the word "ruthless" with mock exaggeration, as if making fun of Farrow's reputation would somehow lessen the danger his rival represented. "You can't underestimate him," Jacob warned.

Keith made a stupid face but didn't respond.

"Without Rousseau, you'll have to rely on my observations to figure out what kind of magic the castle possesses. But something is there," Jacob promised, catching Keith's eye. "Something malevolent. Maybe Rousseau does know something else important, though. Why else would Farrow move against the professor after all these years?"

Keith stopped messing with his computer. "Stay where you are for the time being," he ordered, suddenly sounding very much like a leader. "Get me those pictures right away; then go back to Florida and explore the castle more thoroughly. And I want in. Make the arrangements."

"Of course," Jacob replied.

"You have the necklace back, right?" Keith asked.

Jacob swallowed hard and lied through his teeth. "Absolutely."

Keith paused before disconnecting but gave no other indication that he suspected an untruth. Jacob had to trust that Alexa hadn't truly lost the necklace. Knowing his stepsister as he did, he knew she'd find it. Alexa didn't leave valuables lying around. Ever.

And yet, despite Keith's cluelessness, Jacob was left in his office with an empty pit for a stomach and a serious case of the shakes. He'd gotten himself in deep this time, deeper than ever before. And the only way he was going to survive was to pull himself out on top.

To do that, certain things would have to be sacrificed. Certain people.

But not him. He'd worked too hard, too long, to let opportunity slip away now.

"One mewl and it will be your last, cat," Damon declared the second the ghostly beast poofed into Rogan's drawing room. The room of his entrapment. With the curtains drawn, he'd lost track of how long he'd been sitting on the wing chair with the sorcerer's cloak curved just behind his ear, the plush rugs and velvet trappings of his old enemy pressing in on his consciousness. He imagined he could smell the foul stench of his rival in the fabric. A rival he'd once admired. A rival he'd once hoped to learn from. Damon had been well traveled and immensely educated, but Rogan's life experiences made Damon a churl in contrast.

Now Damon was getting his wish—he was becoming Rogan. Angry. Arrogant. Uncontrollable. Obsessed with fulfilling his own needs without concern about the consequences to others.

The flesh of his palms still sizzled with unused magic. The dark evil that had spawned the magic now infected him, and yet, he had no more means to free himself of the magic's effects than he did to dispel Rogan's curse. He'd tripped into a cycle of impossible choices, and hours of grappling with the contradictions left him no closer to discovering a solution.

Without the ability to re-create the castle, he'd never find the secret to free himself of the curse. Yet the more he utilized Rogan's legacy, the more he lost himself to the evil.

The cat ignored his warning and meowed softly. The beast leaped onto a squat tuffet near the hearth, padded in a wide circle, then curled in the center and eyed him warily. Its thick tail flicked up and down of its own accord, and the feline's amber eyes bored through him mercilessly.

Damon fought to keep his rage in check. Instead, he engaged in a staring contest with the cat, wondering what knowledge existed behind those mysterious golden orbs. He'd always suspected the animal was more than just a companion to Rogan. Ever since Damon's first visit to Rogan's residence in London, the beast managed to turn up whenever Rogan spoke of the Gypsies. Damon had once suspected the cat was more curious about the Romani than the man who kept him as a pet.

Perhaps the cat wasn't a cat at all. More like . . . a familiar?

Damon eased off the chair and stalked stealthily toward the animal, who seemed unalarmed by his drawing closer. Its tail continued to swish to and fro, its eyes staring intensely, its ears perked, but its body perfectly still.

Reaching the tuffet, Damon knelt on the floor and met the cat stare to stare.

"You know, don't you?" he asked.

The cat remained completely still. Except for the tail.

"You heard his curses. You know his secrets. Why, then, would he trap you? Deny you access to the next life? Except, perhaps, to bestow you with immortality?"

The cat raised its paw and took a long, purposeful lick.

Damon turned on his knees and dropped to the ground. Was this what he'd been reduced to? Trying to extract information from an animal? Still, if this cat held the secret he sought, it certainly wasn't going to tell him. He'd done nothing but snap at the feline since its first appearance in his portrait prison so many years ago.

Perhaps this could change?

Damon turned again and, closing his eyes, used a tiny bit of magic to conjure a plate of freshly smoked and salted herring. The cat stopped its grooming and stretched its neck to sniff at the plate.

Damon grinned. "Interested?"

The cat stretched its paws forward, seemingly to elongate its spine, but its paws touched nearer and nearer the plate.

He tugged the pewter serving tray aside.

"It's yours, cat. But for a price."

The cat bounced onto all four paws and let out a protesting howl.

Damon shook his head. "Sorry, but there is a price to be paid."

A price to be paid.

The words crashed back at him with an ocean of meaning. Only two people on this earth would care if Damon's pursuit of freedom turned him evil. He was one. A gentleman of honor, Damon understood that there were times when ruthlessness was unavoidable, when self-preservation or the protection of the family demanded excessive means. But never in his life had he sought revenge or retribution without cause. He had to hope . . . he had to *pray* . . . that no matter what magical blackness swam though his veins, he could resist the total annihilation of his soul.

Then there was Alexa. Damon had meant his initial seduction of the woman to be nothing more than a means to an end—a pleasurable way to ensure that she assisted in his quest to be free from the castle and achieve permanent corporeal form. But while his goal hadn't changed, his emotions toward her had. Even under the influence of Rogan's magic, he acknowledged the great pain and loss she'd suffered in her lifetime. The death of her mother when she was just a child. The tragic demise of her father in an accident that had nearly killed her as well. She cared deeply for her stepbrother, but her love existed with a certain cynicism Damon could hardly understand, since he'd loved both Rafe and Sarina, his half siblings, with just as much ferocity as he had his full-blooded brothers. Alexa was cautious with her feelings, but kind. She possessed all the qualities he'd searched for in his wife and mistresses but had never truly found.

And yet his anger with her before dawn had been both without true merit and all-consuming. Only by removing himself from her presence had he kept from lashing out in ways that, in retrospect, made his stomach turn.

Is this how Rogan had felt toward Sarina, all those years ago? He thought of the broken necklace. The torn charm. Had Rogan ripped it from his sister's neck in anger as Damon had from Alexa's? Had the blackguard sorcerer, with mercenaries closing in, struck out at his sister with murder in his heart instead of the love he'd once professed?

The cat made short work of the fish. Purring contentedly, it strode to Damon and pressed its flattened face against his. The moment it did, his brain burst with an image. Tiles. No. Mosaic. Intricate puzzles of glass and ceramic that formed artistic renderings like no other.

Rogan had been particularly proud of his, themed with tales of Gypsy legend and lore. Why hadn't Damon remembered? Why hadn't he recalled? He could not remember the exact locations of the mosaics, but he'd conjure them sufficiently . . . once he called upon the magic.

20

"Here's your necklace, repaired as you requested."

Alexa looked up from the cost projections and for the first time this morning made eye contact with her assistant, Rose. She closed the report and focused on the young woman standing so eagerly in front of her.

"Thank you, Rose."

"The jeweler said the necklace looked very old. Is it a family heirloom, if you don't mind me asking?"

Alexa slipped the magical charm into the pocket of the bag she'd take with her later to the island. "Definitely a family heirloom."

Just not her family.

"It's very unusual," the young woman said, her voice haunting.

"You have no idea."

Rose glanced at her watch. "Is there anything else, Ms. Chandler?"

Alexa stopped to think. Her world had resumed the calm, focused pace she'd grown accustomed to, likely because Rose had hopped the first plane to Florida with her highly organized and irreplaceable skills packed in a single carry-on suitcase. Alexa had nearly succumbed to the madness of discovering first the castle and then the ghost inside, especially after Damon's strange behavior this morning. But by logging a full day's work, she now felt surprisingly refreshed and balanced. In her element.

Crown Chandler meant the world to her. It was her world. Was that sad or incredibly lucky?

"How long have you been with Crown Chandler?" Alexa asked.

Rose's eyes widened. Her eyes were blue. Had Alexa ever noticed that before?

"Excuse me?"

Alexa stacked the cost projections atop the collection of files on the polished teak desk Rose had had delivered to her suite-turned-office and wondered how often, if ever, she smiled at her assistant. Sure, she said her "pleases" and "thank-yous." Her father had drilled the polite words into her everyday speech since before she'd uttered her first full sentence. But did she make it a habit to look Rose in the eye when she spoke to her, or was she too distracted by her computer, her BlackBerry, her reports, files and phone calls?

She pushed the papers away from her and folded her hands gently on her desk. "How long have you been working for me?"

"Two years, ma'am."

Two years. Two years and Alexa had no idea how old Rose was, if she was seeing anyone or, heck, if she was married. Did she have children? A mother she took care of? A father who came over to her apartment to fix broken pipes? Heck, did she live in an apartment or did she own a house?

"Is there something wrong?" Rose asked.

Alexa leaned back and exhaled deeply. So she wasn't good at interpersonal relationships. Wasn't like she didn't have *any*. There was Cat. Jacob. The members of her upper-management team. She knew all sorts of things about them. Of course, that was more for security reasons than for friendship. Still, the fact that her assistant had been running her office like clockwork for two whole years without Alexa knowing more about her was inexcusable.

"Nothing a chat wouldn't fix." She gestured toward the chair in front of her desk.

Rose eyed her warily. Poised, efficient and smart, Rose reflected the best of Crown Chandler. Alexa wrote Rose's performance reviews in appropriately glowing terms and gave her regular raises and bonuses, but she couldn't remember ever telling the woman in clear and simple terms that she appreciated all her hard work.

"I'm sorry you had to come down to Florida on such short notice," Alexa offered. "Flight okay?"

Rose's mouth dropped open, and she snapped closed the PDA in her hand while she hesitantly made her way to the chair. She didn't sit down immediately.

"Flight was very nice," Rose answered. "The first-class ticket was a nice treat, thank you. And the suite down the hall? It's breathtaking. Bigger than my apartment."

Alexa smiled, relieved. Okay, so she wasn't the twenty-first-century equivalent of Leona Helmsley. Her usually guarded employee was gushing. Gushing was good. Still, there was so much she didn't know.

"Do you have family in Chicago? Someone we should consider bringing down here while you work?"

Rose shook her head and finally lowered herself into the chair. "No, just my cat. I have a friend watching her while I'm away."

"Cat? I like cats," Alexa said. Even ghostly ones with spooky amber eyes and a master who despised him. A master who'd threatened her and her workers with enough conviction that she was chatting with an employee rather than confronting the man, er, phantom, who could waylay her.

"I'm sorry you had to leave your pet," Alexa lamented. "Please let me know if you need help with a pet sitter or boarding. It's really not fair that I dragged you down here with no notice."

Rose's smile was shy but genuine. "I don't mind, Ms. Chandler. I think this project is extremely exciting. A castle! Imagine. What little girl doesn't pretend she's Cinderella or Sleeping Beauty at some point?"

A jolt of enthusiasm shot through Alexa, reminding

her of why she'd originally set her life in Chicago aside to fly to Florida and explore this dream. This . . . fantasy.

"Let's hope scores of people will be willing to pay premium rates to stay in an old castle without having to whip out a passport."

Rose had leaned forward, her tone eager. "Ooh, I think they will."

Ambition glimmered within the soft blue depths of Rose's eyes, and Alexa wondered how much else she'd missed about her assistant. "Let me ask you, Rose. Where do you see yourself with Chandler . . . in the next five years, say?"

Suddenly, Rose's posture snapped straight. She didn't answer immediately, which even Alexa noticed was completely out of character.

"I'm blindsiding you with these questions, aren't I?"

Rose swallowed deeply. "No, I mean, yes. I mean . . . I've always wanted to have this conversation with you. I really love working for you, Ms. Chandler—"

Alexa coughed to hide her snort. She couldn't imagine anyone loving anything about working for her. She supposed she was a fair employer who paid well, but she was also distant and unobservant. She'd never realized. Not truly. Not until Damon had forced her to feel things she hadn't since her accident. Not just sexual desire and pleasure, but empathy and fear. Even the triumphs she'd experienced at work and the loss of her father had been dulled by the walls she'd built around her heart. She hated to admit, even if only to herself, how this phantom of a man had somehow invigorated her hunger for life.

She'd been so sure after her accident that her love of living had pushed her through the surgeries, the therapy, the pain. Now she realized she'd simply been too programmed for success to do anything besides live.

Now she wanted more. She wanted love. In all forms.

"—design really interests me."

Of course, she could start by listening attentively to her employees when they were finally pouring out their hopes and dreams at her urging.

"What perfect timing, then," she declared. "We'll only have a skeleton crew on this project for the time being, until the logistics and materials are in place. Mainly, we'll be planning the furnishings and the layout. If you'd like, I'll have you work closely with the design team."

Rose's face blossomed, and she managed—barely—to contain a squeal of delight. "That would be amazing. Thank you."

"No, Rose. Thank you. This project, if handled correctly, will be magical. I'm sure of it."

Alexa glanced out the ceiling-to-floor picture window behind her and realized the sky was darkening. Soon, Damon would be solid again. She had no idea if he was still in the same foul mood as he had been this morning, but she couldn't imagine letting a night pass with such animosity between them. Besides, she had a little more than a week to calm him down before the first team of workers descended on the castle. She understood his anger, felt for his dilemma—but she still had her own goals to fulfill.

"Let's meet tomorrow morning around ten," she told Rose as she stood to leave the office. "I'll tell you what I envision and you can bring my ideas to the designers."

Rose practically floated across the room, the vividness of her smile rivaling the colors now streaking across the sky. "Thank you, Ms. Chandler."

"Please," she said, wondering why she hadn't insisted on less formality sooner, "call me Alexa."

Rose's ears perked. "The document is finished printing," she announced, beelining toward the outer office.

Alexa stood and listened while Rose retrieved the papers from the printer. "What document?"

"The one Ms. Reyes sent in the encrypted file."

Ten minutes later, Alexa held a spiral-bound copy of Sarina Forsyth's diary in her hands. And two hours after that, she was headed back to her island, the leverage she needed to assuage Damon tucked tightly in her backpack.

With a flashlight clutched in her hands, Alexa pushed her way through the palmetto bushes that blocked the path from the wall to the front door of the castle. She'd just had the plants chopped aside the day before, but apparently, they regrew rather quickly. Either that or Damon was manipulating the magic in order to keep her out.

As if some ancient Gypsy curse could stop her.

She kept her flashlight aimed directly in front of her, focused on the front door, ignoring all the creepy crawlies inside the plants and vines around her. Behind her, the buzz of the retreating boat engine competed with the whine of the mosquitoes swarming through the air. She quickened her pace, cursing the fact that she hadn't thought to include bug spray with her supplies. Oh, well. She wouldn't remain outside for long.

She jogged up the steps and pulled the latch, yelping when the lock did not yield.

"Damon!" she called, banging her fist on the thick door. "Let me in."

Silence whistled into the trees and rolled off the palm fronds, then echoed into the ocean swirling on the other side of the wall. Darkness had descended all around her, though jewel-toned light glowed bright behind the castle's stained-glass windows. He was inside, of course. Denying her entrance.

Well, she'd just see about that.

She put down her backpack and from the pocket withdrew Sarina's necklace. Only Rose could have gotten the chain fixed so quickly. Alexa fastened the jewelry behind her neck, took a deep breath and tried the latch again.

Nothing.

"Damon!"

She banged on the door, but then realized that even if he wanted to let her in, perhaps he could not. In fact, judging by his last attempt at escaping his prison, he'd likely stay as far away from the exit as possible.

So, how did she get in the first time? And the second?

Closing her eyes, Alexa concentrated on the night before. She'd been drawn to the castle because of Damon, because of a powerful lust that drove her to ignore all reason, all logic. All caution. She'd craved entrance to the castle more than anything else.

And on the morning she'd first come in, she'd also been driven by the intense need to find the man in the window, the ghost whose hand had passed through the window without cracking the glass. Both times, she'd wanted not just entrance to the house but access to the man inside.

Tonight, her motives had been skewed away from wanting either Damon the man or Damon the phantom. She'd simply wanted entrance to *her* castle. Her anger with him over his attitude this morning had tempered her desire, forcing her to focus more on manipulating him rather than seducing him.

Maybe that's where she went wrong?

Alexa dug deeper into her bag, this time retrieving the filmy lingerie she'd purchased in the hotel's boutique. Without a thought to the blood-sucking bugs buzzing around her, she undressed and slipped into the gown. The slinky silk slid down her body, igniting every nerve ending with anticipation for when Damon spied her in this sleek black confection. The dark color highlighted her pale skin and the cut emphasized the curves in her breasts and hips. She ran her fingers through her hair, which she'd loosened during the trip from the mainland, and loved the windblown feel of it. How would Damon resist a woman whose entire body thrummed with need?

Licking her lips expectantly, Alexa touched the latch. This time, it pushed open with oiled ease.

She dragged her bag inside, retrieved the diary, and then slammed the door behind her. She looked up and gasped.

While she'd expected Damon, she'd been wholly unprepared to see him standing in the archway to her left, scarlet banners edged in shimmering gold unfurling behind him from the beams crisscrossing the forty-foot ceiling of the dining hall. He was breathtaking in his snug breeches, polished boots and stark white shirt. She swallowed deeply even as her body shook with intensified arousal.

"What are you doing here?" he asked, his volume low but his voice thunderous.

She crossed the distance between the entryway and the hall, the copy of the diary hanging loose at her side, as if unimportant.

"This is my castle," she replied. "I'll come here whenever I damned well please."

With nothing but a sideways glance and a smirk, he turned back into the hall. "Then you are a fool."

Well, that wasn't the greeting she was expecting, was it? Nonetheless, she followed him deeper into the room, which he'd clearly been rebuilding with the aid of Rogan's magic. On the wall between two room-sized fireplaces, a thousand tiny tiles scrambled in the air, adhering to the stone randomly or hovering and darting, as if searching for their proper places.

They were creating a mosaic. She watched until a picture emerged—a Gypsy marketplace, complete with artisans, musicians and scampering children running underfoot with the chickens and cats.

Though the unfolding creation was utterly fascinating, she focused on Damon. "You're a big jerk," she announced.

He spun and faced her. "I am *what*?"

She didn't flinch. "A jerk. A git. A prat. I'm not sure what era or country you need the words from in order to understand. In my century, 'asshole' would be the common term."

His eyes narrowed. She caught a glimpse of the

stormy darkness in his gray irises, but his jaw twitched, as if he was fighting to keep his response to himself.

"Do you want me to define it?" she asked, infuriated at his silence.

"While not in general usage in my time, the word is self-explanatory," he muttered.

"So, do you care to explain why you're acting like a first-class bastard, or shall I guess?"

With a sweep of her hand, she gestured toward the progress he'd made in re-creating the hall. She had to admit, the result was stunning. Long tables dominated the space, with enough chairs to easily seat one hundred people. Or an entire village of Romani, at the very least. Huge fireplaces roared with heat on either side of the nearly completed mosaics, emitting smoky scents into the air and fighting off the strange chill that seemed to leech from the stone.

The remorseless look in his eyes verified her fear.

"Stop it," she said.

"I cannot."

"Yes, you can." She whipped out the diary and tossed it on the table. It slid over the polished oak and came to rest when he slammed his hand on the plain black, faux-leather cover. "What is this?"

"Your sister's diary. She knew Rogan best, didn't she? Perhaps the answer to unraveling the curse is within those pages. Stop using the magic, Damon, before it corrupts you."

Damon chuckled ominously. "Too late."

21

Despite the flash of fear in Alexa's eyes—or perhaps because of it—Damon pressed his hand against the thin book and opened it to the first page. The handwriting looked familiar, but the pages were so white, he was nearly blinded. He tossed the book back at her. "This is not Sarina's journal."

"Not the original, no," she replied, pushing the oddly bound book back at him. "It's what we call a copy. But the words are hers, Damon. Read it."

He grabbed the journal and marched to the head of the table. Even without his attention, the mosaic tiles continued to fly into place. Throwing himself into a chair, he tore open the book and started to read.

Word by word, the fire of resentment burning within him lessened. His breathing came easier. His stomach no longer cramped from pent-up rage. As if Sarina sat beside him at the hearth, some random fairy tale he'd brought her from London clutched to her chest as she recounted to him the adventures of the hero within, his sister sprang to life. Wide-eyed. Naive. And for the most part, lonely.

He saw his name. He recognized the Romani word for "brother." And then the one for "sad." She described him through her eyes, and the assessment stabbed at him just as violently as the sword he'd thrust into Rogan's portrait centuries ago. Never around for long. Never sparing her more than an hour's time. And though he brought her fine presents, he never, ever gave in to her entreaties to return with him to England. She longed to see the estates their father held and meet the glorious lords and ladies of the king's court.

Such optimism and yearning turned his stomach. She'd had no idea how rejected she would have been, simply because of the dark hair and olive skin that marked her as a Gypsy.

Halfway through, he closed the copy and placed it gingerly on the table. At that moment, Alexa slid her hands onto his shoulders.

"You don't need to use the magic, Damon. We can find the answer another way."

He shook his head, even as her fingers dug into his muscles and worked the tension from his neck. "My sister's words are a welcome respite." He smoothed the barren cover with his fingers, regret swelling within him. "Yet they only remind me of my objective on the night I rode with my brothers into the storm, trying to save her from the sorcerer I'd brought into her life. How much did you read?"

"Not much. Her handwriting isn't easy to decipher and she uses a lot of words I don't understand."

"Romani words," Damon told her. "Shortly after my father arrived in Valoren, a beautiful widow named Alyse captured his heart. My brothers and I rebelled against their union . . . until she bore him a son. What a wastrel Rafe was. And then, Sarina." He swallowed thickly, casting off the sentimental memories. "She had a sharp tongue in any language. She wasn't happy that I wouldn't take her to London. Even now, I can hear her tirades. She accused me of trying to keep her prisoner . . ."

The irony slammed him hard. Hadn't he done just that? Hadn't he denied, over and over, each of Sarina's heartfelt requests for freedom from Valoren and her mother's ever-watchful eye? Hadn't she begged him to recount, in painful detail, each and every ball and soiree he'd attended?

Had she, thus denied, entreated Rogan to conjure the curse as retribution for his cold denials?

Suddenly, Alexa's hands were upon his, her palms flat over his knuckles.

"I know what you're thinking," she said.

Forlorn regret gripped his insides. "No, you do—"

"You think she asked Rogan to do this to you. To make you pay for the way you treated her."

"I loved her," he admitted.

"Of course you did. And you were protecting her. You knew what would happen if you brought a Gypsy girl, particularly one half British, to court. Your father would have been reviled. Likely, no one in England even knew he'd taken a Gypsy wife, did they? Sarina would have been marked as illegitimate. Or worse."

He stared at her, amazed at her keen understanding.

"Don't be so surprised," she said. "I *can* read some of the diary and I do know a little about history, remember? And better than anyone, I understand the yearnings of a young girl bound by her position and birth. You told me enough about Valoren for me to put the pieces together. I understood enough of the diary to know that her feelings for you weren't any more vindictive or hateful than the swipes my stepbrother and I toss at each other all the time. I might not like Jacob sometimes, but I love him. He's my only family. I'd never want him hurt. I know he feels the same way about me."

Damon marveled at her even tone, her quiet confidence. Truth be told, Damon knew very little of the workings of a woman's heart, be it sister, wife or mistress. Even his mother, a slave to her station, had spent little time with her children preceding her death, and his stepmother, though open and loving to Rafe and Sarina, the children she'd borne, seemed afraid to truly love her husband's British sons. Could Alexa know more about these matters than he?

"You're so certain?"

She smiled softly. "I'm not certain, no. But I can't imagine that the young girl who fell under the spell of a man you yourself admit was charming and charismatic harbored the hatred it would take to banish her own brother into a painting. She was angry with you and your brothers, Damon. She didn't hate you."

Pulling away from Alexa's touch, he pushed the diary aside. "Then the journal is of no use. The only way to unravel this curse is through the magic itself."

"At what price?" She leaned down and retrieved her bag from beneath her chair. "I have a better idea."

Out of her haversack, she pulled a slim black case.

A grin, devilish and cocky, tilted the corner of her mouth. For the first time since this morning, his anger surrendered to desire. He instantly noticed how the bodice of her gown dipped nearly to her navel, and his entire body tightened in carnal response. If using the magic made him forget his own needs, he clearly needed to find another way to accomplish his goal.

She laid the case gently on the tabletop and flipped a lever that opened the top. After she pressed a button on the side, a green light sparked, and then suddenly, the inside of the top glowed bright blue.

"What is that?" he asked, genuinely curious.

"This, Sir Damon, is a little bit of magic we in the twenty-first century like to call the Internet."

"Topher Pyle? Man, I ain't seen that creep in weeks."

Cat threw back her scotch, the liquid burning down her throat as she boldly eyed the bartender. She'd already found out the man's name was Rock. She'd hoped he wasn't as stupid as one, but so far, things weren't looking good.

"Bullshit," she responded.

Rock's lip curled up at the corner. "You calling me a liar?"

Cat leaned forward, and beside her she felt Ben tense. The bartender, a large man with a patch where one eye should have been and a scar running a jagged edge all around his chin, glanced at Ben, who held up his hands as if her impertinence was none of his affair.

She grabbed the bartender by his marred chin and turned his eye back to her. "Don't look at him. He's just here for the beer. I'm the one who doesn't believe the load of shit you just handed me. If I shell out fifty bucks more for this piss you call booze, you think you might remember something important?"

The man yanked out of her grip. "You're a crazy bitch."

She stepped down from the bar. "I've been called worse by scarier assholes than you."

The huge man shot forward, but Ben jumped between them, kicking back his barstool, which skidded across the sawdust-covered floor. Funny how Professor Rousseau Jr. could look harmlessly charming one minute and the next, he's standing with his hands palm forward—and the sweet side of a .357 magnum sticking convincingly out of his waistband.

"The lady offered you an extra fifty," Ben said, his tone calm.

Rock's one dark eye watched Ben's gun as if it might jump out and do flips. Or deposit a bullet in his forehead.

"Ain't worth it," Rock spat.

"Got someone else who's going to tip you so generously tonight just for information about some prick who probably stiffed you for his tab last time he was here?"

That had been a guess, though Rock's pierced eyebrow rose enough to reveal that she'd hit the mark.

The sleazy dive bar Amber had directed them to was nearly deserted. A few bikers lined up around a faded pool table while two guys played for bragging rights and dollar beers. A couple of drunks gnawed cheap cigars in a corner. A guy in a stark white suit and many gold chains conducted business from a cell phone in the corner, oblivious to the fact that his fashion statement was older than he was. Cat doubted any of the college crowd Austin was famous for went anywhere near this joint ordinarily, yet this was the address Amber had provided for the guy who'd paid her for an introduction to Paschal. She must have been slumming.

Unless, of course, she'd been playing them.

But Cat didn't think that was the case. Since she'd hooked up with Ben, her psychic abilities had intensified in ways they hadn't since she lived with her grandparents. She'd known Amber was telling the truth with the same certainty that she knew this bozo bartender was lying through his crooked teeth.

"Forget it," she said, tossing a couple of bills on the bar. "Old Rock here doesn't know an opportunity when he hears one. His loss, not mine. Someone else with info on Pyle will want our money."

"No, wait." The bartender crowded forward, his single eye glinting both ways to ensure they weren't overheard. "Look, Topher hangs out with real freaks. They rolled into town a few weeks ago and scared off my regulars. They split day before yesterday and I don't want 'em back here, got it?"

Cat slid back into her seat. Ben tossed her a cocky smile over his shoulder.

"Can't guarantee Topher won't come back," Ben said, finishing his bottled beer. "But we won't issue him an invitation. He's got something we want, that's it."

The bartender frowned. "Yeah, well, I've got something of his. Maybe you can work out a trade."

Dipping down beneath the bar, the guy emerged with a scarred leather jacket, which he threw over the battered bar. "He left it here the other night. One of his pals got a phone call and they shot out of here like bats outta hell."

"Know where he lives?" Cat asked.

"Man, this joint ain't Cheers," Rock sniped. "Besides, Topher ain't local. Rental plates on his truck. Drives around with four other freaks, all dressed in black and coats that don't jibe with the weather. Earrings. Black lipstick. Tattoos on their faces. Vampires, if you ask me."

"A bunch of Goth kids scared off your bikers?" Cat asked.

"Weirdest shit you ever saw," Rock said with a nod.

"Even tough-as-nails bikers don't want to mess with sociopaths, got me? Guys like these liable to blow your brains out only seconds before they do the same to each other. I'm glad they've split. Here," Rock said, tossing the jacket at Ben, "take it. Do whatever, but don't lead that jerk's ass back here."

Cat laid a hundred-dollar bill on the bar. "We won't, but if he shows up, his jacket was stolen and you never saw us."

Rock nodded, then, with a greedy sneer, snatched the C-note and turned away as if they'd never walked inside.

She followed Ben out the door. Once outside, she stopped suddenly, grabbed Ben by the sleeve and pushed him against the wall.

His smile was cocky, his body instantly hard. "We've got to stop meeting like this."

"Sorry," she said, not really meaning it. "I can't help it. Your mean cowboy act back there just made me hot."

She pressed her mouth against his and the blast of sensation nearly melted Cat from the inside out. Tense and powerful from the density of his biceps to the firm feel of his chest against hers, Ben's body proved every inch as marvelous as she imagined. She leaned wholly against him, steaming the air around them and leaving little oxygen to feed her lungs. She fed on him instead, tearing her hands into his hair, only barely registering the stab from the zipper of Topher's jacket indenting her skin.

The moment her focus shifted to the jacket, a wave of sensation—decidedly not sexual—crashed over her. She pulled away from Ben as if drowning. Anxiety. Fear. Anger. Emotions so strong, they yanked the lust from her body, leaving a striking pain in their wake.

"Cat?"

Ben grabbed her by the shoulders and led her away from the bar. At the car, he tossed the jacket into the backseat, and suddenly she was able to breathe.

"What happened?"

She shook her head, trying to regain her equilibrium. God, what had just happened? A premonition? She hadn't had an emotional reaction like that since . . . since she'd been a young girl on the verge of puberty, coming into her psychic abilities in haphazard spurts. She'd learned to ignore her gift, pushing the ability deep inside her where it could do no harm.

But now, maybe it could do some good. Was she willing to take the chance?

"The jacket," she said, breathless. "I felt . . . something. I'm guessing emotions of the guy who owned it. He's pissed off. Royally. And he's afraid he's going to lose something he wants very badly."

"Like my father?"

She shook her head, trying to clear the confusion streaming at her from all angles, all sides. She didn't have a clear picture, just impressions.

"I'm not sure, and unfortunately, I know only one way to find out."

"What way is that?" Ben asked, helping her to the passenger side, opening the door and graciously guiding her in.

Cat took a deep breath. She couldn't believe she was going to do this—she couldn't believe that after all this time, she was willing to go this far. One glance up at Ben's expectant eyes told her she had no choice. She *could* help him find his father. But first, she had to take a very wild leap into a world she'd eschewed for many years.

"Do you know what a *botánica* is?" she asked.

Ben eyed her suspiciously. "A store where you buy supplies for certain religious rites."

She nodded. "Like voodoo and Santería. You need to find the nearest one. Fast. Before I lose what might be our only connection to your father."

22

Damon stared at the screen, motionless. He had no idea how long he'd concentrated on the words there, but he knew that when he and Alexa had finally found a listing for the Forsyth family on a . . . Web site . . . tracing the lineage of families associated with the House of Lords, she had still been awake. Now she slept in the chair beside him, her head resting against her arms on the table, the flames from the hearth adding streaks of fire to her glossy red hair.

His gaze returned to the numbers beside his father's name. Born 1684. Died 1767. He'd lived twenty years after the disappearance of his sons, to the ripe age of eighty two. Below his name appeared each of his male offspring born to his first wife, Margaret. Damon. Aiden. Colin. The twins, Logan and Paxton. No mention of Rafe. And of course, none of Sarina or her gypsy mother, Alyse.

And all the sons, including himself, bore a death date of 1747.

His heart ached. Had none of his brothers survived the battle? Had they died at the hands of King George II's mercenaries or in battle with Rogan? The document did not say. And of course, for all he knew, his brothers had simply been cursed as he had.

This brought him no comfort.

He took a measure of relief from knowing that his father did not die in the cellar of the Valoren home.

Had he searched endlessly for his sons, or had he returned to England to serve the Crown until he died? Damon had once aspired to nothing more. But now? Damon could afford to serve no one but himself and his burgeoning desire to piece together all the fragments of his past.

"Have you googled Rogan yet?"

Alexa's voice, thick with sleepiness, startled him. She hadn't moved a muscle. Her hair was a curtain over her face, but through the strands, he saw her eyes flutter open.

"I thought you were asleep."

"I'm catnapping," she replied, shaking her hair out of her way so the dying embers of the fire behind him glistened in her emerald eyes. "I showed you how to google." She yawned. "Didn't you look him up?"

Damon closed the top of the contraption he'd learned was called a laptop computer. The origin of the word perplexed him since Alexa warned him that the lap wasn't a sturdy place to balance such a delicate instrument.

But she certainly hadn't been exaggerating about the magical quality of the thing. The library at Alexandria could not have held half the information available with the click of a button here, the typing of a word there. He'd had trouble adjusting to modern American spellings but, with her help, had found the academic Web site where he'd first discovered his father's name. Clicking subsequent "links," as she called them, led him to the family tree.

And since she had shown him how to "google" not only his family, but hers, the moment she'd drifted to sleep, he'd revisited the many pages that referenced her life story. He now knew what a car looked like— particularly after being squashed by a monstrous vehicle called a semitrailer truck. He'd studied the mangled steel in horror, trying to imagine her body being pulled from the wreckage. In many ways, she'd cheated death more than he. All he'd had to do was remain in a painting for two hundred and sixty years. She'd had her body stitched back together inch by bloody inch.

"I do not wish to know more of Rogan," he answered.

She frowned. "That isn't very smart. 'Know thy enemy' is the first rule of business."

He eyed her carefully and spied a hint of secrecy lingering in her eyes. "Then I suppose you researched him yourself before you came here tonight."

Lifting herself heavily off the table, she stretched and yawned again, her bodice nearly falling open as her back arched. He glanced aside. He had no time for dalliance tonight, despite the wicked desire coursing through him at the sight of her in such a decadent black silk gown. He hadn't had much time to explore the change in fashion from his century to this one, but if all women dressed like her, he had no trouble understanding why the female gender seemed to now rule the roost.

"Of course I did," she replied. "But I couldn't find a damned thing. You didn't give me much to go on."

"I do not know much beyond my personal interactions with the man," he replied. "Rogan shrouded himself in mystery. I do not even know his family name. The man wore inscrutability around him like a cloak. If one had to ask questions of his past and family, one was considered to not be 'in the know,' so to speak. Everyone assumed that everyone else knew the man's history, yet even the gossips were stumped. When someone dared question him too closely, he turned on his considerable charm until the queries were forgotten."

"That may have worked with others, but how did it with you?"

Damon smirked. "I didn't wish to know more. Not knowing was more intriguing."

"But once he went to Valoren with you, he must have told you something. Your father would have asked—"

"Of course my father asked, and Rogan's replies

were rife with words that answered nothing. He was a world traveler, the son of the earth itself and a follower of the moon. The Gypsies loved him, embraced him, despite his high-born wealth. I highly suspected he was a Gypsy himself who had somehow come into a massive fortune."

"So he had no past, but he had money?"

"An unending supply of gold, which made keeping his secrets all the easier." Damon slid the laptop toward her. Dawn would soon approach. He had an hour, perhaps two, with Alexa before he faded from sight and needed rest. Since he had not used magic since her arrival, the anger within him remained at bay. And yet, he knew the peace could not last. He'd tried to reach his goal her way, but they'd accomplished nothing except establishing that his brothers had also disappeared or died the same night as he did—and that Sarina more than likely had never been found. Now more than ever, he had to return to his original plan—conjuring up the entirety of Rogan's castle in order to search for the source of his magic so he could set himself free.

"I appreciate your concern, Alexa, but there is only one way for me to discover the secret to Rogan's curse. I must use the magic."

Her arm shot out and her fingers clasped his wrist. "You can't. The magic is infecting you. Maybe you'll find the magical source, but who will you be once you're free?"

He extricated himself as gently as possible. "The consequences matter not. Only the outcome. I cannot exist this way forever."

Sliding his chair away from the table, he focused on the mosaic, one of the many once scattered throughout the castle. The scene seemed ordinary—a day in the life of the Umgeben village Gypsies. When Rogan didn't take his meals in his private rooms, he often arranged dinner in the main hall. He invited the Gypsies into his fortress so he could revel not only in their adoration but in their tradition and music.

Their magic.

Damon wandered to the fire and stared into the flames. He had to continue re-creating the castle. The infection of evil would invade him, but he'd fight the effects as best he could. But not with Alexa anywhere near him.

He turned to send her away and she was already standing behind him.

"I'm not going," she declared, arms crossed.

"Daylight beckons, my lady. I know you have business to attend to." He reached forward to touch the triangle of gold dangling around her neck, but she jerked away.

"Oh, no, you don't. The necklace is mine now. It allows me entrance to *my* castle, and I'm not about to give that up. You can try and take it from me again," she challenged, loosening her arms by her sides, though he wasn't fooled by her casual stance. She was ready to fight for the talisman, even against him. He knew he could overcome her, but at what price?

"I will not take it, but I will warn you that with this sunrise, you must leave and not return to the castle. It will not be safe."

"No can do," she replied. "I won't let you destroy yourself."

"You mean, what's left of me."

She arched a brow, then sidled forward until her body pressed against his. "You're all the man I need."

Humor and lust battled within the emerald depths of her irises, but Damon had to remain strong in his conviction. "In the night, yes. But in the light of day, I'm no more than a shadow. I cannot exist this way, Alexa. Being locked in the painting—aware, yet unaware—was easier than knowing a whole amazing world exists outside these walls that I cannot experience except through your machines. I have never been a man to be satisfied with living through others. Like my sister, I yearned to explore, learn, enjoy. I finally understand her anger and frustration . . . about three hundred years too late. Perhaps if I'd comprehended earlier, she wouldn't have been susceptible to Rogan's allure."

"You can't change the past," she argued.

"No, but I can alter my future. And I must do so without you."

He closed his eyes and concentrated on Rogan's study. In a sparkle of color, he materialized there. Darkness surged inside him once again, licking at his insides like the tongue of a horrible beast. He took a deep breath and pressed the air downward, forcing the evil to remain at bay. When he opened his eyes, he discovered Dante, the cat, lounging on the chair, his tail flicking aimlessly while his golden gaze regarded Damon with indifference.

Breathless, Alexa charged into the room. She caught the edge of a bookcase to stop her momentum and shouted, "Stop! Don't run from—"

He closed his eyes again, this time transporting himself into the tower. She'd never reach him here—she likely did not even know the way. He paced, trying to determine his next course of action, wondering at what point Alexa would retreat to the mainland and abandon him so he could act without worrying about the consequences to her. A quarter of an hour later, however, he received his answer. Watching the ocean outside for any sign of her boat leaving the island, he heard her steps on the circular stairs behind him.

When she reached the top, she collapsed on the floor, her lips parted halfway between a smile and a snarl.

"You can't get rid of me," she said, panting, "so easily."

His rage spiked. He clenched his fists, pounding them against his sides. "Be clever, Alexa. Leave me while I search for the answers I seek. I do not wish to hurt you."

She pulled herself to her feet and, before he could stop her, threw herself into his arms.

Need, pure and elemental, jolted him so that his

anger instantly receded. He opened his mouth in surprise, and just as shockingly, she grabbed him by the neck and lifted her body until her mouth was on his. The longer they kissed, the harder her tongue battled with his for sensual dominance, the more the evil drained from him.

"What are you doing to me?" he asked once he had the strength to pull away.

She gazed into his eyes with an emotion he might have mistaken for love. "I'm saving you, you big lug. From a fate worse than death."

"Death is preferable to eternal entrapment."

"Maybe, but there has to be another way."

Without the magic, the tower room was cold and drafty. The ocean roared below them and the only light came from the stars and full moon outside the slatted windows. Damon held Alexa close, blocking her from the chill.

"You see?" she asked.

"See what? That you are the most stubborn woman in Christendom?"

"Just Christendom?" she questioned. "You underestimate my bullheadedness."

"I have to find a way out, Alexa. You must know now that I cannot be your hotel ghost, remaining to entertain your guests and enhance the amount of coin in your purse."

She rolled her eyes at him as if he were a simpleton. "That plan went out the window the moment you touched me. Not the hotel. I still want that. But sharing you with others, keeping you captive? Never. I've proved I want to help you escape, but not by allowing you to turn evil. What type of life will you have on the outside if Rogan's magic infects your soul?"

Though it took all his strength, Damon pushed away from her. "Perhaps evil in my veins will help me do what needs to be done."

"Rogan is gone. Who will you exact revenge upon? His great-great-great-grandson? Be reasonable, Damon."

"There is no reason where there is magic."

She snared her bottom lip in her teeth and Damon could see her warring to find a logical reply. God, how this woman intrigued and excited him. Her emotions did not rule her, but she did not deny them, either.

"You're wrong," she declared finally. "Rogan's magic has rules and parameters. That's why you can't leave the castle the same way you left the painting. And if I'm right, when the evil threatens to overtake you, my touch alleviates the anger."

His body shook. God, he wanted her. His mouth dried with thirst for her. His belly ached with hunger. She fed the goodness in him. How or why he did not know, but in a flash, he thought back to the Gypsy woman and her prediction. Alexa Chandler had influenced his destiny. He'd be a fool not to listen to her now.

"What do you propose?" he asked.

Her smile lit her face like the dawn cracking over the horizon outside. "Give me the day. Don't use the magic. Read the rest of Sarina's diary. I promise, Damon. We'll figure this out without sacrificing your soul."

She slid into his arms and Damon buried his nose in her hair, inhaling the scent of her as her body imprinted its softness on every inch of his skin. Despite her pleas, he could make no promises. Not any he knew he could keep.

"I'll wait until nightfall, but no longer."

She took a deep breath and buoyed herself with a confidence he suspected was part of her makeup just as much as her red hair and green eyes. "Then by nightfall, you'll be free. Without the evil magic. I'll figure out a way or die trying."

23

On the porch, Ben paced, allowing Catalina privacy while she prepared, even while he rubbed his anxious hands together and tried to ignore his watch. He'd witnessed many an ancient ceremony in Africa and a few in certain parts of Europe, but his knowledge and experience with voodoo and Santería were nil. Though he drove her to the shop where she'd purchased what she needed for the rite, the rest he'd left up to her. He trusted her instincts—and that shocked him most of all.

On the surface, Catalina Reyes was the kind of woman he had no business messing with—strong willed, adventurous and boldly sexual. He couldn't stop his brain—or more accurately, his heart—from comparing her to Mariah. Biggest difference so far was that Mariah would have split the minute she had the diary, just like she had with the statue in Istabul and the scroll in Luxor.

Cat, on the other hand, had chosen to stay. Even when her friend had twisted emotional screws to lure her back to Florida, she'd resisted. She'd even dug into her seemingly uncomfortable past to perform the ceremony to help him find his father.

On the way to the *botánca*, Cat had explained how she'd seen her grandmother perform the ritual, usually for people trying, on behalf of her Santería followers, to tap into lost bank accounts or find family heirlooms that had been stolen or misplaced. The Santería priestess had never, to Cat's knowledge, used the process to find a missing person—but Cat believed that didn't mean it couldn't be done. Her grandfather, the voodoo practitioner, had once located a kidnapped child after performing a separate rite of his own. Unfortunately, magic that powerful was painful and bloody, so he rarely performed it. Cat guessed that by combining the two traditions, and throwing in a few things she'd learned as a paranormal researcher, she might pull from the cosmos some clue to finding Paschal.

If Cat was willing, who was he to say no? If even the slightest chance existed that her magical mojo could help find his father, he wasn't going to argue.

While Cat got ready, Ben called the detective investigating Paschal's disappearance. Other than verifying that the blood on the driveway did indeed belong to his father, the police had nothing. No activity on his bank accounts. No sightings around town. No ransom demands. With his permission, they'd tapped both his apartment phone and Paschal's home phone, and no one had called. Ben's cell hadn't beeped, either. Whoever had Paschal didn't want him for money.

As each minute passed, Ben knew he'd go to any length to save his father—including trusting Catalina and the psychic powers she only barely trusted herself.

He'd believe enough for both of them. In his travels, he'd seen odder doings than searching for missing loved ones using candles, crystals, herbs and the old, smelly leather jacket of the man who might—emphasis on "might"—have taken him.

Cat opened the front door. "I'm ready."

From across the porch, he couldn't see inside the house. With the door held close to her body, only her head was visible.

A golden glow of candlelight created a halo effect that sapped his breath. Her black hair, worn loose and long, shined against the night. As he neared, he realized she'd painted symbols on her face.

He reached out and touched the representation of a third eye on her forehead.

"It represents the Sight," she explained.

He grinned. "I figured."

The moment burgeoned with tension. When she swung the door wide to allow him entrance, he understood why. She'd transformed the foyer into a lighted path with candles on either side of the staircase. She wore a scarf tied around her waist like a skirt, the fabric bright with slashes of burgundy, orange and pink that glowed against her bare legs and feet. Her blouse, twisted from the same material, bared her belly and cupped her breasts. Beads glistened from around her neck and dropped to her stomach. The charms tied around her ankles jingled when she walked.

At the top of the stairs, Cat turned and pressed her hand flat against his chest.

"I can't guarantee this will work."

Ben laid his hand over hers, knowing she could feel the pulsing of his heartbeat. "I know."

"I haven't—"

He blocked her claim with his other hand, laying it flat over her lips. "Funny, but when we first met yesterday, you didn't strike me as the insecure type."

With a roll of her eyes, she smiled shyly. "I'm confident about a lot of things, but not this. I'm not practiced."

"But you are motivated. I need you, Cat. My father needs you. And you need him to help your friend."

With a resolute nod, she took his hand and led him into his father's study. In the center of the room, lit with candles on all sides, was a small table she'd dragged in from the guest room. On it lay the jacket, a book, a Texas map, a globe, a jewel-handled ceremonial knife, three thick ceramic bowls reeking of dried herbs and one empty bowl with odd carvings around the edge. Though versed in several ancient languages and hieroglyphics, Ben didn't recognize the symbols.

"What is this?" he asked.

She took his hand and led him to the table. "A little Santería, a dash of voodoo."

He glanced around. "No live animals?"

She gave him an annoyed push. "I'm trying to avoid that, thanks."

"But the blood is key," he said, drawing on his scant knowledge of the two religions.

She silenced him with a tired expression. "Like I don't know?" Lifting the sharp athame, she pointed the knife at him for emphasis and he suspected her wicked smile wasn't just for effect. "Trust me, when we need blood, we'll have it. Now, be quiet. I need you to concentrate on your father. Close your eyes and picture him. Picture the last time you spoke to him. Hear his voice in your ears. Inhale the scent of his cigar. Taste the flavor of his favorite wine."

Ben did as she asked, opening his eyes only briefly when she clicked on the CD player. Drums beat a haunting tattoo that echoed in the silence of the rest of the house. Chanting began, first from the CD, and then from Cat. The language, though foreign, rang with need. The timbre of her voice, deep and resonant, spoke of intense desire. So much so that his lower body tightened and he had to shift his stance.

He struggled against his selfishness and redirected his attention to his father. Paschal Rousseau. Quick to laugh. Gentle. Cerebral. Images of his father barely visible behind a mound of old books popped into his head. Memory snapshots of Paschal throwing a few mismatched shirts and slacks into a suitcase and rushing out the door to catch a plane to some secret European location flashed in his mind. His father's guttural chuckle rang in his ears, along with the sound of his incessant humming. Old music—tunes that might have been played on a lute or a harpsichord.

As long as he kept his eyes shut, he managed to ignore the heat building in the room around him, in Catalina's needful vocals and the desires she inspired.

Then, she grew silent. The chanting on the CD continued, but though he sensed she was standing close by, Cat had stopped chanting, stopped moving. Stopped . . . breathing?

He opened his eyes. She stood directly across from him, her hands pressed against both the jacket and the diary, her head arched back so that his gaze immediately fell upon her slim neck and generous breasts. He squeezed his eyes tight, conjuring images of his father again when a light laugh escaped her lips.

"What's so funny?" he asked.

"I have him," she replied.

"You know where he is?"

She inhaled deeply. "Give me the map."

He picked up the folded map as she tossed the jacket aside, her hands held out as if the vibrations of his father's location remained on her palms. Moving the bowls and the knife aside, he spread the map on the table.

"The athame," she said, extending her left hand.

He placed the hilt in her palm, but she made no move to tighten her grip around it. Instead, she waved the knife loosely above the map, as if waiting for the blade to tumble out of her hand and fall.

Nothing happened.

She chanted. Words Ben had never heard, phrases he couldn't begin to understand. Then, a bit of Latin. To find. To seek. To need.

"Take the knife."

Ben grabbed the hilt.

"Cut me."

"What?"

She held her hand out, palm up. "Think of your father and slice my skin." She'd started to sway with the rhythm of the repetitious mantra, her hair sliding against her body, the strands teasing the edges of the candle flames.

"Cat, no—"

She cut off his protest with a glare so intense, he wondered about her supposed inexperience with her psychic powers. Her eyes flashed with power, with determination. If he didn't cut her, she'd cut herself. Nothing would stop her from finding Paschal, especially not a moment's pain.

The minute he touched the sharpened tip of the

athame to her skin, she closed her eyes and chanted louder. With an unspoken curse, he sliced the blade across her skin and watched, horrified, as her bright red blood beaded, then streamed across her palm. She held her hand over the empty bowl, her chanting and swaying building to a wild crescendo that grabbed him by the throat. He turned the knife on himself and sliced his hand, mingling his blood—Paschal's blood—with hers, then, after listening intently, he repeated the prayer to her voodoo gods.

She squeezed her injured hand tightly, cutting off the flow of blood. He did the same. Still chanting, Cat dipped her uninjured hand into the herbs and added the tiny dried leaves to the bloody bowl. She grabbed a candle, held it high above her head, invoked the goddess Orunmila, and threw the flame into the bowl. The herbs ignited and the scent of coppery blood was immediately swallowed by a burst of pungency. She stirred the tip of the blade in the charred remnants, then held the knife over the map yet again.

Slowly, Ben became aware of how he swayed with Cat, how their bodies moved in synchronized rhythm with the melodious mantra on the CD. His palm stung and his shirt stuck to his body with cold sweat. But before he could register any other detail, the knife fell from her hand and punctured the map.

At this, she stopped. Her eyes flew open, and from the way her irises darted from side to side, he realized she wasn't entirely aware of what had happened. She'd fallen into a powerful trance, one that he wouldn't have believed possible if he hadn't witnessed the scene himself.

She glanced at the map, shaking. Gingerly, he took her injured hand in his.

"He's here," she said.

Ben glanced at the location, sighing in relief when he realized his father wasn't so far away that they couldn't reach him before dawn. She'd done it. She'd found him. She'd endured both physical and emotional pain on his behalf—for a man she'd never met.

Driven by emotions he couldn't name, he lifted her hand in his and pried her fingers until her fist unclenched and he could see the wound within.

He kissed her hand, directly above the cut, then led her wordlessly into the guest bathroom, where he rinsed her wound, then did the same to his. In silence, he retrieved antibiotic ointment from the medicine cabinet, applied it to her cut, then wrapped the gash in gauze. She returned the favor, slowly, carefully, without a breath of a word spoken.

When she was done, the tiny bathroom seemed to shrink. Their bodies barely fit in the enclosed space, and yet fit perfectly.

"Thank you," he said, finally breaking the quiet ringing in his ears, drumming out the flare of passion that ignited the moment he realized she was just a few inches away from him, wearing next to nothing, dizzy from the magic she'd invoked on his father's behalf.

"We haven't found him yet," she said, ducking away and returning to the study. She removed the knife and was examining the map by candlelight when Ben mustered the strength to follow.

"He's close."

"Not too far," she replied. "Hill Country. But we have to get there fast, Ben. He doesn't have much time."

24

"Don't stand too close to the edge," a voice warned, startling Alexa so that she nearly lost her balance on the dock.

She spun to find her stepbrother standing behind her, his walnut leather duffel bag slung over his shoulder while he puffed on a Dunhill cigarette.

"What are you doing here?"

"The problem in Boston was resolved," he said. "Apparently, we don't pay certain maintenance men what they think they're worth."

Alexa had to muster all her brainpower to remember what he was talking about. Oh, yeah. The sabotage in Boston. Just a disgruntled worker. Good. But that information could easily have been conveyed by phone. Which left a question. "That doesn't explain why you're back in Florida."

"Bored." He took one last drag on his cigarette, then flicked the butt into the ocean.

"Of course," she said, turning away from her brother and taking a deep breath. She loved Jacob, but his timing sucked.

She'd stayed later than planned at the suite, trying to come up with a plan for securing Damon's freedom without invoking Rogan's magic. Distance from Damon had allowed her to attack the problem with all her business acumen. Without experts, she made lists of what they knew about the castle, the magic, the diary, Paschal Rousseau and Lord Rogan. Each bit of information they'd gathered produced questions—questions that might lead to the elusive solution, if Damon cooperated.

Her brief conversation with Cat told her that Paschal Rousseau still had not been located, but that she and Paschal's son, Ben, were nearly certain the crime was related to the researcher's knowledge of Valoren. Meaning, he might know a way to set Damon free, if, as she suspected, he knew about Rogan and his curse.

She supposed magic like Rogan's would be very valuable. Look at what Damon could conjure from thin air. She'd known people who had sold their souls for less—had that been why Paschal Rousseau had been taken hostage without any request for ransom? To unlock the secrets to Lord Rogan's sorcery? And she couldn't help but wonder why now . . . just after Cat had started poking around. Coincidence of timing or not, until Cat and Ben recovered Paschal, Alexa had to keep Damon from using Rogan's magic. If the black evil infected him completely, she might never break him free.

In the distance, she saw the boat she'd chartered approaching the dock after refueling. Paulie, a saucy blond grad student with salt water in her veins, waved warmly from the captain's chair.

Alexa picked up her bag. "Go back to the hotel, then," she told Jacob. "We'll talk in the morning."

"We'll talk now," Jacob said. "I'm going with you."

"Excuse me?"

Jacob dug his hands into the pockets of his jeans. "Rumor has it you've been spending every night at the castle since I left. I want to see you sleep on a hard stone floor."

"I had a room done up," she lied. "A room that sleeps one. And since I'm perfectly safe in *my* castle on *my* own, I'll see you in the morning."

She grabbed her bag and proceeded down the pier, relieved when she didn't hear Jacob's footsteps behind her. As she boarded the boat, he saluted. Only after

Paulie shoved off did Jacob sprint down the pier and jump onto the deck, grinning at his own moxie.

The young captain dashed in front of Alexa. "Who the hell are you?"

"Ask her," he said.

Alexa cursed. "I didn't invite you along, Jacob."

"Since when does family need an invitation?"

Since I'm going to see my phantom lover, you twit.

"Since I need some time alone," she answered.

He stepped closer, but apparently, Paulie's expression made him stop before he was too close. "What secret are you keeping?" he asked. "You've never been reticent with me before."

Only because she'd never had secrets worth keeping until now. Work, work and more work didn't require caution. Now larger-than-life, amazing, unbelievable, intimate things had been happening to her. Things she might never have believed less than a week ago.

And she wasn't thinking about the magic.

"I'm not being secretive; I'm being private. There's a difference. Unless, of course, you want to pour your heart out to me about where you go on those jaunts of yours every other weekend? Or the large packages that arrive at the house every month with no return address? Or maybe you'd like to show me the second cell phone you keep, the one that never rings with numbers I recognize?"

Jacob stared at her, expressionless. "I don't know what you're talking about."

She crossed her arms tightly on her chest and told Paulie she could stand down. The captain headed back to her helm, out of earshot, but watching Jacob keenly. Alexa stepped closer so Jacob wouldn't miss a single syllable of her response. "Let's just say that our brother-sister relationship isn't about one of us being *bound* to the other. I mean, I may have tried to *whip* you into corporate shape for the good of the company, but I don't expect you to act *submissive* to me."

Jacob forced a chuckle at her seemingly nonsensical response, but his discomfort oozed from the pores on his forehead and above his lip. "My personal life is none of your business."

"Exactly. And mine is none of yours."

Paulie leaped onto the pier and resecured the bow line to the cleat. When Jacob made no move to disembark, the captain cleared her throat. Jacob spared her a glance and quickly accepted that two stubborn women weren't worth the trouble. He gave Alexa another salute, grabbed his bag and returned to the dock.

Seconds later, Paulie joined her on the boat, her gloved hands automatically coiling the line. "You okay?"

Alexa swallowed deeply, but her throat remained dry. Something in Jacob's eyes seemed different . . . and yet, familiar. Like the Jacob of the old days, when he cared more about rebellion than he did about his Rolex.

"I'm fine. My brother is overprotective sometimes."

Paulie smirked as she climbed into the captain's chair. "Is that what you call that look? Cause, hon, it looked like pure, unadulterated hatred to me."

The young captain turned her attention to the helm, her observation hanging heavy in the air. As the boat pulled away from the dock, Alexa watched Jacob laze his way toward the marina. He watched them depart. The distance was too great for her to gauge his expression, but a chill chased up her spine anyway. With a shake, she banished the reaction to the back of her mind. She had more important things to think about right now than her stepbrother.

Like Damon.

She wanted him to stay. In her castle. In her bed. Not to fulfill some fantasy and not to haunt her hotel guests. She wanted him with her, fully flesh and blood, to share her life. But once they secured his complete freedom, she knew he'd leave. She expected him to set off immediately to discover what happened to his family, to Rogan, to his estate and title. Roles reversed, she'd do the same. He had no tie to her. No obligation.

Too bad she felt inexorably tied to him.

The whole affair had started as a fairy-tale fantasy, but now their connection was painfully real. At least to her. He'd made her face things about herself, about her life—about her future—that she couldn't ignore. For the first time in years, she looked forward to the next day, the next hour, the next minute—not because of the money she'd make or the expectations she'd satisfy, but because of the man who'd traveled across centuries and landed in her life like a gift.

And Alexa knew better than to ever refuse a gift.

Time slowed, a contrast to the swiftness of the wind against her face. Nightfall had come and gone. She'd run late and then had been delayed by Jacob. When Paulie slowed the vessel near the entrance to the lagoon, Alexa's gaze locked on the castle looming above a wall of prickly tropical plants and prayed she wasn't too late.

Once Paulie released the anchor, Alexa grabbed her bag and joined her captain at the stern of the boat, where she kept an inflatable skiff. Paulie had made the journey with her once without incident, yet Alexa noticed the younger woman still looked nervous, even after the motorized raft's hull scraped against the bleached white lagoon sand.

The sunset had turned the sky into a brilliant prism of reds, pinks and oranges while she'd been arguing with Jacob, but now a deep indigo overtook what would be a starry sky. "You look nervous," Alexa said, climbing out and accepting her bag from Paulie. "You know I'm safe here, right?"

Paulie glanced at the castle. "On this island, I think safety may be relative. I'm not from around here originally, so I didn't grow up with all the legends and lore, but those salts at the marina have a good time filling my head with horror stories."

Alexa tried to stifle a grin. "Do you believe these tales of ghosts and curses?"

Paulie snickered. "Do you want me to?"

Just a few days ago, Alexa would have said yes. She would have wanted to feed the fables until no one could resist making a reservation at her castle, if only to find out if the stories were true. Now thoughts of establishing her independent reputation outside of her father's legacy meant next to nothing. Not when a man's soul was at stake.

Paulie floated the skiff back into the water. "Check your phone. Make sure you can reach me if you need rescuing."

Alexa did as her captain instructed. The satellite device responded perfectly, so with her usual promise to call when she wanted to leave, she waved good-bye.

With her flashlight skimming the area as she moved, she followed the now familiar path to the fissure in the wall that would lead her to the castle. Again, the overgrowth snapped at her, and again, she persevered until the castle was only a few yards away.

The moon hung like a priceless pearl in the sky, the glow electrifying the castle walls with a thousand points of diamond light. Candle- and firelight burned inside the stained-glass windows, igniting a rainbow of color against the glittering stone. She couldn't help but think that all future guests to the island should arrive on a full moon so they could witness the castle as she did now.

Joyful. Magnificent. Magical.

She approached warily, but this time, before she even touched the latch, the door slowly swung open.

As if someone had thrust a knife into her windpipe, she faltered. From the foyer to the stairwell and both grand rooms on either side, period furnishings, tapestries, paintings, mosaics and plush carpets overflowed with rich elegance. Damon had spared no detail. Even the cat seemed inordinately pleased as it pranced across the landing, flicking its thick, fluffed tail.

"Damon," she whispered, her stomach aching from what he'd done. "No."

She dropped her pack and shot forward to find him,

then stopped before she had gone six paces. Remembering her brother's odd appearance at the dock, she turned and secured the door. She then dug into her pack and retrieved her satellite phone and, as an afterthought, the flare gun. Despite her warnings and his promises, Damon had re-created every inch of the main floor. What had the magic taken from him in return?

25

Searching for him took more than an hour. Every corner she turned provided yet another stab in her heart, another blow to her ability to hope. Only a few small rooms on the upper floors and a row of small chambers beyond what she learned was the kitchen remained untouched. She was about to backtrack when a frustrated shout rent the air.

She followed the sound through an archway at the very back of the castle. On the other side, she discovered an odd circular room she didn't remember from her initial explorations. Very little distinguished the space from an outdoor patio, except that it had a roof and curved walls on all sides. Otherwise, the floor-to-ceiling windows invited the outdoors in so much that she was shocked to see Damon collapsed onto his knees in the center of the room, his head buried in his hands.

She called his name.

"Leave, Alexa. Now. Before it's too late," he muttered, though even the thready words brimmed with barely checked fury.

Disappointment and loss flooded through her. How could he use the magic so thoughtlessly? He'd known the consequences. How could he risk everything without first giving her a chance?

"What have you done?"

He slapped his hands against the polished marble

floor, and pushed to his feet. He did not face her, but his shoulders bunched with barely contained tension.

"Go."

The word was more growl than command. He'd done so much magic. Did she dare stay?

She took a step forward, her hand outstretched. If she could only . . .

He spun on her. "Go!"

"I won't!"

He charged toward her, slashing his arm as if he meant her to fly backward with the momentum of his movement. She didn't move, but a large urn near the doorway rose into the air and crashed against the wall.

She jumped, startled, but held her ground. He slashed his arm again and the urn's partner exploded. A hailstorm of ceramic shards rained against her legs but did no damage.

Only inches in front her, Damon panted, furious, then stared at his hands. Horror was etched into the stunning planes of his face. Horror at what he'd tried to do? Or at his impotence to hurt her?

When he looked up, his eyes burned. A red glaze had formed over his irises.

"Get. Out," he ordered.

Her heart cracked and the emotional pain nearly doubled her over. Then, completely on instinct, she grabbed his shirt and yanked until her lips crashed against his.

The contact lasted only seconds. He threw her backward and she lost her footing, falling and sliding across the floor. Debris from the shattered urns bit at her hands, but not enough to scare her off.

She stood and dusted the dirt off her slacks. "I won't go."

"Then you'll suffer unspeakable pain," he responded, but the voice wasn't his. He'd clearly gone too far. Too much of Rogan's magic had infected him. Was there any of him left?

"Like you are?" she challenged. "You can't leave,

can you? All that magic, all that power, and you're
still trapped like an animal. Only through me can you
find your way out."

He yelled, fury raising his voice to painful levels.
Lifting his hands, he focused his gaze on the wrought-
iron chandelier hanging above them. The masonry
shook. The stone cracked. The heavy collection of
candles and metal plummeted toward her.

Alexa threw up her hands. Any second now, she
expected the excruciating pain of being crushed beneath solid iron, but nothing happened. She looked
up. Just above her canopied arms, the chandelier had
stopped in midair.

Instantly, she dashed out of the way. The moment
she was clear of danger, the light fixture crashed to
the ground. She flattened herself against the wall,
gasping for breath, while Damon stared at the twisted
remnants, blinking wildly, rubbing his eyes, trying, she
hoped, to break free of the dark infection.

"How did I . . . stop you?" she asked, the question
meant more for herself than the monster Damon had
become. He'd tried to kill her, hadn't he? But he had
not succeeded. Why?

She couldn't assume she'd lived because his heart
wasn't in it. The chandelier would have crushed her
if she hadn't stopped its momentum.

Heat burned between her breasts. She tore her
blouse aside, expecting an injury, but finding the
charm. The charm was protecting her.

But for how long?

After a second, her body and brain caught up with
each other. She could not stay any longer. She ran,
dashing around and through doorways, jumping over
footstools and trunks, knocking over knickknacks, her
entire focus on escaping the castle before Damon
snapped out of his odd trance and pursued. Once at
the front door, she reached for the latch only to find
her way blocked by Damon's materializing form.

She stumbled back. "Leave me alone. You wanted
me to leave."

Sweat splashed down his face and glued his shirt to his body. His eyes continued to glow red, as if a veil of blood had descended over the stormy gray irises. His breathing was heavy. His fists clenched and unclenched. Was he fighting the evil he'd unleashed by using the magic so completely? Or was it too late to help him break free?

With no other option, she tossed herself against him. Her lips crashed against his as she grabbed the damp stays on his shirt and ripped it free from his body. If touches and kisses had cleansed him of Rogan's evil before, then she'd have to go farther to save him this time.

He shoved his hands between them and pushed her away.

"Don't touch me!" he ordered.

She tore off her blouse and kicked off her shoes. "Touch me, then," she countered, just as forcefully.

He took a step away from her, but didn't dematerialize or strike out at her again. As she unclipped her bra, his gaze feasted on her bare breasts. She could feel his eyes rake a path over her, and for a split second, she glimpsed the Damon within. Her nipples hardened and a surge of need flooded through her until her blood burned.

She shimmied out of her slacks and panties. Bare to him in the dazzling light from the torches, Alexa experienced a vulnerability that nearly broke her down. Her legs shook. Her knees threatened to buckle. Her heart pounded so hard, her chest ached. A war played across his face and she knew she'd made the only choice.

She drew her hands up her body, sliding her palms from her thighs to her abdomen, then lifting her breasts tauntingly. "You know you need me," she whispered, flicking her thumbs across her thick, dark nipples. "Take what you want."

In a split second, his clothes flashed off his body. His sex jutted from his groin. Hunger raged behind his eyes. She braced herself, but when his hands clamped over her shoulders and his mouth descended on her neck, she hooked one leg around his waist and gave in to the need.

She couldn't hold back. She couldn't allow her fear to waylay her passion. In a leap of faith unlike any other, she surrendered to the madness of his lust. She speared her hands into his hair, lifted his head and kissed him wildly, their tongues battling without surrender. She streaked her nails down his muscled back, then gripped his buttocks with keen possession, grinding her sex into his until he could resist no longer. He spun them and lifted her flat against the door, then thrust inside her, his hardness blinding her with rough sensations she'd never known.

He grabbed her thighs, buoying her against him as he found a rampant rhythm. Clutching her arms around his neck, she lifted herself high. Hungrily, he took her breasts into his mouth even as he drove deep, long and hard. He bit. He pumped. Awareness of anything beyond him and the ecstasy building in her body disappeared. She lost track of time—lost track even of her purpose.

She only knew she wanted him. For now. For always.

When he came, he howled, arching his back and shouting to the ceiling as hot fire burned inside her. When he looked down at her again, wet streaks cut grooves into his face.

And the only color in his eyes was silvery, stormy gray.

26

Paschal stood beside the barred window, his profile even more striking with moonlight playing across the planes of his face.

"Nice place," he said as Gemma shut the door behind her and raised the volume on the piped-in music. "Though I find it hard to believe that all this security is just for me. How inept must you people be if you need armed guards and security bars to keep an old man from slipping away?"

She turned so her face wasn't visible to the not-so-hidden camera. "I don't much care if you escape, Monsieur Rousseau, not so long as you tell me the location of the Queen's Charm before you leave."

Paschal arched a curious, if not stunned, brow. Gemma had calculated that her use of the necklace's proper name would evoke a response from the Gypsy researcher. Even Farrow didn't know what the golden triangle was called, and thanks to her, he had no clue as to its potential power.

"I'm disappointed," he said finally, his expression cool and inscrutable, "No seductive come-ons? No womanly wiles meant to loosen my tongue? I've used the facilities and brushed my teeth for nothing, then?"

She narrowed her gaze. Any other man wouldn't dare mock her, and yet, this one made her laugh. At him. At the situation. And admittedly, at herself. "There's no time, I'm afraid. I just intercepted news that a hotelier by the name of Alexa Chandler has taken possession of property that is rightfully mine. I can only get it back with the Queen's Charm."

"How is this property yours?"

"By birth," she stated simply, but then her bitterness broke through and she allowed her tone to drip with it. "Though no one around here believes I deserve it because I lack a Y chromosome."

His gaze locked on her. She nearly shrank back under his scrutiny—but only nearly.

"Where is this place?"

"An island off the coast of Florida."

A corner of his mouth quirked. Not in a grin, exactly, but he knew what she was talking about, that was for sure. "So you're a child of Valoren?"

She sneered. "I'm not Gypsy, if that's what you mean."

"Then what are you?"

She stepped fully into his personal space. "A woman who is running out of patience. I want the charm."

"I don't know where it is," he replied.

"You're lying," she insisted.

"I wish I were. I had the necklace years ago, but I'm afraid it was stolen. You're one step behind your rival, I'm afraid. Who is, I suspect," he said, the lilt of a guess in his voice, "your brother?"

Gemma's heart clenched in her chest. There was a family resemblance. Supposedly around the eyes, though she didn't see it. "You know Keith?"

Paschal rubbed his chin, his strong, square jaw speckled with white stubble. "We've met. He took my class at the university. I don't think he realized that I knew who he was. Honestly, took some time for me to figure it out. He had a tattoo. Gave him away."

Gemma nodded. She had that same tattoo, but not in a place visible to the general public.

"So he has the Queen's Charm?" she asked, her tone bitter. She'd wondered, when she'd taken Farrow's side in the schism, why Keith hadn't been more upset. He'd been one step ahead of her, the prick.

"I assume he has it, but I do not know for sure. The necklace was, however, stolen from me before he was born. Twenty years ago now. I'd returned to Germany to figure out where I went wrong in unlocking Rogan's secrets. A common thief snatched it from my hotel room safe. Poor bugger likely had no idea of its true purpose and power. Probably pawned it for a pint. Then, a few months ago," he said, his eyes twinkling as if she'd find this portion of the tale amusing, "the charm surfaced with a jewelry dealer in Berlin. Unfortunately, by the time I arrived at the shop, a young American man had paid an obscene amount to entice the dealer to sell it to him rather than to me."

"Keith doesn't have obscene amounts of money," she argued.

"I suspect, though, he has friends who do?"

Click. Alexa Chandler. Jacob Sharpe. He was the hotelier's stepbrother and he had at least as much money as Farrow, likely more, at his disposal.

"At first," Paschal went on, oblivious to Gemma's revelation, "I supposed this American thought it would be a nice trinket for his girlfriend. But then I heard about the fractious doings within the K'vr—"

She gasped.

"Yes," he said with a nod, "I know of the K'vr. One cannot explore the history and legacy of Lord Rogan without knowing of the K'vr, my dear. Charming group, yours."

Paschal's dismissive attitude infuriated her, but she held her tongue. This wily old man could prove even more useful than she'd originally imagined, even without the Queen's Charm. If her brother had it, she'd need to rethink her alliances. If Farrow had somehow acquired it and his quest to recover it through her had simply been a ruse to keep her busy while he usurped all the power for himself, that changed things as well.

She'd always assumed that her techno-addicted baby brother had not taken the time, as she had, to read the actual books, letters, diaries and sociological

papers about the history of Lord Rogan and the followers of the K'vr that had been handed down
through generations. According to her studies, the
K'vr had possessed the charm sometime in the eighteen hundreds. The leader at the time—a great-great
uncle twice removed or some such—had explored the
charm's magic to near obsession.

He'd learned that the necklace that had once belonged to a Hanoverian queen who'd then bestowed
the trinket upon a British nobleman sent as governor
to the Gypsy haven of Valoren, was literally a key.
The magic woven into the links of the gold chain and
the delicate points of the interlocked triangles not only
provided a powerful protection spell, but had been
enhanced by Rogan himself to immunize the wearer
against his magic.

With the key in her possession, Gemma would finally enter the castle of Valoren, now rebuilt on an
island off the Florida coast. And inside, Rogan's magic
existed. The source of his legendary power would be
hers for the taking. Once she was inside.

"So you know what it does?" she asked.

"Quite," he replied.

Gemma grabbed Paschal by the arm. "Does the
source of the magic exist in the castle? Will the charm
get me what I want?"

He countered her move and wrapped his hand
around her wrist, his thumb pressed painfully between
her wrist bones. Strength surged through his wrinkled
skin. "You know what I know, don't you?"

"Let go of me," she ordered.

The corner of his mouth tilted into a sardonic smile.
"You weren't so adverse to my touch yesterday."

"Yesterday, I thought you had what I wanted." He
loosened his grip and she yanked free. "Now you're
useless."

"Am I?"

She marched toward the door, but the cockiness in
his voice stopped her. She turned. If ever a man re-

sembled a cat who ate the canary, it was Paschal Rousseau.

"What aren't you telling me?"

With a flick of his gaze, Paschal alerted Gemma that he knew about the surveillance equipment. Clearly, he wasn't simply an erudite professor with obscure tastes in Gypsy artifacts. He knew about the K'vr. About the inner strife for leadership. About her brother. Though a copy had been hard to find, she'd read his paper on the existence of Valoren and the cover-up by the court of King George II to erase its existence from the history books. Apparently, he knew, as she did, that the colony had been a breeding ground for unparalleled magic—magic she intended to take for herself.

"The charm alone will not invoke the magic you seek," he informed her casually. "I know. I tried."

"You?"

"Twice. Once in Germany, and once"—he moved forward, wrapped his arms around her waist, thrust her close and whispered into her ear—"after *I* moved the castle to Florida."

He nibbled on her neck, which she supposed played well for the camera. Thankfully, she was facing the window, so her shocked expression remained out of anyone's view. Farrow himself likely wasn't watching, since he'd called a meeting with the elders of the K'vr—a gathering he'd kept her from attending by demanding she get answers from Rousseau before the night was through. She suspected his blind faith in her had started to falter. Between that and the news about Alexa Chandler, which she'd intercepted, Gemma was running out of time. No more games. She needed Rousseau's knowledge, but not here. If Farrow had even an inkling of suspicion that she planned to double-cross him, they'd both be dead within the hour.

She closed her eyes and, for a few moments, allowed Paschal's skilled lips to soothe away the tension in her neck and shoulders. She supposed she'd made worse bargains than trading sexual favors for information from a fascinating man like Paschal. He clearly knew more than even Farrow suspected. Her smartest move would be to get him out of the estate now, while Farrow was occupied and darkness was on her side.

"If your brother has the charm," he murmured, "he's one step ahead of you."

She retrieved Paschal's hand from kneading into her buttocks and pulled him toward the door. "Come on," she instructed.

"Where are we going?"

She looked straight at the hidden camera. "To tell Farrow what you just told me. He'll be eternally grateful, *monsieur*."

She glanced at the barred window, at the door, then winked. Paschal's crooked grin told her he understood. Once they'd escaped, she'd pump him for the rest of the information he undoubtedly possessed. If he knew the charm wasn't enough to gain entrance to the castle, did he know what else she'd need?

Tearing open the door, she was immediately confronted by two of Farrow's armed guards.

She grabbed the muzzle of one's gun and shoved it out of her face. "How dare you! Professor Rousseau has important information for Farrow. Move out of my way."

They complied. Walking proudly, Gemma strutted down the corridor, Paschal's hand still tight in hers. Once at the archway, a right turn would lead them to Farrow's suite. Left led into the main rooms of the house, through which they could access the grounds and, if lucky, escape.

At the end of the hall, Gemma moved to the left, but Paschal tugged her hard toward the right.

She opened her mouth to protest, but he placed a soft finger over her lips and moved her out of the sight of the guards.

"If there's one thing I've learned in my many years, my dear, it's that subtlety can be a valuable skill."

They had to keep moving. Security cameras were everywhere. If they hesitated too long, they'd be found.

"So you really want to tell Farrow what you told me?" she asked.

"Farrow Pryce? That power-hungry upstart? Good God, no. But I also don't think his associates will allow us to waltz out the front door, no matter how incredibly persuasive you are."

"I haven't persuaded you of anything."

"Don't underestimate yourself. You've persuaded me to help you." He glanced briefly down the hall, then reached up and tapped a decorative tile on the wall. A panel immediately swung open and he yanked her inside mere seconds before it slid shut again.

They were drowned in darkness. "How did you know this was here?" she whispered.

His chuckle belonged to a much younger man. "I know something about secret passageways. Judging by the fortified armaments, I guessed this hacienda was owned by a drug lord or other unscrupulous type. And drug lords always have secret passageways."

"That doesn't explain—"

"Is now the time, or should we simply make a run for it?"

At that moment, an alarm sounded. Screeching wails blasted around them, though the painful pitch was muted by the walls behind which they hid.

"I guess someone figured out we're up to no good," she said.

"It's been years since I've been up to no good," Paschal said wistfully, then tugged her tight into his arms. "Let's make the most of it, shall we?"

"This is Mariah. You know what to do."

With a curse, Ben snapped his cell phone shut. He'd already left three messages. Why he'd thought for five seconds that his ex would be hanging around town, twiddling her thumbs, waiting to provide aid in his personal crisis, he didn't know. Mariah Hunter was a lot of things, but accessible wasn't one of them—not unless she had something to gain.

"Any luck?" Cat asked, glancing at him from the driver's seat.

He shoved the phone into his pocket. "No, but keep going. I know where she keeps her bird. I'm sure she won't mind if I borrow it for a few hours."

"What if she's taken it?"

Ben would deal with that contingency when and if necessary. Born into a family of bush pilots from the Northern Territory of Australia, Mariah preferred her Cessna to her Eurocopter. She'd won the chopper in a poker game and the craft had saved both their asses more than once during their string of retrieval operations in southern Mexico. Ben hoped the whirlybird would provide the same good luck this time. If Cat's visions were accurate—and he had no reason to believe they weren't—they didn't have much time to rescue Paschal from the Hill Country before all hell broke loose.

"If she's got the bird," he replied, "we'll take her Cessna and make do."

"Do you always go around stealing your ex-girlfriend's flying machines?"

He eyed her suspiciously. "I didn't say she was my ex-girlfriend."

"You didn't have to. There's a growl in your voice when you say her name. Not a sexy growl, either. More like a mad dog."

"I don't growl," he claimed, but even he heard the guttural undertone in his voice.

Cat snickered and Ben just shook his head. He should have known better than to try and be coy around a gifted psychic like Cat, whose abilities were growing every minute.

"Ma-ri-ah," he said, stringing out the name so he could enunciate each syllable without snarling, "owes me. And right now, she's all we've got."

Without his reminding her, Cat switched lanes and

took the exit that led to Mariah's hangar. "I called Alexa," she offered. "She's not answering her satellite phone, but her assistant is on alert and can arrange a ride for us in thirty minutes, tops. Crown Chandler has all sorts of private transportation at its disposal."

Ben checked his watch. They were only ten minutes from the private airport on the outskirts of San Antonio where many of the pilots had questionable pasts, so for the right price, few questions were asked. If the guards remembered him, they would be able to get in and out with minimal fuss.

"That'll be Plan B, but we're too close to Mariah's place to wait for Alexa to pull her strings and get us a lift. Let's just hope we won't need a Plan C."

As they pulled off the highway onto an unlit, single-lane road, Ben had to face the fact that seeking out Mariah was more than just necessary to save his father. Until Cat came into his life, Ben had thought that his ex had destroyed his ability to trust and his ability to care about a woman who, with her innate sensual power, had the means to carve even the strongest man's heart into a bitter shell. Ben hadn't realized how high he'd valued his romantic ideals until Mariah had torn them down.

His mother had loved his father in ways Ben never could completely understand. And his father had capitulated to his mother's every whim—except when it conflicted with one of his mysterious jaunts to retrieve this or that item related to Gypsy lore. Ben had taken up antiquities hunting honestly, so to speak, then had fallen hard for Mariah the first time she'd acted as his partner in crime. He'd been a fool, but so what? He was done hating himself for wearing his heart on his sleeve, where Mariah had had easy access to rip it to shreds. In the four years since their definitive breakup, he'd healed. He'd kept his relationships superficial, but he'd healed.

If he hadn't, Cat wouldn't have seeped into his bloodstream so easily.

Luckily for Ben, Cat was as resourceful as she was

beautiful. With a wad of cash provided by her heiress friend, Cat bought them onto the airfield property. Two hidden keys, three security codes and a picked lock later, and they were in Mariah's hangar. Thanks to his ex's obsessive need to be ready to depart in the shortest amount of time, Ben and Cat were in the air in less than an hour.

"She's going to kill you, isn't she?" Cat asked into the speaker that fed into Ben's headphones.

"If she hasn't killed me by now, taking her bird in an emergency isn't going to push her over the edge."

Cat flashed him a dubious look, then opened the map across her lap. She'd circled the area where she'd sensed Paschal was being held, and Ben had already charted the coordinates into the navigation system. Compared to Mariah, he was a rank amateur as a pilot, but he could get them there.

Question was, could he get them back?

Even at dicey airstrips like Mariah's, security kept him from bringing his gun with him. Fortunately, he'd known where to look for Mariah's. He had a high-powered rifle for himself and a pistol for Cat, though she'd refused to touch the weapon unless absolutely necessary. Another difference between her and Mariah.

They seemed to be adding up, which forced Ben to realize that he was, like so many men before him, a complete and total idiot.

After twenty minutes in the air, Cat asked, "We should be close now, right?"

He checked the navigation computer and found she was correct. "You've got a great sense of direction."

Catalina smirked. "Thanks to this," she said, holding up the catalog of swords she had taken from his father's secret room. Of all of Paschal's belongings, including the diary, she'd claimed this one had given off the most intense vibrations. His father hadn't shown much interest in weaponry before. Gypsies weren't the types to sign up for anyone's war. But he didn't waste time questioning her. Not with his father's life on the line.

"We need to go in low," he said, scanning the countryside, "and look for a clearing where we can put this down as close to the place where they're holding him as possible. Since they didn't ask for ransom or contact anyone, they're likely not expecting a rescue attempt."

And yet, as they flew over the estate where Cat sensed Paschal was being held, Ben spotted fortifications that made his skin crawl. Far from any lit road, the spacious hacienda was surrounded by a tall fence, likely electrified, judging by the red lights on the posts that blinked at regular intervals. The land abutted a shadowy ravine. The rock slope, even from a distance, looked difficult to traverse without equipment, and while Mariah was an accomplished climber, he doubted she stored her gear on board the whirlybird.

Otherwise, he'd done the right thing in hijacking Mariah's helicopter. By land, they'd be spotted easily. Trouble was, how could they possibly put down inside the grounds without being seen? They couldn't. But if they landed nearby and hiked in, how would they get past the electrified fence?

"We could always knock on the front door," Cat suggested.

He understood the irony in her tone when he saw armed men standing in the lit entryway. Unfortunately, they saw him as well. One fired. The other tore inside.

Ben pulled up and spun away from the estate. Once clear, he found a safe spot to hover while he organized his thoughts.

"We're not ready for this kind of operation," Ben said. He loved his father. He couldn't bear to think he'd be hurt simply because his son failed to come up with a decent plan.

Cat reached across and laid her hand on his leg. "Too bad for us. We either move in now or never."

"Did you sense something?"

Closing her eyes, Cat paused before replying. "Anxiety. Trouble is, I don't know if it's mine or your father's. Or even yours."

"I'm not nervous."

"Of course you are. You're diving headfirst into a dangerous situation with no reconnaissance and no clue if my vision is even remotely accurate. For all you know, your father is hundreds of miles away and I'm just some freak who has delusions of grandeur."

Ben laughed, covering her hand with his. "You? Not possible. You're just an average nutcase. Beautiful, sexy and resourceful, but still crazy as hell for hanging out with me."

"Now isn't the time to discuss the advantages of mental health," Cat said, scanning the landscape below them. "I say we put this baby down on the other side of those trees, kill the engine and figure out what to do next."

"Have you got a plan?"

"I thought that was your specialty."

Ben piloted the chopper to the clearing she'd indicated, grinning as ideas started spinning through his head, each crazier and riskier than the last.

27

As the secret panel leading into the garage slid open, Gemma tucked her blouse back into her slacks. The alarms had stopped. An army of footsteps had stomped out of the hacienda, including, if she wasn't mistaken, the cool, clipped gait of Farrow Pryce. If she was going to move Paschal, she had to act without delay.

He eased up behind her, the scent of his cologne screwing with her senses in ways she didn't want to admit.

"Now what, Mata Hari?"

"We get the hell out of here," she replied.

"You don't think Pryce alerted his guards to stop us?"

"Probably. That's why we need to act fast."

The garage was deserted. The security cameras inside this portion of the house activated when a garage door was opened—either the one from the house or the one that led outside. They had a few minutes to work out a plan—but no more.

Though the garage was designed to hold four vehicles, only one car, a luxury Lexus, was parked inside.

She retrieved the spare key from the utility closet and popped the trunk.

"Get in," she instructed.

He eyed her warily. "You expect me to fold this old body into that cramped space?"

She scoffed noisily. "I just experienced what you

can do with that so-called old body of yours in another cramped space. Don't wimp out on me now."

"I do not," he grumbled, swinging one leg into the trunk, "wimp out. Ever."

"Explain what happened in the passageway, then," she challenged.

"Alas, no time," he answered cockily. "I'm not quite as young as I used to be. Besides, certain things should not be rushed."

"So you say," she countered, helping him in the rest of the way while trying to forget just how skillful he'd been up to the point where he couldn't finish what he started. "One of these days, you're going to have to prove it."

He winked as she grabbed the top of the trunk. "One of these days, I will."

She slammed the trunk, closed the secret panel, then dashed into the driver's seat. She'd always planned to turn the tables on Farrow and betray him, but she'd had a coup d'état in mind, not an unplanned, reckless escape. But Paschal Rousseau had the information she needed, and if Farrow got it before she did, she'd have no chance to take the leadership of the K'vr. Better to escape with the man now and hope she could beat Farrow at another time.

She'd have to think on her feet. She'd always been more of a planner, but if her pleasurable, though incomplete, time in the dark passageway with Paschal Rousseau had taught her anything, it was that preconceived notions meant nothing when someone was properly motivated.

With a deep breath for fortification, she opened the garage door at the same time she turned on the engine.

"Here we go," she said loudly, intending for Paschal to hear but not respond. "Hang on."

She backed out with lightning speed, flinging the car into a controlled half circle and then shooting down the long driveway, past the dozen or so armed guards jogging across the lawn. No one fired at her. Good.

The order to consider her a traitor had not yet gone out.

She proceeded unchallenged until the guard gate loomed in front of her. If she burst through, a hail of gunfire would pepper the back of the car, negating her need for an escape in the first place, since Paschal would be Swiss cheese. She had to stop and talk her way out of Farrow's compound, just as she'd talked her way in all those months ago.

And to that end, she unbuttoned the top of her blouse.

"Where's Farrow?" she asked as her window automatically lowered. "I was just out of the shower when the alarm sounded. Paschal still missing?"

"A helicopter buzzed the building," the guard told her even as he aimed his pistol directly at her head. "Rousseau's not in his room. Pryce said he was with you."

She glanced down at her cleavage, knowing the guard would follow her eyes.

He did, though he didn't lower his gun.

"I was on my way to interrogate him when I"—she lowered her lashes and her voice seductively—"decided to . . . freshen up a bit first. I hardly had time to dress." She giggled girlishly.

When the guard leaned forward to leer into the car, she slammed the door open, knocking the man in the gut at the same time she grabbed the barrel of his gun and tugged it from his grip. He twisted to grab the rifle leaning against the guardhouse. One shot at close range later and Gemma was peeling from the driveway yet again.

"We're clear!" she shouted.

The backseat tilted down. "You shot the poor man," Paschal reproached.

"Him or me, *monsieur*. Stay down. We're not clear yet."

Headlights gleamed behind her. She jammed the gas pedal to the floor of the car, kicking up dirt from the unpaved road as she accelerated. She had no idea where she was going or how she was supposed to outrun the legion of four-by-fours Farrow had when she was driving a luxury Lexus. Then she remembered the guard. A helicopter buzzing the property in the middle of the night? That was no accident.

"Did you hear what the guard said about the chopper? Could someone be coming to your rescue?"

"My son pilots various aircraft, but he'd have no way of knowing where I was, unless your people were sloppy. Were they?"

She had no clue. Her part in the kidnapping hadn't commenced until after Paschal had been delivered to the hacienda. Though she had met the young K'vr neophyte who'd executed the crime. Mean, yes. Devious, clearly. Overly bright? Not so much.

"Good chance."

Paschal was silent for a moment, prompting Gemma to adjust the rearview away from the nearing headlights in order to focus on Paschal's face. In the darkness, she could see nothing.

"Paschal?"

"Yes, it's him. Head"—he paused, then after a few moments finished with—"east. On the other side of a thick ridge of cypress. Along a river. Very lush."

She knew the trees. They bordered the property on the east side, but they were now heading south. "That ridge is behind us. And how do you know where they are?"

Paschal chuckled as if she'd just told him a quaint joke during a leisurely drive rather than asking him an unanswerable question in the midst of a car chase. Seconds later, gunfire pinged off the back bumper. With a yelp, Paschal pushed his way through to the inside of the car, then with a series of grunts and curses, into the front seat.

"A little birdie told me," he replied.

She twisted the steering wheel, throwing the car into a sharp bank to the left around a clump of scrub oak. Behind her, one truck sped by. The second completed the turn and remained about fifty yards behind.

"I hope this little birdie can fly us out of here."

Paschal gulped audibly, bracing his hands on the dashboard. "That's the idea."

She tossed Paschal the gun.

"Take out the tires," she ordered.

He glared at her. "Do you know how difficult that is to do? This isn't a movie."

"And you're not Sean Connery, yet I find you strangely attractive."

Gunfire pierced the car again, this time shattering their back window.

"Not Sean Connery, indeed," he said with a huff, rolling down his window and shifting his body so he could fire behind him.

Gemma lowered herself in the seat and concentrated on moving forward. She glanced at the sky but saw nothing resembling a hovering helicopter. Paschal cursed each time his bullets whizzed impotently past their mark. When one finally connected with the front passenger tire of their pursuers' vehicle, he slid back into the car with an enthusiastic pump of his fist.

The sport utility vehicle behind them swerved, hit a tree stump, then flipped and spun before landing with a thud along the trail. Gemma slammed to a halt.

She hadn't realized how wildly her heart had been pumping inside her ribs until a dead silence, invaded only by the running engine, settled over the scene.

And then—chopper blades.

Paschal got out of the car. The wind kicked up dirt, sand and leaves, causing him to duck back in. Only after the helicopter landed and a stunning brunette jumped out of the vehicle did he emerge again, Gemma with him.

"Professor Rousseau, I presume?" the dark-haired woman said, running in a half crouch toward them, her hand extended.

"Just as I presume you're my little bird," he replied.

"I'm more cat than canary, but I'm glad you received my message."

"That's a potent psychic power you have there, my dear."

She waved at the pilot. "It's becoming damned useful, but it won't stop bullets. The SUV you eluded doubled back. We saw them from the air. We need to get you out now."

Gemma's heart lurched and she pushed Paschal toward the waiting helicopter. "Get out of here. I'll delay them."

"And you are?" the woman asked.

"Someone who's about to ensure not only an escape, but that you have a clear shot from here to Rogan's castle."

"How did you—?" the woman questioned.

"Never mind," Gemma said.

In the distance, headlights broke through the darkness. They ducked and ran toward the copter. The woman slid open the door and waved Paschal inside.

He stopped, turned, grabbed Gemma by the shoulders and kissed her soundly.

In an instant, she visualized him in his youth. Virile. Charming. Irresistible. If only she'd met him then, she might not have focused on such single-minded pursuits as magic and power and legacies. She might have, once in her life, wanted to have sex for reasons beyond working her way up the K'vr ladder of leadership.

"Come with us," Paschal said, shouting over the increased grind from the rotor blades.

"I'll meet up with you," she promised. "But first, I have to throw Farrow off the scent. Send him in another direction."

"What if he doesn't believe you?"

She laughed and yanked him toward the door. "You underestimate my powers of persuasion. Go! Unlock the magic. But don't forget who it rightfully belongs to."

Finally, he ducked inside the copter, and gave the pilot—who she assumed was his son—a pat on the shoulder before buckling himself in. The dark-haired woman turned to her. The headlights were close

enough so that Gemma could see the outline of Farrow's personal Cadillac Escalade.

"Punch me," she yelled at the woman.

"What?"

Gemma threw a swing, connecting with the side of
the woman's head. She stumbled but didn't fall.

"You did *not* just do that," the woman yelled.

"Yes, I did. And I'll do it again if it means saving
my damned life. And yours. Now punch me."

In a blurred spin, the woman kicked. Gemma felt
her jaw snap just before she hit the ground hard.

In a haze of pain and disorientation, she watched
the helicopter rise into the air. As the sound of the
blades receded, she registered commands coming from
the direction of the car.

"Gemma? Gemma?"

Farrow.

She attempted to grin, but the pain spiked and she
rolled onto her stomach.

"What happened, baby? Were they headed to that
island? I just got a communiqué. Where's Rousseau
going?"

Mustering all her strength, will, resolve and stubbornness, Gemma pushed one more lie through her
bleeding mouth before she surrendered to the darkness.

"What have I—?"

Alexa cut off his shock with a kiss.

He indulged her for a moment, then pulled away.

"I nearly . . ." Shame shook his voice and turned
his eyes to liquid silver.

She splayed her hands on either side of his face.
"But you didn't. You're free of the evil, Damon. Now,
finish what you've started."

She clutched him tighter with her legs and he immediately knew what she needed. Back against the door,
he thrust inside her again, this time more gently, until
she tumbled over the brink into ecstasy.

Still holding tight to her, he braced his forehead against hers and tried to catch his breath.

"I—"

"Don't say anything."

"We can't stay here."

She lifted his chin. "You can take me anywhere, just not by magic. No. More. Magic."

He lowered her to the ground, swept up their clothes and then lifted her back into his arms, this time cradling her against his chest. As he marched up the stairs and into the study, he said nothing. He tossed the remnants of their clothes onto the chair, then laid her gently on the chair near the fire.

She started to speak, but he'd already turned away. He filled two goblets with wine, downed one, refilled, then handed one to her. He grabbed the cloak from the corner of the chair and spread it over her to chase off the chill. The brooch, a massive fire opal that flamed in the light from the hearth, sat heavy on her shoulder.

"I am sorry, Alexa."

She reached for his hand, but he stared down at her fingers as if she were poison. Or, more accurately, as if he was.

She took a sip of the bold red wine, closing her eyes as the flavors of oak and berry washed over her tongue, quelling the shivers running up and down her spine.

"You should have waited for me," she said softly. "You shouldn't have used the magic."

She patted the plush footstool in front of her, but he clearly preferred to pace.

"I could have killed you."

She twisted her fingers into the necklace with the triangle charm. "No, I don't think you could."

She relaxed against the cushioned wingback and lazed in her nudity, enjoying the way the wine warmed her from the inside out. She wondered how and if Damon, who now knew not to call upon Rogan's magic, was going to reclaim his clothes, besides the ripped shirt that now lay tangled with her mangled outfit. He'd vanished his breeches, his last act of magic before she'd coaxed the evil out of him using her most powerful weapon—her sexuality.

Who knew?

The thought, coupled with the wine and the headiness of victory, made her chuckle.

"I see nothing funny about what just happened," he chastised.

She waved her hand at him. "I was just wondering about your pants. Poof!"

Frowning, he glanced down at his naked body. This, for some unknown reason, made her laugh harder.

"You're incorrigible," he said, pointing his finger before stalking to the wardrobe, where he pulled out a new pair of breeches and punched his arms into the sleeves of a white shirt.

"No, I've just learned that life is too precious to waste on regrets. The charm protected me, Damon, but there's no telling what the magic might have done to you if I hadn't thought to ravish you."

"It's safe to say," he said, tying the stays on his breeches with a firm tug, "ravishment is a welcome defense against the evil, but I'd rather avoid that situation in the future."

"Agreed."

In the quiet lull, she hooked her finger and motioned him to join her. Not quite as resistant as before, he managed to settle on the footstool in front of her, his long legs stretched across the carpet, nearly touching the fireplace grate. She hooked her arms around his neck and eased him back against her. Seconds later, the cat poofed into the room and immediately settled into Damon's lap.

No matter how much wine she drank, a difficult question sat like a weight in the pit of her stomach. "Why did you risk everything? All you had to do was wait."

Damon buried his fingers in the cat's fur. "I've waited two hundred and sixty years to be free. Darkness came. You were not here. I rationalized that you could not find an answer, so you chose not to come."

She rolled her eyes. Men, even those from the eighteenth century, could be so incredibly stupid. "I was running late. Women do that from time to time. I'd think I'd be worth waiting for."

He took her hand and kissed each of her fingers. "No one who knew me in my time would deny I'm a fool where women are concerned."

Chuckling at his own joke, he retreated to silence, and they enjoyed a rare and comfortable moment. So many struggles were ahead of them—the least of which was his transference from phantom to living and breathing man, but Alexa had no doubt they could face the challenges together. Even now, she suspected he was keeping something from her, but she wouldn't force him to share. What had just happened between them, what had been happening over the course of the last week, had sapped her emotionally. She needed time to sort through the aftermath. She figured he needed the same.

But that didn't give either of them a reprieve from discovering a way to counteract the magic. "What was that room down there? It was practically outside."

Damon gave the cat a generous scratch behind his ears. "Practically, but not quite. Rogan used it for spiritual purposes, I understand. I'd completely forgotten about it until I read more of Sarina's diary. She wrote that he called it the castle's heart. He invoked the magic of the Gypsies there. I thought perhaps—"

"Now, see, that's where you're going wrong," she said, gesturing with her goblet, which was suddenly in need of a refill.

He quirked a brow. "Excuse me?"

"Not in reading the diary," she insisted. "It's actually about time you did that, after all the trouble Cat and Rousseau's son went to in order to get it. But I have my doubts about you re-creating the castle and its furnishings in order to locate the source of the magic. I understand what you meant to accomplish, but you've done every room now, haven't you? Have you found anything?"

Damon cradled the cat in his arms as he stood and retrieved the decanter. "I thought perhaps the answer was in the mosaics. Rogan had several of them, nearly one in every room. I re-created them tile by tile, but when I called to the magic, nothing responded."

"Maybe what's wrong is that what you're re-creating is just that—a re-creation. You're not conjuring the actual objects, are you?"

He frowned. "I cannot say one way or another with any certainty."

After dropping the cat, who curled up near Alexa, Damon poured her wine and then abandoned the decanter. Hooking his hands behind his back, he paced the room with long, pensive strides, his unfastened shirt billowing around him, his bared chest gleaming in the firelight. His skin still shimmered with sweat, and Alexa's mouth watered for a salty taste of him. She'd come so close to losing him—perhaps forever.

She cleared her throat. "Then let's assume the objects you conjured are just magical copies. Nothing could exist for nearly three hundred years without fading or cracking or being destroyed. Everything you've created looks brand-new."

He gave a curt nod. "Go on," he urged.

"As I promised," she said, not hiding the reproach in her voice, "I spent the day trying to work out a solution. And I realized that while re-creating the castle might give you a clue as to the location of the magical source, you are working on too many suppositions and not enough facts."

"And what are the facts?"

"That when you materialized in this castle, there was only one object here with you."

Damon crunched his brow. "The cat?"

Dante mewed nastily.

"No, he's ghostly like you."

"You mean the painting?"

She nodded. Instantly, Damon dashed out of the room.

"Damon, wait!"

He did not. Still naked, she wrapped the cloak around herself and ran toward the landing.

Damon had removed the painting from the wall. His likeness, frozen in oil, stared back at him, but he didn't seem to notice. He was peering close to the canvas, looking over every single detail. In the shadowed corner where he'd claimed to have first spotted the redheaded woman. Along the edges where the canvas tucked tightly into the frame. In every fruit basket and representation of fire.

"The answer has to be here," he muttered.

Banging sounded on the front door. Alexa jumped. Daylight was at least an hour away. Who could be on her island?

"Paulie?" she called, walking cautiously down the steps.

The reply was muffled.

Damon pointed at the door.

"Let no one in!" he shouted.

The thumping continued. The rhythm was unmistakably frantic.

Damon had turned back to the painting. Alexa hurried down the steps. The closer she got, the clearer the muffled voice became.

"Alexa, it's Cat! Open up! We have Rousseau."

She struggled with the latch, but once the door opened, Cat flew into her arms. Their hug conveyed a backlash of emotion neither of them had time to process. Relief. Fear. Desperation. Elation. Suddenly, Cat pushed her back but kept her hands on her shoulders.

"What are you wearing?" Cat asked.

Alexa tugged at the dark material, pulling the sides close around her naked body. "Um, a cloak?"

Cat arched a brow. "I can see that. And you got this cloak from whom?"

Alexa glanced over her shoulder. Damon had the painting held high above his head, as if about to smash it to the ground.

"Damon!" she screamed.

Her shout didn't deter him. He stalked to the railing, frustration etched deep into every line on his face. He was on the verge of hurling the cursed painting over the landing when another voice, this one male and booming, echoed against the stone walls.

"Stop or you'll never be free of Rogan's curse!"

"What?" Alexa asked, shocked. How did they know? "Damon!"

He jerked to a halt, but the weight of the frame and the forward momentum stole the painting from his hands. Alexa screamed as the key to Damon's freedom flew over the banister and shattered on the stone floor below.

28

Standing at the end of the dock, Jacob watched the yacht's stern lights until they were nothing more than tiny pinpoints. Sure. Take the witch bitch and her new posse to Alexa, but don't take him. See if he cared.

He turned away from the water, but the fact that he did care about his sister vexed him more than Cat's frantic arrival at the marina just before dawn or the way both the guy in the bomber jacket and the old man stuck to his ex like glue. He'd considered confronting them, challenging them when they'd ordered Alexa's feisty captain to shuttle them to the island, but he'd decided to keep his mouth shut. He also needed to get to the island so he could find the magic source for the K'vr. He only hoped he could keep Alexa out of the cross fire.

Sitting on the dock, he dangled his feet over the edge, just inches from the sloshing salt water, and tried to remember the man he used to be—the boy, really—who'd been so consumed with jealousy and hatred toward his stepsister that he'd arranged to have her killed. He'd siphoned thousands of dollars out of a little-used Chandler account and paid off not only an ex-con with auto mechanic experience to tamper with the brakes on the company limo, but the driver of the semi whose job it had been to run the car off the road. He'd had no idea his mother and stepfather would be running late for a trip to Bermuda and that they'd hop into Alexa's limousine to share the ride.

He'd watched them drive away, frozen, too afraid to stop them before they left with Alexa or waylay their departure or even volunteer to drive them himself so only his stepsister would die in the crash. All the options had come to him only later. At that time, he'd been paralyzed by his fear. The first hour passed in a frantic blur.

The waiting. The dread. The oh-so-secret delight.

He'd snorted his way through that hour. Shot up through the next. Drank through the third. It wasn't until morning when he'd learned that Richard Chandler and his beloved second wife had died while Alexa, his target, had only sustained serious injuries.

He'd learned a hard lesson that day. About fate. About retribution. About karma. As he'd helped his sister recover, he'd searched for spiritual cleansing. He'd found it with the K'vr.

"Toss aside past sins. Embrace the future power."

That mantra had saved his life. And Alexa's. He'd studied hard, often alongside the leader's odd but intelligent son. Over time, the kid—on his father's orders, probably—had encouraged Jacob to get close to his sister, not knowing the devious teen would call on him later to use Alexa to build his road to power. But then, Jacob hadn't objected. He'd agreed.

Now he had to figure out how to get her out of the mix without getting her killed.

"Waiting for the sunrise?"

Jacob spun so fast, he nearly lost his balance. Alexa's assistant grabbed him by the shirt and tugged him away from a cold, dark dunking.

"What are you doing here?" he asked, trying to remember the girl's name.

Her hands buried deep in the pockets of a long windbreaker, she hugged herself against the salt-scented breeze. "Couldn't pass up a chance to see dawn over the Atlantic."

He twisted so he faced the water again. He really didn't need or want company right now. He had to figure out what to do about Keith and Alexa and the charm and the castle and who knew what else. Keith had been calling his cell phone for hours. He could claim bad reception for only so long. He didn't need his sister's gopher interrupting his thoughts.

"The view's likely better over there," Jacob replied, pointing to the main pier, which jutted farther into the water.

"Company's better here."

The sensual tone in her voice caught his attention. He'd interacted with the woman many times, but in Alexa's presence, he'd never gotten more out of her than a curt brush-off.

"What's your name again?"

"Rose," she replied, scooting down onto the edge of the pier beside him.

"Rose," he repeated. He glanced sideways at her, but she was staring intently across the inky black ocean. The stars that had blanketed the sky when he'd first decided to wait at the marina rather than return to his hotel room were fading from view. Unless Cat fucked things up, Alexa would soon return to the mainland. If Jacob wanted her safe, which he was growing more certain he did, he'd have to convince her to abandon this project until he could get the situation under control.

"You been here all night?" Rose asked.

"Hard to beat the view," he said.

"You can't see anything in the dark. I thought maybe you were avoiding someone."

He stared at her, but she still hadn't turned her face away from the water. "Why would you think that?"

"You're not answering your cell phone."

"You called me?"

"He's not pleased that you're avoiding him," she said cryptically. "Not pleased at all."

When she finally faced him, her cold stare chilled him to the marrow.

"Who are you?" he asked, but the answer popped into his head before her mouth curved into a self-satisfied smile.

The mole?

"How do you know Keith?" He asked the question on the off chance Rose was relaying an innocent phone message.

"Same way you do."

No such luck.

She twirled a blond lock behind her ear and revealed a tattoo—a hawk carrying a fire red jewel—along the base of her neck. Most K'vr members had the brand in inconspicuous places or hidden among other, more mundane tattoos. That this woman wore hers so boldly spoke to her devotion.

"I've never noticed that before," he said.

"Makeup does wonders." She glanced behind her, as if waiting for someone, and seconds later, Jacob saw a stretch Hummer pull up the marina drive, gaudy lights trimming the windows and a purple glow emanating from underneath. Crass and juvenile.

Keith.

Jacob moved to stand, but an icy steel jab in his side stopped him cold. The weapon, clutched confidently in Rose's hand, dispelled any thought he might have of escape.

For him . . . or for Alexa.

With a deafening slam, the portrait shattered against the marble floor. Gold-leafed wood splintered in every direction. Damon watched as Alexa ran forward, her hands shielding her face from the spray of sharp spikes.

"Alexa, no!" Damon commanded.

She skidded a few feet away from the ruined portrait, the cloak flapping around her, revealing her nude body in a flash of fabric. His throat tightened. His heart raced. His image lay amid the ruins, wilted and torn, and still he felt nothing.

He was still a phantom. Trapped. Captured by a curse set by his greatest enemy—forbidden by fate to have a life with Alexa. A life outside these thick stone walls.

Damon had acted on instinct, hoping and praying that the destruction of the painting would set him free. But as he looked down at his hands and then back up at the windows, still dark, he anticipated the change that would soon twist through his body—but not the change he'd strived for.

Soon, the sun would rise and he would fade.

Below him, a dark-haired woman with round black eyes placed her arms protectively on Alexa's shoulders.

The old man who'd come in behind them shuffled toward the painting, throwing aside the broken bits of frame to reach the canvas beneath. He muttered to himself while Cat assured herself that her friend was all in one piece.

"I take it this is your ghost," she said wryly, looking up at him.

Alexa spared her a half grin. "Well, he's not exactly ghostlike during the night."

"Which explains your lack of apparel beneath that cloak," she cracked.

Damon cleared his throat and stood taller. "Surely women in this time do not gossip so openly."

The women exchanged bemused glances. "Yes, actually, we do," Alexa informed him.

He frowned. "Then I assume you are Cat."

"None other," Cat replied, uncertainty and distrust evident on her olive-skinned face. She could have been a Gyspy, this one. She had quick eyes, he could tell. Likely missed very little—a good friend for Alexa to have.

"I appreciate your hesitation," he said, starting toward the stairs. He hadn't much time before the sun rose and banished him again to the shadows. If Alexa's friends had arrived to help his pursuit, there was no time to waste. "The portrait was my prison. I thought by destroying it, I might find my freedom."

"That's not the way," replied a gruff voice.

The old man looked up, his stare accusatory.

"And you are?"

The man hesitated. Damon was sure he'd never seen anyone quite so old, yet possessing such strength of spine.

"Paschal Rousseau," he informed him, his chin tilted upward.

Damon locked his gaze with that of the man who assessed him so boldly. Alexa slid next to Damon and took his arm. No doubt, she recognized the meeting for what it was—each man taking the measure of the other.

"You are the reported expert on the Romani of Valoren?"

A quick, enthusiastic grin spread across the man's face, but only for a moment. Just as quickly, he pursed his lips and averted his eyes. The hair on the back of Damon's neck rose. He pushed Alexa behind him.

"You should dress," he said to her, though his eyes never broke from Paschal Rousseau.

"My bag is by the door," she replied.

Damon lifted his hand to summon the bag, but she immediately slapped his arm.

"Don't. You. Dare."

Surprised by his actions, he lowered his hand immediately. Was the magic so entwined within him now that his instincts reverted to it without thought? How many times could he tempt his soul with the magic before he lost his center completely? Alexa's inventive means of restoring his humanity had worked well once, but he had no guarantee the strategy would work forever.

And he didn't have forever. He would have rather endured the foggy half awareness of the painting than knowing that a world existed beyond these castle walls of which he could not partake. He looked down at the broken portrait frame and realized, with no disappointment whatsoever, that he could not retreat. He wanted his freedom above all else.

Even more than he wanted Alexa, he acknowledged sadly. He could be no man to her if he dissolved into nothing with the coming of every dawn.

Damon turned his focus to the younger man, who'd remained in the doorway.

"What is your name?" Damon demanded.

The man crossed his arms. "Ben Rousseau."

Damon nodded toward the old man. "This is your father, then?"

"Yes, and he's come a long way and endured more than a man his age should in order to help you, so I suggest you soften your tone."

Damon quirked an eyebrow. Assertive, this one. Quick to anger. Reminded him of himself. He supposed some allowances had to be made for the professor's advanced age and reputedly useful knowledge.

"You know of the Gypsy curse as well?"

Ben shook his head. "I only know what my father told us on the way here. Bottom line is, we're here to help you. Whatever you are."

"Ben," Paschal chastised, "mind your manners."

Tension seeped into Damon's neck, and when he held out his hand to Ben, who'd picked up Alexa's bag and brought it to her, Damon wondered why he felt so ill at ease with strangers who claimed to want to help him. When Ben turned away, Damon grabbed his arm and gazed into eyes, trying to read his true intentions.

Ben tugged his arm free. "What are you? A ghost?"

"No, son," Paschal interjected. "He's not dead."

Cat tugged Alexa toward the dining hall to dress, but she hesitated until Damon assured her all would be peaceful until her return. In the meantime, he meant to extract what information he could, knowing he could not trust either of these men until they had proved their worth.

"How do you know I am not dead, sir?" he questioned Paschal. "It is my understanding that your knowledge of my predicament has been gleaned entirely from books and heresay."

Paschal chuckled and, while raspy, the sound was hauntingly familiar. "That is a misconception I myself created. For obvious reasons."

"Obvious to whom?"

"You're just as haughty and overbearing as ever, aren't you?" Paschal accused, though his tone lilted with humor.

Alexa and Cat returned to the foyer. Dressed hastily in pants and a blouse, Alexa cradled Rogan's cloak over her arm. The fire opal broach on the collar flamed in the light from the torch beside her. Damon turned back to Paschal, whose eyes suddenly looked even more familiar than his son's—because they looked so very much like his own.

"Who are you?" he asked.

They could not be descendants, could they? All his brothers had died or disappeared, though he imagined Aiden or Logan might have had an illegitimate son at some point. He'd had no uncles. To the best of his knowledge, thanks to Alexa's computer, the Forsyth line had died that night in Valoren.

Or had it?

Paschal's smile, so easy, so full and relaxed, instantly gave him away.

"Good Lord above," Damon said, his gut tightening as if he'd just been pummeled. "Paxton? You bloody, duplicitous whelp!"

"Paxton?" Ben asked, planting himself firmly between Damon and his father. "Who the hell is Paxton? This is Paschal Rousseau, the noted Gypsy researcher."

"Like hell," Damon shot back. "This old coot is Paxton Forsyth, my devious younger brother."

29

The collective gasps in the vast entryway nearly sucked the air from Alexa's lungs. She searched her memory for information about Paxton, recalling only that he was one of the twins, the youngest of the sons borne to John Forsyth and his first wife. But what were the chances that her Gypsy expert and Damon's assumed dead brother were one and the same?

"Your brother?" she asked. "How is that possible?"

"It's not," Ben insisted.

Paschal leveled his steely gaze at his son. "It's more than possible, son. It's *true*." He then spun on his brother, his arms akimbo in a jaunty pose that shaved twenty years off his reputed age. "I'd wondered if after all these centuries, my arrogant, self-centered git of a brother would recognize me."

Alexa searched Paschal's expression for signs of real resentment but found nothing but twinkling eyes and a devilish grin. After a tense moment, a similar smile lit Damon's face and he laughed heartily. With a push, he removed his grown nephew from his path and enveloped his long lost brother in a massive hug.

Cat grabbed the back of Ben's jacket to ensure he didn't interfere.

"This isn't possible," Ben muttered.

Cat patted him lovingly on the shoulder. "Just four hours ago, I contacted your father using a catalog of swords as my psychic telephone line. Just four days ago, Alexa walked into this monstrosity of a castle and freed a cursed phantom from a painting. The fact that your father is just under three centuries old seems par for the course." She turned to Alexa. "Small world, huh?"

Alexa exhaled a whoosh of air. "So he's an expert on Valoren because he *lived* there."

Cat bounced on the balls of her feet. She always loved a good cosmic connection. "Who better? Still planning on turning this magic magnet," she said, gesturing to the castle, "into your flagship hotel?"

Alexa's smile nearly hurt her face. Suddenly, the banners flapping on the walls looked brighter, the tapestries richer, the carpets more lush. Even the sparkling stone and its incessant chill seemed warmer when filled with the people she cared about—Cat, of course. Damon, particularly. Even Ben and Paschal— er, Paxton—as they were Damon's family. She suddenly felt a connection to her castle that went beyond business, beyond ambition, beyond pride. This was where she'd found him. And this was where, with Paschal's help, she would set him free.

"Absolutely," she replied.

"He was supposed to be your resident ghost," Cat reminded her.

"The guests can get their own ghost," Alexa quipped.

"I don't know . . . he was your big draw." The doubt on Cat's face and her singsong voice were clearly for comic effect.

Alexa watched Damon and Paschal part, then after a moment of checking each other out from head to toe, they fell into another fraternal embrace.

"He'll always be my big draw," Alexa mused, her hopes helplessly pinned on Paschal Rousseau—or Paxton Forsyth, as the case may be—to reveal the secret that would set Damon completely free. "As for my previous plans, I believe I'll look into the possibility of special effects."

Cutting their banter short when Paschal and Damon finally released each other, Alexa sent Ben into the dining hall to retrieve a chair for his father, who seemed wiped out from the explosion of emotion, not to mention the aftereffects of a kidnapping and rescue, all of which Cat recounted. Ben wordlessly placed the high-backed oak chair near his father. Paschal sneered at the seat, but took it nonetheless.

"What happened?" Damon asked, a hint of a frown tilting his mouth as he knelt beside Paschal, his hand protectively atop his brother's knee.

"You mean, why am I so old?"

Damon's brow creased his face severely.

Paschal clapped his brother heartily on the shoulder. "Think this is what awaits you, do you? Immediate aging once you are free of the curse? If I'd aged to where I should be chronologically, I'd be nothing more than a pile of dust. No, I was freed of the curse over sixty years ago at the height of the Second World War, thanks to a lovely French girl who had an eye for beauty even amid the ravages of war."

Damon glanced at Alexa, a grin teasing his lips. Her own eye for stunning lines and magnificent symmetry, along with her penchant for fantasy and an insatiable hunger for a secret lover, had drawn her to the castle and into Damon's world with just as much romanticism as the lilt in Paschal's voice.

"White blond hair," Paschal mused. "The shapeliest legs I've ever seen. Since women in our time were scandalized by the exhibition of a well-turned ankle, you can imagine how the shortage of fabric in Europe worked to my advantage."

He waggled his eyebrows and Alexa had to admit that Paschal's impression of history was much more passionate than hers. In her catch-up session with Damon two days before, Alexa had barely touched on the world wars, not to mention the radical changes in women's fashion since the Georgian era, but over the next fifteen minutes, Paschal regaled them with adventurous recollections of the French Resistance against the Nazis and of the brave and trusting twenty-year-old girl who'd found a mirror in an abandoned shop in Provence that had, because of Rogan's magic, contained Paxton's soul.

His voice adopted an increasingly dreamy quality as he slipped farther back into his memory and described the night Damon and his brothers had stormed into Umgeben to free their kidnapped sister.

"As you ordered, Logan and I went in search of the tinker," he said. "His shop had been abandoned, just like the village square. We searched for any sign of evacuation, but everything seemed to be exactly where it belonged. Except for two stunning mirrors in a velvet-lined case, sitting in plain view. Logan couldn't believe anyone would leave such wonders of workmanship behind. Or out in the open. They were, admittedly, brilliant pieces of silverwork, with jeweled handles. And since Logan was always in search of a new gift to offer his latest conquest, he grabbed them. Handed one to me. For a split second, we looked at each other. Then, a bright white light. And that was that."

He finished his story with a nonchalant shrug.

"That was that?" Ben repeated incredulously. "That was *what*?"

Positioned behind his father, Ben's arms were so tightly crossed over his chest that Alexa thought the constricting pressure was the only thing keeping the vein on his neck from bursting. She glanced at Cat, who sidled over and placed a hand quietly on his back.

Quietly and . . . intimately.

What exactly had her best friend been doing with this guy during his father's rescue, hm?

Paschal threw an exasperated glare over his shoulder. "Loosen up, Benjamin. You weren't born yesterday. This is your uncle. This is your history. You should be very interested."

"If this fairy tale is so important," Ben challenged, "why haven't I heard any of this before now?"

Paschal's snow-white brows rose high over clear gray eyes. "You would have thought I'd lost my mind and had me committed—and don't say you wouldn't have, because that's precisely what I would have done had the roles been reversed. Your mother and I considered telling you years ago—"

"Mother knew?"

"Good God, boy, of course she knew! She's the one who freed me from the curse, just as I suspect Miss Chandler here did for your uncle." He turned back to Damon and spoke directly to him, though behind his hand, as if everyone couldn't overhear. "He's a handsome boy, and bright, too, but has a nasty stubborn streak. It's in the genes."

"The what?" Damon questioned.

Paschal waved a hand dismissively. "You can learn about genetic studies later. Of the lot of us, you always were the book learner. Funny. Now I'm the one with the knowledge you need. The one who used to put toads in your bed."

Damon and Paschal laughed, but Ben remained in stunned silence. The merriment didn't die down until Paschal turned his gaze to Alexa's throat. Instinctively, she drew her hand to the charm Jacob had given her. Paschal's stare narrowed, then he waved her forward.

She bent low so he could examine the necklace. "Ah, yes. The Queen's Charm. I highly suspected, after Miss Reyes explained your circumstances, that you'd somehow gotten ahold of it."

"My brother gave it to me," she explained. "For protection."

He nodded knowingly. "The primary purpose of the Queen's Charm is protection, but I gather you've already learned as much."

Damon scooted closer. "The Queen's Charm, you say? I thought this was but a trinket Father gave to Sarina."

"So did I," Paschal reported, "until circumstances forced me to find out where Father got it in the first place. Apparently, the old King George's queen, Sophia, before her banishment, received the charm from a Gypsy artisan she'd done an accidental kindness to.

The Gypsy claimed it was a key to unlock a woman's greatest desires. The queen must have passed the trinket to our father before he left to oversee the colony at Valoren. Rumor has it, she was fond of our father. But the poor woman likely didn't believe in the magic. Nevertheless, Father gave the charm to Sarina years later as a gift."

"How do you know all this?"

"Sarina wrote about it in her diary," he answered. "I take it you haven't read it." Paschal nodded knowingly. "Delving into our sister's secret passions was not easy for me, either, not when we don't even know what became of her. But I can tell you—after Rogan fell in love with her, he further enchanted the charm to protect Sarina from his magic."

"Fell in love?" Damon spat, shoving to his feet. "The mere thought is as revolting as it is insane. Rogan lacked the heart to love anyone."

Paschal shrugged. Clearly, his spite and anger toward Rogan had lessened with time. Or else he'd never experienced the same all-encompassing rage Damon struggled so hard against, since Rogan had been his friend.

"Why did this sorcerer need to protect your sister from his magic?" Cat asked. "If he cared for her—even if he only meant to seduce her," she amended, witnessing the affronted look on Damon's face at the implication that Rogan might have genuinely loved Sarina, "why would she be in danger from him?"

Damon, Alexa and Paschal all sighed knowingly.

"The magic," Alexa piped up, laying her hand softly against Damon's arm, "comes with a price. It corrupts the sorcerer who wields it. Makes him very dangerous."

"Very good, Miss Chandler," Paschal said, ignoring the flash of regret that streaked across Damon's face. "You figured out in a matter of days what took me years to learn. Once I got my hands on the necklace again sixty years ago, I was able to breach the castle's defenses and move the structure here. Seem to remember I procured this island during a rather dicey poker game."

"You gamble, too?" Ben asked incredulously.

"Life's a gamble, my boy," Paschal said with a dismissive snort. "I brought the castle out of Valoren because a nasty group of cultists had been trying to take the castle for their own nefarious intentions. I anticipated I'd need years to sort out Rogan's magic. I'd hoped my brothers had been trapped as I was, and I, of course, intended to free them. I took the castle as far away from Germany as I could, knowing it might be the key—the source of the curse."

"Cultists?" Alexa asked, confused.

"They're called the K'vr," Cat told her. "They're followers of this Lord Rogan and they've been searching for the source of his magic for centuries. They kidnapped Paschal."

Alexa stared at Damon. They'd spoken at length about Rogan, but he'd never claimed his enemy to be any sort of religious leader. "Rogan had followers?"

Damon shook his head, clearly as amazed as she. "Not in his lifetime. The Gypsies adored him, but—"

"The cult was actually started by his brother," Paschal explained. "Lukyan Roganov was a greedy landowner in Hungary who used his brother's reputed magic to scare his tenants into paying inflated tithes. The power of influence was something he couldn't give up even after his brother disappeared, so he played upon the fears of the illiterate peasants and started a secret society that lasts until this day."

Paschal eyed the charm again. "The group that kidnapped me wants that," he warned, pointing a gnarled finger at her chest.

Alexa flattened her palm over the gold triangle. "Sarina's necklace?"

"The K'vr believe that Rogan bequeathed his magic to the Gypsies, and on the night of their mass disappearance from Valoren, he somehow left the magic inside the castle to be reclaimed by his devoted followers. They believe the magic was encased in an item

Rogan owned, one he'd found during his extensive travels. They believed, at first, that the Queen's Charm was the source. After they possessed it, which they did a century ago, they realized that wasn't the case— although I've recently learned that that knowledge had been lost. Only a select few realize that the source of the magic lies elsewhere."

Alexa tried to process centuries' worth of subter- fuge and treachery and magic and came up woefully confused. She combed her hand through her hair and for the first time since the castle was invaded by visi- tors, wondered what she must look like in wrinkled clothes, sans makeup and lacking sleep.

Damon shot a glance at Ben, who, with a groan, disappeared into the dining hall and returned with a chair for Alexa. She sat and leaned on her elbows to be nearer to Paschal. "You mean some of the K'vr still want my necklace?"

Paschal stretched and rubbed his back. She couldn't imagine that a terrifying kidnapping, a harrowing es- cape via helicopter and private plane from Texas and brief, but frantic ocean travel added up to comfort for a man Paschal's age. She wondered if they could delay the rest of this conversation, but one glance at the stained-glass window in the room behind them told her they could not. Daylight was coming. And since Cat and Ben had stolen Paschal back from his captors, there was a good chance those goons were headed this way, too.

"The K'vr has since split into factions," Paschal ex- plained. "One is quite aware that the necklace is only a key. The other took me captive."

"And they let you go once you could not produce the charm?" Damon asked.

"One of the faction leaders—or at the very least, someone who aspires to the job—aided in my escape and stayed behind to waylay the others. But I doubt I've seen the last of her—or them. They are led by a power-hungry parvenu named Farrow Pryce. The sec- ond group has the bloodlines. The leader, Keith Von

Roan, is barely a man, but he's descended from Lukyan Roganov. His father, grandfather and beyond led the K'vr for years. That gives him extreme sway. His is the group that knows the charm's true purpose, and I suspect they will move against us soon. They must have orchestrated you getting the necklace so you could bypass the castle's protective spell for them. That's why you need to take Rogan's power now, before anyone else."

Damon scowled. "You think I have not been trying? Finding the source will release me fully, will it not?"

Cat blew out a frustrated breath, and Alexa could see dark circles beneath her friend's eyes. Paschal wore a matched set. Ben didn't exactly look ready to run a marathon. They'd been through so much, but sunrise loomed. The time to solve this mystery was now.

"Why wasn't Damon released the way you were?" she asked. "Why is he trapped in the castle?"

Paschal's expression turned pensive. "I believe, though I am not certain, that Damon has suffered from a second magical curse because the portrait was more important than the mirror that entrapped me. I don't believe the painting was intended to capture my brother or any of the other raiders heading toward Valoren that night. I believe the painting was meant as a hiding place for Rogan himself."

Damon stood and, in his usual, thoughtful manner, began to pace a tight circle around his brother.

"Because Rogan was in the portrait originally?"

"Yes," Paschal replied. "He kept that painting at the precise center of the house. The best place to hide something of value is in plain sight, agreed? Rogan manipulated the magic most skillfully so that anyone who stumbled upon his cursed items, perhaps the raiding horde on their way to massacre the Gypsies, would suffer centuries of loneliness trapped inside the valuable items he'd enchanted, but they would not control his power. That, he'd keep for himself."

Damon sat back on his haunches. "So you knew I was trapped in the painting when you found it?"

"I suspected," Paschal said, rubbing his stubbled chin. "But nothing I did released you. Even my dear Collette tried, to no avail. That's when I decided to use the money Collette's family had amassed before the war to bring the painting back to its home. Here, in the castle, but out of reach. I'd hoped the surroundings would trigger the magic." His tone dipped low as his failure hit him hard. "Nothing worked. Then the charm was stolen from me and I could no longer enter the castle. I had to abandon your portrait. I decided then to work toward retrieving every item I could associate with Valoren, in hopes I'd free one of our brothers, and together, we'd find a way to free you."

"So you left?"

Alexa wished she could erase the pain from Damon's voice, but Paschal stood and put his hand on his brother's shoulder. "I had to keep searching for the answers. I believed Rogan had created the ultimate catch-22. He could hide in the painting, in a sleeplike state, for as long as he needed. He would not age. He would not waste away from hunger or thirst. But to break free of the painting, someone, most likely Sarina, had to unlock the magic with the key—the Queen's Charm. When he was out, he would destroy the protection spells and go about his life. Apparently, things did not go as he planned."

"But how does this help us find the source of Rogan's power?" Alexa asked, her eyes darting to the window.

"Rogan never would have strayed far from the source of his magic. If he planned to hide from the raiders in the portrait, it stands to reason that the source is there as well."

"Do you mean . . . ," Damon asked, his eyes as round as silver coins.

"Yes," Paschal verified. "You've had the source all along."

"And the necklace? If it's the key, why didn't it work for you?"

"It did. To a point. I was able to breech the castle's

defenses. But to release the portrait's subject, Rogan had introduced a failsafe I've only now figured out." His eyes darted between Damon and Alexa and a smile, curved with naughty innuendo, spread across his face. "Clearly, the charm only works when in the hands of a person who desires the person within. Collette caught a glimpse of me in the mirror the day she found me. The way she told it, she was instantly, well"—he cleared his throat and cast a guilty look toward his son—"intrigued by me. She'd found the mirror at a time in her life when she was yearning for some delight to cancel the horrors of war. Sarina would have, at least in Rogan's mind," Paschal said politically, "desired to be with him. Need, I'm afraid, is the crucial element."

"You mean lust," Cat quipped. "He meant for Sarina to free him all along and he was counting on her being hot for him."

Everyone ignored Damon's growl.

"Possibly," Paschal replied. "She did have the key and she did—the diary proves it," he directed at Damon, "want to be with Rogan more than anything."

Damon's nostrils flared. He stomped nearer to his brother and punctuated his words by jabbing his finger in the air. "The night I was entrapped, I found the necklace on the floor at the bottom of the stairs. She abandoned him. She left him."

"Possibly," Paschal conceded. "We may never know."

Tempted as she was, Alexa couldn't allow herself to be swept into the romance of Sarina and Rogan's affair. For one, the topic infuriated Damon. And second, it did nothing to save her lover, who was even now growing paler with the sunrise.

"This is a great story," she snapped, "but now we need to find the magic. Tell us where it is."

Paschal looked at her, shocked. "I have no idea where it is, my dear. But Damon does."

30

Damon's skin felt as if it were wrapped in cotton. Muffled. Light. Soon, he'd lose his corporeal form. He had no idea if he could free himself in that state, and frankly, he didn't want to try. He'd waited long enough.

He'd missed so much. His younger brother, the shadow twin to the loquacious Logan, had grown old and had searched for his missing brothers entirely alone. He'd made great progress, but now Damon had to take the torch. With his preserved youth and Paxton's superior research, they could track down Aiden, Colin, Logan and Rafe and free them from the curse that had likely captured them all.

Unless they'd been freed already, as Paxton had. Unless they'd already lived out their lives and died?

Not willing to risk an overload of emotions when time was so short, he pushed that possibility away. He wanted the source and he wanted it now. He thought hard. What was in the painting? The cat?

He called to the beast, but it did not materialize.

"I do not think the cat was the source. To put something so valuable in a living thing would be risky indeed," Paschal offered.

Damon's mind swirled. His gaze roamed across the room until he spotted Alexa's bag, over which she'd draped Rogan's cloak.

The cloak! Of course. It had been with him in the portrait the entire time. With purposeful strides, he crossed the room and retrieved the cursed fabric with an insistent yank. The brooch on the collar flamed to life, mocking him with its blatancy.

"How could I not have known?" He shook the cloak angrily.

Alexa glanced up at him, perplexed, for only a moment before all the pieces fell together in her mind.

"The opal?" she asked.

Paxton hummed. "A wise possibility. A beautiful stone. Very valuable, in and of itself. And I don't think I ever saw Rogan without it. He used to toy with it, remember, Damon? Roll it in his hand after dinner when he'd sit by the fire with you and Father over port and politics. I venture to guess that no matter how lovely or precious the gem, you left the cloak precisely where it was, hanging over Rogan's chair, never touching it, never wanting anything associated with Rogan near your skin."

Cat crossed her arms and whistled at Rogan's cleverness. "The perfect hiding place. He put it in the painting. Only by releasing you could anyone retrieve it—and once you were out, the place where he'd hidden the stone was the last place you'd want to be."

Damon allowed himself a second to admire his enemy's brilliance, then another realization hit him.

"I've always had the power to free myself. It was right beside me the whole time."

Paxton clucked his tongue. "No, you needed Alexa to awaken you. And you needed me to fill in the blanks. Of course, all we have right now is supposition based on an old man's educated guesses. We won't know if my theory is true until you take the stone and will yourself free."

Stepping back, Damon shook out the cloak and spun it so it would fall across his shoulders. But before the material could settle against his shirt, Alexa ripped the cape from his hands.

"No, wait!"

He yanked the cloak back. "There's no time for delay." Grabbing her by the arm, he led her into the dining hall to the nearest window. The stained glass glowed with the rising sun.

"Why are you stopping me?"

"The magic, Damon. The cloak and the opal are filled with it. Even Paschal isn't sure the magic will set you free. And even if it does, it could corrupt your soul for good. We need to wait. Slow down. Think about this."

Alexa clutched the cloak against her chest with such desperation, her fingers turned red, matching the rise in her cheeks.

He grabbed one of her hands, stroking it softly until the muscles in her fingers relaxed. "You know there is no time, my love." He glanced over his shoulder at Paxton, Ben and Cat, who were watching them expectantly. "If the K'vr went to great lengths to capture my brother, we cannot assume they will stop pursuing him or the magic's source. And Paxton said the other faction is also searching and that it was they who had the necklace before and perhaps saw to it that you . . ."

He let his words die away, but Alexa wasn't a fool. She knew exactly what he meant.

"Jacob isn't a member of any cult," she claimed, but the words sounded entirely hollow.

"You told me yourself you are not close with him, that you do not delve into his private life. Judging by his actions in the past, a sect devoted to an ancient sorcerer might be very seductive to your brother."

"Stepbrother." This came from Cat, who'd stopped at the doorway. "He gave you the necklace, Alexa. And right after you put it on, you were miraculously allowed entrance to both the island and the house. That's no coincidence. And then there's the matter of the island itself. He's the one who brought you the codicil. You say you own this island—"

"I do," Alexa insisted. "I have the deeds. Chandler Enterprises has been paying the taxes on the land for years. Jacob"—she stumbled over the name—"showed me the records himself."

"Then the state of Florida is getting more than its fair share," Ben said, sidling up behind Cat. "My father never sold this land, Miss Chandler. This castle, this island, belong to him."

With Damon at her heels, Alexa stomped into the other room. She stopped hard when she saw Paxton relaxed in the chair, his eyes fixed on some faraway place. Perhaps into the past. He snapped to attention once he sensed their presence.

"What? Did the cloak work?"

"You still own the island?" she asked. "You didn't sell it to my father or lose it in another poker game or—?"

Paxton frowned, as if he hated imparting the truth to Alexa. "I'm sorry, Miss Chandler. I never would have sold this land, knowing that my brother might possibly be trapped here. Documents such as deeds can be forged, apparently. I'm afraid you've been duped."

Alexa dropped back, flush against Damon's chest. He longed to wrap his arms around her and help her through this heartbreak. More than anyone in the room, with the possible exception of Cat, he knew how she'd pinned more than just her financial hopes on the castle she'd inherited from her father. The discovery of the deed had not only reawakened old fantasies, but connected her on a deeply personal level to a man she missed more than she'd admit to anyone. Even herself.

But Damon couldn't be the man she needed now if he was nothing more than a phantom, locked in the night. Perhaps that was the rub in this whole scenario. No matter how much he cared for her—loved her, even—Damon could not be Alexa's lover beyond these seductive castle walls until and unless he risked his soul to become whole again.

Cat slipped next to Alexa and threw her arm lovingly across her shoulders. Damon stepped aside and, with his eyes locked with his brother's, drew Rogan's cloak around him and fastened the clasp. He then laid his hand over the opal brooch, closed his eyes and called to the magic to restore him to a full and free life.

Instantly, waves of prickly heat shot through his body, starting at his hand and spreading like wildfire. His heartbeat accelerated and his lungs seemed to enlarge so that they felt entirely too thick and full to be contained in his chest. Bright flashes of light appeared in his eyes, but no one else in the room moved or reacted, so he knew only he could see the fireworks. The explosions came faster and faster until his muscles constricted and he threw his fists against his eyes to keep them from popping out of his head.

"Damon?"

The voice pierced through the pounding in his brain. He felt a hand wrap around his wrist and knew it must be her. But if the magic did corrupt him, she couldn't be the closest. He might hurt her. He tore out of her grip and staggered away.

Fire coursed through his blood like knives, stripping him from the inside out. He could no longer contain a scream, and seconds later, the agonized sounds echoed against the sparkling stone all around him.

Somewhere beyond the pain, he heard Alexa's voice. Was she calling him? Cursing him?

He collapsed. In a fog of awareness, he heard Alexa demanding that Ben help her remove the cloak. Paxton argued vehemently, ordering them away.

"Let him be!" Paxton shouted.

And yet, he could feel Alexa cradling his head in her lap. He struggled, but opened his eyes to a growing brightness, and in the center of his vision was the woman he loved. Her red hair gleamed in the streaming sunlight. She had, indeed, affected his destiny, as the Gypsy woman predicted. In every way possible.

"Damon? Say something. Are you all right?"

He groaned, then tested his tongue against the roof of his mouth. "I believe . . . I am."

Control returned to his muscles. Pain receded, and after a deep breath, he raised himself off the floor.

The cloak now felt like a soft caress around his shoulders.

Otherwise, nothing else had changed.

Alexa's eyes brimmed with moisture. She hadn't yet cried, but was on the verge. He chose his words carefully, holding his hand out to her. "I'm fine, Alexa."

She hiccupped and then laughed. "You don't feel an irresistible urge to kill me?"

He chuckled. "No."

Cat clucked her tongue. "Just wait. The time will come."

Alexa rushed into his arms, and the sensations of her embrace erased any memory of the agony he'd experienced.

"But how do we know you're alive?" she asked, looking up at him expectantly. "You're solid now, but how long will it last?"

He stared at the sunlight now turning the crimson glass in the window into bright scarlet. "There's only one way to find out for sure."

Despite the apprehension marring Alexa's lovely face, he marched to the door and touched the handle. The sky remained bright. No storm brewed. He felt no resistance as he pressed the latch. He sucked in a breath, tugged and was instantly bathed in new morning sunlight.

He blinked, then, realizing he was holding his breath, he exhaled audibly. He reached behind him and Alexa instantly took his hand. He stood there with her, in the doorway between his former prison and freedom, breathing in the fresh salt air and listening to the gentle rustling of the wind through the strange, spiky plants that surrounded the castle. His life, after nearly three centuries, had finally begun.

Tentatively, he took a step outside the threshold. He glanced up at the sky, which was blossoming with an array of colors, from lavender to pink to tangerine, with hints of blue that foretold a clear and brilliant day. As his boot crunched on the step, covered in sand and crushed shell, he turned toward Alexa, and with no words to express his elation, bent down to kiss her sweet lips and make his rebirth complete.

But before his mouth could press against hers, pain tore into him, the hot agony preceded by a sharp report. The world rocked. His legs buckled. His vision swirled. His knees slammed hard on the stone when he fell, but the only sound he could hear was Alexa screaming his name.

31

Alexa drew her hand away from the hot, slick liquid oozing from Damon's back. Blood. Oh, God. He was real. And he was dying.

On the path leading up to the castle, she saw the barrel of a gun. Pointed at her. A man. Two, maybe. With nowhere to hide, she tried to drag Damon's body inside. The weight of his unconscious body overwhelmed her. Suddenly four hands dragged them both inside. The door slammed closed behind them.

Ben cursed. "There's no lock!"

Alexa saw Damon's eyelids flutter. Ben had immediately rolled him over and was applying pressure to the wound.

"He's alive."

"But for how long?" Alexa cried. "Whoever shot him is coming this way."

"Barricade the door," Paschal shouted, limping fast to his brother's side.

"With what?" Cat screamed.

Alexa watched Damon weakly stretch his fingers toward the door. He mumbled, then fell silent.

Ben tugged again on the latch. It wouldn't budge.

Alexa's heart froze. Damon had just broken free of the curse and the castle without surrendering his soul. But what would happen now if he employed the magic?

"No more magic!" she begged him, even as he struggled with consciousness.

Cat tore off the shirt she wore over her tank top and handed the material to Ben to staunch the bleeding. "Can we use it to heal him?"

Alexa shook her head wildly. "He tried to use the magic to heal himself before and it didn't work. Now he's too weak." She stamped her foot and shouted in frustration. "This isn't fair! He'd just gotten his life back. Who would do this?"

Paschal hurried back into the dining hall and dragged a chair to the window so he could peer out of the few clear strips in the stained glass. "There's a whole group. At least four. Maybe five."

Alexa looked desperately at Cat, who nodded at her reassuringly. Ben seemed to know what he was doing. She had to take control of finding out who had just shot her lover. And why.

"He can't heal himself," she offered, "but he might be able to conjure what you need to help him."

She rationalized that small magic wouldn't affect him. It hadn't before. Only when he'd pushed beyond the limits of a quick conjure or a fast disappearance had he suffered the aftereffects of the evil.

"He's not entirely conscious," Ben said, his eyes—so like Damon's, she now noticed—flashing with hopelessness and fear.

"Try," Alexa ordered before running into the other room to join Paschal at the window.

"Will the charm protect me from guns?" she asked.

Paschal frowned. "Only from Rogan's magic. I'm sorry."

"Who are they?"

"K'vr, undoubtedly. Trouble is, which side?"

"Does it matter?"

"I was not the soldier in the family, but I have learned that the identity of your enemy always matters. We could hole up here indefinitely, I suppose, with the magic at our disposal, but they'd only send reinforcements. And though Ben has picked up some battlefield medicine during his days as an adventurer, he's no surgeon."

"My phone!"

Alexa dashed back into the other room and dug into her bag until she found her satellite phone. She dialed so quickly, she missed a number and had to start again. Finally, she had Paulie on the other end of the line. She explained as quickly as possible and her captain promised to send the Coast Guard right away. Alexa then threatened Paulie with the loss of her job, her captain's license, her lease and her student loans if she came anywhere near the island alone.

"Help's coming," Alexa told them, but with no sense of relief. Damon was still hurt, though he had regained consciousness.

Ben and Cat had rolled Damon onto his back, though they'd elevated him against the chair they'd dragged into the hallway. Cat tilted a bottle of something into Damon's mouth. He grimaced, but swallowed.

"I went three centuries," he coughed, "without sustaining a mortal wound. I don't intend to die today."

Alexa allowed herself a dose of happiness, her heart bursting with love for this man—yes, a man!—who'd come into her life as nothing more than a fantasy. "You won't die. As soon as the Coast Guard comes—"

Alexa jumped when someone pounded on the door from the other side, then ducked out of the way when what sounded like a hail of gunfire blasted against the thick wood. All of them ducked, but the bullets failed to penetrate the castle's defenses, magical or physical.

She looked up when the hammering stopped.

"Alexa Chandler!"

The voice was muffled, but the name was clear.

"Alexa, please!"

"Jacob," she breathed, her stomach dropping.

Cat ran toward her. "This could be a trap."

"It's Jacob," she insisted.

"With the gunmen," Cat pointed out.

Alexa gaped at her friend. "He'd never hurt me.

They must have forced him to come. I know your history with him is ugly and hurtful, but—"

Cat's lips drew into a severe line. "You have no idea how ugly, Alexa."

"Don't I? He's into weird shit," Alexa said, anxious and angry and on the brink of an emotional meltdown. Damon was hurt. Jacob was in danger. She had to fix this and she couldn't let Cat or her pride stand in her way. "He wanted you to join him and you refused. I don't blame you. And since then, he's been mean and spiteful. But he doesn't deserve to die because he's got fetishes neither one of us understands."

Cat's dark eyes widened. "You knew?"

"The staff to the rich and famous have ears, though thankfully, they also have confidentiality agreements and excessively high salaries." After gulping a deep breath, Alexa forced herself to calm down. Cat wasn't her enemy, and though Alexa had downplayed Jacob's questionable tastes, she knew her friend had every reason not to trust Jacob. "I'm sorry I let you think I didn't know, but I figured you'd tell me if you wanted to, and since you didn't, I just respected your need to be mean right back to my brother ever since."

"Your stepbrother."

"But still a brother."

Again, Jacob called from the other side of the door. Alexa pressed her ear against the wood to hear him more clearly. The other voices were muffled, as if the gunmen stood at the bottom of the stairs.

"Jacob, I'm here," she shouted. "What's happening?"

Silence ensued, followed by a thud and vibration of the door, as if someone had thrown his body against it.

"Jacob?"

"They'll kill me, Alexa. They'll shoot me right here if you don't give them what they want."

She glanced over her shoulder at Damon. At the fire opal still glittering on the heavy black cloak.

"What do they want?"

A jumble of voices argued on the other side. Alexa's chest ached as she held her breath. The answer would determine their course of action. Or inaction? She couldn't wait. She couldn't allow Jacob to die.

"They want the magic," Jacob said.

Cat rushed to her side. "Don't buy this. Jacob's not in any real danger," she insisted. "Those are his people. He gave you the necklace. He wants the magic, too. He's working with the K'vr."

"One faction perhaps," Paschal said, shuffling toward the door. "But that doesn't mean he hasn't been captured by the other. We don't know who's out there. They might not have been aiming for Damon at all or even know who he is. They might have been aiming for you."

Alexa turned her face toward the door, pressing her palm against the thick wood, trying to divine what to do. Under other circumstances, she'd wait for the Coast Guard to arrive, but she had no idea how long it would take Paulie to contact the authorities and not only convince them of the severity of the situation, but order a cutter with armed men to the island. If they were off on another call . . .

"I have to go out there," she decided.

"What?" Cat shouted.

"You will not!" Damon insisted in the same breath.

She darted across the floor to Damon's side. His color had returned, but his breathing was still thready. "He's my brother." She glanced at Paschal, who'd returned to the window in the dining hall. "You'd do the same for yours."

"My brother didn't get me into this predicament," he replied, indicating the necklace with his eyes.

"No, your sister did," she shot back.

Damon scowled. "That's a blow unworthy of you."

"It's the truth. You were willing to die that night you rode after Sarina, if it meant saving her from Rogan. How can I not do the very same for Jacob?"

Again, Jacob shouted her name, each time sounding more and more pained.

She splayed her hands on Damon's cheeks and took strength from the heat on his skin. "I have to negotiate, but I don't have to give them what they want."

With that, she ripped the fire opal off the cloak, amazed at how the gem buzzed in the palm of her hand. She held the jewel toward Ben. "Take this. Keep it on you, but don't invoke the magic."

"The gem is not required to call the magic," Damon said.

"When you were still tied to the castle through the curse, you didn't need the gem. But now you're free. Try doing magic now without it."

Damon complied. Nothing happened. He placed his hand over the stone in Alexa's hand, and instantly, he faded from sight. Ben tripped backward. Alexa could still feel the warmth of his skin on hers.

"You're scaring your nephew."

When Damon reappeared, a sly grin battled with the pain in his eyes.

"Any side effects?" she asked.

"A mild annoyance offset entirely by your touch." Damon drew Alexa's fingers to his lips, kissed them, then snatched the stone back. "I'll keep the source with me. I can protect it."

"How?" she questioned. "You're barely able to move."

"My strength is returning, thanks to my nephew's skill. You will not attempt to save your brother alone."

"No, she won't," Cat said. Alexa recognized the change in her friend's demeanor immediately. Though frowning, Cat pointed toward Paschal but addressed her words to Ben. "Get your father somewhere safe. This castle is huge. Find a good hiding place and stay in it."

Damon cleared his throat. "There's a storeroom beyond the kitchens," he said, indicating the direction with a minimal wave of his hand. "It's well hidden. You should be safe there."

"I can't bail," Ben said. "In case you haven't noticed, I'm the only able-bodied male around this place."

"You're not bailing," Cat reassured him, grabbing him by the shirt, her eyes betraying her determination to send him away. "But your father is the most vulnerable of all of us. The K'vr has already captured him once. I'd suggest Damon take him, but he's hurt. And he won't go anyway."

"You take him," Ben suggested.

Cat shook her head. "He won't go with me. Besides, Alexa might need my parlor tricks. You never know."

The kiss that followed was short in duration but powerful in emotion. Even Alexa looked away, mildly embarrassed by the intimacy.

Damon broke up their affectionate display with a cough.

Alexa smiled and took Cat by the hand, tugging her away from Ben, who'd left to convince Paschal to cooperate with their plan. "What changed your mind?"

"Jacob."

In the briefest retelling possible, Cat explained how her psychic powers—the ones Alexa had doubted so strongly before—had grown since her departure for Texas.

"It's the magic," Paschal offered. "You spent a great deal of time in my house, around my things. So many of those items had been touched with Rogan's magic, I've no doubt they amplified your natural abilities."

Cat glanced lovingly at Ben. "Or else I was just properly motivated by someone who believed in me." With a breath, her dreamy expression disappeared, replaced by her usual determined glare. "Either way, I can feel Jacob's fear. The threat to him is very real. If we don't act, he'll die."

"I thought you hated him," Alexa said.

"I do," Cat shot back. "But you don't. And you're my friend. Tell me what to do and I'll do it."

After a heartfelt shaking of hands among the re-united Forsyth men, Paschal and Ben headed toward the kitchen. Cat and Alexa helped move Damon so that when they opened the door, he'd remain hidden from view. Jacob had said the gunmen wanted the magic. Did they know about the stone? Did they know about Damon? Were they using her to get to him—or at the very least, to the magical source that he'd tucked into his pocket?

"A bit of Rogan's evil might go far right about now," Damon muttered as he leaned heavily on a thick stone column.

Alexa grinned. "The magic itself will be enough."

"I don't know that I can control it."

Her heart skipped a beat. "You locked the door. And you just made yourself invisible."

Pain caused tight ridges around his mouth. "Rogan had a lifetime to learn how to manipulate this stone to keep the magic from turning him mad. Now, I'm just a man who doesn't want the woman he loves to step into danger."

The woman he loves.

The woman he loves.

With each repetition in her head, Alexa's confidence grew. She took a moment to kiss Damon strongly and thoroughly, then pulled away before he could wrap his arms around her and keep her inside.

She took two steps back and nodded toward Cat at the door, who shouted to the party outside that they were on their way.

"Hold that thought," she said. "And don't use the magic unless you have to. I just got you, Damon. As a man. In my life. I can't lose you."

He patted his pocket. "You won't. I promise."

But as Alexa turned toward the door and nodded for Damon to unlock the castle, she wondered if she already had.

32

With a click, the door slowly swung open. Alexa squinted against the sunshine, but as the day had just dawned, her eyes adjusted quickly. She spotted Jacob lying across the top step, his eye blackened, his lip bloody and a nasty gash running across the top of his nose.

She squelched the instinct to run to him and instead focused her gaze on the raiding party below—two big men carrying equally big rifles. One shifted nervously, even as he kept his gun trained on Jacob. The other, pointing the weapon toward her, appeared steady and sure.

She opened her mouth to speak, but stopped when Rose walked out from behind one of the large armed men.

"No one has to get hurt here, Ms. Chandler."

Alexa gaped. It was one thing to be attacked by strangers, but a trusted employee? Clearly, there had been a reason why she'd been reticent about getting close to Rose.

"It's a little late to claim nonviolence, don't you think?" she asked, holding up her hands, still red with Damon's blood.

Rose sneered, then gave a little shrug. "A necessary show of strength. We want the source of the magic and we want it now."

Alexa stared at her boldly. "I don't know what you're talking about."

You're . . . pissing her . . . off.

Alexa wavered, the intrusion of Cat's voice into her mind distressing on so many levels, she didn't know where to start. But with few weapons at her disposal, she had no choice but to exploit Cat's newly honed psychic abilities to try to get the upper hand against their attackers.

"Tell me something I don't know," she whispered out of the corner of her mouth.

Cat stood only a few feet away from her, flush against the threshold, trying to interpret the feelings and emotions swirling around them.

Jacob's terrified. He . . . doesn't . . . trust . . .

For a split second, a backwash of emotion rushed into Alexa's brain. The events of the last two days and warring emotions between saving Jacob and letting him rot had exhausted Cat to the point where she was not reliable. Cat knew it. Alexa knew it, too. With an imperceptible wave of her hand, she sent her friend farther into the castle.

She'd relied too much on everyone else so far. On Damon's magic. Cat's abilities. Even Paschal's superior knowledge and Ben's medical skills. Rose had been her assistant, but Alexa was an expert negotiator. She should be able to work this out on her own.

Rose marched between her goons and placed one foot on the bottom step.

"You're anything but stupid, Ms. Chandler. You know exactly what we want. Hand it over, along with the castle, and your brother will be safe."

"She's . . . ," Jacob said, his breath coming hard from his bloodied mouth, "lying."

Alexa raised an eyebrow.

Rose shrugged prettily. "Perhaps I am; perhaps I'm not. We want what we want and we mean to get it. By any means possible."

"Who's *we*?"

"The K'vr," Rose answered, though almost imperceptibly, her eyes darted toward the path that led to the lagoon. "We're the rightful heirs to this castle and everything within it, including the source of Lord Rogan's magic."

Alexa squinted, trying to see if someone was hiding amid the overgrown plants, but she saw nothing but the rustle created by the ocean breeze.

"What is that source?" Alexa challenged, sidestepping closer to her brother, who was struggling to his feet. "You've been incredibly vague for someone who wants it so badly. It's almost as if you expect me to tell you what it is. Don't you know?"

"*You* know," Rose insisted.

"I do? Why are you so sure?"

"Because you've manipulated the magic for days," Rose replied. "Your brother here has seen it, seen him. Felt him, anyway. The phantom within. Now your time is up."

Alexa bent down next to Jacob and shifted so that her shoulder tucked under his arm. Up close, their eyes met and Alexa watched as his gaze shifted from pained to regretful to icy cold.

Cat jumped out from behind the door and screamed, "No!" but her warning came a split second too late. Jacob grabbed the Queen's Charm and yanked it from Alexa's neck.

Gunfire erupted. Alexa tucked her head beneath her hands and dropped to the ground just as blood spurted from a bullet drilling into Cat's arm. The impact threw her friend hard against the stone. Alexa rolled toward her, yelping when a bullet exploded just above where her head had been.

Jacob ordered the attack to stop, but when it didn't, he jumped in front of her. Blood splattered from his stomach, raining bright red drops over her.

"Jacob!"

Shocked, he turned to Alexa and mouthed, "I'm sorry." Then, as if time stopped cold, he crumpled forward and tumbled down the steps, only to unfurl, wide-eyed and bleeding, on the shell-encrusted ground at Rose's feet.

Coldly, Rose stepped over him, stopping only to

retrieve the Queen's Charm from his hand. Alexa turned her face away from her fallen brother, knowing he'd betrayed her even as he'd tried to save her. A mass of contradictions assailed her, none of which she had time to sort through. Was Rose from the faction of the K'vr that believed the necklace was the source of the power, or did they understand the true nature of the charm?

"You didn't have to kill him!" she screamed.

Rose gave Jacob a cursory glance. "He was in the way."

"Meaning you meant to kill me," Alexa surmised.

Rose took the steps slowly.

Cat had rolled so that the advancing enemy could not see her face. She had one hand gripped tightly around her wound, but the blood seeping through her fingers wasn't bad. A flesh wound, likely. Alexa wished Cat would verify her suspicion with a thought, but she could see her friend was too hurt to wrangle her psychic energy. Alexa had to get them out of this. Rose had the necklace. There was a chance she might be able to enter the castle without worry about the magic on the other side of the door.

But the gunmen couldn't.

Just as Rose's foot touched the top step, Damon appeared and in two flashes of blue light, disarmed the gunmen below. The rifles flew high into the air, then landed in melted, mangled heaps on the ground. With a frightening battle cry, he leveled another set of flares toward the men themselves. One fell. The other ran, singed, into the tangle of trees. Knowing Damon could do nothing to stop Rose with his magic, Alexa launched herself into the woman's side, sending her flying.

If Damon was experiencing uncontrollable rage since he had called upon Rogan's magic again, Alexa imagined the eruption of emotion was nothing compared to the fury flooding through her as she tussled with her former assistant. Though formidable when flanked by armed gunmen, Rose wilted beneath Alexa's

well-placed strikes to her nose and ribs. Applying
pressure to the woman's wrist, she released the necklace from her grip and snatched it back.

"You're so fired," Alexa said, before delivering one
more blow to Rose's chin, which left her unconscious.

When she spun on Damon, she saw the fire building
in his eyes, even as he leaned against the door. He
was both weakened and powerful. Reluctant and determined. His gaze had drifted to Cat, who'd scuttled
as far away from Damon as she could. With the
Queen's Charm firmly in her hand, Alexa shouted
his name.

He turned. She moved to kiss him, to release the
evil coursing through him, but he pushed her away.
She tripped down the stairs, falling to where Jacob lay
dead, her body aching and her mind confused. Was
she too late?

"Alexa?" Cat called desperately as Damon turned
back toward her.

"Damon, no!"

She stood, opening her arms wide. "If you're going
to hurt someone, hurt me."

Below her, she heard a croaked, "No."

"Jacob?"

Though blood soaked his shirt and his skin had
paled so that he nearly blended into the sandy ground,
Jacob turned his face a quarter of an inch and blinked.
He didn't have much time. He knew. Fear streaked in
his glossy gaze, scaring her as much as the anger and
rage building in Damon just a few feet above her.

"Not Rose," Jacob said, his voice barely audible.
"Keith."

"Who?"

Just beyond the edge of the trees, Alexa heard rustling again. Not the breeze this time. Not even the
soldier who'd deserted. Someone else. The Coast
Guard? Another accomplice?

She glanced at Damon, who stared woefully at his
hands, which sparked with the same blue flame he'd
used to disarm the gunmen.

Jacob gasped for air. "Rogan's . . ." He gulped in another painful breath, then exhaled with the word "heir" dying on his lips.

Alexa turned toward the trees and spied a dark head bobbing beyond the thicket of palmetto. "Keith!" she called, thinking fast. "You coward! Rogan's heir wouldn't run from a fight, would he?"

The dark head stopped its retreat and with infinite slowness turned toward her. He was a kid. A teenager. But the hatred in his eyes was unmistakable. He didn't move, didn't speak, but his sneer spoke volumes. And so did the fact that he'd watched this entire confrontation from the sidelines. He expected Jacob and Rose, two people once close to her, to do his dirty work. Well, if there was one thing Alexa knew about, it was how to properly take on a legacy of power—and this punk had a hell of a lot to learn.

"You did this," she accused. "You killed my brother. You caused this bloodshed and you hide in the bushes like a snake? Take it from someone who runs a multimillion-dollar empire, kid. If you want something done right, you have to do it yourself."

The young man accepted her challenge. He came out of the trees, his chin jutted forward. Only then did Alexa notice the automatic pistol clutched in his hand.

"You should have let me go when you had the chance," he taunted.

Damon started down the steps. Keith held his gun higher. "You may have my magic, but you're not impervious to bullets. And neither is she."

33

He turned the gun yet again on Alexa, who'd managed to back up a few feet, but not nearly enough to avoid being shot at close range if the kid had even halfway-decent aim.

Damon stopped. The fire in his eyes flickered, flaming and then burning out, then flaming again. He was struggling against the evil infection of Rogan's magic. Struggling, but not winning. Sweat dripped down his face, soaking his shirt to his body. His hands shook.

Out of the corner of her eye, Alexa saw Cat crawl back into the castle. *One less person in the line of fire*, she thought. Now it was up to her and Damon to bring this to a close.

"Damon," she said, turning to face him completely. "I love you."

Behind her, Keith laughed. "How romantic, wasting your last breath on sappy shit. Go on," he urged Damon. "Declare your love for her, too, so I can shoot you both and claim what is mine."

"You can't kill him," Alexa said, her voice balanced and calm. She'd negotiated business deals with sultans and despots. She could certainly manage one homicidal teenager. "He's the source of the magic. You need him or you'll have nothing."

The lie tripped off her tongue easily, and from the horrified look on the kid's face, she knew he'd bought her story instantly.

"Is he?" he asked, his eyes wide and mouth agape.

"Rogan?" Alexa turned back to Damon, the fire still flickering in the stormy gray depths of his eyes. "I don't know. Are you?"

Two words. One short question, but enough to push Damon over the threshold between victim and master. With a guttural shout that called up a mighty wind, Damon lifted his hand high, and Keith's feet were ripped out from beneath him. He flew one way and the gun the other. Alexa dove over Jacob's lifeless body, retrieved the weapon and threw it as far as she could into the bramble.

In the distance, she heard sirens. A bullhorn. The rattle of gunfire.

The Coast Guard.

And through the howling of Damon's conjured tempest, a young man screamed for mercy.

"Damon, stop!"

She battled through the wind and threw her arms around him from behind, willing all the love she felt for him to pass through her and into him.

"I. Am. Nothing. Like. Rogan," he shouted; then his voice turned icy cold as Keith cowered below him, tucked into the fetal position, whimpering. "If I were Rogan, you'd be dead."

The wind died. The sand and shells stopped attacking Alexa's arms and face like angry hornets, and when she gazed into Damon's eyes, she saw nothing but silvery gray. Throwing her arms around his neck, she pulled him down until their lips were but inches apart.

"But you are Damon Forsyth. And you're all mine," she said.

The longer and more luxurious their kisses, the more the atmosphere around them stilled. Soon the only sound was the Coast Guard rushing toward them, guns drawn. Paulie broke through the line of seamen to reach her side.

"Are you all right?" the young woman asked.

Alexa pulled back from Damon, glanced woefully at Jacob's body, then with hope toward the castle, and

then into the eyes of the former phantom she'd grown
to love.

"I will be. Now I truly will be."

From a chair set just in the arch of the main door,
neither inside nor out, Damon watched the sailors zip
Jacob's body into a dark bag. The doctors that had
arrived in the flying machine had tended to him, halt-
ing his bleeding and staunching the pain with something called an injection. While he waited for Alexa
to supervise the removal of her brother's body, he
perused the island from his perch, wondering at the
exotic plants that bordered the castle and imprinted
the piquant scent of sea salt in his nose. He glanced
at Alexa, who stood a few feet away, her arms
wrapped tight around her middle and silent tears
streaming down her face.

He wanted to cradle her in his arms and quiet her
heartbreak with soft words, but he knew she wouldn't
welcome the affection just now. Her brother had worked
against her, betrayed her. In the end, he'd sought to
save her, but his previous machinations had caused the
conflagration in the first place. Damon would not soon
forget having to draw from Rogan's evil magic in order
to save her—nearly losing himself in the process.

"She loved him," Cat said, balancing her injured
arm, newly bandaged, with her healthy one. "I never
understood how deeply."

"He was her family," he said simply.

Cat eyed him narrowly, then tossed a look over to
Ben and Paxton, who had strolled into the dining hall
to examine the mosaic at the precise point where Rogan's cloak and the magic fire opal were depicted.
"Family is important to you?"

Damon stared at her, wondering at the odd question. "Of course."

"And what about Alexa? If you run off now to try
and find the rest of your brothers, your sister or even
that Rogan creep, where does that leave her?"

Damon shifted in the chair, the ache of his injury

nothing compared to the idea of losing Alexa. Even for a day. An hour. A minute.

"She shall be with me, Miss Reyes."

Cat plopped down on the top step, then tilted her head so that her long hair brushed over her knees. "She needs to heal. She's not only lost the last member of her family; she's lost this," she said, indicating the castle. "She's put more than money and thought into rehabilitating this old castle into a hotel. To you and me, it's just business. But to Alexa, it's her—"

"Life," Damon provided, then patted Cat's shoulder reassuringly. "I understand her, Miss Reyes. She's a woman driven by many goals, not the least of which is financial. I have no doubt Alexa and I will be able to merge our ambitions, but because I know you worry, I will not rush her. My brother took sixty years to find me, and while I'm not willing to wait quite that long, I will not abandon Alexa in my quest."

"You won't have to abandon her at all," Ben said, joining them outside. "We'll look for your brothers," he finished.

Damon regarded his nephew quizzically. "Paxton is not of an age to go running about this new world searching for trinkets any longer. He is better served by remaining here, with—"

"I didn't mean my father," Ben clarified. "I meant Catalina."

"Excuse me?" Cat asked.

Ben grinned and Damon had the sudden urge to leave, but when he moved, Cat jumped to her feet and pushed down on his shoulder, making it quite clear she didn't wish him to go anywhere.

"Why not?" Ben asked excitedly. "We make an excellent team, you have to admit. And my father and I think I've put my life on hold long enough. Paschal knows he can't go jaunting around the world in search of his brothers anymore. After today's fireworks and finding Damon, he's agreed to let me take on this mission. He has a good lead on a sword that his research shows was forged in Valoren."

Cat listened, then a smile bloomed slowly on her face. "Yes," she said confidently. "I think I might like roaming the world with you. You're a fun guy, when you're not stuffed up in some classroom."

He smirked. "And you can be fairly exciting yourself, when you're not trying to run the world."

Ben opened his hand to Cat, who placed her palm in his and screeched delightedly when he pulled her into his arms. They both turned expectantly toward Damon.

"So," Ben asked, "does this plan work for you?"

Alexa started up the stairs. "What plan?"

After a moment of thick silence, Damon explained the proposal to Alexa. The more he allowed the idea to take root in his head, the more he thought the plan sound. Ben and Cat would take charge of the search while Alexa and he remained at the castle, ensuring that her dream to turn the structure into a luxury hotel went forward as planned.

"I can't ask you to abandon your dream," Alexa said, kneeling at his side after she'd asked Cat and Ben to give them a few moments alone. "You waited three hundred years to leave this place, to explore the world. To find your brothers."

"Then you believe they may still exist?"

She rolled her eyes. "You exist. Paschal, um, Paxton exists. Chances are good, I suppose."

"And Rogan as well?"

She winced, fear skittering across her face.

"But I'll not search for them without you," he declared. "And first, you need to see your dream to its fruition."

With a withering sigh, Alexa sat on the step and dragged her hands through her hair. Hands still marred with stains from his blood. And Jacob's. "I don't know," she said finally.

"Paschal said you could do with the island and the castle whatever you wished," Damon reminded her.

"I know, but what's the point? Jacob's gone."

"You did not want to do this for Jacob."

"I don't know what I want anymore."

He leaned closer. "Are you so sure?"

Despite her heartbreak, she managed an intimate smile. He'd lost his brothers, too, but he hadn't had to witness their betrayal or their violent death. Alexa had healed once physically, but now it was her heart that had been battered and bruised. And more than any ambitions he had to reunite with his brothers or avenge his family on Rogan or his murderous heirs, Damon wanted to help Alexa find her joy again. If she could find her happiness in him, so much the better.

She'd changed his destiny. Now it was time for him to repay the debt.

"I want you," she answered simply.

"Good," he said. "I was hoping that would be your answer."

He ignored the pain from his injury and wrapped his arm around her. She climbed gingerly onto his lap and pressed her cheek softly to his. "I can't ask you to stay here. You have a whole world to see."

"And I'm sure you will be an excellent guide. We'll explore the world, Alexa. Together. For centuries, I thought I had no time at all to act, to take revenge, to live again. Now I realize, even if I have only fifty years, that's all the time in the world, as long as I'm with you."

Her smile rivaled the sun, and when she kissed him, he could think of nothing but stripping away her torn and bloodied clothing and washing her clean with his own hungry hands.

For an instant, he thought he might have inadvertently transported them inside the castle, but when he fluttered his eyes open, he found them sitting still on the steps, the ocean waves crashing on the rocks nearby, the sun beating softly on their shoulders and the sky a brilliant and unrivaled blue.

She pulled away softly. "That reminds me," she said ruefully. "What are we going to do about the magic?

Judging by Keith's threats before he and Rose were carted off to jail, the K'vr will be back. One faction or the other, they're going to be trouble."

Damon patted his pocket, where the magical source still thrummed against his skin. "And we'll be ready for them."

"How?"

Unsteady, but determined, Damon stood and enveloped her as tightly in his arms as his wound would allow. "I'll master the magic, my lady. With your . . . *assistance*," he said delicately, "I'm quite certain I'll learn to keep the evil—and Rogan's followers—at bay."

The grin curving her lips reached her eyes so that they sparkled. "That might mean a whole lot of lovemaking."

Damon suddenly forgot all about pain or suffering or curses. He thought only of magic. Not the type created through the fire opal still hidden in his pocket, but the rare and wonderful kind he'd invoke with Alexa at his side. "Yes, my lady. It will, indeed."

Read on for a preview
of Julie Leto's next book,

PHANTOM'S TOUCH

Coming from Signet Eclipse
in December 2008

"You're all mine."

Lauren Cole chuckled greedily, holding the package close to her chest as she flipped the light switch and locked the door behind her. No one would think to look for her here. With her new movie scheduled to start filming in a week, the studio soundstage was normally a beehive of activity, but not in the middle of the night. She had less than six hours to enjoy her stolen treasure.

She kicked off her shoes and, with a squeal of delight, fell to her knees on the nearest mat in the studio exercise room, clutching the object of her desire tight. Even wrapped in a cashmere throw, the metal underneath bit into her skin. It was the most delicious pain she'd ever felt.

The sword was hers. The last and final gift she'd ever accept—or in this case, take—from her exhusband. Her body thrummed with excitement and she had to remind herself to breathe. Adrenaline overload caused some of her dizziness, but mostly, she was simply jazzed to have returned, even for just one night, to the Lauren she was before she'd met Ross Marchand. Lauren, the conniver. The street kid. The thief.

Her ex-husband had made it his business, literally,

to drum her felonious tendencies out of her and teach her to speak properly, dress with style and channel her expert lying skills into genuine acting talent. In the end, she'd worked the red carpets and movie premieres so adeptly, every paparazzo within a two-mile radius had wanted to know everything about her—especially the name of her first film, which, of course, the internationally known Marchand would produce. Thanks to Ross, she'd glided onto the Hollywood A-list instead of falling through the cracks in some stinking lockup.

But as she caressed the cashmere, she knew that sometimes being bad again felt oh, so good.

A sudden knock on the door broke into her silent revelry.

"Hello?"

The pounding in her ears kept her from identifying the voice until he said, "Who's in there?"

She exhaled. Marco. Studio security. Diligent, but sweet. She scrambled across the workout mats, unlocked the door, but opened it only a few inches, desperate to keep the sword hidden.

"Hey, Marco," she said, using all of her considerable acting skill to appear relaxed, if not slightly guilty for breaking a rule she and the security guard had confronted on more than one occasion.

The older man arched a bushy salt-and-pepper eyebrow. "Ms. Cole, you know you're not supposed to be on the set alone."

She grinned at him prettily, having learned the power of her smile years ago. "Technically, I'm not *on* the set. I'm in my favorite rehearsal room."

"The one with all the weapons," he pointed out, attempting to look over her shoulder, but at five foot nine, Lauren had a few inches on the guy. Tightening her grip on the door, she blocked his view.

"We're shooting the first fight scene day after tomorrow," she explained in a whisper that echoed in the cavernous silence of the soundstage just behind him. Though the building was filled with lighting, sets and equipment, no one but Marco was supposed to be here after hours. Lauren had taken a chance coming here, but risk wasn't anything new to her. She was rusty, but not out of practice altogether. "I just wanted to get in some more workout time."

"Without your trainer?"

Lauren suppressed a smirk. "I've done how many of these Athena movies now, Marco? I could train the trainer."

Marco snorted. "You could kick my ass, and I'm the one carrying the gun."

She squeezed her arm through the opening, and then laid her hand on Marco's shoulder. "That's about the nicest thing any man has ever said to me."

She batted her eyelashes, which increased Marco's laughter enough so that he forgot she wasn't supposed to be where she was, particularly with the item she'd lifted from the film producer's private study. Well, used to be her study, too. She'd shared his home and his bed until a year ago, when she'd caught him fucking her ingenue costar in the cabana by the pool.

The divorce had been relatively quick and pain free, the final papers having been delivered just this morning. Thanks to Ross, she'd learned how to manage her own money, and California law and an ironclad prenup had taken care of the rest. She got the town house in Beverly Hills. He kept the Malibu beach house. She got the dog, a Rottweiler whose favorite pastime was chewing on Ross's Bruno Maglis, and he'd taken the art. All the art. Including, unfortunately, the sword they'd purchased together from a shady Dresden antiques dealer in a dicey part of the bustling German town.

From the moment she'd caught sight of the intricate inlaid gold handle glittering above a polished steel blade, she'd wanted it. Needed it. The tug in her chest had instantly reminded her of her days on the streets when she'd been so hungry, her entire body ached. And Ross, so magnanimous and generous (she'd thought at the time), had paid the exorbitant price in cash to appease her ravenous need for the sword. Only he'd then snatched the prize away before she'd even touched it, insisting that the sword be authenticated before anyone handled it.

Once the ancient weapon had arrived in Los Angeles with papers declaring it an amazing design of a double-edged long sword likely forged in the fifteenth century, he'd had it immediately sealed in an unbreakable glass case.

Only not so unbreakable, as she'd learned tonight.

The familiar pull of the sword forced her to cut her conversation with Marco short.

"Thanks for not snitching on me," she said, hopeful that the security guard would comply. "I think I owe you another case of that Australian wine your wife likes so much."

He frowned deeply at first, glanced at his watch, and then patted his nightstick.

"You don't have to do that, Ms. Cole," he answered.

"Don't you have your daughter's wedding coming up? I bet that wine would be perfect for the rehearsal dinner."

His grin returned, and after assuring her that no one would interrupt her private workout session, he left. She released the pent-up breath clutching her chest, then relocked the door. It was barely midnight. She had until at least five a.m. to figure out what the heck she was going to do next.

Because stealing the sword was one thing. Keeping it was something else entirely.

She slid across the mat and dropped to her knees again. She'd barely had time to remove it from the case and wrap it in the blanket before she'd had to hightail it out of her former home without getting caught by anyone on Ross's staff. She had the legal right to the sword. Her attorneys had assured her that she was entitled to anything Ross had purchased for her as a gift during their marriage. Legal rights aside, taking the sword could mean the end of her career.

Ross had been indulgent during their marriage, but only when it suited his needs. Right now, he needed her to star in the final Athena film. She'd agreed, since pocketing her generous salary, as well as a healthy portion of all residuals, had been her plan all along. One more movie with her ex, and then she'd be free of him forever. But he'd balked at letting her use the sword for the film. He'd laughed at her request during a preproduction meeting in front of everyone from the director to the key grip.

In private, he'd reminded her with pointed ruthlessness of what he could do to her career if she challenged him so boldly again. There were things he alone knew about her past that could destroy her career. One tip from him to the tabloids and she'd be done.

That threat had been the final straw.

The old Lauren, the Lauren who'd once made her own way in the world and didn't depend on anyone else—ever—would not have asked permission to use the sword. She wouldn't have worried about consequences or folded under some jerk's bullying. She wanted. She took.

And even if Ross gave her up, he'd pay a hefty price himself. Not only for revealing her secret, but for harboring a few of his own.

Grasping the edges of the soft, camel-colored blanket gingerly, she peeled aside the buttery soft wool until the lights above her flashed off the sword's polished blade. She gasped, then moved to touch the steel, stopping when she realized that her fingerprints would mar its beauty. No, the only part of this sword she needed to touch was the handle.

She shifted so that her fingers slipped into the masterfully crafted grip, which seemed to close around her hand when she firmly grasped the hilt. Immediately, warmth spread through her skin, causing her fingers to buzz, as if she were gripping . . . her vibrator? She snickered at the thought, but instead of the erotic images bursting out of her brain from the humor, the pictures deepened. Darkened. Expanded.

Naked bodies intertwined like the gold on the handle. A man's hard sex pressing against her skin like the pommel and hilt of this magnificent sword.

She released the weapon, but her nipples had tightened painfully. A gentle throbbing intensified between her legs.

What the hell? She knew swords were the ultimate phallic symbol, but she'd been around the damned things since her first turn as Athena six years ago. She enjoyed swordplay, but she certainly never got all hot and bothered because of it.

Laying the blade gently on the blanket, she tore off the jacket she'd worn over two snug tank tops. The room had suddenly become stifling, so she scrambled to the door, lowered the thermostat and doused all but the few dim, blue lights her trainers used to simulate fighting in the dark. When she turned and eyed the sword, she gasped. The handle sparkled and glowed as if she hadn't just adjusted the wattage to nearly nothing.

Intrigued, she crept forward, her weight on the mat shifting the sword as she walked. Tiny jewels in the handle, fiery red, captured the dismal light and reflected back a brilliance that was nothing short of ethereal.

Damn, she'd known the sword was beautiful, but she'd never truly seen it, had she? The antiques shop had been dingy and dusty and gray. The case that Ross had enclosed the sword in had diminished its real beauty. Now she could see it. Now she could touch it. And the effect had been nothing short of orgasmic.

She wanted to fight with it. Cut the air with the blade, balance the weight against her toned arm muscles, learn how to make the weapon dance as she parried and thrust. This was the weapon Athena would carry during this film, her final hurrah as the warrior goddess traveled to an alternate universe to smite the sadistic and pummel the impure. Invigorated with excitement, she twirled over to the video camera and activated the machinery. Once Ross saw how she used the sword, once he witnessed the magnificence of it, he'd never deny her.

Not, at least, in front of the production crew, who would be wholly bowled over by the way the sword would capture the light and reflect back the power associated with Athena. They'd save a bundle on special effects, she was sure. At least, that was the argument she fully intended to use.

Ross wouldn't be able to deny her. Not in front of everyone. Not when the sword was so incredibly perfect.

Once she had the video rolling, she dashed back to the sword and lifted it again, this time holding the weapon with a straightened arm to get a full feel of the weight. She'd never held anything so perfectly balanced. Warmth washed over her again, and in response, her heartbeat accelerated.

She sliced the sword through the air once, then twice, instantly finding a controlled rhythm marked by the quiet swish of the blade through the increasingly thick atmosphere. She spun and chopped downward, skillfully pulling up before the blade touched the ground. She counterturned and with precision that shocked even her, stopped dead before she connected with the hanging workout bag she imagined was an attacking foe.

"Wow," she said, breathing hard, not from the exertion of lifting or wielding the sword, but from the overpowering surge of electricity shooting through the handle and into her arms. The steel caught the blue lights overhead and reflected a luminous sapphire gleam. It was as if the blade was . . . alive.

I am alive.

The voice was deep, masculine, but so quick, so soft, she knew she'd imagined the words. She was alone. Wasn't she?

"Marco?" she called out.

No response.

She bent her arms at the elbows, bringing the sword parallel with her body, the blade shining blue in her eyes. Leaning close and then gazing upward, she realized the steel couldn't reflect the light from this angle.

The light was coming from . . . within?

Touch me. Don't be afraid.

The voice, louder and more insistent this time, echoed in her brain. She hadn't heard the command; instead the message had vibrated up her arms like words on a taut string. She tried to drop the sword, but the handle seemed to curve tighter around her hands, tangling her fingers, encircling her wrists, holding her captive the harder she tried to escape.

She bounced against the hard canvas workout bag, then, flying on the momentum, threw herself hard against the wall. Nothing would dislodge the sword from her hand. Her vision swam. The blue lights above her merged with the luster of the blade, nearly blinding her in azure flashes. She turned the sword again, more slowly this time, trying to find a way out of the twist of metal, when she saw them.

Eyes.

As silver as the blade.

Powerful. Hypnotic. Yet . . . sad?

Do not forsake me, Lauren. Only you can set me free.

Desperate and afraid, Lauren ran toward the light switches. Was this some sort of trick? Special effects? Was Ross paying her back for stealing his sword, or was her guilty conscience twisting her triumph? But Ross couldn't know she was here. And even if Marco had alerted him, he wouldn't have had time to do anything more than burst in and demand his weapon back.

Forget him. You want me.

"Who are you?" she asked desperately, uncertain if she should address the sword or the room in general.

Embrace me and find out.

Lauren struggled all the way to the door. She reached for the lock, but her left hand betrayed her and dropped to her side, frozen. Sliding to the ground, she lifted the blade again. She'd seen those eyes before. In dreams. Dark, erotic dreams.

Images flashed again. The naked bodies. The hard sex. The muscled man with hair the color of night and eyes as silver as storm clouds skittering across a full moon. She knew him. She'd wanted him.

Did she want him now?

"Tell me who you are," she demanded.

Touch me and know.

She swallowed thickly. Her heart slammed hard against her ribs. She squeezed her eyes shut, then forced them open, trying to see clearly, trying to figure out what the hell was going on. The blue light had not diminished. If anything, as her sanity slipped, the glow intensified.

And so did her desire.

She dropped the blade. The flat side of the metal touched her calf and stretched over her thigh. Intense sensations nailed her to the floor. Not pain. Not blood. She hadn't been cut. She'd been . . . captured?

"I . . . can't . . . breathe."

Who was she talking to? Why couldn't she keep her thick, suddenly lead-heavy eyelids from dropping down over her unfocused eyes?

Would she ever wake up to find out?

Spirited Away

Cindy Miles

Knight Tristan de Barre and his men were murdered in 1292, their souls cursed to roam Dreadmoor Castle forever.

Forensic archeologist Andi Monroe is excavating the site and studying the legend of a medieval knight who disappeared. But although she's usually rational, Andi could swear she's met the handsome knight's ghost.

Until she finds a way to lift the curse, though, love doesn't stand a ghost of a chance.